THUNDER

IN THE

MORNING

CALM

BOOKS BY DON BROWN

The Black Sea Affair
The Malacca Conspiracy

The Navy Justice Series
Treason
Hostage
Defiance

ZONDERVAN

Thunder in the Morning Calm
Copyright © 2011 by Don Brown

This title is also available as a Zondervan ebook. Visit www.zondervan.com/ebooks.

This title is also available in a Zondervan audio edition. Visit www.zondervan.fm.

Requests for information should be addressed to:

Zondervan, *Grand Rapids, Michigan 49530*

Library of Congress Cataloging-in-Publication Data

Brown, Don, 1960-
    Thunder in the morning calm / Don Brown.
       p. cm. — (Pacific Rim series)
    ISBN 978-0-310-33014-1 (pbk.)
     1. United States. Navy — Intelligence specialists — Fiction. 2. Grandfathers — Fiction.
3. Korean War, 1950-1953 — Prisoners and prisons, North Korea — Fiction. 4. Prisoners of
war — United States — Fiction. 5. Korea (North) — Fiction. I. Title.
PS3602.R6947T48 2011
813'.6 — dc22   2011012855

Maps created by Jane Haradine. Copyright © Don Brown.

Cover design: Extra Credit Projects
Cover photography: istockphoto©, photo.com™
Interior design: Michelle Espinoza

Printed in the United States of America

11 12 13 14 15 16 17 18 /DCI/ 22 21 20 19 18 17 16 15 14 13 12 11 10 9 8 7 6 5 4 3 2 1

DON BROWN

THUNDER
IN THE
MORNING
CALM

PACIFIC  SERIES

ZONDERVAN®

ZONDERVAN.com/
AUTHORTRACKER
follow your favorite authors

This novel is dedicated to my grandfathers

Walter Lawrence Brown, October 4, 1898–March 25, 1989

William Arthur Hardison, April 8, 1909–December 12, 1995

ACKNOWLEDGMENTS

For his superb editorial assistance, a special thanks to US Army veteran Jack Miller of La Mesa, California, who, with his wife, Linda, is a generous benefactor of the San Diego Zoo and the Lambs Theatre of Coronado, California. With grateful appreciation for the behind-the-scenes tours with the giraffes and the magical musical performances by the Pacific.

A special and warm thanks to Sue Brower, acquisitions editor of Zondervan, and to Lori Vanden Bosch, both of whom, quite frankly, were born to be editors, and whose comments, feedback, and strategic input during the editorial process have been an oasis of wisdom. Also, special thanks to Jane Haradine not only for her superb editorial assistance, but also for her superb talent and artistry in the preparation of the various maps found throughout the novel.

TO THOSE AMERICANS WHO SERVED

This novel is released in conjunction with the sixtieth anniversary of the Korean War. You who are still alive who fought in that war liberated a nation that Communist forces had invaded, smothered, and occupied totally, with the exception of a small amount of land on the far southeastern corner of the country around Pusan. But you, brave soldiers and marines and sailors and airmen, hit the enemy hard in one of history's most daring amphibious landings, at a place called Inchon, where tides rise and fall rapidly, making the precision and execution of your operation a matter of life or death. You ended the Communist strangulation of South Korea and pushed the freedom-hating invaders back north of the 38th parallel.

Yes, some troops from other nations were involved, and yes, some call the war a UN "police action." Some have even called it "the Korean Conflict."

But then there is the truth. Korea was neither a "police action" nor was it a "conflict." Korea was war in its bloodiest and most brutal form. Although other countries fought in the war, American blood saved South Korea. Nearly 37,000 of your brothers-in-arms gave their lives in Korea. That's ten times the sacrifice of all other nations combined who sent forces there. More than eight thousand Americans are still missing to this day. No, despite what some say, Korea is not the "Forgotten War." Korea was an American war. And you who served shall never be forgotten.

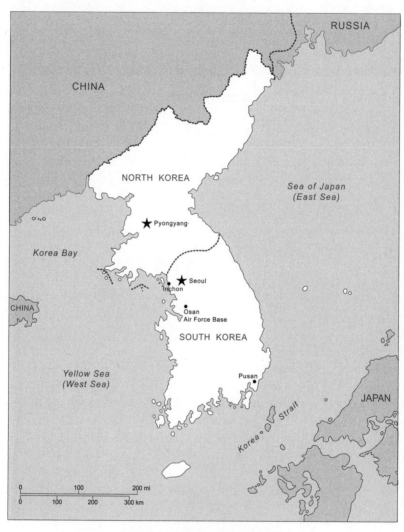

North and South Korea, Seoul,
Osan Air Force Base, Inchon, Pusan, Pyongyang

All that is required for evil to triumph is for good men to do nothing.

Edmund Burke

PROLOGUE

Kim Yŏng-nam Military Prison Camp
Hamgyŏng-Namdo Province
120 miles north of the Demilitarized Zone
the Democratic People's Republic of Korea (North Korea)

early twenty-first century

The morning sunlight beamed through the barred windowpane above the bunk. Feeling its slight warmth on his face, Keith opened his eyes and squinted into the glare.

Another morning. Another day.

He rubbed his eyes and rolled slowly to his side. The aches and cricks had worsened over the years, but arthritis had not debilitated him. Not yet anyway.

His mission was not yet done.

He pushed himself up from the hard mattress. Hot, searing pain flared and burned within his elbows. He would have bitten a bullet, but four of his teeth had fallen out and three more were half chipped or broken. And even if he had all his teeth, they took his bullets from him long ago. He exhaled, blowing through the red-hot fire flashing from his elbows and his knees.

Mornings were the hardest. He would feel better in a moment. But not yet. He grimaced, grabbed his left knee, and squeezed hard. He glanced over at the two figures covered by gray blankets on the other side of the room. Robert and Frank, his only living links to a happier world, were not yet awake.

The sun's rays had not reached their bunks. They were not yet stirring. Their blankets rose and fell, up and down, ever so slightly, barely visible, providing evidence of the breath of life. For this, the first blessing of a cold autumn day, Keith closed his eyes and thanked his Creator.

Once there were ten of them.

Now, only three.

Death claimed them over the years, one by one, whittling their numbers to a fragile trio of the fading elderly. He guessed that they had reached their eighties by now, although he was unsure even of that. The seasons and the years had marched slower with time. The earth had slowed her axial spin so as to prolong the torture to which they had been condemned. There was no way to track time. Not anymore. Keith never feared death, yet fear had not escaped him. Indeed, the fear of outliving the others, of remaining as the last man standing, loomed always as his greatest nightmare.

Blam! Clang-a-lang-a-clang-a-lang-a-clang-a-lang. The metal trash can bounced across the concrete floor, down the middle aisle between the bunks.

"Get up, old dogs!" The guard loomed in the doorway with a bullwhip in hand. Like every new whipmaster over the years, this one too would prove himself on this, his first day on the job. "Water time! Move! Move!"

The guard clicked his heels. He was standing just in front of two other jackbooted guards with semiautomatic rifles. "Get up, swine! Perhaps today we will shoot you all!" He laughed. "Or perhaps we shall cut you up and sell you at the market."

Self-bemused at his own ranting monologue, the guard stepped into the cell and kicked the trash can again.

Clang-a-lang-a-clang-a-lang-a-clang-a-lang. Then *whap whap* against the concrete floor.

Keith swung his feet over the edge of the bunk.

His buddies shifted in their bunks. Robert's arms shook and his face twisted with pain as he tried to get up. His weathered forehead showed deep lines and wrinkles. He opened his mouth wide, desperately trying to suck oxygen into his lungs. The whipmaster ignored Robert, at least for the moment. He turned and marched back outside the prisoners' concrete barracks and perched himself at the entrance, where he continued to bark a string of orders.

Keith's feet found his worn leather sandals on the concrete floor. He slipped into them and stood up.

Robert wheezed, coughed, and again tried to stand. His legs shook as he pushed himself up from the low-lying cot. Keith reached out, found Robert's elbow, and helped steady his friend. Frank fell into line.

Wearing only heavy black-garb pajamas, they shuffled out the door toward the waiting guards.

Keith always tried to focus on things of the Creation … the sunshine, the colors of the trees, the moon and stars when he could see them—

Whap! The whip cracked on the ground behind them. "Faster, old goats!"

These things—the moon, the stars—reminded Keith of the Creator … somewhere … still in control … somehow. But now, each day it was harder somehow than in the years when he had relied on the strength in a younger body to survive. Now each day was—

Whap!

Sometimes classical music played in his mind and gave him inspiration. Sometimes he heard the great hymns of the faith. This morning the lyrics and words of Beethoven's Ninth danced in his head … "Joyful, joyful, we adore Thee, God of glory—"

Whap!

"Ooooooooooooooeeeeeeehhh!!!" Keith dropped to the rocky ground. The whip had opened a gash in the top of his foot. He grabbed his foot and lay there. Above him, the world spun in a painful blur.

Angry voices of three guards filled the air. The two with the rifles yelled at the one with the whip, who yelled back. One of the rifle bearers knelt down, pulled a handkerchief from his pocket, and tied it around Keith's bleeding foot as a makeshift bandage.

Blood soon soaked the handkerchief, its white cloth yielding to the crimson flow.

"Get up, old dog! Get moving or there will be more of that."

The whipmaster's voice had lost part of its anger. Keith thought the strike to his foot probably was an accident. Poor aim. Most of the guards' tactics these days were more psychological than physical. And this guy was new. *Has to show who's boss.*

Keith pushed himself back to his feet, grateful the whip had not struck Robert. He limped back into line with his buddies, the aching in his knees now throbbing in a rhythmic, synchronized cadence with the throbbing pain in his foot.

They shuffled up a hill to a long wooden trough, the kind that horses and pigs drank from back home.

"On your knees!"

The three men dropped down and, like dogs lapping from a mud puddle, began licking water from the trough with their tongues. At least the water was fresh.

"Enough!" the whipmaster yelled. "Into formation. To the latrine!"

Keith and Frank got back on their feet. But when Robert pushed himself up against the front of the trough, trying to stand, he lost his balance and tumbled to the ground. He lay there, wheezing and coughing. One of the guards, the one who had bandaged Keith's foot with his handkerchief, laid down his weapon and helped Robert back to his feet.

"*Kamsamnida*," Robert said.

The guard responded with a stern-faced nod.

Robert's wheezing was getting much worse. He had another coughing jag and turned a dusky blue.

The wind brought a whiff of the latrines over to the right. The three old men were used to it and shuffled in line toward the stench of human excrement.

Whap!

Again the bullwhip slapped the ground.

Not far beyond the drinking trough, off to the right, were the unmarked graves of their buddies. Each day as he walked by, Keith prayed for their families. Keith had considered taking his own life, as one man had done years ago. The man had fashioned a makeshift noose from strips of a sheet he tied together and hanged himself.

But Keith could not abandon Robert and Frank. Not now. Robert likely would not survive another frigid Korean winter. Keith was certain of that. And he wanted to be able to bury him, as he had the others. And he wanted to bless Robert's grave with the love and respect he deserved from his countrymen.

No, he could not abandon them, not now or ever. Cowards chose suicide. And suicide was an affront to the very faith that had kept him alive all these years.

They would hang together until the end.

Semper Fidelis.

Once a Marine, always a Marine.

CHAPTER 1

Office of Naval Intelligence (ONI)
Suitland, Maryland

The massive Suitland Federal Center, located in suburban Maryland just eight miles southeast of the Pentagon, sprawled across 226 acres of grass, well-manicured shrubbery, and brick-and-mortar federal office buildings.

Reachable by subway off the Washington Metro's Green Line, yet unknown to most Americans, the center is home to several federal agencies, the most recognizable being the United States Census Bureau.

From the Pentagon, the ride to Suitland by car was scenic, even on a barren mid-November day. Crossing the Potomac River, the government-issued Ford Taurus passed by the Jefferson Memorial and the Tidal Basin, the reflections in the pools and basins of Washington's great monuments a reminder of the great force for freedom that America had been, still is, and, hopefully, will remain.

But in a few short minutes, the images of grandeur disappeared as the Taurus left behind the glamorous buildings of government and drove into the crime-infested southeast sector of the city, past the Washington Navy Yard to the right and slumlord government housing to the left.

In the front passenger seat, Lieutenant Commander Gunner McCormick, United States Navy, checked his watch. They had departed the Pentagon thirty minutes after the end of rush hour, with plenty of time to spare, unless one of those notoriously inconvenient Washington-area fender benders paralyzed traffic.

"We've got a few minutes, sir," said the senior chief petty officer driving the Taurus. "Be happy to stop and buy you a coffee."

"Sounds great, Senior Chief," the commander said. "I could use the caffeine. Come to think of it, I could use a smoke." He checked his watch again. "But I'd rather be early than take any chances. How about on the way back I buy you a coffee or, better yet, maybe something a little more substantial."

"That'll work," the senior chief said, sporting a sly grin as the Taurus rolled east across the Pennsylvania Avenue bridge spanning the Anacostia River.

Not much was said for the rest of the trip as the commander gathered his thoughts. Three days ago, they plucked him off his ship in the Pacific, flew him to Hawaii, then to San Diego, and then to the Pentagon for one day. And now they were driving him over to Suitland, to the Office of Naval Intelligence, for a top-secret meeting about a top-secret subject. He still had no clue why he had been called.

His boss at sea, Rear Admiral James S. Hampton Jr., had not been too happy about it. But then, Admiral Hampton had not been happy about much lately. Gunner thought the admiral had been on his case over just about anything and everything. He had no idea what was bothering him. Who knew? He'd learned long ago that in the Navy, you don't second-guess the orders of your superiors. Half those orders never made sense anyway. And you don't try to read officers' minds. Flag officers, especially, could change their minds as quickly as the wind shifts directions. So what was the point?

They crossed the Maryland state line into Prince George's County. They made a right and then a left on Branch and Alabama Avenues, then stayed to the right for the final stretch along Suitland Road Southeast. As they approached Gate 1, the driver slowed down, then turned in. After presenting their credentials, they drove onto the grounds of Suitland Federal Center. The road dead-ended at Swan Road, the main corridor within the center. Most of the signs pointed to the left, toward the buildings of the giant US Census Bureau. But the senior chief clicked on the right-turn signal and made a sharp right turn.

A moment later, they reached Gate 9, with its armed Marine Corps guards. A Marine staff sergeant snapped to attention and shot a sharp salute.

"Good morning, sir," the sergeant said. "May I help you?"

"I've got a meeting with the admiral at ONI," Gunner said, referring to the Office of Naval Intelligence.

"Aye, aye, sir," the sergeant said. "Your identification and orders, please."

"Senior Chief," the commander said, "show the sergeant our papers."

"Aye, sir." The senior chief passed the orders out the window.

The sergeant studied the papers, then passed them back. He shot another perfectly stiff salute with precision-like bearing. "You may proceed through the gate. ONI is in the building straight ahead. The duty officer is awaiting your arrival, Commander, and will escort you to the admiral's spaces."

"Thank you, Sergeant," Gunner replied, and the Taurus rolled through Gate 9 past two other Marine guards and parked near the National Maritime Intelligence Center building.

Gunner stepped through the double doors into the marble-floored foyer. Flanking the entryway to the left was the flag of the United States. To the right was the US Navy flag.

"Lieutenant Commander McCormick?" A Navy lieutenant smiled and extended her hand. The gold cord hanging from her left epaulette designated her as an aide to an admiral.

"That's me. My friends call me Gunner."

"Yes, I've heard." Hers was a dimple-accentuated smile. "I'm Lieutenant Mary Jefferies."

"You're the admiral's aide?"

"That's right."

"Nice to meet you, Lieutenant." He released her handshake.

"You too, Commander. I'll take you up to the conference room on the sixth deck. We have some background information for you to read. Then the admiral and I will brief you."

"Excellent," Gunner said and followed her onto the elevator. "But you can call me Gunner if you'd like."

Lieutenant Jefferies punched a button and the elevator lifted quickly to the sixth floor—the sixth *deck*—where the doors parted and Jefferies stepped into the hallway just ahead of Gunner.

"Right this way," Jefferies said, holding her hand out to the left.

They walked down to the end of the long hallway. Jefferies stopped in front of a door, punched a combination lock, and pushed open the door to a windowless rectangular conference room, complete with table and chairs. In the middle of the long table was an 8-by-10-inch envelope with the words *TOP SECRET* in red.

"In the envelope you'll find your orders, Commander, along with general background on the political and military situation surrounding your next assignment. I'll leave you here to go over the material. I'll be back in a few minutes to let you know when the admiral will be ready."

"Excellent," he said, "but you can call me Gunner."

Jefferies beamed at him. "Very persistent, I see. Just like your dossier says."

"You've read my dossier?"

"Would you expect otherwise?"

"I think you're bluffing, Lieutenant. You don't have an actual dossier on me."

"Oh, I'm bluffing, am I?" She raised one eyebrow.

"So just what about me have you read?"

"Hmm. Let's see what I can recall. Graduated from Virginia Tech. Four-year backup quarterback on the football team, but didn't play much. You got to carry a clipboard and wear a headset and send in plays to the starter."

"Ooh, that hurt."

"Did it now?" She smiled at him. "You got tired of not seeing any action, so you joined the Navy."

"I just want you to know I'm in better shape now than I was when I played on the football team. We had a wimpy strength-and-conditioning coach. The guy didn't know how to teach power lifting. An hour a day on weights now does more than two hours in the gym back then."

"Okay. Let's see. You attended Officer Candidate School in Newport, and after OCS, you got picked up for intel, where you finished, unimpressively I might add, in the middle of your class at Dam Neck."

"Unimpressively? Hey, I was a football jock! At least I passed."

"Then you got yourself assigned to a Cruiser Destroyer Group, where you met your surface warfare obligations. Again bored, you got out of the Navy. Took a high-paying job as a commodities analyst in New York. But then you got bored with that too."

"What can I say?" Gunner quipped. "I get bored easily."

"Yes, of course you do. This time you tried something a little less boring. You returned to active duty from the reserves and volunteered as an intel officer attached to a SEAL unit in Afghanistan."

Gunner shrugged. "I flipped on the TV one morning and saw the commercial that said, 'The Navy—it's not just a job. It's an adventure.' Guess I missed that the first time."

"You certainly made it an adventure the second time, Commander. Let's see. What did it say? While attached to the SEALs, you jumped in a hole, grabbed a live grenade tossed in by the enemy, and tossed it out half a second before it exploded, saving the life of the injured Marine waiting to be medevaced out. You were cited for heroism and bravery and awarded the Navy Cross."

"You're embarrassing me, Lieutenant. Why do you bring this up?"

"You're the one who said I hadn't read your dossier. Just proving I did my homework."

"I would expect nothing less."

"Well, then, I'm sure you know the admiral will expect you to have these papers read prior to your meeting."

"That your way of telling me to shut up and get to work?" He chuckled.

"That is correct," she said. She opened the door to step out, then turned back. "I hope you will find a suitable level of excitement there."

"You did nail me."

She tried suppressing a smile but failed. "I'll see you in a few minutes, sir." She stepped out of the room and the door closed behind her.

Gunner sat down. Time to get to work. He opened the envelope and spread its contents on the table.

Date: November 17
From: Deputy Chief of Naval Operations for Information Dominance (N2/N6) and Director of Naval Intelligence (DNI)
To: LCDR Christianson Pendleton McCormick, USN, Staff Intelligence Officer, Carrier Strike Group Ten
Subj: Initial Intelligence Briefing Carrier Strike Group Ten Yellow Sea Deployment
Classification: TOP SECRET

1. Due to increasing hostilities on the Korean Peninsula, the Republic of Korea has requested joint naval exercises with the United States Navy in the Yellow Sea as a show of unity, solidarity, and force between the US and the ROK to deter possible aggression from North Korea.

2. The National Command Authority has ordered Carrier Strike Group Ten (USS *Harry S. Truman* Battle Group) into the Yellow Sea to conduct joint naval exercises with the ROK Navy. Commander Strike Group Ten shall be informed of these orders imminently.

3. As senior intelligence officer for the Strike Group, the purpose of this communiqué is to brief you on (a) the historical and political situation of the conflict as relevant to the Strike Group's mission; (b) the positioning of North Korean shore batteries that may pose a threat to the Strike Group; and (c) the positioning of North Korean naval and air forces that are a potential threat to United States naval forces.

4. A summary of the historical and political background is as follows:

KOREAN CRISIS
HISTORICAL AND POLITICAL BACKGROUND

In 1910, Japan attacked and conquered Korea. The brutal military occupation ended more than one thousand years of Korea's sovereignty as a nation and was a major source of shame to Koreans.

Thirty-five years later, Japan lost Korea in World War II. Just as Europe was divided along the "Iron Curtain," Korea was divided along the 38th parallel into the American-backed Republic of Korea in the south (ROK) and the Communist-backed Democratic People's Republic of Korea (DPRK) in the north. The DPRK was led by a young rebel and disciple of Joseph Stalin named Kim Il-sung.

In 1950, Kim Il-sung invaded the South to unify the country. North Korean Communist forces rapidly drove south, gaining control of almost the entire country before American and United Nations forces, under General Douglas MacArthur, executed a daring amphibious landing at Inchon, which decapitated the Communist supply lines into the South.

After Inchon, the military pendulum swung to the West. American forces pushed the Communists back, driving them back into North

Korea—their goal to obliterate the dictatorial regime in Pyongyang. But the surprise entry of overwhelming Communist Chinese forces secretly crossing the border into North Korea changed the dynamic of the war. The US and Korean forces that had advanced north toward the Yalu River border with China on the western side of the peninsula were driven back by the surprise entry of Chinese soldiers, who had crossed secretly into Korea. On the eastern side of the peninsula, Chinese forces attacked the First Marine Division commanded by Major General O. P. Smith near the Chosin Reservoir on their push north. Surprised and surrounded by Chinese forces outnumbering it eight-to-one, the division, fighting in subzero conditions, rallied around General Smith and battled through Chinese fortifications, inflicting mortal damage to the enemy before returning south. Many have said that the Battle of Chosin Reservoir was the Marines' finest hour.

In 1953, after three years of fighting, Korea remained divided in almost exactly the same place it had been divided before the war began.

The 38th parallel.

The armistice kept the two heavily armed warring armies separated, 2,500 yards apart, by a no-man's land now known as the "Demilitarized Zone," the DMZ.

As many as four million people died in the Korean War, which had some of the most brutal warfare the world has ever known. The US dropped nearly one million gallons of napalm on North Korea. Eighteen of twenty-two major cities in the North were at least half obliterated.

While most people think the war ended almost sixty years ago, there never was a peace treaty. More than 21,000 days later, the long cease-fire continues.

North Korea remains the most oppressive regime on the planet. Although intelligence is somewhat sketchy, best evidence from eyewitness reports suggests that North Korea maintains several dozen forced-labor prison camps, reserved primarily for political dissidents who dare to challenge the regime. These camps have been used over the years to dissuade political opposition.

Even to this day, rumors have circulated and circumstantial evidence from the North has suggested that North Korea may be holding a few elderly American prisoners never returned from the war.

"What?" Gunner mumbled aloud. He rubbed his eyes and reread the last paragraph.

Even to this day, rumors have circulated and circumstantial evidence from the North has suggested that North Korea may be holding a few elderly American prisoners never returned from the war.

"I can't believe this." He looked back at the communiqué.

Due to the highly sensitive political nature surrounding enforcement of the tenuous nature of the armistice, the US has been unable to confirm or deny the validity of such rumors.

"What the heck is that supposed to mean ... 'Unable to confirm or deny'?"

A knock on the door. Gunner heard someone working the combination lock, then the door opened. Lieutenant Jefferies was standing alone in the passageway. "The admiral is ready for you now, Commander. If you will come with me, please."

Gunner stood, grabbed the folder, and joined Lieutenant Jefferies out in the hall. His briefing with the admiral would be interesting. But he knew that nothing the admiral could say would erase the idea growing in his mind.

American Marines could be alive in North Korea. And he intended to find them and bring them home.

CHAPTER 2

Kim Yŏng-nam Military Prison Camp

Keith knelt on the concrete floor, leaned over the cot, and laid his hand on his friend's forehead. The skin was hot, dry. Over the last few days, Robert's hacking cough had grown worse. His lungs sounded full of phlegm that he couldn't cough out.

"That you, Keith?" More coughing. More wheezing. "Mama? Mama? You there?"

"He's delirious," Frank said. He was sitting on a bunk across the aisle.

"It's the fever talking," Keith said. "He's on fire. If we don't get his temp down, it's over." He lifted Robert's wrist and felt for a pulse. "His pulse is firing like a machine gun."

For Keith, the thought of losing Robert triggered a flash of memories—memories of bygone days when they were young, strong, and idealistic.

Robert *was* a Marine. And in his younger days, he was a Marine's Marine.

It happened in November 1950 at a place called Chosin Reservoir near the border between Korea and China. The First Marine Division was pinned down, surrounded by overwhelming Chinese forces. Their situation was hopeless. But Brigadier General O. P. Smith, the commander of the division, had rallied the leathernecks with a jolting war cry: "Retreat, hell! We're not retreating! We're just advancing in a different direction!"

Although the Chinese had the Marines surrounded, the Marines rallied around their general and began a daring and thunderous advance through enemy lines.

That day, Keith was covering the rear of his advancing platoon. They were moving south, back toward the 38th parallel, and his job was to provide the first line of fire if the Chinese or North Koreans attacked from the rear. He had cocked his M-1 carbine and was moving low and swift just behind his leatherneck comrades. They had just fought through a North Korean platoon when a deafening shot rang out behind his head.

Startled, he pivoted and brought his carbine into firing position.

A Chinese soldier lay dead on the ground from a bullet to the head. Robert was off to one side, pistol in hand, barrel still smoking. That sight would forever be burned in Keith's memory.

Somehow, the Chinese soldier had slipped into the Marines' rear guard and was about to shoot Keith in the back of the head at point-blank range when Robert fired, killing him. Robert saved his life.

They left the body on the ground and moved out, trying to catch up with their platoon. But suddenly, out of nowhere, they were surrounded by Chinese soldiers with rifles aimed right at them.

Had the Chinese witnessed Robert shoot their buddy, both Keith and Robert would have been shot. Instead, the Chinese turned the two Americans over to the North Koreans, dooming them to an eternity of hell on earth.

At first, hope lived. Hope of release. Hope of a rescue. Hope of a prisoner exchange.

But as months turned into years, and the years into decades, their hopes and dreams of freedom faded and finally vanished. America, the beacon of light among nations, the hope of freedom on earth, morphed into a faint and distant memory. Images of family frozen in time at first haunted the deep recesses of their minds. Crazed wonderings — whether family was dead or alive, whether a spouse was remarried or still waiting, whether markers had been placed on their empty graves in some lush green war cemetery somewhere back in a place they once called home — had once tortured them. But as the decades passed, their thoughts of ever returning home had dimmed.

Now they had only each other—Keith and Robert and Frank. They had become closer than brothers.

Two quick knocks on the door brought Keith back to the present. The door swung open and a swirl of snow rode in on a gust of cold air. Two guards were standing out in the yard smoking cigarettes. A petite woman, perhaps midthirties, walked in with a large wooden tray that held three bowls of beans and rice and three tin cups of water from the trough. She held out the food and said, "Eat, eat, eat."

Keith's eyes met the woman's, and he said, "*Ahn yang haseo*, Pak."

"Hello. Hello. You hungry?"

"Very sick." Keith pointed to Robert, who groaned and rolled over toward the wall, away from the food and the water.

"Oh, sick?" Pak leaned over and touched Robert. She frowned and looked concerned. Pak had been bringing them food for the last few years, and unlike the whipmaster and the other uniformed guards, she often showed kindness to the men, but only when the guards were not looking. "Oh, hot," she said. "Needs drink."

"Right," Keith said. He took a jar of water and put his hand behind Robert's head. "Can you lean up, buddy?"

Robert's head shook and bobbed as Keith raised him to a slight angle off the hard pillow. Fighting the burning pain in his own arms, Keith brought the jar of water to Robert's lips.

"Take a sip," Keith whispered, tilting the jar up. A small amount, maybe two or three tablespoons, drained into Robert's mouth. A gulping came from his throat. "That's good. Drink some more." He tipped the jar again.

"*Uh-kuh ... uh-kuh ...*" Water poured from the sides of Robert's mouth. Keith jerked the jar away.

"I think he got some in his lungs," Frank said. "Easy. It's gonna be okay."

Keith eased Robert's head back down to the pillow.

"*Uh-kuh ... uh-kuh ...*"

Keith rolled Robert on his side and popped him between the shoulder blades a couple of times. More coughing was followed by fast, heavy breathing. "You're going to be fine."

"Keith, your foot." Frank pointed down.

Keith looked down. "Oh, crap." Blood oozed from the lash mark on the top of his foot. "I must've caught it on the edge of that steel bar under the bed."

"Here, here." Pak removed her apron, knelt on the floor, and pressed the folded cloth down on the foot.

"Thank you, Pak," Keith said. "I'm okay." He reached down and pushed the apron against his foot and looked into her black eyes. "Please, Pak. Robert is sick. Can you get medicine? Please."

She stood up. Her face flashed a nervous look.

"Please," Keith pleaded. "Whatever you can bring. We won't say anything."

Her eyes shifted to the left and then to the right. "I try," she whispered, then turned and walked out of the barracks.

"She's worried about sticking her neck out," Frank said. "I don't blame her."

"Me neither," Keith said. "Let's pray she does it, though." He dabbed cold water from the jar on a towel and laid the cool, wet towel on Robert's forehead. "I'm worried about him making it through the night, let alone dealing with Sergeant Jack-Thug when he barges in here in the morning." He pulled the blanket up and covered Robert's neck, leaving only his head exposed. "Robert's in no shape to march down to the pig trough, and that guy's gonna have to back off."

"Maybe he'll cool his jets by morning," Frank said.

"Somehow I doubt it. We'll see."

Colonel Song Kwang-sun, the senior commander and military warden of the prestigious Kim Ying-nam Military Prison Camp, opened his eyes and squinted at the shapely silhouette hovering over him. When his blurry vision sharpened, he saw a smiling Mang Hyo-Sonn leaning up, her chin supported by her hand and her long hair draped over her shoulder. She gazed at him with the look of a teenager in love.

Colonel Song pulled clean white sheets up over their shoulders to break the slight chill in the air. He looked into Mang's black eyes and gently pushed a lock of brown hair from her face.

As she gazed into his eyes, a slight smile teased the corners of her mouth. "Have I not been enough to keep you warm?" She ran her fingers across his arm and moved her lips to his. Her kiss, as luscious as the sweetest vial of pure honey, made him feel half his age.

"You are more than enough to keep me warm, my dear, but that is not the question."

"No?" She toyed with his chin. "Then what is the question?"

"The question is whether I keep *you* warm," he said, chuckling at himself.

She smiled and whispered, her lips right next to his ear, "Of course my big strong man keeps me warm."

"This is good to know, but just in case"—he pushed himself up and reached for the clear bottle half full of soju on the small table beside the bed—"have another sip."

"Thank you, my colonel." She took a gulp. "You are a most generous commander."

"Of course I am." He laughed. "Give me that." He snatched the bottle from her and brought it to his lips. Delicious, potent soju poured down his throat. He capped the bottle and turned to Mang, his aide and his lover.

"I have a prison to run. We must return to work before someone suspects something."

"Of course, my colonel," Mang said, running a soft hand across his forehead.

He sat up on the side of the bed and stuck his legs through his long Army-green uniform trousers. His feet went into his boots. He stood up and put on his Army jacket, buttoning it carefully and adjusting the red pin bearing the photo of Kim Il-sung, the "Eternal President" of the Democratic People's Republic of Korea. Finally he buckled the shiny belt carrying his holstered pistol.

"Get dressed. I will leave first. Wait ten minutes, then leave. Make sure that no one sees you."

"Yes, my colonel."

Song stepped into the hallway and turned right. He headed for the WC to get rid of some of the soju.

Pak walked into the commander's office. A silent testament of braggadocio adorned the walls, various photographs of goose-stepping soldiers, military medals and citations framed in boxes, and pictures of a younger Colonel Song Kwang-sun smiling and shaking hands with dignitaries and accepting whatever awards they gave out to high-ranking Communists of the North Korean Army. His sharp eyes, emanating a steely and evil glare, seemed to follow her from every photograph.

"They are only pictures," she mumbled softly. "Fear not, for I am with you."

She glanced at the clock on the wall. Three o'clock. She knew the colonel usually was out of his office at this time of the afternoon. Still, she needed to hurry. He was not far away.

The worst-kept secret in all the prison was Colonel Song Kwang-sun's daily rendezvous with Mang Hyo-Sonn, the twenty-two-year-old North Korean flower half his age. A staff sergeant, Mang had been detailed as a guard in the military prison system. But because there were no female prisoners to guard, Mang served as administrative secretary to Song. She arrived a month ago.

Their daily midafternoon dalliance had started two weeks ago. They would slip into the small sleeping room down the hall, ostensibly on their lunch hour. Sometimes he would return in an hour. Sometimes he would not.

Everyone knew. Even the colonel's wife knew, they said.

The only secret was what Mang Hyo-Sonn didn't know. When the colonel grew tired of her, and he would, she would be shipped off to another facility—if she was lucky. One of his four mistresses wound up a few miles from the prison with a bullet in her head.

Pak prayed that Mang Hyo-Sonn would be especially distracting today.

She walked across the outer office, through another door, and into the office of the colonel-warden himself. More photographs on the wall showed the colonel in Pyongyang. Several showed the colonel standing between the Dear Leader, Kim Jong-il, and his son the madman heir apparent, Kim Jong-un. Others showed Kim's father, the "Eternal President" of North Korea, Kim Il-sung.

With a feather brush in hand, Pak dusted the colonel's desk, then his chair, and then along the inside of the barred windows looking out onto the courtyard. Finally she darted into the small bathroom next to the office and pushed the door closed behind her. After turning on the faucet to muffle the sound, she pulled open the door to the medicine cabinet.

The colonel normally kept several bottles of aspirin on the bottom shelf. But the bottom shelf was empty.

She reached up and felt on the second shelf. A razor. Another razor. A bar of soap. "Please, Lord Jesus, help me find something," she whispered. Her hand moved to the top shelf. She felt two plastic bottles. She took the bottles off the shelf and examined them. Aspirin. Penicillin.

She heard the sound of boots walking in the outer office. A door closed.

Cold panic rushed through her body. She had planned to take just a few pills. No chance of that now. She put the aspirin back on the shelf and stashed the penicillin bottle in her pants. She turned off the running water in the sink.

What could she do? Climb through the window into the courtyard? That is crazy, she thought. One of the guards would see me. Or the colonel would come in here. She muttered a fast prayer, put her hand on the doorknob, turned it, and opened the door.

"Colonel!"

He stood there in the office, an angry look on his face. Fear gripped her at the sight of him. She noticed his vein-bulged neck, his drab-green officer's uniform resplendent with all his medals pinned upon his chest. His look was cold, his glare menacing. "You are still here?" he asked.

"Yes, Colonel. I was cleaning in your bathroom."

"You always clean this late?" He pressed his hand against his forehead.

"I was just finishing, Colonel."

"Very well," he snapped.

"I must attend to other duties," she said. "Please excuse me." Without awaiting his permission to be excused, she walked past him, past the large desk in the outer office, and out into the hallway.

Her heart was pounding like a battering ram. She quickened her pace down the long hallway, praying that she would not hear his footsteps behind her. The empty offices along the hallway were closed and dark in this antiquated facility that now had more guards than prisoners.

A door on her left creaked open.

Pak saw the young woman in the drab brownish-green North Korean uniform step out into the hallway.

The colonel's mistress eyed Pak as she walked by. But Pak ignored Mang and, pretending not to see her, kept looking straight ahead and walked briskly toward the door at the end of the building. A moment later, she pushed open the door. The air temperature had dropped since the morning. Swirls of snow greeted her as she stepped outside. She walked down the four concrete steps, then glanced behind to see if she had been followed.

Nobody was there.

Thank God.

She headed up the hill toward the concrete barracks that housed the prisoners. The front door would be unlocked this time of day. Everyone knew the old men in the barracks could not get through the fence surrounding the compound even if they wanted to.

Three armed guards in long greenish-brown trench coats stood in a circle about a hundred feet from the barracks, smoking cigarettes and laughing and chatting. A fourth stood a few feet away, smoking on his own.

She prayed again as she approached the door of the prisoners' barracks, then she stepped into the barracks and closed the door behind her.

The old prisoner named Keith was sitting on a wooden chair at the bedside of his sick friend. He was holding a wet towel to his friend's forehead. The other prisoner, Frank, was lying on his cot, watching Keith sponge Robert's head.

"Pak." Keith stood up.

"*Shhhhhhhhhh!* I bring medicine," she said. She pulled the bottle from her pocket and thrust it into Keith's hand. "Penicillin."

He looked at the bottle. His old eyes gazed into her face. "God bless you, Pak."

"I go. I must go."

"Thank you," he said. Then he turned to his friend. "Robert. There's good news. We've got medicine. I need you to try and lean up for a second."

Pak started to walk out, but turned and looked back. The sight stopped her in her tracks. Keith was cradling Robert's head in his arm and, almost like a father cradling a baby son, he was speaking tenderly to his old friend. "Here, open up." Robert opened his mouth, barely, and when he did, Keith dropped a penicillin tablet onto his tongue. "Hang on, I'll get you some water."

Propping his friend's head with his left hand, Keith reached for a tin cup half full of water. "Here, drink this."

A splash spilled down the side of Robert's face. Keith poured a little water into his mouth. The old man coughed twice, then swallowed.

Keith looked at Pak. "Thank you."

She stepped back out into the thickening snowfall.

Now what? Stay and finish cleaning? Perhaps. But, of course, no one would know if she left now. Unless ... if the colonel noticed ... Her instincts took over. She took a scarf from her pocket and draped it over her shoulders. Through the thickening snow, she walked a straight line across the camp toward the front gate.

As she approached the gate, two stone-faced guards stood at the entrance. Were they looking for her already? Her breathing quickened.

The wind whipped up and blew cold snow against her face. The first guard seemed to lock eyes on her.

Walk straight. Look normal, she told herself.

"Leaving early today, Pak?"

"Finished already." She smiled, nodded, and kept walking.

The second guard stared at her, then, without saying a word, swung open the gate. She walked straight through and hurried onto the road in front of the prison camp. Across the road, two steel poles rose perhaps ten feet into the air, and five bicycles were chained to them. She reached for her bicycle and felt for the combination lock.

Her hands shook as she fidgeted with the combination: 14 – 16 ...

"Pak! Halt!" boomed a voice from the guard shack.

She looked back. One of the guards, his rifle strapped on his back, was marching toward her through the wind and snow.

The colonel has discovered me, she told herself. They will shoot me for rendering aid to the enemy.

"Wait!" he ordered, now so close that she could hear his jackboots clicking as he walked. "Something is missing?"

"I do not know what you are talking about, Sergeant." She felt herself shaking.

The sergeant extended his hand and held the scarf out to her. "You walked so fast through the gate that it blew off your shoulder. You did not notice."

She reached out to take it, hoping he would not see her panic. "I did not notice. Thank you, Sergeant."

"The snow is getting worse. You should go before the road gets too icy." He nodded at her bicycle. "We will see you tomorrow."

"Thank you, Sergeant." She turned back to the combination lock: ... 18–27.

The lock opened and the chain fell off the post. She unthreaded it from around the wheel, put it in the basket, and pedaled off into the wind and snow.

CHAPTER 3

USS Harry S. Truman
the Yellow Sea
sixty-five miles west of the North Korean coastline

The long flight from the East Coast across eleven time zones was the perfect recipe for jetlag. Back out on the carrier on station in the Yellow Sea just off the Korean coast, Gunner was somewhat relieved to be back aboard the ship but still trying to force his body to readjust to the local time. He swigged steaming black coffee as he stepped out onto the sun-drenched observation deck.

The great ship plowed through rolling waters, and an odd mix of cool and warm breezes whipped off the sea. Scattered white cumulus clouds waltzed across the morning sky, and from them wind whistled over the flight deck and swirled around the ship's one-hundred-fifty-foot control tower that looked like a giant steel-and-electronic beanstalk.

The odd breezes grabbed the red-and-white pennant hoisted just under the Stars and Stripes, setting it to flapping and snapping, proclaiming the great ship's battle cry, "Give 'em Hell!"—the phrase immortalized by the man for whom the ship had been named.

Gunner gazed almost hypnotically at the furiously flapping pennant, and his conscience raged within him. Did he really want to risk his career? Perhaps even his life? Maybe start a war? Leaning on the railing high above the flight deck, Gunner squinted against the glare of the morning sun, then slipped on his sunglasses.

"Lieutenant Commander McCormick to the flag bridge! Lieutenant Commander McCormick to the flag bridge!"

"That's my cue," Gunner said to himself as he checked his watch. He stepped from the observation deck onto the flybridge, which was the highest navigational bridge on the carrier, and then descended two levels, first past the operational bridge, then down to the flag bridge, the admiral's command post. Rear Admiral James S. Hampton Jr., the highest-ranking officer aboard the *Harry S. Truman* and the commander of Strike Force Ten, was Gunner's boss.

Two Marine guards were posted outside the door of the flag bridge. "They're waiting for you inside, sir," one said.

"Thank you, Staff Sergeant," Gunner said as the Marine opened the door. Gunner stepped inside and stood at attention. "Lieutenant Commander McCormick reporting as ordered, sir."

"At ease, Gunner." Admiral Hampton was standing with his arms crossed, two silver stars glistening from each collar.

"Thank you, sir," Gunner said.

The other officers on the bridge were all seated. Awaiting his report were Captain Tony Farrow, Hampton's chief of staff; Captain Charles Harrison, commanding officer of the *Harry Truman*; Captain Mark "Maverick" Garcia, the carrier air group commander, or CAG; and Lieutenant Jim Porter, the junior intelligence officer and Gunner's assistant.

Porter was holding an envelope with the words *TOP SECRET* in bold red ink. Porter had done what Gunner had told him to do. He had brought with him the papers Gunner had retrieved from Suitland.

"How was your trip to the States?" Captain Harrison asked.

"Excellent, Skipper," Gunner said. "After my briefing at Suitland, I managed to get down to Virginia for a day to spend some time with my mother, who just about hog-tied me to keep me home for Thanksgiving. She isn't feeling too kindly toward the Navy just now."

The admiral chuckled. "I expect not, Gunner. But I understand this briefing couldn't wait." The admiral switched to his let's-get-down-to-business tone. "What do you have for us?"

"Lieutenant Porter, would you please pass out a packet to each of the officers?"

"Aye, aye, sir." Porter began retrieving packets of information from the top-secret envelope and handing them out.

Gunner waited until the admiral had received his packet, then began his report.

"Lieutenant Porter is passing out operational packets that I obtained on my trip to Suitland three days ago. As you gentlemen go through the packets, I'll begin with a summary of our operational orders.

"The government of South Korea has requested the United States conduct joint naval exercises with the South Korean Navy in the Yellow Sea.

"This request is made as a result of increasing acts of belligerence on the part of North Korea in recent months. Tensions between the two countries have continued to rise, and as you know, as recently as November 2010, North Korea fired dozens of rounds of naval fire into Yeonpyeong Island in the Yellow Sea near the North Korean coastline.

"Yeonpyeong lies near the Northern Limit Line, which as you know is the maritime boundary between North and South Korea in the Yellow Sea, set forth by the 1953 armistice agreement, which brought about a cease-fire in that war. The Northern Limit Line extends out into the sea as an extension of the Military Demarcation Line dividing North and South Korea roughly along the 38th parallel.

"Lieutenant Porter, could you get a chart of this up on the Power-Point?"

"Yes, sir."

A few moments later, a nautical chart of the area flashed up on the screen.

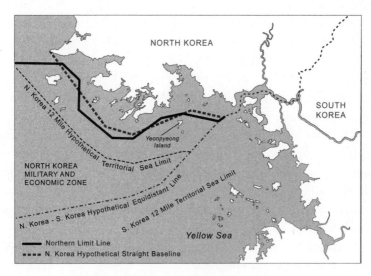

Northern Limit Line with Yeonpyeong Island

"Gentlemen, on this chart, which is included in your packet, you can see what I'm talking about. The Northern Limit Line is marked very clearly in the solid dark line. That line marks the extent and the border of North Korea's maritime claim, as set forth in the 1953 Armistice Agreement, which North Korea signed. Anything outside that is international waters. Starting in the mid-1990s, however, Pyongyang reneged on its agreement and claimed the waters out to the dashed line, which is twelve nautical miles off the coast.

"If you'll note from this chart, there are five islands in this disputed zone, from Paengnyong-do in the northwest corner of the chart, all the way to Yeonpyeong to the east.

"Yeonpyeong, where the attack took place, is only seven and a half miles from the North Korean coast. The armistice agreement specified that those five islands, including Yeonpyeong, would remain under South Korean control.

"North Korea now claims a border farther south that encompasses all five islands and valuable fishing grounds. In other words, while North Korea has not to date claimed Yeonpyeong or the other islands shown here, it is claiming the waters around them. North Korea's claim is not accepted in the international community. Not even the Chinese, who are Pyongyang's principal benefactors, accept it.

"Of course, lack of support in the international community has never stopped Dear Leader from saber rattling. He has a history of firing missiles on the Fourth of July to defy the United States. He fired a barrage of missiles on July 4, 2006, and then on July 4, 2009, he fired at least seven missiles over Japan, toward Hawaii. Fortunately, those missiles fell harmlessly in the Pacific.

"On November 23, 2010, North Korea shelled Yeonpyeong Island, and the South fired back. This shelling set buildings ablaze and left dozens of homes damaged. Two South Korean Marines and two civilians were killed. Eighteen others were wounded. All this hit the international news. You may recall seeing images of billowing black smoke coming from the island."

"I remember it well," Captain Harrison said. "Looked like the Korean War was going to reignite."

Admiral Hampton added, "I was just finishing my stint as naval attaché to our embassy in Seoul. They extended me another sixty days. We thought the roof was about to blow."

"Well, the South Koreans are concerned that the roof may be about to blow again," Gunner said.

"How's that?" Hampton asked.

"Well, this is the reason they called me back to Suitland, sir. If you gentlemen would have a look at Exhibits 4, 5, and 6 in your packets." Gunner waited for a moment as the senior officers shuffled through their classified documents.

"Looks like satellite photos of troop movements," Captain Farrow said.

"More like troops massing in a concentrated area," Hampton said.

"You are both right," Gunner said. "These are satellite photos, filmed by US spy satellites, of North Korean army units amassing along the Yellow Sea coastline just a few miles from these islands. North Korea does not maintain a separate marine corps, but it operates two amphibious sniper brigades. These units are a cross between our Marine Corps and our SEAL units, although they cannot match the firepower or training of either our SEALs or our Marines.

"Still, they could be deadly against South Korea. Their mission is to infiltrate and attack targets such as military bases, ports, and infrastructure, like nuclear power plants and industrial centers. Ordinarily, the North Koreans station one of these brigades on the east coast, to guard the Sea of Japan, and the other on the west coast, guarding the Yellow Sea. But in these photos, both amphibious sniper brigades are stationed in close proximity to one another and are drilling with regular army units."

"Hmm," Captain Harrison mused, flipping back and forth between the satellite photos in his packet. "And I suppose that both these units are amassing along the Yellow Sea with regular army units for a friendly turkey shoot between them with the winner buying the loser a Big Mac."

"They'd have to defect to buy a Big Mac," Admiral Hampton quipped. "And they'd get shot by their own guards if they came within two miles of the DMZ."

"You got that right, sir," Captain Garcia added.

"Okay, Gunner," Admiral Hampton said, "what's the scoop? Let me guess. Suitland thinks, based on these photos, that the Communists may be planning something."

"Actually, sir, not just based on these photos. We've intercepted encrypted message traffic that the North Koreans are planning an amphibious invasion of the five islands, including Yeonpyeong."

No one said a word. The senior officers exchanged glances.

"That could tip the balance," Hampton observed.

"Yes, it could, sir," Gunner said.

"When are they planning this attack? Is this invasion imminent?"

"We don't know, Admiral. The intercepted message traffic doesn't reveal a time frame. Could be tomorrow. Could be six months. But the movement of forces on the ground makes us think sooner rather than later. Food, supplies, fuel—all the things that an invading force would need to occupy and hold territory—have all been trucked into the staging area within the last two weeks. They've even given the invasion a name. Operation Sea Lion."

More exchanged glances of concern. The admiral walked over to the other side of the bridge.

"Care for my seat, sir?" Captain Garcia stood.

"No, Pete. Sit down." The admiral stroked his chin and stared out the starboard window. "Operation Sea Lion," he muttered, then turned and looked at Gunner. "So, Commander, what exactly do they want us to do about this?"

"As you know, Admiral, we've been invited by the South Korean government to conduct naval exercises with their navy in the Yellow Sea. Both Washington and Seoul think the Communists won't try an invasion with a US carrier task force nearby. But the exercises could get dicey. They want us to fly our warplanes into the zone that North Korea is trying to claim, with close-in overflights above Yeonpyeong and the other islands to display a show of force that the US will not accept North Korea's attempt to invade these islands and deviate from the 1953 armistice. That would send a message that if they do try to invade, the US would step in and help our friends in the South."

"So it's send in the Navy," Captain Farrow said.

"The plan of virtually every American president in times of crisis since the beginning of the republic," Captain Harrison added. "Speak softly, and show 'em the big stick. In this case, the big stick is the *Harry S. Truman*."

"Sounds simple enough," Hampton said. "Captain Garcia?" He turned and looked at the CAG. "Your pilots ready for some fun?"

"My pilots are always ready to rock 'n' roll, Admiral."

The admiral chuckled. "I figured that's what you'd say." He looked at Gunner. "Commander, do the intel people anticipate resistance from the Commies?"

"Sir, we don't think they are stupid enough to fire on us. We expect the typical type of activity you see in war games. Our planes chasing their planes. Their planes trying to chase ours. Just like their other daddies, the Russians, tried in the Cold War. And while we don't expect live fire, there's always a risk that some antsy North Korean pilot could get trigger-happy with our planes operating in such close quarters near the coast, over this area that they dispute."

"Okay," Hampton said. "Our mission, in addition to conducting joint naval exercises, is to spend at least two weeks flying into the hot zone to preserve international airspace and to deter the North Koreans from attacking these islands."

Gunner nodded. "That's exactly right, sir."

"We're within flight distance of Yeonpyeong right now," Admiral Hampton said. "Captain Garcia, let's get our planes in the air as soon as we break. Go below and brief your squadron commanders. Let's carry out our orders."

"Aye, sir," the CAG said.

"Captain Farrow, let's get a classified communiqué to all ships in the battle group that overflights are to begin within the hour. Be on alert in the event of hostile response."

"Yes, sir," the chief of staff said.

"Gentlemen, any questions for Lieutenant Commander McCormick?"

"No, sir," Captain Harrison said, as the others shook their heads in the negative.

"Commander McCormick, is there anything else we need to know?"

Gunner's stomach knotted, his mind again riveted to the classified rumors that had haunted him for the last few days. Why even mention the rumors of elderly Americans being held? This information was presented within the context of general background and, in Gunner's judgment, was not all that relevant to the mission at hand. No one here needed to know, not the Navy pilots, not the ship's captains, not even the admiral. The rumors, even if they knew about them, would not help any of the naval personnel carry out their stated mission of deterring a North Korean invasion of Yeonpyeong and the other islands. In fact, Gunner decided it probably was a dumb idea that some securities analyst had included that information as part of the background for the briefing.

"Commander?"

"Yes, sir."

"Was there anything else?"

Gunner hesitated. "Yes, sir, there was one other item."

"Shoot."

"Well, sir, when I was back in the States, I had sent you a message with a request for approval of leave."

"Yes, Captain Farrow brought that to me. You want to take leave in Seoul?"

"Yes, sir. I've never been to Seoul, and I haven't burned any leave in a year. I thought it would be a good opportunity not only to check out the country but also to keep my ear to the ground for any intel that might be of use to the task force. Korea is a real military hotspot right now, and I think it would be helpful to our intelligence if I got a firsthand look on the ground, maybe visit a couple of our bases ... speak with the intel guys there. Besides, Lieutenant Porter here has been well-versed on our current situation and would be more than capable in my absence."

"You're asking for thirty days?"

"Probably wouldn't use all that, sir. But you know how it is. If I don't use it, I lose it."

"Hmm ..." Hampton crossed his arms again. "I never like to deny leave to a well-deserving officer. Of course, I'm a little reluctant in this case because of the exercises we're about to begin. Let me think about it and I'll get back with you."

"Aye, aye, sir."

"Thanks for the briefing, Gunner. You're dismissed."

"Thank you, sir."

Two hours later, after a lunch of meatloaf, mashed potatoes, and green beans in the officers' wardroom, Gunner had still not heard from the admiral regarding his leave request. The carrier was now operating off the area near the disputed waters, and as flight operations over Yeon-pyeong had been underway for about an hour, he decided to head back up to the bridge to watch a few takeoffs ... and to think.

With a mug of coffee in his hand, he stepped out onto the observation deck outside the flight bridge to join the others already there. A cool breeze was whipping off the sea. The sun had reached its midday zenith slightly south of overhead as the earth tilted to within weeks of her winter solstice. Below, on the flight deck, a crew was positioning an F/A-18 Super Hornet for takeoff.

Good thing the admiral could not read his mind, Gunner thought, as he watched helmet-clad crew members rushing around the plane, wisps of steam coming from the steel deck. Not only would the admiral deny his leave request, he might order him shot and dumped to the sharks.

Gunner knew well that wealth had its benefits. The wealthy enjoyed choices beyond the imagination of the poor. On the other hand, the temptations accompanying fortune if not carefully checked could wreak self-destruction. Such had been the fate of many millionaire playboys whose adventures only money could buy. JFK Jr., Dodi Fayed, Davey Allison, John Walton, John Denver.

Not that Gunner considered himself a playboy. But to the charge of multimillionaire? To that charge, he would plead guilty. Indeed, he had made his money the old-fashioned way.

He had inherited it.

Over the generations, his family's giant peanut-farming operation at Corbin Hall Plantation, near Suffolk, Virginia, had given him the luxury of never having to work, had he so chosen.

And now the fortune had helped rocket his imagination on a super-highway to the danger zone.

This was crazy. He should nix the idea, here and now, and take leave somewhere else. Perhaps Hawaii. Maybe Tahiti or Europe. His playground was the world.

He soaked his esophagus with more hot caffeine, swallowed hard, and tried to stop thinking about what he was planning to do.

Seventy-five feet below the observation deck, down on the flight deck, high-pressure steam catapults hissed and pierced the air. The wind, blowing in from the bow, pushed the steam back across the deck like a blanket covering all the way to the stern.

Gunner gazed off to the horizon. Somewhere out there, beyond the wide expanse of blue waters, lay Korea, the "Land of the Morning Calm," and within its borders ...

"Morning, Commander." An ensign, with binoculars draped around his neck, nodded and smiled.

"Mister Roberts." Gunner nodded, sipped more coffee, and resumed his thoughts.

Still, if the rumors were true ... he had done his homework, he was an intelligence officer, and he had reason to believe ...

"Clear the flight deck! Prepare to launch!" The voice from the 1MC, the ship's public-address system, boomed across the flight deck. Navy crew members, sporting kelly-green vests, helmets, and jackets, and wearing camouflage pants and black boots, sprinted away from the jet. One crew member, designated the shooter, knelt on the runway beside the cockpit and pointed his finger straight out over the end of the flight deck toward the sea.

Flames roared full thrust from the jet's twin afterburners, and ... *swooooooooosh.* The giant steel catapult, propelled by thousands of tons of compressed steam, slung the roaring jet off the bow of the ship. The Hornet dipped a bit over the water, as if about to drop into the sea, and then, with flames thrusting from its afterburners, peeled off to the left and shot almost like a rocket up into the sun-drenched blue sky.

"MiG-21s inbound! Nine o'clock! Cover your ears!" The senior chief pointed off the carrier's port side. Two airborne objects, glistening about five hundred feet above the water, roared in toward the ship like attacking missiles. The aerial game of cat and mouse had begun. Gunner was about to get his first close-up view of the North Korean military.

He held his hand up to block the glare from the sun. "Where'd they go? I lost 'em."

"Here they come!" the ensign said.

Gunner put down his coffee and covered his ears.

Swoooosh.

Swooosh.

Boom!

Gunner leaned out over the steel railing and craned his head skyward. Two sleek-backed jet fighters, each with a red star painted in a white circle on its fuselage, streaked like rockets straight over the ship, trailed by the booming thunder of their roaring jet engines bouncing off the flight deck.

"Here come the good guys!" someone shouted over the diminishing roar from the MiGs.

Swoooosh.

Swooosh.

Boom!

Two Navy F/A-18s shot across *Harry Truman*'s bow.

"Wooo, doggie! Ride 'em, cowboy!" a senior chief yelled, yanking his ball cap from his head and making circles in the air to cheer on the Americans. More jet-engine thunder shook the ship as the Hornets rocketed through the sky off to the right, then began banking right, hot on the tails of the Commies.

Gunner brought his mug to his lips, but the adrenaline shaking his hand made it impossible to take a sip.

"They're getting bold!" the lieutenant to Gunner's left blurted out. "Right over the top of the ship!"

"Too bad our boys can't just splash 'em," the senior chief said. "These are the wimpiest rules of engagement I ever saw!"

"International airspace," the lieutenant, the junior JAG officer on the ship, responded. "They can fly wherever they want until and unless the president changes the rules of engagement. We're out here to protect and preserve international airspace."

"Lawyers," the senior chief mumbled in a sarcasm-tinged tone, reflecting a universal disgust for lawyers, even on the high seas. "They could launch a missile at the carrier, and all our boys could do is splash 'em. That'd be trading a fighter jet with one man for a supercarrier with five thousand men." He grunted. "This politically correct crap is a bunch of—" He stopped himself. "I'm not gonna cuss in the presence of officers." He pulled a cigarette from his pocket.

"You know"—the senior chief fiddled in his pocket for his lighter—

"Ole Harry Truman said in the Korean War that he might just nuke 'em." He struck the lighter, firing up the cigarette. "They don't make 'em like Give 'Em Hell Harry anymore."

"Actually," Gunner said, "I think if they take out our carrier, we take out Pyongyang. And that'd be trading five thousand Americans for 3.2 million Commies. I'm not sure they're *that* crazy."

"Maybe so, Commander"—the senior chief blew a smoke ring into the sky—"but I don't want to be their guinea pig."

"Attention on deck!" someone shouted.

All hands jumped to attention. The officer, two silver stars on the shoulders of his nearly black Eisenhower-style jacket, walked out on the observation deck. "At ease, gentlemen." Rear Admiral James Hampton sported a confident smile. "Everybody pumped up yet?"

Gunner nodded at the carrier strike group commander. "Afternoon, sir."

"Afternoon, Gunner," Admiral Hampton said. He turned to the senior chief. "Spare a cigarette, Senior Chief?"

"Absolutely, sir." The senior chief spoke with an enthusiasm that reflected a higher regard for Navy admirals than for Navy lawyers.

The admiral watched the activity on the flight deck for a while, then turned to Gunner. "I came up to let you know I'm granting your leave request."

Gunner's heart jumped. "Thank you, sir."

"But I'm doing so with the stipulation that if things get too hot out here, we cancel your leave immediately and fly you back out to the ship. Leave contact information with Captain Farrow and be prepared to get to Osan if I need to send a plane for you."

"Of course, Admiral."

"And Gunner, before you leave, the air wing commander needs some updated intel on how many squadrons have switched from east coast to west coast bases in North Korea and their potential strike capabilities against the task force if something goes wrong. We need the latest intel."

"Absolutely, Admiral. I'll also make sure Lieutenant Porter is more than up to speed on all locations of enemy forces."

"Just be prepared to fly back out if we need you, son."

The thunder of another F/A-18, roaring its engines to full power for launch, muffled the admiral's voice. He waited as the jet *swooshed* off the end of the flight deck and started its climb.

"We've got an E-2C Hawkeye launching for Osan Air Base at zero-seven-hundred hours tomorrow. Why don't you get me that report, pack your seabag, and go enjoy the sights of the city. Who knows? You may even pick up some intel that would help our mission here."

"Aye, sir. I'll have that report for you within the hour." And Gunner surrendered to whatever fate lay before him.

"Good man." Admiral Hampton delivered an enthusiastic slap to Gunner's back. "You got a place to stay?"

"Yes, sir. When I was in Virginia, I took the liberty of contacting some folks just in case you approved my leave. I'll go up and get a message off and let them know I'm coming."

"Excellent," Hampton said. "Keep your eyes and ears peeled, Gunner. Be safe. And don't do anything dangerous."

"I'll be careful, Admiral. Nothing dangerous."

CHAPTER 4

Osan Air Base
South Korea

Strapped into a less-than-comfortable jump seat as the plane began its final approach, Lieutenant Commander Gunner McCormick craned his neck for a peek through the third small porthole on the right side of the twin-engine E-2C Hawkeye. He caught his first glimpse of the distant South Korean landscape, bathed in the early morning sun.

As he gazed at South Korea, his thoughts reverted again to his last conversation with the admiral.

"Keep your eyes and ears peeled, Gunner. Be safe. And don't do anything dangerous."

"I'll be careful, Admiral. Nothing dangerous."

Did the admiral know something? Did he have a premonition? Lying was against Gunner's religion. And flat-out lying to an admiral, as Gunner had done when he promised nothing dangerous, was downright stupid.

His conscience was bothering him. But this was no time to cop a conscience.

Shake it off, Gunner.

The pilot banked right, and and the twin nine-thousand-foot runways of the sprawling Osan Air Base came into view. They were surrounded by rice paddies and ran parallel to the snaking Chinwi River. Home to the US Air Force's Fifty-First Fighter Wing, Osan was the most forward-deployed US military base in Korea, only forty-five miles south of the Demilitarized Zone. Air Force F-16s at Osan formed an aerial vanguard to protect the capital city of Seoul if the Communists struck across the DMZ.

The Hawkeye banked again, displaying the mountainous terrain beyond the low-lying peninsula. From two thousand feet, in the midst of a sun-drenched afternoon, and in the distance, was a panoramic display of majestic snow-capped mountains.

"We're on final approach for landing at Osan," the pilot said over the loudspeaker. "We'll be on the ground in about two minutes."

Gunner tightened his shoulder harness and sat back. The plane descended through bumping turbulence and, a moment later, *bump* ... A slight bounce on the runway was followed by the sound of rubber wheels spinning against concrete, and then the *whooshing* sound of a braking aircraft decelerating on the ground.

"Welcome to South Korea," the Navy pilot said. "For those of you who've never been to Osan, you'll find that the Air Force is usually accommodating. They're supposed to have a couple of Humvees to ferry us over to Building 772. From there, you can check in if you're staying on base or take a taxi or bus into Seoul."

The plane rolled to a stop. The whine of its two engines diminished. Then, silence.

"One other thing." The pilot's voice boomed again over the PA system. "If you're taking a bus into Seoul, they won't take dollars. Only won. They'll do an exchange for you there in Building 772. Cab drivers will take dollars."

The side door opened, and the cold gust of air was like a sudden slap on the face, reminding Gunner that he was now on Korean soil. His heart was pounding. Second thoughts raced through his mind.

From his shirt pocket, he extracted the small photograph that he kept over his heart. The colors had faded over time, but the image of the young Marine officer in dress blues, seated before the American flag, helped calm his nerves. "Focus," he whispered. "Eyes on the goal. Remember your mission."

Another blast of cold air brought shivering goose bumps up the back of his neck. Gunner stood and donned his wool Navy bridgecoat, which knocked down the chill a bit, and then his Navy officer's visored cover.

"Hope to see you back on board soon," the pilot said.

Gunner picked up his carry-on, waited for the supply corps commander to leave, and then stepped down onto the gusty tarmac. Four Air Force Humvees sat parked in a half-moon formation beside the plane. Several enlisted men milled about, moving luggage from the Navy plane into the Humvees.

"Commander McCormick!" The gruff-sounding voice coming from near the tail section was barely audible against the roaring engine of an F-16 out on the runway.

Gunner turned and saw a civilian walking toward him. The man wore a black pullover cap and a black pullover sweater under an unbuttoned black leather jacket and black pants. The two-inch scar along the left side of his jutting jaw was visible even from twenty feet away. His graying hair blew in the wind. He stuck his hand out toward Gunner. "You Commander McCormick?"

"That's me," Gunner said.

"John Davenport." The man's grip was like a steel vice. "My friends call me Jackrabbit. I got your message."

"I've heard a lot about you," Gunner said as the man mercifully loosened the crushing handshake. "Nice to meet you, Mr. Davenport."

"Mister Davenport was my daddy," the man responded in a gruff Southern dialect. "Where's your bags?"

"Just a carry-on." Gunner lifted the seabag off the tarmac. "You prefer John or Jackrabbit?"

"Don't give a durn." The man pointed at a muddy black pickup truck with a crew cab behind one of the Humvees. "That's our ride."

"That's great, John," Gunner said. "I thought I might have to take a bus to Seoul."

"Like I said, my friends call me Jackrabbit," the man snapped in an almost irritated tone. "Throw your bag in the back and hop in. Our contact is waiting for us."

"Roger that." Gunner unzipped just enough of the bag to extract a bottle of water, tossed the suitcase into the bed of the truck, then opened the passenger-side door. Toasty warm air from the truck's heater bathed his face and neck as he slid onto the seat and slammed the door.

Behind the seat, two black automatic rifles—US-issued M-16s with magazines—lay on the floor. Jackrabbit stepped on the accelerator, and the truck moved out across the tarmac, away from the plane and through an open gate guarded by two enlisted Air Force MPs.

Jackrabbit swung the truck left onto the main road.

"I appreciate the roadside service," Gunner said.

"For what you're paying, not a problem." The truck rolled along a main road paralleling the runways.

"You have any problem getting on base?"

"Nah. Still some benefits to being retired military living outside the US." Jackrabbit rapped the horn. "Move it, lady!" Another beep.

The Korean woman driving the Toyota hatchback turned off the road.

"Your dossier is impressive," Gunner said. "Purple Heart twice. Defense Distinguished Service Medal. Distinguished Service Cross times two for service in Afghanistan. Once in Iraq. Nominated for the Medal of Honor. Special Forces. Special Ops." He unscrewed the cap on the water and took a swig. "Remarkable."

"It's a bunch of bunk." Jackrabbit snorted. "Means I've been shot at a lot."

"Well, Jackrabbit," Gunner said, "you're too modest, considering your history. I'm glad you're on our team."

A stoplight along the main road turned yellow, then red. Jackrabbit tapped the brakes, and the truck rolled to a stop behind an Air Force Humvee. "Look, Commander, let's get one thing straight." Jackrabbit looked straight ahead through the windshield. "I'm in this thing for two reasons. First, for the money. Second, to kill Communists." An angry tone seemed to take over. "I can't decide which I like more. Green dollars or dead Communists. Now if it just so happens that your interests ... whatever they are ... coincide with mine ... well, then, I guess I'm on the team. But I want you to understand one thing."

The light turned green, and the truck accelerated through the heavily guarded gate leading off base.

"What's that?"

"If you're suggesting what I think you're suggesting, you're flirting with a suicide mission. See, for me, it's a sport. Killing Communists. I don't care if they kill me. But Commander, you're a younger man than me. You've not lost what I've lost. If I were you, I'd think long and hard before I went through with this. It's not too late to change your mind."

They came to another stoplight. "We drive through this light, we're on the freeway to Seoul. I can still turn back around. That Hawkeye can take you right back out to the carrier, and you can celebrate the weekend in a warmer spot."

Gunner let that thought sink in. Call it off. He's probably dead. Why risk your life? Why risk war? He thought of his family, fourteen hours behind on the other side of the International Date Line, getting ready to celebrate the most American of holidays, Thanksgiving. Soon his mother would be putting the turkey in the oven to roast overnight. Then she'd be up early to prepare the rest of the feast.

For a moment he felt a twinge of homesickness. He reached back into his pocket and pulled out the faded color picture of the young Marine and just looked at it. His mother swore they had the same eyes, the same facial features. Indeed, he had part of the man's name.

The not knowing was the worst. Someone had to reach out. Someone had to get some sort of an answer. It was obvious the government was not going to help. He put the picture back into his pocket. "Let's roll, Jackrabbit. If we die, we die."

"Rock 'n' roll, Commander. Rock 'n' roll." Jackrabbit popped the clutch, the truck jumped, then sped onto the ramp headed north for the Korean Expressway.

In less than an hour, they arrived in Seoul. The black pickup weaved its way through crowded streets full of brake lights and small Korean cars, all beeping their horns and flashing their taillights. The colorful, chaotic swirl of early morning metropolitan Asia revealed an ultramodern city that seemed visibly torn between her Asian roots and an ever-present Western influence.

Gunner looked up and saw a street sign written in Korean, Chinese, and English. The English proclaimed: "Parking Lot Street."

Jackrabbit rapped down on the horn. "Move, lady!" he yelled at the car ahead, then pulled the pickup over in front of a parking meter and turned off the engine.

"Let's go," he said as he opened his door.

Gunner stepped out onto the sidewalk into the hustle and bustle of olive-skinned humanity, students with book bags, jacketed men with briefcases, and black-haired Korean women with shopping bags moving in every direction.

"Where are we?"

"Seoul. Hongade Section. Real posh section of the city. Over there's Hongik University. Real artsy private university. Follow me." They stepped into an old brick building and got into an elevator. Jackrabbit pushed the button for the third floor. The doors closed. A moment later, the doors reopened on a hallway with an old stone wall lined with photographs and rusted steel plates covering the windows.

"This way," Jackrabbit said. They turned right and walked down a few paces to the entrance of a bar-restaurant.

"What's this place?"

"This is Moonyang Bar. Popular hangout with the locals. You got to know about it to find it."

"They open this early?"

"Nah. The place isn't open yet. Don't worry, you've got it all to yourself for a while."

They walked through two glass doors into a darkened lobby where, off to the right, unmanned electronic cash registers sat on a counter in front of black-and-white photographs hanging on a back wall, presumably of famous Koreans who had frequented the joint. The front of the place was barely illuminated by subdued light from the hallway. A couple of candles flickered on the counter, their flames twisting under a slight breeze generated by a couple of ceiling fans. To the left of the photographs, carefully placed in dozens of iron racks bolted to the wall, were hundreds of liquor and wine bottles.

More light seeped in under a door toward the back of the building. To the left of the door, black-and-gold curtains hung, leading into another area in back of the bar. A faint light glowed behind the curtains.

The place was empty.

Gunner followed Jackrabbit to a small table way back in a corner. A pitcher of water sat in the middle of it, and three glasses of water had been poured, as if someone were preparing for a meeting. "Have a seat," Jackrabbit said. "Be right back."

Jackrabbit stepped over to the wall and flipped a switch. A globe light hanging on a chain over the table came on. He then disappeared through the hanging curtains at the back of the room.

Gunner barely had time to look around before the curtains stirred and Jackrabbit walked back in. Behind him was a Korean man, fifties-looking, of average height. He had on a black T-shirt and looked pretty muscular for a man of his age. He walked over to the table, but did not sit.

"Commander, this is Jung-Hoon Sohn."

Gunner stood and extended his hand. "I'm Lieutenant Commander Gunner McCormick, United States Navy. I've heard of you, Colonel Jung-Hoon. It's an honor."

The Korean bowed slightly but did not take Gunner's hand. "How may I help you, Commander?" His voice was low and his English was nearly impeccable. He had piercing black eyes.

"I want to talk to you about North Korea. There are rumors I have heard. They come up occasionally in discussions about the North—"

The tattoo on Jung-Hoon's bicep sprang forth like an angry rattlesnake. Gunner's eyes shifted back and forth between the identical tattoos on the biceps of the Korean and the American. The Korean's tattoo was smaller than Jackrabbit's, but it obviously was the product of the same skin artist. The flag in the tattoos had three horizontal stripes—blue, thicker red, small blue—and in the midst of the red field, a white circle, and in it a red star. The flag of North Korea. Just above the flag was the image of a man shoveling dirt on the North Korean flag.

"I have heard that somewhere in the North," Gunner said, "the Communists may be holding some old Americans captive from the Korean War."

Jung-Hoon and Jackrabbit exchanged glances. "Please sit, Commander," Jung-Hoon said as he pulled out a chair. Jackrabbit and Gunner both sat down.

"It is unusual for an American to hear of such things, Commander McCormick," Jung-Hoon said. "Over the years our governments have suppressed such stories." The Korean scratched his chin. "I am curious." A raised eyebrow. "Where did you hear such a thing?"

"I am an intelligence officer. I have top-secret clearance and came across a briefing that mentioned the possibility."

Jung-Hoon leaned back and crossed his arms. "You are talking about something that happened sixty years ago. With all the other issues that threaten the peninsula—a possible invasion from the North, shootings along the DMZ, North Korea's nuclear program—tell me, Commander, why would you come here to ask me about such rumors that so few even know about?"

Gunner leaned forward ever so slightly. "Tell me, Jung-Hoon, is it customary for such a legendary warrior of the Land of the Morning Calm to answer the questions of a lowly admirer by asking another question?"

The Korean's stone face morphed into a chuckle. "This must be a day for rumors. The 'legendary warrior' story is a rumor of the past. This bar is my life now." He grinned. And then, as quickly as the chuckle had appeared, the stone face returned. "I believe my question was ... why come so far, Commander, to ask a bar owner about a rumor, a very implausible rumor?"

Gunner hesitated. He reached into his pocket and placed the faded color photograph of the young warrior in dress blues on the table. As Jung-Hoon and Jackrabbit stared down at the photo, Gunner said, "This gentleman is my grandfather." They looked up at him. "Second Lieutenant Robert K. Pendleton, United States Marine Corps. He disappeared at the Battle of Chosin Reservoir. They never found his body. His disappearance has haunted my family for years." He paused. "I don't know what happened to him. But whether he's dead or alive—and I know the chances are slim that he's alive—I am going to find him."

Silence.

The three men sat there, as if playing Russian roulette to see who would speak first. Jung-Hoon picked up the photograph. He held it up and studied it. "In Asia, it is noble to fight for the honor of our elders."

Another silence.

"I'm from a place called Virginia," Gunner said. "And in Virginia, it is likewise noble to defend the honor of our forefathers. That longing is in my blood, Jung-Hoon. My grandfather disappeared there at Chosin Reservoir and was never heard from again. And if I have to go north of the DMZ myself, I'm prepared to do that."

Jung-Hoon studied the photograph again, then slid it back toward Gunner. "These rumors have circulated for years. Such rumors are passed on to a very few Koreans, mostly military and a few government officials with top-secret clearances. But there are witnesses who were on covert operations across the lines who claim to have credible information that this once was the case."

Gunner looked at his grandfather's picture. Anger shot through him. "If you believe the evidence is credible, why has your government done nothing about it?"

Jung-Hoon raised an eyebrow. "Commander. Please. The rumor was that elderly Americans were being held, not elderly South Koreans. These rumors are classified as top secret by your government and mine, as I am sure you have seen in your capacity as an intelligence officer. If there is any truth to them, doing something about them after the armistice agreement was signed would risk another war. Our governments have kept quiet partly because of the sketchiness of the data and partly because of the supposed location of the prison camps."

Gunner let that sink in. He picked up the photo of the young Marine officer and put it back in his pocket. "What location?"

"Rumor placed the camps somewhere northeast of Pyongyang, near the city of Hamhung."

Gunner thought about that. "I'm familiar with Pyongyang. Hamhung doesn't ring a bell."

"Hamhung is the capital of South Hamgyŏng Province." He looked at Jackrabbit. "My friend, would you go look in the upper right drawer of my desk? There is a map of North Korea in there."

"No problem," Jackrabbit said. He headed back through the curtains and disappeared.

"The war almost destroyed the city," Jung-Hoon said. "They rebuilt Hamhung during the midfifties and early sixties. Then, in the nineties, a great famine struck North Korea, which devastated Hamhung more than any other city. Thousands died of starvation. Dear Leader could not feed his people. There is talk of rebellious factions within the city."

"Really?"

"Yes. Some reports claimed seventy thousand people died during the famine. Reports surfaced of children dying of malnutrition and thousands of freshly dug shallow graves in the hillsides. In 1995, a group of North Korean soldiers began marching toward Pyongyang to challenge the government. This is the only documented challenge to the North Korean government by elements of its army. Of course the rebellion was quickly put down."

Jackrabbit returned with a map. He spread it out on the table.

North Korea, Pyongyang,
Taedong River, Hamhung, Hungnam

"Thank you," Jung-Hoon said. "As you can see, Commander, the Taedong River flows from the northeast to the southwest, through the capital at Pyongyang, where your ship the *Pueblo* remains, and out to the west into the Yellow Sea.

"Now if you look over here to the Sea of Japan, just south of the 40th parallel, you see the city of Hungnam. From Hungnam port, all UN forces and thousands of refugees were evacuated after the Battle of Chosin Reservoir in 1950."

"I remember reading that," Gunner said.

"Eight miles to the north is Hamhung, the city I told you about.

And somewhere to the west or north of that"—he pointed at the map—"are the rumored sites of these secret camps."

"Hmm." Gunner studied the map. His eyes fixed on Hamhung. I wonder if . . . He looked up at Jung-Hoon. "Do you think any camps are still there?"

"I think the camps were once there," the Korean said, "but I doubt that they are still there, at least not to hold captured Americans. Most if not all of the Americans should have died by now."

Gunner studied the map again, then looked up. "So . . . let me ask it this way. Do you think they are still holding any Americans?"

Jung-Hoon met his eyes. He glanced at Jackrabbit, then back at Gunner. "A year ago, I heard rumors that a few might still be alive. These rumors came from reports floating over from the North. Since then . . . nothing. But do I believe that there still may be elderly Americans somewhere behind the lines?" He stopped for a moment, as if weighing the odds. "If someone put a gun to my head and made me guess, I would say yes. I would not think many were still alive, but too many reports surfaced over the years for there not to be some truth to these rumors."

The three men sat there, seemingly in a speechless stalemate. Gunner finally said, "How can I get into that area to find out?"

"You'd need a pile of money and a suicide wish," Jackrabbit said.

"Money's no problem," Gunner said. "Let's say I wanted to take a small team in behind the lines, unnoticed, with the mission of discovering whether these rumors are true . . . and, if so, bringing one or two of the men out alive."

Jung-Hoon and Jackrabbit again eyed each other. Then Jung-Hoon nodded, yielding the floor to the American expat. "You'd need a light aircraft you could ditch in the sea. A rubber floatable Zodiac boat. Light weaponry. Sophisticated communications equipment with jammers. Maps. Dagger military GPS devices with updated crypto key. Light plastic explosives with remote detonators. Heavy-duty wire cutters. Plenty of cash. US dollars and even more North Korean won. And, of course, if you're caught, you're executed on the spot."

Gunner looked at the American he had just met, then at the Korean. "I know your background, gentlemen. I know how each of you feels about the Communist regime in Pyongyang. Will you help me? I will pay you more in a month than you would make in a year."

Eyes shifted again between Jung-Hoon and Jackrabbit. "When you're asking for help," Jackrabbit said, "you mean you want us to cross the lines with you?"

"Why not?" Gunner said. "Both of you have faced dangerous situations with Special Forces on top-secret missions all over the world. If the money's right ... and it will be ... why not this mission? You're both fearless. And you have a chance to accomplish something worthwhile."

"But Commander," Jung-Hoon said, "we are both retired warriors. I live a peaceful life running this bar. And my friend here" — he nodded to Jackrabbit — "he can speak for himself, but I have known him for years. He is trying to live a quiet life here in Korea, away from the fast life back in the USA. Besides, while neither of us fears dying, if we are caught, the stakes would be greater than our own lives. The North would claim that we are government spies and use this as a pretext for attacking the South. If that happens, innocent women and children would die. So you see, Commander, this is not only about money. Tell me why we should consider this."

The Korean had made a good point.

Would Gunner lose his most valuable team members before even getting started? Perhaps he should go back to the *Truman* or spend a week or two in Seoul and then leave. He prayed for the right words.

"I'm from Virginia. I wasn't much on reading the Good Book back then, but every night my mother made me memorize a Bible verse. One that she made me repeat every day for a year was very simple." He paused. "Deuteronomy 6:18: 'Do what is right.'" He looked at Jackrabbit. "You're an American. You live here in South Korea now, but you will always be an American. Now I know our country has undergone considerable change." He stopped. "A lot of that change has not been for the good. But there was a time when our government would never leave Americans behind enemy lines to rot. Politics or not, international ramifications or not, that is plain wrong. And if our government won't get to the bottom of it, somebody must have the courage to do the right thing. Do what is right. Americans don't leave Americans behind enemy lines to rot." He paused. "Not in the America I grew up in, anyway. You're a decorated war hero, and I'm just an intelligence officer. But whether you go with me or not, somehow, someway, I'm crossing that line to the North, and I'll get some answers ... even if it costs me my life."

The *whirr* of the overhead ceiling fans filled the silence.

"Is this not about your grandfather," Jung-Hoon asked, "making this a personal mission for you? Forgive my bluntness, but North Korea is a barren, famine-ravished, poverty-stricken wasteland. Your grandfather probably died long ago."

"I understand that," Gunner said, meeting the gaze of the Korean. "And yes, this is personal. But maybe it is for you too." Jung-Hoon raised an eyebrow. "I've done my homework, Jung-Hoon. I know what they did to your brother."

Jung-Hoon shifted on his chair.

"And also to your wife, Jackrabbit," Gunner said.

Anger flashed across the ex-pat's lips and eyebrows.

"My apologies for evoking bitter memories. But your brother, Jung-Hoon, and your wife, Jackrabbit, gave their lives fighting this regime. And their work was not sponsored by the government. They fought injustice out of a brave commitment to do what was right." Gunner stopped to let them think of the past. "I don't know about the two of you, but I'm willing to risk my life for the memory of your wife"—he eyed Jackrabbit—"and the memory of your brother"—a glance at Jung-Hoon—"and yes, for the memory of my grandfather too."

The light *whirr* of the overhead fan hummed on as the triumvirate engaged in an awkward silent negotiation, each with his own thoughts of right and wrong.

Gunner broke the silence. "If either or both of you gentlemen do not wish to join me, I understand. I will find someone else who will."

He waited. There was no response. Finally he stood. "I'll be leaving now. Jackrabbit, don't worry about driving me back. I'll catch a cab."

"Wait," Jung-Hoon said. "Meet me at Grace Fellowship Evangelical Baptist Church in Seoul. Seven o'clock tonight."

"At a Baptist church?"

"Yes," Jung-Hoon said. "Jackrabbit knows the church. My brother attended there. So did Jackrabbit's wife. I do not attend, but they are good people. The pastor is closing speaker at a conference tonight. Meet me in front of the church sanctuary at seven, just after the speech. I will introduce you to the pastor."

"Who is this pastor?" Gunner asked. "We need to be careful about who we talk to."

Jung-Hoon looked irritated. "You asked for my help. Do you still wish to have it?"

"Of course."

"Then trust me," the Korean said as he stood. "We are—what do you Americans say?—on the same page here. I would not compromise the sensitive nature of these discussions."

"Forgive me," Gunner said, extending his hand to the Korean and bowing slightly. "Of course I trust you."

"Very well," Jung-Hoon said. "Meet me there. Jackrabbit will drive you."

"I will see you at seven."

CHAPTER 5

Seoul, South Korea

Gunner sat alone in the hotel restaurant in downtown Seoul. His American companion had dumped him at the hotel and told him to be ready at 6:30 for the drive to meet the South Korean pastor. Then he left.

Gunner tried his best to force down a Korean dinner of bulgogi and rice. Although the beef was tender, he had no appetite. His stomach churned at the thought of what the next few days might bring. He stirred the shallow puddle of cooling coffee at the bottom of his cup.

"More coffee?" The smiling young Korean waitress seemed pleased to be able to practice her English.

Gunner nodded. "*Ano*," he said, taking a stab at the most basic word in his limited Korean vocabulary.

The woman smiled and half bowed, then poured more coffee into his mug.

Gunner's thoughts focused again on the resumé of Jackrabbit Davenport, the man who could make the difference between failure and success in the next few days. Special Forces. Green Beret. Multiple kills in Afghanistan and Iraq before transferring to South Korea. Met a Korean woman. Married her. She died. He stayed. Mercenary work in Myanmar and Thailand. Then back to South Korea.

But for what? His wife was gone.

Maybe professional killers don't talk. Jackrabbit barely said a word on their drive into Seoul. This odd-looking man, though American by birth and by appearance, seemed distant. Angry ...

Gunner took another swallow of the hot coffee.

"Ready to roll, Commander?"

Gunner turned and saw the expatriate, dressed in his signature tight black T-shirt and black pants, a leather jacket plopped over his shoulder, making quick strides toward him.

Gunner stood. "Just need to pay. Then I'm good to go."

"Make it fast," Jackrabbit barked. "Jung-Hoon Sohn doesn't like to be kept waiting."

"You bet." Gunner swigged the rest of his coffee.

He stepped to the counter and handed a credit card to the clerk to pay for his meal. As the clerk swiped Gunner's Visa, the smell of beer breath made Gunner turn to see the source.

The familiar tattooed bicep brushed against him. "Truck's out front," Jackrabbit announced, then headed toward the revolving door at the hotel's entrance. "Like I said, the man doesn't like waitin'."

Gunner rushed back to the table, grabbed the black leather jacket he'd left draped over the chair, put it on, and jogged out the front door. Already behind the wheel of the black pickup, Jackrabbit was staring straight ahead.

"Ready, Commander?" Jackrabbit revved the engine, and the truck screeched through the circular driveway, nearly striking a bellman, who jumped aside just in time.

"Strap up, Commander. We got thirty minutes to make it through this traffic."

The church was huge. They parked on the sixth floor of the garage, descended to ground level in a fast-moving elevator, then rode up three escalators to reach the church lobby.

The room was enormous, three stories high, with a row of chandeliers hanging down from the arched ceiling. Only a few men and women were milling about, watching the activity on six large video screens mounted on the walls. The screens, all showing different angles, displayed live images of a sea of people packed into the seats in the sanctuary, all gazing up at a middle-aged man standing behind the pulpit, waving his hands as he spoke.

Gunner didn't understand a word. "That's some conference. There must be two thousand people in there," he said.

"The place seats four thousand," Jackrabbit said.

"Jung-Hoon said your wife went here. You ever go with her?"

"Nah. She came all the time. She dragged me with her once in a while. I didn't go very much. Easter. Christmas. You know?"

Gunner glanced back up at a screen. The conference appeared to be over. One camera showed a dozen conference attendees gathered around the pastor near the pulpit. He patted some on the shoulder and leaned over to perhaps whisper in the ears of others.

"You know him?"

"Quite well," Jackrabbit said. "Met him through my wife. He's tried to get me to come to church, especially after she died. But I never bothered."

"He must be a good speaker. What's his name?"

"Lee. Pastor John-Floyd Lee."

"Hmm. I understand the Lee part. But John-Floyd doesn't sound Korean to me."

"His granddaddy was American. Married a Korean lady working at Osan. He's named for his granddaddy."

"So he's one-fourth American," Gunner said.

"By blood, that's right. Although you can't tell it by looking at him."

Just then a half-dozen double doors flew open all at once. The conference attendees began filing into the lobby, heading for the pots of tea and trays of refreshments laid out on tables.

"That's our cue," Jackrabbit said. "Let's go."

Gunner followed Jackrabbit into the back of the half-moon-shaped sanctuary, moving against the heavy flow of humanity pouring out. In minutes they stood in the presence of the charismatic man himself, the Reverend John-Floyd Lee.

"Reverend, this is Commander Gunner McCormick," Jackrabbit said.

"Welcome to Korea, Commander." The pastor's English and his accent made Gunner think he could have been from the American Midwest. "And in the name of our Lord and Savior, welcome to Grace Church." Lee extended his hand to Gunner.

"Thank you, Pastor. This is a beautiful church."

"Thank you." Lee smiled. "It is beautiful indeed, but only because the risen Lord is at work here."

"Amen to that," Gunner said, feeling a bit awkward. This was the only response he could muster.

"Commander McCormick is the man that Jung-Hoon Sohn called about."

"Ah, yes." A look of recollection crossed Lee's face. "Jung-Hoon will be meeting us in my office. Follow me, my brothers," he said as he headed toward a side door and led the way down a hallway.

A number of conference goers were milling about in the area, and the pastor smiled and shook their hands, but did not stop to chat. Fifty feet down the hall, they entered an elevator that took them up. A few moments later, the doors opened. Only a few people were standing in the hall.

"This is the sixth floor. The church offices are up here," Lee said. They turned right, walked down a blue-carpeted hallway, then through a door into an office reception area.

A smiling woman sat behind the reception desk. She handed the pastor a note, he looked at it and put it in his pocket, then turned to Gunner and Jackrabbit. "Come into my office."

The pastor's office overlooked the boulevard in front of the church.

Jung-Hoon, who had been sitting on one of the two blue leather sofas, stood as they entered.

"Jung-Hoon Sohn." The pastor bowed at the aging warrior.

"Nice to see you, Pastor Lee." Jung-Hoon returned the bow.

"I look for you every Sunday," Pastor Lee chided.

"Perhaps if you come to my bar on Saturday night, I come to your church on Sunday morning, Pastor Lee."

Lee chuckled. "I understand you wanted me to meet with Commander McCormick."

"Yes, I wanted him to meet you because he is proposing a mission that is similar to the mission that my brother and Jackrabbit's wife were on."

The pastor's friendly expression changed, and his bubbly countenance went solemn.

"I thought," Jung-Hoon said, "perhaps you might provide us some assistance through your network or, better yet, perhaps talk him out of it."

"I see," the pastor said. "Everyone, please sit."

They sat down, and the pastor walked over and sat behind the large wooden desk flanked on each side by the South Korean flag and the white-blue-and-red Christian flag.

"Tell me. How may I help?"

Jung-Hoon said, "Pastor, the commander wants to finance a small mission into the North. His grandfather and other Americans disappeared there during the Korean War. He has heard the rumors that the Dear Leader may still be holding American soldiers, and he wants to find out for himself."

Lee looked at Gunner. "I am sorry about your grandfather. My grandfather was American, and he too fought in the North. But he was lucky. He made it home and married my grandmother, whom he met at the American base. He died twenty years ago, but I got to know him well, and it is his memory that has inspired this special ministry of ours."

Gunner looked at Jackrabbit and Jung-Hoon.

"Pastor, I have not told the commander about your ministry," Jung-Hoon said, "so he does not know what you do."

"Of course," Lee said. "Commander, our church secretly finances rescues of our brothers and sisters from the North."

A pause.

"Really?" Gunner said. "I'd heard of this type of activity going on, but I didn't know ..."

"Actually," the pastor said, "we try to fly under the radar screen. Several Christian organizations are involved."

"You go through ... where? ... China?"

"Exactly," Lee said. "It is impossible to get anyone out of North Korea through the DMZ. So we use our contacts to sneak them across the border between North Korea and China. We move them through China to the northern tip of Laos, then across the Mekong River into Thailand. If we get them to Bangkok, they are usually arrested, but then they are given the choice of refuge in Europe, the USA, or Seoul. Most choose Seoul."

"Wow," Gunner said. "That's got to be a couple of thousand miles from the North Korean border to Bangkok."

"Closer to four thousand," Lee said. "Hang on." He reached into a cabinet and pulled out a map mounted on foam board. He set the map on an easel beside his desk.

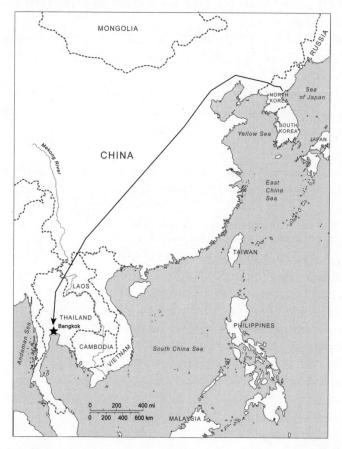

Escape route from North Korea through China, Laos, and Thailand to Bangkok

"This map shows our rescue route through China. As you can see, our normal route takes us west of China's major population centers, then down across the northern tip of Laos, across the Mekong River, and into Thailand. Bangkok is at the tip of the arrow."

Gunner got up to study the map. With his finger, he traced down the line of the arrow leading into Thailand. "That has to be very risky. Do your church members actually go?"

"It is dangerous, and yes, a small number of our members go. They risk their lives."

Jackrabbit seemed to tighten up.

"Only a select few know about our program. Jackrabbit lost his wife on one of these missions."

Gunner looked at Jackrabbit. "She died doing what she wanted to do," Jackrabbit said. "A North Korean border guard shot her at the Yalu River border."

"And I lost my brother near the same border," Jung-Hoon said. "He was on a church mission trip too." No one said anything for a moment. "Pastor, do you have a map of the border?"

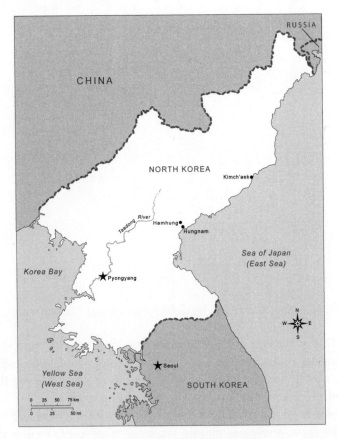

North Korea showing border with China

"Certainly," Lee said. He set another map on the easel. "This is the North Korean–Chinese border. It runs from the southwest to the northeast for a distance of about 880 miles. Parts of the border are fenced off on both sides and heavily guarded to stem the flow of North Koreans trying to escape. Parts of it are not as heavily guarded.

"We have established several different crossing points to make our rescue operations unpredictable. Most of the border, about five hundred miles of it, is marked by the Amnok River, as we call it, or the Yalu River, as the Chinese call it. It empties into Korea Bay, just beyond the town of Sinŭiju.

"Here is another map showing just the Amnok River, or the Yalu, as you call it.

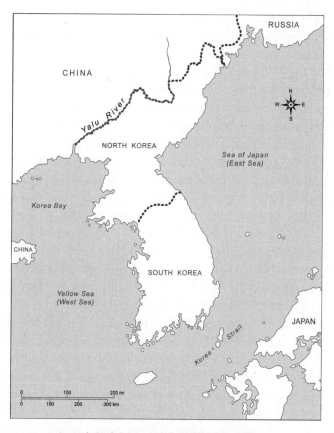

Amnok (Yalu) River on border of North Korea

"Most of our refugees have crossed this river around the midsection. Unfortunately, in recent years, North Korean border patrols have increased, making escapes much more dangerous. They've begun firing across the river into China, shooting at North Koreans fleeing. They sometimes have hit rescuers. That is what happened to Jackrabbit's wife and Jung-Hoon's brother."

"Now you know why we hate the North Koreans so much," Jackrabbit said.

"I understand," Gunner said.

"Still," the pastor continued, "as dangerous as this route is, at least there is a chance, and with a little luck and a lot of prayer ... If you try to cross the DMZ, you've got no chance."

The pastor paused.

Jung-Hoon looked at Gunner. "If you undertake this mission, I wanted Pastor Lee to get you to understand how deadly dangerous it can be, and, if you do decide to go ahead"—he turned from Gunner to Pastor Lee—"to see if the church might provide assistance, either intelligence, or manpower, or other means."

"Hmm." Pastor Lee crossed his arms and rocked back in his big black leather chair. "I have heard the rumors of these secret prison camps," he said. "And I believe them to have been true. At least at one time, I think they were true. And I believe the few members of the church who are involved in these rescue efforts would be sympathetic to your mission. But your proposed mission is different in several respects from the basic model under which we operate."

"I think I understand those differences," Jung-Hoon said, "but perhaps you could explain them to the commander."

"Of course," Lee said. "First, it seems that yours would be a paramilitary mission. Forgive me, but you would be crazy to undertake this type of rescue attempt unarmed. Is that correct?"

Gunner said, "You're right, Pastor. My team will need to be armed."

"Well," Lee responded, "our rescue missions do not carry weapons. Our weapon is cash. Bribes go a long way in cash-starved countries like China, Laos, Thailand, and North Korea. But no guns. Not for a church group. We rescue. We don't kill. Also, we don't cross the border into North Korea. We send messages through secret Christian networks to families there who wish to escape. But our people go only as far as the

North Korean–Chinese border. The refugee has to cross the river, then we help them to freedom. But I imagine that you will have to cross into North Korea to search for what you are looking for." Again he looked at Gunner and waited for a reply.

"Yes, Pastor. We will cross into the North."

Lee seemed to think for a moment. "I would not hesitate to rescue an American or anyone else held in that place. But your proposed mission does not match our model. I do not know how members of the committee would react."

"But what do you think about it?" Jung-Hoon pressed the issue.

"I don't know," Lee said. "I'd have to know more about it, and I'd have to pray about it. What did you have in mind, Jung-Hoon?"

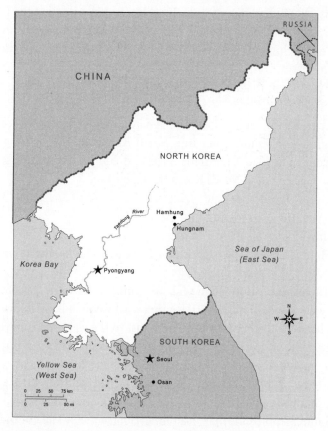

North Korea with Hungnam, Hamhung, Kimch'aek, Pyongyang, Seoul

"Well, the commander here says that money is no object. Thus, I propose that we infiltrate by a combination of air and sea, striking the coastline somewhere northeast of ... could you put the map of the border back up again, Pastor?"

"Certainly." He retrieved the map.

"Now, then," Jung-Hoon continued, "without getting into any details at this point, my plan involves striking the coast along the Sea of Japan, somewhere between Hungnam and Kimch'aek, then heading inland toward Hamhung. These camps are rumored to be in that area. We don't need the church's help to get in. It's your contacts on the ground in North Korea and the getting-out part that I want to explore."

"I take it your escape route would be into China?" Pastor Lee asked.

"As you pointed out, Pastor," Jung-Hoon said, "crossing the DMZ is suicide. And somehow, I do not think we will be purchasing a one-way ticket out of Sunan International Airport. That leaves China as the logical choice."

"Even if you make it into China," Lee said, "you are still far from the arms of safety."

"True, Pastor," Jung-Hoon said. A pause. "Which is why we are here. If I can get the commander into North Korea without us all getting shot, your network of Christians is the best-equipped contact organization for escape out of North Korea through China."

"I see," Pastor Lee said. "Hmm." He looked at the map. "Where would you propose crossing into China?"

Jung-Hoon walked over to the map.

"Here is a grease pencil," Pastor Lee said as he handed a pencil to him.

"Thank you," Jung-Hoon said. "We come in from the Sea of Japan, then head toward Hamhung. If we find what we're looking for, then we could head for the border somewhere just to the west of Kanggye. Perhaps something like this." With the grease pencil, he began outlining an escape route.

"There." Jung-Hoon put the grease pencil on the pastor's desk. "That should do it."

Gunner studied the map. Had Jung-Hoon actually laid out the plan? And was he taking charge of planning the whole mission? No one in all of Korea would be better suited to lead such a deadly mission than Jung-Hoon.

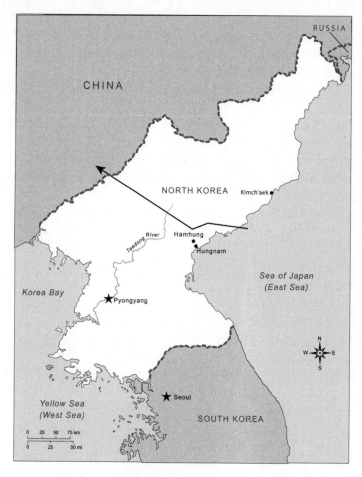

North Korea with route from Sea of Japan to China,
angling toward Hamhung

"Interesting," Pastor Lee said after a minute of studying the map. "Of course you understand that the escape route you are proposing is extremely mountainous."

"Everything in Korea is mountainous," Jung-Hoon said. "But at least we're avoiding population centers."

Gunner sensed a spark of passion in Jung-Hoon's voice. He looked over and saw Jackrabbit nodding.

The pastor studied Jung-Hoon's route, then said, "I will mention this to two elders who head up our rescue program. Regardless of their decision, I want you to know that I am with you in spirit, and if you undertake this brave and daring mission, I pray that the Lord will allow us to be a part of helping you to succeed."

"Thank you, Pastor," Jung-Hoon said. "When can we expect to hear from you?"

Pastor Lee scratched his chin. "I will call you as soon as I have a decision."

"Thank you," Jung-Hoon said. He looked at Jackrabbit and Gunner. "Let us return to the hotel. We have some planning to do for this suicide mission."

CHAPTER 6

Corbin Hall
Suffolk, Virginia

The aroma of roasting turkey saturated the rooms of the house. The familiar warm fragrance of Thanksgiving brought a smile to her face. She swung her legs over the side of the bed and her feet found her slippers. She stood and reached for her robe, which she had draped over the side of the pink wingback chair.

The clock beside the bed showed that the turkey had been in the oven on low heat for over eight hours already and had four hours to go. The house would soon be bustling with activity and laughter and fellowship. The family would begin arriving soon, and she still had tons of preparation to do. She headed for the kitchen.

Darkness filled the small bathroom adjoining the large kitchen of the grand country home. She stepped in and flipped on the light.

The mirror did not lie.

Her beauty had not faded, not totally anyway, even in the more than half a century of years that would be credited to her on her next birthday. Somewhere, in the back of her mind, she could produce, if demanded, information relating to the exact number of years that she had endured upon this earth. But when she hit fifty a little over a decade ago, her strong will had made her forget her exact age.

Still, the mirror did not lie.

The high cheekbones, once the topic of male suitors over the years, were still set against an olive skin marred by few wrinkles. Even the streaks of gray were not all that unattractive, she thought, as she pulled her hair back into a ponytail and began to apply makeup. Her hands showed the wrinkling and ropey veins of age. Her wrists were now boney. Yet arthritis had not beset her, as it had other members of her family, and she remained grateful for the strength she had heading into her sunset years.

As she put on a comfortable pair of jeans and the red sweater Gunner had given her last Christmas, she thought about the last ten years. Had she made a mistake by rejecting two proposals of marriage after her husband died? The last one, a rather dashing and handsome suitor, was wealthy to boot. But marrying him would have required her to trade the serenity of Corbin Hall for the West Coast.

The ties of family and the pull of Corbin Hall had never allowed her the luxury of starting anew. The new would never be like the old.

Enough reminiscing. Today was Thanksgiving. Time to liven up. She left the bathroom and entered the kitchen. She reached for the remote control and turned on the TV. A small flat-screen television on the kitchen counter came to life with the sight of a giant smiling Bambi bobbing in the sunlit skies between skyscrapers of Madison Avenue. Ah ... the sights and sounds of the Macy's Thanksgiving Day Parade in New York made her feel better. Over a light breakfast of coffee and toast, she watched the colorful floats brighten the dull gray exteriors of New York skyscrapers.

Breakfast over, she turned down the volume and perused the checklist on the counter.

Peel potatoes.
Prepare dressing.
Sweet tea ... two gallons.
Set table.

Set table. Yes, of course. The hard part.

For the next several hours, she worked on her list, peeling potatoes, chopping celery and onion for the dressing, and brewing the tea. With the food well in hand, she moved to the dining room for the next step.

The placemats, silverware, and Waterford crystal glasses already adorned the table. To be sure, she counted in her head again the number of plates she would need ... Gorman and Bri, Little Tyler and sis Jill, and one for her.

She counted again. One, two, three, four, five … plus one.

She reached into the china cabinet and extracted six dinner plates. Five were of a now-defunct but beautiful pattern called Chinoisserie, with black-and-gold banding around the white center and colorful Japanese lettering and figurines on the black banding.

She set four plates around the old mahogany table, then set the fifth at one end.

One plate remained in her hand. It was different from the others. She looked at the plate and then looked at the chair at the head of the table.

The white envelope lay on the placemat, waiting to be covered by the plate. Folded inside was the letter she penned years ago, during an hour of deep self-reflection, after some traumatic and emotional changes in her life.

She walked to the head of the table and kissed the plate that was unlike the others. She had ordered it from the Marine Corps Exchange at Camp Lejeune several years ago. Engraved in the middle of it was a gold globe-and-anchor, the symbol of the United States Marine Corps.

With the dignity of a soldier guarding the Tomb of the Unknown at Arlington, she set the plate down over the top of the envelope.

There. All done.

Back to the kitchen, back to the checklist. She reached for her scissors and snipped open the plastic bag in the box of brown sugar. She dug a tablespoon into the sugar and sprinkled the sugar on the sweet potatoes in a Pyrex bowl.

How could she not read the letter? She had written it, and it had meant so much to her then.

She dropped the spoon on the sweet potatoes and went back to the dining room.

She stood at the head of the table for a moment, then sat down in the chair. Carefully removing the plate, she picked up the envelope, extracted its contents, and began to read.

Dear Daddy,

I was almost five years old when you went missing in action in 1950. They say you disappeared in a place called the Chosin Reservoir. Mama was left with me and my twin brother Jeffrey.

I only remember one thing about you — your arms reaching out to me to pick me up at Thanksgiving, and I remember you holding me in your arms and smearing my face with chocolate pie! At least I think I remember. Mama is gone now too. She always had trouble talking about you. Jeffrey is gone too. I learned more about you from your brother Bill and sister Maydie than from anyone else.

I know you were a great athlete in high school, that you were a star quarterback, and that you were a young Marine officer who loved this country. They said you'd planned on getting out of the Marines and coming back to Virginia to run Corbin Hall. They said you would return to us. I believed them.

We moved around a lot, Daddy. We lived in Iowa, New Mexico, California, and South Carolina. Mama always said I looked like you. She never could deal with the thought of you being gone for good. She never remarried. Finally, when Granddaddy got sick, she agreed to come back to Corbin Hall to take over the business. She did a fine job. She bore the family name with strength and pride.

I went to school in all those places, graduated from high school in South Carolina, and went on to beautician school. I practiced ten years as a cosmetologist and married Gorman McCormick, a Naval Academy grad and Navy pilot who flew in Vietnam. We married in 1968. He was a wonderful person, gave me two beautiful sons — your grandsons — but he died of cancer in 1999.

I worked for a while after Gorman died, but when Mama started getting sick, I came back to Corbin Hall to help her with the business. Gorman Jr., your oldest grandson, went off to Virginia Tech, studied agriculture, and came back to help me run Corbin Hall. He married Brianna, and we call her Bri. She's very pretty. From down around Edenton. She and Gorman have two great children, Tyler and Jill. They're your great-grandchildren.

You'd be proud of your grandsons!

Gunner worked in a fancy finance job in New York. But he quit to follow your footsteps and his daddy's in the military. We named him Christianson Pendleton McCormick. The name Christianson came from a Marine, Stanley Christianson, who won the Medal of Honor in Korea. And of course his middle name, Pendleton, well that's for another Marine who went to Korea, his beloved grandfather. He picked up the name Gunner when he won the Tidewater Shooting Championship sponsored by the Junior NRA at age sixteen. He became quite the marksman with a .22 rifle! You'd be proud of him, Daddy!

He's now an officer on an aircraft carrier named for the man who was president when you left for Korea. I expect he'll come back and help Gorman with the farm after he leaves the Navy.

I still miss you. You were so young and never got a chance to live.

I know where Mama is, and I know where Jeffrey is, and I know where Gorman is. But I don't know where you've gone, Daddy. So I set a plate for you every Thanksgiving at the head of the table. I do it because Thanksgiving was the last time I remember even the littlest bit about you. I don't expect you to ever sit there or ever to walk in this house again, but I promised years ago that I would always remember you. And although my hope of seeing you has faded with each passing year, I'll cling to the last dimming rays of a fading hope until I draw my very last breath.

Your disappearance rocked us all, Daddy. Mama. Me. We never got over it. I love you always.

See you in heaven, Daddy.

Your Baby Girl,
Margaret Pendleton McCormick

Four fresh teardrops had smudged the blue ink on the letter.

The doorbell rang. Then the sound of the front door opening. "Mother, we're here!" Gorman Jr. called out.

"We've got desserts!" The chipper voice of her daughter-in-law, Bri.

She refolded the letter, slipped it back into the envelope, and laid the letter back under his special plate. She dabbed her eyes with a napkin.

"Be right there!" Pushing her father from her thoughts, she hurried to greet her family.

CHAPTER 7

Kim Yŏng-nam Military Prison Camp

Staff Sergeant Kang Ho-soon glanced at his watch—0800 hours. Time to get the old dogs moving.

He looked over at Chung Nam-gyu and Cho Doo-soon, the two comrades assigned with him to oversee the prisoners. They were drinking coffee in the mess hall and yakking. He knew they were just putting in their time until retirement. Chung and Cho had been at this job in the prison camp too long. They'd lost their ambition.

Not so for Kang Ho-soon. Although he was new, he saw his assignment to the top-secret prison camp as a testament to the Army's confidence in his leadership abilities. Before being considered for duty in this top-secret program, Kang had been subjected to extreme physical and psychological tests, all of which he passed. After a second round of interviews with Army psychiatrists and Communist party investigators, he received the North Korean Army's prestigious top-secret clearance and was awarded a medal for meritorious service.

He would never forget the day of the ceremony. They had ordered him to report in full dress uniform to party headquarters in his home city of Chongjin in North Hamgyŏng Province. His father and mother, both factory workers at the Chongjin Steel Company, were invited. They knew in advance only that he was being promoted to staff sergeant. But when he received the prestigious medal for meritorious service, his parents were shocked. His mother, her hands rough from years of glorious labor in service to the party, shed tears when they pinned the dangling medal with the red star on his jacket.

Of course, his parents never knew the real reason why he had earned the medal, nor did they know that he had received the prestigious top-secret clearance. Indeed they could not know—nor could anyone else know. Perhaps one day his children would know of his new assignment.

Kang remembered the day they led him into a secure chamber and told him of his assignment to the top-secret camp. He then had spent six months learning English in Pyongyang before reporting to Kim Yŏng-nam Military Prison Camp.

At first, Kang had not understood it all. And then it hit him. He had been chosen to be among North Korea's elite! His star was rocketing upward! This was his chance.

Kang eyed his comrades sitting there at the table, more interested in their coffee and their bellies than their duty, he thought. Part of the problem was that the two standing guard with him were his superiors, but not by much. They were one stripe and pay grade above him. He *technically* was subject to their orders.

Kang had decided that the North Korean High Command had erred by bestowing on them the same top-secret clearance that he had just received and now had recognized that mistake. But rather than relieve them of their duties and send them elsewhere or shoot them, they had brought *him* in to clear things up. Yes, Kang Ho-soon planned to take command here. His leadership abilities would propel him to the officer ranks of the Army and, from there, assignment to the highest places of power in Pyongyang. Kang smiled as he envisioned his rise to power.

He was certain his new commanding officer, Colonel Song Kwang-sun, had high connections within the Army and the party. He hoped Colonel Song had already heard of his no-nonsense discipline of the rebellious prisoner yesterday. What better way to grab attention than a quick whipping to the foot? A slash across the back would come next.

"Comrades! Time to go get them up," he snapped.

Chung looked up at him. "Comrade, why such a hurry? They are old men. They are not going anywhere. So what if they have to pee? They can wait." He rolled his eyes at Cho, who chuckled.

"Excuse me, Comrade First Sergeant," Kang shot back, "but I have examined the regulations, and the regulations require them to be up and marching for morning latrine visits no later than zero-eight-hundred hours."

"Regulations. Please." This was from the other one, Cho, responding in the same lackadaisical, lazy tone used by Chung. "What will they do? File a complaint?"

"Should we take this up with the colonel?" Kang asked.

Cho eyed Chung, who shook his head. "Very well, my young and ambitious friend. Let us get moving."

"I will wait outside," Kang said. He marched across the dining area, pushed open the door, and stepped out into the snow. A moment later, Chung came outside. Cho followed him like a sheep following its master, Kang thought.

Chung headed across the courtyard toward the prisoners' barracks. He had taken about three steps in a shuffling, nonmilitary bearing when Kang could bear it no more.

"Halt!" Kang screamed.

Chung stopped and turned to look at Kang. "What do you mean, 'Halt'?"

"Are you not forgetting something?" Kang said.

"Forgetting something?" Cho said. "You were anxious to awaken the old fools. And now you say 'Halt'?"

"I must insist that we proceed in accordance to regulations," Kang said.

"Regulations? What now?" Chung moaned.

"The regulations require marching in formation across the grounds for the initial dealings with the prisoners during the day. According to the regulations, this keeps up the all-important message that this is a military prison camp. It sends the strong message to the prisoners that they are to obey."

"We have never marched across the parade grounds just to begin the process of taking the prisoners to the latrine," Chung said. "That regulation was written long ago when there were more prisoners and the prisoners were much younger and needed more force." Chung stepped toward Kang. "Who do you think you are? You have no right to order us around. You are junior to both of us! We tell *you* what to do!"

Kang hesitated. Chung was right. But . . . if he backed down now . . . He could not. He would not. A true leader was not a mere stripe on a uniform sleeve.

"My obligation is to obey regulations!" Kang almost screamed. "You cannot give me a lawful order that is contrary to the regulations. And the regulations of this camp are promulgated by written decree of the commanding officer!" He moved closer to get into Chung's face. "Now, First Sergeant Chung"—he blew his breath directly into Chung's face—"would you like to take this up with the commanding officer?"

Chung bit his lower lip but said nothing.

"I thought not," Kang said, a sneer playing at the corner of his mouth. "Strap your rifles over your shoulders and get into formation. As the junior officer present, I will lead you across the parade grounds in a three-man triangle vanguard formation."

Kang had taken charge.

"Chung, to my back-right five paces! Cho, to my back-left five paces!" Kang took his position as the point man leading the triangle. "Company. Atten-hut!"

Kang heard the cracking sound of two rifles slapped into place behind him—proof that the two guards were complying with his orders.

"Mark time! March!"

Crunch. Crunch. Crunch. Crunch.

"Forwaaard march!"

A lready dressed, Keith knelt on the floor, next to Robert, who was breathing with difficulty. He put his hand on Robert's forehead.

"How ya feeling, buddy?"

Robert groaned.

"Little Kim Il-sung will be here any second," Frank said.

"Good name for him," Keith said. He spread out the wet towel on Robert's forehead. "Why didn't I think of that? Another Kim Il-sung wannabe."

"Aren't they all?" Frank said. "How's he feeling?"

"Feverish. But not as hot as yesterday."

"How's your foot?"

"Fine." Keith lied. Marines never complain. Master the pain. He moved the wet cloth from Robert's forehead to his neck. "There, that'll cool you off a bit."

Another groan.

"What the heck?" This from Frank.

Keith looked up. Frank was peering out the barred window beside his bunk. "Unbelievable!" Frank said. "They're marching in formation ... actually doing the Communist goosestep!"

"Who?"

"The three amigos. Our Little Kim Il-sung is out in front. They're headed this way."

"Oh, great," Keith said. "I've got a feeling Little Kim Il-sung will be a challenge."

Rap Rap Rap. The door flew open. "Get up, old dogs!" Kang Ho-soon stood in the doorway. The other two guards stood at attention behind him.

Keith rose to his feet. Frank slid off the bunk and stood beside him. They were in the middle of the concrete floor, standing shoulder to shoulder, facing the exuberant new whipmaster who had stepped just inside the open door. Fresh snow blanketed the grounds. Frigid air whipped in, carrying snow with it.

"I said get up!" Kang Ho-soon snapped. He glared at Robert, who was rolled over on his side, covered with a blanket, his back to the door. The whipmaster stomped over toward Robert's bunk, screaming, "Get up! Get up!"

Keith stepped in front of him, eyes carefully lowered. "Sir, he is sick. Very sick. He cannot get up."

"Move, old man!" The guard delivered a hard shove to Keith's chest, knocking him onto the edge of Robert's bunk, where his butt crash-landed on Robert's feet.

"Oooh." Robert groaned.

"Get up!" The whipmaster bent over Robert, relentless in his demands.

"What are you doing?" Chung asked. "They are old men. They move slowly."

Kang blurted out a Korean profanity and kicked the locker by Keith's bunk. A white plastic bottle fell on the floor.

Kang quickly bent down and picked up the bottle. "Penicillin! How did you get this?" He looked at Keith, then at Frank. Both had their heads bowed, their eyes looking down at the floor. "This is illegal contraband! Who is responsible for this?"

Silence.

"It was you!" Kang glared at Keith, who kept his eyes averted. "We shall get to the bottom of this. Out of the barracks! Now! Into the courtyard!" Kang bent down and shook Robert. "You! Outside!"

Cho grabbed the whipmaster's arm and pulled him away from Robert. "Let him stay. He is very sick."

"No! He is a suspect!" Kang screamed. "I will take this up with the colonel!"

"Then take it up with the colonel," Chung said. "I am overruling you on this one."

Kang grumbled something in Korean, then shifted back to English. "I will report this contraband to the colonel. You two stand guard until I return."

Then Little Kim Il-sung pivoted and marched out.

Keith knew the reprieve would be brief, but he welcomed it nonetheless.

S taff Sergeant Kang Ho-soon walked briskly through the dark hallway of the military prison's administration building. He had not yet found the man he was looking for. He quickened his pace, his clicking boots echoing down the long hallway. He stopped in front of the closed door of the colonel's office. He could see through the opaque glass that a light was on. Someone must be inside. He clenched a fist and delivered two sharp raps on the door.

"Enter!" a shrill female voice said.

Kang opened the door and stepped forward with two precise goosesteps, then stamped his feet together and came to attention. Staff Sergeant Mang Hyo-Sonn, the colonel's assistant, was seated at the desk.

"Staff Sergeant Kang Ho-soon reporting for the colonel."

"The colonel is occupied," Mang said. "May I be of assistance to you?"

"Tell the colonel that I have discovered a crime against the state that I must report to him."

"A crime against the state?" She looked up at him with a questioning expression.

"Yes," Kang said. "Contraband stolen by the prisoners."

"What sort of contraband?"

"Medicine," he announced. "I caught the prisoners with medicine belonging to the state."

Mang Hyo-Sonn raised an eyebrow. "Wait here, Staff Sergeant ... state your name again?"

"Staff Sergeant Kang Ho-soon!"

The woman disappeared into the inner office.

Why cannot the stupid woman remember my name! Soon she will have no choice, Kang thought as he looked around the outer office of the colonel. He was just about to turn when he heard the *click* of a door latch.

The door to the inner office swung open and the commanding officer of the prison camp, Colonel Song Kwang-sun, with his assistant a few steps behind him, walked toward Kang. "What is this about unauthorized medicine being found with the prisoners?" he asked.

"Colonel, while doing my morning inspection, I began to demand that the prisoners respect proper military decorum, that they would in fact—"

"Get to the point!" the colonel snapped. "What did you find ... Staff Sergeant ... what is your name?"

"Staff Sergeant Kang Ho-soon, my colonel!"

"Right. Tell me about this medicine you found."

"The prisoners possessed contraband. I confiscated it. Here, sir." He took the bottle of penicillin from his pocket and held it straight out in front of him.

The colonel took the bottle and held it up to the light. "This is my medicine! Someone stole this from my personal medicine cabinet!"

"Yes, Colonel. The medicine was in the possession of the old one—"

"They're all old!" the colonel snapped. "Get my jacket, Sergeant Mang! We will get to the bottom of this!" The colonel, grabbing his jacket from his assistant, walked out the door, Mang and Kang following him.

"The prisoners are lined up at my direction," Kang said. "I will be happy to assist with the investigation or to conduct the interrogation, my colonel."

Sergeant Mang shot Kang a warning look as they headed toward the exit into the courtyard.

Mounds of snow, glistening in the early morning sun, were piled on each side of the gate at the entrance of the prison. Pak squinted her eyes to protect them from the glare. She held her breath as she approached the gate. Two stiff-necked, rifle-bearing guards in drab-green uniforms were in the guard shack. Pak prayed that no one had noticed the missing medicine. These were not the same guards who had been at the gate when she left the night before. One she recognized. The other she did not. The one she recognized opened the gate for her, and she thanked him.

She walked into the prison compound and headed for the prisoners' barracks, her heart pounding. She held her breath as she walked rapidly away from the guard shack through the newly fallen snow, half expecting a guard to shout, to stop her, to escort her at gunpoint to the colonel's office when he realized that she was the one who had stolen the bottle of medicine.

When neither guard stopped her, she exhaled and took a deep breath. "Thank you, Lord," she mumbled. As she approached the courtyard, she thought about the sick old man—the one they called Robert. His head had felt like a hot iron and his body had shaken with chills. Stealing was wrong. Pak knew that. But not taking care of the sick was also wrong. She had just tried to give him some comfort in his last days. The poor old man would not live much longer. She was sure of that. Almost all the others had died here in the camp.

When she was halfway across the courtyard, she heard angry voices yelling near the administration building. She quickened her pace but lost her footing and landed butt first in the snow and fell backward.

"Did you take it?" she heard a man yell as she got back on her feet and dusted the snow off.

"Answer me. Did you take it?"

Pak walked quickly in the direction of the voice. When she passed the corner of the administration building, she saw them. They were about twenty feet in front of her. Two prisoners were standing side by side, shivering in the cold. The colonel, flanked by the three guards and his assistant, stood facing the prisoners and was yelling at the top of his lungs.

"I ask you once more!" He held up something ...

What is that? Pak thought.

"You *do* recognize this! Do you not? It is medicine from my personal cabinet. It was found on the floor by your locker. I demand to know! Who stole it?"

The colonel began pacing in front of the two old men.

Keith stared at the ground and said nothing.

"Very well," the colonel said. "Perhaps this will revive your memory." He turned to the guard who had found the bottle of penicillin. "What is your name?"

"Kang! Sir!" The guard jumped to a stiff position of attention. "Staff Sergeant Kang Ho-soon!"

"Right," the colonel snapped. "Revive the prisoner's memory!"

"Yes, sir!" Kang responded with enthusiasm. He stepped in front of Keith. "Answer the colonel's question!"

Nothing from Keith except a blank face, eyes down.

"Answer!"

Still nothing.

Kang hauled back with his hand and slapped the old man on the face, sending him tumbling into the snow.

"Where did you get the medicine?" Kang screamed as he stood over the man.

Keith raised his head. Blood was running from his nose.

"Answer me!" Kang cursed. "I will teach you to steal from the Army of the Democratic People's Republic of Korea!" He grabbed a bullwhip and lashed down perilously close to the old man.

WHAP!

"Stop!" Pak screamed. "Stop it! Stop it!"

They all turned around. The colonel said, "Woman, if you know what is best for you, do not interfere with the state's administration of justice."

"Please, Colonel! Do not strike the old man!" she begged through her sobs. "I did it!"

"What do you mean?"

"I stole the medicine! Please, do not whip him. I did it." She dropped to her knees and sobbed. "Please. Do not beat the old man."

Silence.

Pak hung her head and looked down as a torrent of tears rained down in the snow.

"You two!" She heard the voice of the colonel. "Take these men back to the barracks."

"Yes, sir!"

"Kang, arrest this woman and take her to my office!"

"With pleasure, sir!"

Pak flinched as Kang grabbed her arm and began to drag her across the yard toward the colonel's office.

Kang stood at attention in front of the colonel's desk. This time, Kang thought, he had been invited into the colonel's *inner* office. This time, he was not stopped outside, in the office of his commander's military-mistress-secretary. By proving himself, he had earned the right to be here. He looked over at the other guard, Chung Nam-gyu, who was standing at attention at the other end of the colonel's desk. Kang considered Chung's presence a mere formality, present as a practical necessity. He thought back to that morning, how he had taught the two incompetent and spineless guards a real lesson. One he was sure they wouldn't soon forget.

The colonel was seated behind his desk. Standing between the two guards and facing the colonel was Pak.

This sobbing, worthless, traitorous thief-of-a-woman, Kang thought. The point of this whole meeting, he reasoned, was to draw attention to the fact that *he* — not Chung Nam-gyu — had uncovered the theft of this woman, this traitor to the state, and the colonel knew it and would reward him greatly.

Kang decided that the colonel had brought Chung in only as a second bodyguard. After all, neither Chung Nam-gyu nor the other incompetent excuse-for-a-guard Cho Doo-soon had been selected to interrogate the old-dog prisoner. Only *he*, Kang, had been so selected! And *his* interrogation technique had been so effective that he had psychologically pressured the sobbing heap now standing here to confess her crime.

He wondered what medal he would receive this time. His eyes scanned the photos on the walls, of the colonel standing beside Dear Leader, of the colonel with other decorated leaders of the state.

"Why did you take it?" the colonel's demanding tone brought Kang's eyes back on the traitor.

"I ... I do not know," she said through a torrent of tears.

"You do not know?"

"No, sir."

"You do not know! Well, then, perhaps this will refresh your memory!" The colonel looked at Kang. "Refresh this traitor's memory!"

"Sir! Colonel! With pleasure!"

He raised his hand and swung.

Whap!

The slap across her face sent Pak spinning. She tumbled to the floor, landing at the feet of Chung, who stepped back. The woman was a sobbing ball at Chung's feet.

Pathetic against pathetic, Kang thought.

"Get her up!" the colonel ordered.

Kang watched as Chung bent down and pulled Pak to her knees.

Finally, Chung was given a job, Kang thought. What a contrast the colonel must see in us. On his right, an authoritarian, dashing, rising young leader, one capable of uncovering crimes against the state and extracting confessions from those who would oppose Dear Leader. On his left, an incompetent fool in uniform, a man whose only usefulness is to steady a soon-to-be-dead traitor.

"I demand an answer!" the colonel screamed. His face was red and blood vessels bulged on his neck. "Why did you steal property of the state?"

"I ... I ..." Sobbing, Pak tried to wipe the tears from her face.

"Get your face out of your hands!"

Pak looked up. "I am sorry, Colonel. I felt sorry ... for the old man."

"Ha ha ha ha!" The colonel burst into mocking laughter. "You felt sorry for the old man. So you stole from me?"

"I am so sorry, Colonel. I will not do it again."

"You felt sorry for an enemy prisoner? Well, how does this feel?" He looked at Kang. "Staff Sergeant?"

"Yes, sir!"

Pak looked at him. She was terrified. Her hands were shaking, her lips were quivering. She mouthed a silent "Please, no."

Kang drew his arm back again. The second slap struck her face harder than the first had. Again she tumbled like a rag doll.

The colonel smiled. He sat back in his chair and watched while the other guard just stood there, looking down at the traitor sobbing at his feet.

The colonel's eyes caught Kang's, and the two men, though separated by a gulf of rank and age, both grinned.

Oh, to be on the same wavelength as leadership! Kang thought. He had already received a medal for meritorious service for his actions at the border last year. He was proud of the fact that he had fired across the river, even fired bravely across the border into China, killing one or two of the Bible-thumping traitors who were helping escapees leave the great Democratic People's Republic without authority. A few did escape that day, but he knew that his actions served as a mighty deterrent against such treachery in the future! They decorated him, but not to the extent that he deserved. He was "too young," they said, to receive the highest award of the republic.

But the action he took at the border, he was certain, got him noticed and got him this new assignment. What medal might he receive as a result of his heroism today? he wondered. What promotion was he due for? This was his destiny. This he knew he deserved.

"Get her up!" the colonel shouted.

And again, the other guard put his hands under Pak's armpits and hauled her back to her feet.

Excellent! Kang thought as he saw his handprint on her face. He considered the mark visible evidence that he shared the mind-set of party leadership toward those hostile to the state.

The colonel glared at Pak. "Stand at attention!"

The woman stood, then bent forward, appearing suddenly dizzy.

"Do not slump in my presence, you piece of traitorous trash! This court-marital of the Army of the Democratic People's Republic of Korea is hereby convened. Stand at attention!" He nodded at Kang, who nodded back and stepped behind Pak. He put one hand in the center of her back and with his other hand pulled her shoulders back, forcing her to stand in an upright position for her sentencing.

"This court-martial, based upon the evidence having been

considered, including the evidence produced from the prisoner and recovered by the staff sergeant, and based upon your own confession, does hereby find you guilty of the high crimes of stealing the property of the state and rendering aid to the enemy. I, and I alone, possess the authority now to sentence you to your fate." The colonel glared at Pak, whose eyes seemed glazed, unseeing. "And included within my authority is the power to have you executed or to let you go free. Is there anything you wish to say in your defense?"

Tears rained down the red handprint on Pak's cheek. She brought her hand to her face, wiping the tears away. "I ... I meant no harm. I promise not to steal again." Her voice faded under the sound of more sniffling.

"That is it?" the colonel snapped.

Blood flowed from her nose. She wiped it on her sleeve.

"Very well," the colonel said. "Having found you guilty on all charges as set forth in the indictment against you, this military court-martial does hereby sentence you to be executed by firing squad."

"Ah, nooooooooo!!"

"Shut her up! Take her. Lock her up. The sentence shall be carried out at noon! At my direction!"

Kang smiled. "Yes, Colonel!"

CHAPTER 8

**US Navy F/A-18s
on patrol over the Yellow Sea**

Lieutenant Commander Corey Jacobs, USN, known by his handle as "Werewolf," pushed down on the stick of the supersonic fighter and banked the plane to his right. Bright rays of midmorning sun streamed through the top of the clear-glass canopy and into the cockpit. The blue waters of the Yellow Sea glistened ten thousand feet below.

Down to his left and trailing by one hundred feet, his wingman, Lieutenant Bill "Bobcat" Morrison, mimicked the banking maneuver of his senior officer. Morrison's F/A-18 Super Hornet, its gray wings swept back, flew a broad swoop through the skies, like a graceful gull following its leader.

Today marked the duo's third mission in three days of high-stakes, cat-and-mouse war games with the Korean People's Air Force, the official name of the Air Force of North Korea. Each day, the mission had been the same. Launch from USS *Harry S. Truman* in the middle of the northern Yellow Sea, fly due east toward the North Korean coastline, then start a swooping maneuver, turning back thirteen nautical miles from the coastline, just one mile short of entering Communist airspace.

These "fly-ins," designed to keep the Communists guessing if American jets would invade their airspace, had started in retaliation for the North Koreans buzzing over the top of the USS *Harry S. Truman*, invading its airspace. The rules of engagement, or ROE, called for avoiding North Korean airspace and no firing except in self-defense.

Yet, despite the current rules of engagement, Jacobs, Morrison, and the other pilots in the air wing had contingency orders to change the ROE—to penetrate North Korean airspace, launch missiles against selected military and industrial targets in and around Pyongyang, then break for the safety of Osan Air Base just south of Seoul.

These contingency orders would be implemented only if the Dear Leader's Air Force took a shot at the *Harry S. Truman*, something they had not yet dared try. But the North Koreans tended to strike on cherished American holidays, like the Fourth of July. And with it being Thanksgiving weekend back home, they just might try something extra.

These round-the-clock flights by the carrier's air wing to the edge of North Korean territorial airspace would continue until someone with more brass on their collar than Jacobs ordered them to stop.

For the last three days, the war-game routine on both sides had become a repetitive chorus. As Jacobs and his fellow Navy fighter pilots bore down at supersonic speed on Dear Leader's airspace, MiG-21s of the Korean People's Air Force would scramble, rocketing out to greet the Super Hornets. The MiG-21s would chase the Super Hornets back to the west, toward the carrier, where the MiGs would be intercepted by two more eastbound Super Hornets flying toward them in defense of the ship.

A testy game of high stakes, such high-speed maneuvering through the skies made for an aerial powder keg that could blow at any moment.

"Werewolf. Bobcat. Here they come." The voice boomed through the plane's air-to-air radio control and into Jacob's headset.

"Roger that, Bobcat. Got 'em on my radar. Looks like a couple of 'em. Same drill. Hang on. Let's get out of this bank and break for the ship."

"I'm with ya, boss," Morrison said. "I feel the need for speed!"

North Korean MiG-21s
on patrol over the Yellow Sea

Lieutenant No Chul-Su, Korean People's Air Force, eyed the two inbound American fighters on his cockpit radar screen. The jets were rocketing toward the coastline, but in the excited rush of the moment, he could not determine their intentions.

He switched his broadcast radio to international frequency. "American F-18s! You are violating the sovereign airspace of the Democratic People's Republic of Korea. Turn back or you will be fired on!"

US Navy F/A-18s
over the Yellow Sea

Did you hear that sucker?" Morrison asked.

"Yeah, I heard him," Jacobs said. "Those MiGs have screwed-up radar. Let's get the heck out of here. Set course two-seven-zero degrees and hit afterburners ... On my mark."

"Roger that, boss. Setting course two-seven-zero degrees."

North Korean MiG-21s
over the Yellow Sea

No response from the Americans. Had they heard him? They were banking, slightly. But were they turning to fly back out to sea? Or were they altering their course from Namp'o to Pyongyang? At this speed, they could drop a concussion bomb or a laser-guided missile on the palace of Dear Leader within minutes!

There was no room for error. He could take no chances. He had been trained for instances like this, and when in doubt, he was called to defend the Motherland!

He had no choice. He reached down and activated the plane's fire-control radar. Then he reached for the "missile launch" button.

US Navy F/A-18s
over the Yellow Sea

B*eep-beep-beep-beep*
Beep-beep-beep-beep

Beep-beep-beep-beep

The cacophonous rapid beeping drew Commander Jacobs's eyes to the missile-lock alarm.

"Skipper, he's locked on!" Morrison yelled.

"I see that!" Jacobs said. "On my mark! Hit afterburner!"

"Roger that."

"Two ... one ... now!" Jacobs pushed down the plane's throttle, and the jet's afterburner kicked in, firing the Hornet through the skies with a missile-like burst.

"Skipper, we got a missile in the air! Running up our rear! Right now!"

"Okay! Follow me! Climb to the sun!"

"With ya, Skipper!"

Jacobs pulled back on the stick and the Super Hornet climbed at a steep angle. He steered the nose straight into the overhead sun. The rays were so bright that he could barely make out the climbing altitude on his altimeter: 10,500 feet ... 11,000 feet ... 11,500 ... The idea was to pull the heat-seeking missile into the sun's rays.

"You still with me, Bobcat?"

"Still with ya, Werewolf, just off your wing. But that missile's still closing!"

"Okay okay ... it hasn't decided which one of us it's gonna lock on. Feed range updates!"

"Range three hundred yards and closing, sir ... Range ... two hundred fifty yards ... range two hundred yards ... Missile closing fast, sir!"

Jacobs glanced at his altimeter: 13,000 feet ... 13,500 feet.

"Okay, stick with me, Bobcat. Don't panic. On my mark, break hard right and launch chaff and flares. I'll break left. Got it?"

"Got it, skipper! On your mark."

"Range!"

"Range one hundred yards ..."

"Stand by ... be ready ..."

"Range seventy-five yards ... Range fifty yards and closing ... Skipper?"

"Hang on ..."

"Range twenty-five yards ..."

"Now! Break! Break!" Jacobs bulled the stick to the left and fired chaff and flares out the rear of the jet. The jet pulled hard to the left, like a peeling stripped off a giant banana. Powerful g-forces pushed him back into his seat. He looked back and saw an explosion lighting the blue sky.

"Dear Jesus, please not Morrison."

North Korean MiG-21s
over the Yellow Sea

Lieutenant No looked up through the cockpit glass. The bright explosion several thousand feet above his head meant a direct strike! His wingman, Lieutenant Lee Ung-Pyong, flying about twenty yards off his right, had a wide grin on his face and flashed a thumbs-up.

The adrenaline flowing through No's body had taken control. His hands shook and his mind rushed with a thousand thoughts. He had just destroyed a vaunted fighter jet of the United States Navy!

In a matter of hours, he would become a hero of the Korean people! He, and he alone, had now sent a message to the cowboy fliers from the aircraft carriers to think twice about taunting the coastline of the Motherland. Soon, he would be sitting in the presence of Dear Leader himself, receiving all the accolades that he had earned and deserved for this act of heroism. This would be hailed as the greatest North Korean military victory since long before his birth, when the Navy captured the American spy ship the USS *Pueblo*.

Indeed, this would be an even greater feat than the *Pueblo*. For there, the Americans were only spying. But here, the Americans had invaded the airspace of the DPRK with hostile jet warplanes. What a difference a matter of seconds had made. His star would rise faster than a blazing comet! He would be immortalized as the pilot who single-handedly saved the Democratic People's Republic of Korea.

US Navy F/A-18s
over the Yellow Sea

Truman Control. Viper Leader." Jacobs had switched to the direct frequency for the ship. "We've been fired upon by North Korean MiGs!

Repeat, we've been fired upon. Evasive maneuvers taken. Status of Viper Two uncertain."

"Viper Leader. Truman. Copy that. Damage report?"

"Truman. Viper Leader. Uncertain. I'm fine. Haven't located Viper Two."

"Viper Leader. Truman. Roger that. You are authorized to release weapons and use force to defend yourself. Repeat. You are authorized to use force to defend yourself."

"Truman. Viper Leader. Roger that. Understood. Understand upgraded rules of engagement. Authorized to use force."

Jacobs armed his missiles and looked back over the horizon for a parachute. A staticky crackling came through his headset.

"Werewolf! Bobcat! You okay?"

"Bill!" Jacobs felt himself exhale at the radio call from his junior partner. "Thank God! You okay?"

"I'm fine. That missile hit one of our flares and blew. I got bounced around a bit, but I'm airborne."

"You need to head back to the ship?"

"Negative. Unless you order me back," Morrison said.

"You up for a fight?"

"Let's go get 'em. I don't appreciate getting shot at."

"Good!" Jacobs felt himself grinning. "Then let's go kill a Commie!"

"Sounds like a plan, boss! I'm right behind you!"

Jacobs pulled back on the stick again, turning the plane back toward the last known location of the MiGs.

North Korean MiG-21s
over the Yellow Sea

Kaech'on Control. Red Vulture One." Lieutenant No radioed his home air base, located fifty miles north of the national capital of Pyongyang. Kaech'on was the headquarters for the First Combat Air Command, which was responsible for defense of the capital city.

"Red Vulture One. Kaech'on Control. Go ahead."

"Kaech'on Control. Red Vulture One. Be advised we have engaged enemy aircraft ... US Navy F/A-18s violating DPRK airspace. I ordered them to turn back. They refused. I fired. Advised, one enemy jet destroyed per visual confirmation."

"Red Vulture One. Kaech'on Control. Copy that. Return to base."

"Kaech'on Control. Red Vulture One. Roger that. Setting course for home base. We're on our way."

"Red Vulture One! Red Vulture Two! Second enemy fighter is on radar!"

"What?" No looked down and saw the same two blips on his radar screen that his wingman had just reported. How could this be? He had seen the explosion himself! And now, somehow, two American jets were on his tail!

Beep-beep-beep-beep
Beep-beep-beep-beep
Beep-beep-beep-beep

The missile-lock alarm cut a panicky static throughout his cockpit. The Americans had locked on to him! A cold sweat washed over his body.

"Red Vulture Two! They've locked on to us! Hit afterburners."

US Navy F/A-18s
over the Yellow Sea

Range to target, two miles," Jacobs said, his eyes focused on his fire-control radar and his right thumb resting on the missile-fire button. "Morrison, I'll take the one on the left. You take the one on the right. Copy that?"

"Copy that, boss," Morrison said from the cockpit of his F/A-18. "Ready to fire on your command."

"Roger ... on my mark ... fire!" Jacobs pressed the missile-fire button. The plane jumped, and less than a second later an AIM-9 Sidewinder air-to-air missile pasted a white streak of smoke through the skies at two-and-a-half times the speed of sound. Off to the right, an identical smoke streak trailed a Sidewinder shooting out from Morrison's plane.

"Let's see if you can get out of this one, suckers!"

North Korean MiG-21s
over the Yellow Sea

Red Vulture One!... Missile in air!... Check that ... two heat-seeking missiles on our tails!"

"Red Vulture Two! Pull up! Pull up! Into the sun!" Lieutenant No grabbed the stick on the MiG-21 and pulled back frantically, causing the jet to point upward. "Hit afterburners!" The plane shot up into the sky, climbing like a rocket. "Prepare to fire chaff!"

US Navy F/A-18s
over the Yellow Sea

Commander Jacobs craned his head skyward and squinted against the brightness as he watched the two MiG-21 "Fishbeds" rocket upward toward the sun, trying to replicate the same evasive maneuver that he and Morrison had just pulled off by the skin of their collective teeth.

"Range to target, 100 yards!... Range to target, fifty yards!"

The "Fishbeds"—as MiG-21s are referred to by American fighter pilots—suddenly broke in different directions, launching chaff and flares into the sky.

But the Sidewinders honed onto their afterburners.

BOOM!

The first jet exploded in a fireball. Then the second Sidewinder ran up the tail of the other Fishbed.

BOOM!

Twin fireballs lit the sky as the flaming hulks of what moments ago had been sleek fighter jets dropped through the air.

"Truman Control. Viper Leader. We have a confirmed kill on two MiG-21 Fishbeds. Repeat, confirm kill on two MiG-21s."

"Viper Leader. Truman Control. Roger that. Confirm two MiG-21s shot down. You are instructed to return for debriefing."

"Truman Control. Viper Leader. Roger that. We're on our way."

CHAPTER 9

Kim Yŏng-nam Military Prison Camp

The hard trunk of the old birch tree pressed into her back. The rope was cutting into her arms and wrists. Around her waist and feet was more rope, and the rope around her chest and abdomen was so tight she could barely breathe. In a few hours, they would shoot her. She would die against this old tree that she had admired for its natural beauty. Thinking this, her heart raced and tears slid down her face.

Death loomed. Her death. She knew it. She thought of her mother, who had taught her in secret, away from the prying eyes of the Communists, to always do what was right and not to worry or fear. She knew her mother would be proud. For she had done the right thing. She had tried to save the life of the dying old man, even if it now meant facing a firing squad.

She closed her eyes and tried whispering verses from the New Testament she had kept hidden in her government-issued apartment. "In this you greatly rejoice, though now for a little while you may have had to suffer grief in all kinds of trials. These have come so that your faith — of greater worth than gold, which perishes even though refined by fire — may be proved genuine and may result in praise, glory and honor when Jesus Christ is revealed."

Reciting these verses from the first letter of Peter brought a sense of calm that cascaded from her head down. She smiled and began repeating the passage.

"In this you greatly rejoice, though now for a little while you may have had to suffer grief ..."

Tongy'mak Municipal Airport
South Korea

The man watched the red-and-white Cessna 150 circle the west end of the runway, then line up for final approach.

Another slow morning, he thought. Just four takeoffs and three landings on this Friday, counting the Cessna that was about to touch down. No flight plans filed for the afternoon. The larger airports up the coast, at Samcheok and Donghae and Gangneung, had nearly driven him out of business.

Kim Jung-man knew that business was stagnant everywhere. Flight lessons, which accounted for more than half of his income in the previous year, had been in free fall the past few months. Many of his clients had moved their planes to the airports up the coast. Others, unable to afford the maintenance cost of keeping a private aircraft flightworthy, had sold their planes or, in some cases, simply abandoned them. The prolonged recession had crippled his charter service, driving customers to commercial air, their automobiles, or mass transit.

And now, faced with an onslaught of calls from impatient creditors, both business and personal, Kim Jung-man was being forced to make some hard decisions about the future of the airport.

He owned three planes that he used for his general aviation business. These included the Cessna 150 he used for beginning flight lessons and an Aero Commander 500 and a Beechcraft Bonanza G36. The latter two had been used for charter flights around South Korea and to Japan back when such flights were more plentiful.

Kim Jung-man loved flying. He could not imagine any other profession for himself. Flying was his life. Yet he had put all three airplanes for sale on various aviation websites on the Internet. The planes had been for sale for two weeks. There had been no calls.

This lack of interest from purchasers would have relieved him if the bank had not threatened to recall his line of credit, now more than six months behind, and if the mortgage company had not threatened to foreclose on his home. If only there were some other way. He did not want to sell any of his planes. A pilot develops a sentimental attachment to his planes. Selling even one was almost like choosing which of his children to sell. His choice, however, was unavoidable. Either sell one of the planes or file for bankruptcy.

The phone rang.

"Tongy'mak Aviation."

The caller asked about one of the planes, the Bonanza G36. He answered a string of questions. Yes, it was available. Capacity, five passengers plus the pilot. Seaworthy?

What a strange question, he thought.

"Well, yes, we have sealed the aircraft to make it as seaworthy as possible in the event of an emergency water landing, but as you know, it is an aircraft and not a boat, and it won't float very long. The aircraft does come with several flotation devices and an inflatable rubber raft in the event of a water landing. Plus, there is an emergency waterproof homing beacon, so if the plane goes down . . .

"The price?"

Suddenly he couldn't bear to let the aircraft go. He upped the price. "We are asking six hundred thousand dollars."

Kim held the phone away from his ear as the caller ranted about the higher-than-advertised price tag. But if the deal fell through, at least he would keep his precious Bonanza. "Yes, yes, I know that is fifty thousand more than we advertised, but we have gotten numerous inquiries, and I already have one offer above the listed price. It is contingent on the buyer getting financing, which looks good right now. But if that financing comes through—. . . What? Your buyer is prepared to pay cash?"

I should have asked for more, he thought. Farewell, sweet Bonanza . . .

"Okay, okay . . . Yes, I can meet you here this afternoon."

He hung up the phone.

Strange call, he thought. Then he realized he had neglected to get the caller's name and contact information. He checked the phone and hit redial. The phone rang. A beep but no voice mail. Kim hung up. Perhaps this was a hoax.

He shrugged. He would know soon.

Seoul, South Korea

Gunner leaned back in his chair, surveying his newly assembled team. They sat around the table in the kitchenette area of Gunner's hotel room. Jung-Hoon worked the telephones in Korean, speaking with the rapid-fire velocity of a stockbroker, one call after another. Jackrabbit gulped a Coke as he scribbled notes on a legal pad, creating a list of supplies.

Gunner returned his gaze to a map of North Korea, focusing his eyes on the area around the cities of Hungnam, on the east coast, and Hamhung, just inland. He was also looking for potential escape routes across the Chinese border—if they made it that far alive. Pastor Lee had called with the information they would need if they got to China.

They had returned to the hotel last night and, after a good night's sleep, arisen early to make their plans. Jung-Hoon, as Gunner had hoped, had started putting together the mission. Whether his motivation was the money he'd been promised or his innate hatred of the North, Gunner didn't know.

Not that it mattered. Jung-Hoon was *the* man of all men in South Korea uniquely qualified to spearhead a daring privately financed armed commando mission into the most dangerous country in the world.

"I think we have found an aircraft," Jung-Hoon said as he hung up the telephone.

"Oh, yeah?" Jackrabbit said. "Whatcha got?"

"A Beechcraft Bonanza for sale. Model G36. Located at Tongy'mak Municipal Airport on the east coast."

Jackrabbit set the Coke down on the table and raised an eyebrow. "Bonanza Model G36 would seem to be perfect. Two men in the cockpit. One in the back. And plenty of room for weapons, rafts, and electronics."

"Exactly," Jung-Hoon said. "Speaking of weapons, have you been working on that supply list?"

"Here." Jackrabbit slid a piece of paper across the table. "That ought to do it."

Jung-Hoon picked up the paper and began reading.

"Should be enough fireworks in there to light up Pyongyang if we have to but not too much to carry on the plane," Jackrabbit said.

Jung-Hoon began reading the list out loud. "Three M-16 rifles with noise suppressors. Concussion grenades. Ninety MREs. Handheld dagger military GPS devices. Updated crypto key. Wire cutters. Plastic explosives. Remote detonator. Three US Navy SEAL combat knives. Handheld electronic jamming device. Three thousand rounds .223-caliber ammo. Pup tent with portable heater and blankets." Jung-Hoon looked up. "You don't ask for much, do you?"

"I'd ask for more if we had the room and the manpower."

Jung-Hoon looked at Gunner. "We'll have to get all this from black-market arms distributors. It's illegal to make these purchases in South Korea. We'll pay a big premium for that. And then to have all this delivered in short order, there's another premium. We're talking big money here."

"How quickly can this be assembled and delivered?" Gunner asked.

"I suppose that depends on how quick you want it, Commander."

"Say twelve to twenty-four hours. Maybe sooner if the price is right."

"Ooohhh. You are asking a lot," Jung-Hoon said.

"I am asking."

"Understand that you are asking a lot of people to stick their necks out. I would have to make a call to get a quote for you."

"Make the call, please."

Jung-Hoon nodded. "As you wish."

From the corner of the room, the muted television, set on CNN International, flashed images of two US Navy fighter jets. "Hey, Jackrabbit, turn that up, will you?"

"Sure, boss." He punched the remote.

"Repeat ... this news breaking from CNN International. We have unconfirmed reports of an air-to-air combat exchange between US Navy combat jets and combat jets of the North Korean Air Force. Eyewitnesses from civilian South Korean fishing vessels in the area report witnessing a dogfight, and one vessel shot this video, which appears to be footage of two jets being brought down by air-to-air missiles."

"Unreal!" Gunner muttered. He stared at amateur footage of two jets appearing to blow into fireballs in the sky. The footage kept repeating.

"Looks like the real thing to me, Commander," Jackrabbit said.

Gunner nodded in the direction of Jung-Hoon, who was talking on the phone. "How good is he in the cockpit?"

"I've flown with him," Jackrabbit said. "He's all right. Put it this way. We never crashed or anything even close."

"Can he fly below radar?"

"You'll have to ask him that."

Jung-Hoon hung up the phone.

"Looks like a couple of Hornets just splashed a couple of Fishbeds," Gunner said.

"Not good for us," Jung-Hoon said. "Makes the situation even more dangerous. They'll be shooting surface-to-air missiles at everything that's flying."

"Yes, we were just discussing that," Gunner said. "How did it go with your weapons contact?"

"Expensive."

"How much? We're running out of time."

"He can deliver within four hours, but he says it is very dangerous for him. He will risk being arrested. I tried to get him to lower the price."

"Jung-Hoon, if you don't tell me how much, they're going to call me back out to the carrier before we can get out of here."

"One hundred thousand US dollars. Wants cash."

"Ouch!" Gunner said. "I'll be bankrupt before this thing gets off the ground."

"That too much, Commander?"

"No. Not yet. But we've got to work fast. Get me the wiring instructions for the weapons people and the plane."

The CNN report continued: "The footage you are watching was taken from a camera phone onboard a South Korean fishing vessel, operating in international waters in the Yellow Sea. Off the North Korean coastline." Repeated footage of missiles streaking into the backs of two fighter jets, followed by fireballs. "This footage was sent to a South Korean television station in Inchon. This is officially unconfirmed. Neither the US Navy nor the South Korean armed forces have commented. However, it appears the American and South Korean military have both gone to a higher stage of alert readiness. We have received reports of some South Korean reserve units being called in, which, if true, would indicate a potential escalation with the North."

"Shut it off, Jackrabbit," Gunner said.

Jackrabbit complied. "At least it isn't on the east coast."

"We've got ships off the west coast, in the Yellow Sea," Gunner said. "That won't stop them from scouring all air routes. Especially at a time like this."

"You having second thoughts, Commander?" Jackrabbit asked.

"Not a chance," Gunner said. "But we're gonna have to get moving before the admiral calls me back to the ship. Jung-Hoon, what's the total cash we're going to need?"

"Six hundred thousand for plane. One hundred thousand for weapons. Plus another fifty thousand should be more than enough for bribes and payment for cooperation in North Korea."

Gunner's heart pounded. In his mind, his limit had been perhaps a half a million dollars to finance the whole operation. But now the price tag had risen to three-quarters of a million.

Even with his land holdings in Virginia, worth several million dollars, this was a huge chunk out of operating cash. His thoughts turned to his mother back home at Corbin Hall and another Thanksgiving having passed with more painful memories of the unknown. He recalled the years growing up, the empty plate for his grandfather, how his mother always honored him with a few words before the meal was served. "He was a brave man and a good man," she would say. "He may be gone, but he will never be forgotten." And then, in homage to the United States Marine Corps, each year she would close her reminiscing with the words *Semper Fi*, followed by "Let us pray." And then, Thanksgiving would proceed, although his mother would often wipe a tear or two before passing the turkey.

He again took the picture of the young Marine from his pocket, gazed at it for a couple of seconds, and stuck it back.

"Jung-Hoon, if I turn all this money over to your friend, how do I know he will deliver the weapons and keep his mouth shut?"

"He will."

"How can you be so sure?"

"Because I will slit his throat if he betrays me in any way. He knows this."

"Remind me not to cross you," Gunner said. "We'll wire him the money. Have your contact meet us at the plane. Make sure he's got everything there or it won't be a pretty sight. We need to check the stuff, then load the plane and go. We don't have any time to waste."

"No time for a test flight?"

"No time for anything. We've got to take off this afternoon," Gunner said. "If you can't fly that thing, I need to know it."

"I can fly it," Jung-Hoon said. "I can fly anything. I like to take a test flight before I fly with passengers."

"No time. I'll take my chances." He glanced at Jackrabbit. "You okay with flying with him without a test flight?"

"What the heck," Jackrabbit muttered, "we all got to go sometime."

The three men looked at each other, then Jung-Hoon said, "Very well, Commander. I will call my man and tell him to meet us at the airstrip."

Kim Yŏng-nam Military Prison Camp

Are you ready for the execution, my dear one?" Colonel Song polished the last brass button on his drab-green Army jacket as he glanced over at his assistant, Mang Hyo-Sonn, who was getting dressed. Aroused by the events of the morning, they had had their tryst earlier than usual.

Mang pulled on her green enlisted uniform, alpha class, which on a woman meant a drab-green skirt matching her uniform blouse. The fit was tight. Her legs, he thought, were as luscious as they had been the first time he had noticed them. All this reminded him again of the privileges of rank, and although Mang Hyo-Sonn was the latest in a line of fine-looking conquests, something about her made him want her more than the others.

"Almost ready, my colonel," she said as she buttoned the top of her blouse. "And I cannot wait for the execution."

He pulled her close and their lips met. The total effect—his power over life and death, his ability to have the most beautiful of women at his command—sent his head swirling with an intoxicating euphoria.

"My big and powerful man." Her finger traced across his chin. "A thought did occur to me about something."

"A thought? What thought, my love?"

"That poor stupid girl. Don't you think in an odd way she may have done us a favor by what she did?"

"A favor?"

"Yes. I was thinking that this might be the case."

"What kind of favor?" He relaxed his grip and rested his hands on her shoulders. The sparkle in her black eyes roused his curiosity.

"My colonel." She toyed with the dimple in his chin. "This is the most prestigious military encampment in all the DPRK, is it not?"

"Yes, of course. Nothing compares in terms of prestige. Not in the Democratic People's Republic."

"Umm. It makes me love you that much more, my colonel, that you can wield such power, that you command the confidence of Dear Leader. But tell me, you have now been commandant for three years, no?"

"Yes, it will be three years at the end of next month."

"And because of your leadership here, your excellent record, there is a good chance that you will be promoted to general, is that not right?"

"I see that you have studied the career paths of my predecessors at this post."

"I do my homework." She flashed a sexy wink. "I want to fully understand the man of power I serve."

"What is your point, my beautiful one?"

"Well, in the three years since you have commanded this encampment, not one of the old Americans has died, is this not true?"

"That is true. Prisoners have died over the years. Some were executed before I assumed command. But no one has died on my watch."

"Precisely, my colonel. This exemplifies why you are so brilliant." She blinked and smiled.

Song hesitated. He was about to order a three-man firing squad to fire a round of bullets into the heart of a traitorous pig, but now, in the moment, he felt mesmerized. "Many have accused me of brilliance, my dear, but how does the fact that no prisoner has died yet also exemplify my brilliance? These are old men. They could die at any time."

"Think about it, my colonel. As long as they are alive, the DPRK has a valuable national treasure. The prisoners are a living symbol of our dominance over America in the war. Over the years, as they have dwindled in number, each prisoner has become more valuable to the DPRK.

"Once they are gone, I would be concerned that some in Pyongyang might not be so happy about such a loss. Anyone opposing your nomination to become a general might make an issue about it even though we both know it is truly a red-herring issue."

"Go on," he said.

"I do not wish to overstep my boundaries." Her eyes filled with passion. "I believe that the DPRK is best served by your promotion, finally, to the rank of general. I know you are preparing for the execution of the girl. I do not wish to delay you as you carry out the work of Dear Leader.

But I believe perhaps the girl is mentally deranged, and I would not want you to be accused in any way of ignoring that possibility."

Either this girl was interested in promoting his career or she was the finest actress in all of the Democratic People's Republic, Song thought. He studied her eyes for a moment. Either way, she exuded incredible intelligence, which magnified her desirability.

"You are not overstating your boundaries, my dear. I would reprimand you if you were. And we will proceed with the execution of this skinny piglet only when I say we will proceed. She can sweat a bit longer." He released Mang from his arms and walked over to the mantel. He poured himself a shot of soju. The liquor slid down his throat, warming him instantly and making him feel just a little lightheaded—which was a good thing.

He walked back over to his irresistible flower. "Now then, my pretty, what were you saying about all this?"

"My colonel"—she tipped her head and blinked up at him several times—"you are in a predicament of fate. As the commandant of the most prestigious military prison camp, the only one holding Americans, one must instill discipline against prisoners and not appear to go too soft on them. Yet, on the other hand, because of their value to the DPRK, one must be very careful to keep them alive, especially at their age, without appearing too friendly to them. That is why, ironically, someone like this stupid traitorous piglet that you are about to have shot could continue to be valuable to you."

"You think this American-loving backstabber can be *valuable* to me?" He sipped more soju. "My dear, *I* am the one who has been drinking." He chuckled. "If you are attempting to persuade me to stay the execution of this little hog because she is somehow of value to me, you had better make it fast. My three overanxious firing-squad members could get so excited that they wet their pants. We need to get moving."

"No. I would never suggest such a thing, my colonel. No. No. I would only suggest that you do have an option that could serve you well either way. If you proceed with the execution, you will have shown that there will be no toleration of stealing in your camp.

"On the other hand, if you decide to teach her a hard lesson short of execution, you can use her again, as a tool, as one willing to secretly help the old Americans survive. Using someone like her helps to make sure that the old prisoners do not die on your watch, my colonel. That would crush any arguments your political enemies might throw against you with Dear Leader when you are nominated for general."

"Hmm. Interesting, my lovely." He decided that his sexy little kitten clearly hoped to someday become the wife of a general. "But I have already sentenced her to death. I can hardly afford to look weak before my men."

She smiled and gently ran two fingers down his face. "I am not suggesting that you not execute her. That is your decision. But there are many ways to prove that you are a strict disciplinarian—many measures that you can take whether you have her shot or not. I believe you can use such a meaningless rodent to your advantage if you so choose." She planted an electrifying peck on his cheek. "I am sure that whatever you choose will be irresistibly exciting, and I cannot wait to see how you dispose of this little swine!" She draped herself against him. Her kiss was atomic. He let it linger for a moment, then pushed her away. Duty called. The execution loomed. But she had given him much to think over.

"Later, my love. We must deal with the traitor." He slipped on his coat and stepped out the door.

Downtown hotel
Seoul, South Korea

Commander. Excuse me, Commander!" the hotel clerk said as the trio rushed past the front desk, out toward the black pickup parked out front.

"Gotta go!" Gunner waved at the attendant.

"You have a telephone call."

"Who from?" Gunner shouted back across the lobby, walking quickly away from the check-in area and toward the revolving doors.

"The USS *Harry S. Truman*."

That announcement stopped him dead in his tracks. Frigid air blew in every time the front doors were opened.

"Sounds like they want you back on board the ship with all this shootin' going on," Jackrabbit said.

Jackrabbit was right. Gunner's mind shot into hyperdrive. If the Navy ordered him back to the ship, any chance of finding a clue about his grandfather would be forever lost. Yet he was a naval officer and duty called.

Still ... the US government had ignored these secret rumors all these years ...

Plus, the admiral had granted him thirty days' leave. But he had said that if the situation heated up, he would call him back to duty. Cancel his leave.

Of course, the call could be about anything. No message was left. Nothing like "Commander McCormick, contact the ship immediately." If they wanted him back immediately ...

"Better make up your mind, Commander," Jackrabbit said.

Jackrabbit was right. A decision beckoned. And he was a naval officer. And duty called. He turned back toward the desk.

But the image of his young grandfather in uniform stopped him. Perhaps they were only trying to verify his address. After all, he was on leave. They would call back if they needed him.

"Tell them that I have already left, please."

"Yes, Commander."

Gunner turned and stepped through the front door into the frigid air.

CHAPTER 10

USS Harry S. Truman
the Yellow Sea

Geneeral quarters! General quarters! General quarters! Man your battle stations! Prepare to launch jets!"

The booming voice of the *Truman*'s executive officer thundered over 1MC, the ship's public-address system. His words blared into every compartment of the giant supercarrier, echoing against the steel bulkheads and off the flight decks. Five thousand United States Navy crew members scrambled in chaotic precision to various parts of the ship, manning stations to defend her from enemy attack.

Rear Admiral James Hampton was taking no chances. Now that two Super Hornets had been fired on by North Korean MiGs and the Hornets had blown both MiGs out of the air, an attack on the *Truman* could be imminent.

"Has anybody found Commander McCormick yet?" Hampton demanded as he paced back and forth, checking his watch. He glanced down at the latest intelligence communiqué generated by Lieutenant Jim Porter. As a junior lieutenant, Porter was bright enough, but he was young and green. Hampton preferred the experienced McCormick at his side if missiles started flying. McCormick may have been distracted recently, but Hampton had supreme confidence in him.

"We made a couple ship-to-shore calls to the hotel he's registered at, Admiral," said Captain Anthony Farrow, Hampton's chief of staff. "They said he just left."

That brought a short burst of profanity from the admiral. "Did he get a South Korean cell phone?"

"Don't know about that, sir."

"Shouldn't we have worked that little detail out before we sent him ashore?"

"Well, yes, sir, Admiral. We should've ordered him to pick up a South Korean cell and provide us the number. My apologies, sir."

"All right. Don't worry about it, Tony. I'm the one who granted his leave to begin with. Keep trying to raise him."

"Aye, aye, Admiral."

"When you find him, tell him I've canceled his leave and he needs to report back here ASAP."

"Will do, sir."

The 1MC broke in. "Now hear this! This is the XO! Two inbound missiles approaching! Repeat: two inbounds approaching! Prepare for evasive maneuvers and brace for impact!"

"Throw me my helmet, Tony! I'm headed to the bridge."

"Sir, with all due respect, we need you to move below decks. It's too dangerous topside if there's impact."

"Tony, you can go below decks if you want, but I'm going topside. I need to see what's going on. Now throw me my battle helmet. That's an order!"

"Aye, aye, sir! ... I'm coming with you!"

Kim Yŏng-nam Military Prison Camp

The steady cold wind from the north numbed his lips and fingers. But for Staff Sergeant Kang Ho-soon, the cold gave him renewed strength. As he awaited the order for the execution, he patroled the camp with a sense of purpose and resolve.

Where was the colonel? Undoubtedly detained for an excellent reason. He decided the colonel probably had begun the paperwork for the commendation or medal he would receive for his discovery of the slimy pill thief. Or maybe the colonel was even considering a promotion for him. Yes, of course. That was it.

Bullets would soon explode into the twisting, worthless snake of a woman. Kang imagined how the colonel would announce his promotion, standing at attention in the courtyard. Perhaps the colonel would even call him into his office and announce that finally, he, Staff Sergeant Kang Ho-soon, would be given the opportunity to meet Dear Leader himself! He glanced over at his two colleagues, their AK-47s strapped over their shoulders, rubbing their hands together like a couple of idiotic chickens shivering in the elements. "Chung! Cho!" he snapped. "Check your rifles! They must be ready for the execution!"

They looked at each other and shrugged. Neither one said a word.

Kang was about to give another order when Chung pulled his AK-47 from his shoulder and Cho did the same. And just as Kang had ordered them to do, they each began checking the safety mechanism on the side of their rifles.

Good. His leadership was now unquestioned. The execution of the pig would seal his position and earn him his much-deserved promotion.

USS Lake Erie
the Yellow Sea
on patrol twenty miles east of USS Harry S. Truman

Inbound missiles, range twenty-five miles and closing, Captain!" the weapons officer announced.

Captain Hugh Bennett, the skipper of the Aegis-class heavy cruiser USS *Lake Erie*, looked through his binoculars toward the eastern horizon. Somewhere out there, not yet visible to the human eye, in the airspace above the line where the sea gave way to the sky, two enemy missiles were closing rapidly on the ships of the United States Carrier Strike Group Ten.

The missiles, fired from somewhere in North Korea, were either Chinese-made CSSC-3 "Seersuckers" or KN-01s, the North Korean enhanced version of the Seersucker. Either one had a potential range of up to two hundred kilometers and enough firepower to obliterate any ship in the battle group.

But Bennett knew, as did every member of his crew, that the North Korean missiles were targeting the biggest prize that any enemy of the United States could hope to claim—a nuclear supercarrier, this time the USS *Harry S. Truman*, with five thousand souls aboard and a carrier air wing consisting of more than fifty jet aircraft, eight helicopters, and enough firepower to single-handedly wipe out the functional operating structure of most nations on the face of the earth.

A supercarrier would be the ultimate trophy for any of America's enemies. Bennett's mission, indeed the principle mission of his ship and crew, was to protect that carrier at all costs. And while his ship and crew had drilled for this scenario on dozens of occasions, this was the *Lake Erie's* first life-and-death encounter against live missiles fired at the carrier.

Bennett dropped his binoculars and swiped beads of sweat off his forehead. With every eye on the bridge riveted on the eastern horizon, the weapons officer tracked the position of the inbound missiles.

"Inbound missiles, range twenty miles and closing, Captain," the weapons officer announced.

"Launch interceptors."

"Launch interceptors. Aye, Captain."

The aft section of the *Lake Erie* lit up with two sudden bursts of fire and billowing white smoke. Out of the fire and clouds of smoke, two SM-3 antiballistic missiles shot straight up and away from the back deck, kept climbing high above the ship, and then curved out from a vertical trajectory into a horizontal one, now flying parallel to the contour of the sea. Behind them trailed white streaks of smoke, marking their rapid race across the sky to the east. Computers within their internal guidance systems, interfacing with data being fed by radar from the ship, steered the missiles in their flight on an intercept course with the inbound enemy missiles.

That was the theory anyway.

Now Bennett could only pray. And wait. The life-or-death fate of thousands of sailors depended on the accuracy of those interceptors.

"Fifteen seconds to impact ..."

Dear Jesus, help us, he prayed.

"Ten seconds to impact, Captain.

"Still inbound, Skipper. Five seconds to impact. Four ... Three ... Two ..."

Bennett brought the binoculars back to his eyes just in time to witness a fireball explode in the sky. Cheering erupted on the bridge.

"Quiet!" Bennett ordered. "Weps! Status!"

"Sir, we got one! The other's still inbound. Course locked on the *Truman*!"

Swooooooooooosh!!!!

The second North Korean rocket shot right over the top of the *Lake Erie*, flying from port to starboard at an altitude of perhaps two hundred feet. Bennett watched it streak in the direction of the carrier. "Give me that!" He snatched the ship-to-ship radio that was already dialed in to the carrier's frequency. *"Truman! Lake Erie!* One missile still inbound! Repeat: missile still inbound! Emergency evasive maneuvers!"

USS Harry S. Truman
the Yellow Sea

Admiral's on the bridge!" the bridge watch officer shouted, as Admiral Hampton stepped onto the bridge.

"Forget me!" Hampton barked. "Carry on!"

"Right full rudder! All ahead flank!"

"Right full rudder! All ahead flank! Aye, Captain!"

The ship's nuclear-powered engines screamed at full power. The ship banked hard to her right, cutting so hard and steep in the water that the port edge of the runway rose up toward the sun. Captain Charles Harrison, a rugged sea veteran, sat in his captain's chair in the middle of the bridge.

"Grab your hats!" Captain Harrison yelled.

Admiral Hampton lost his balance but had a tight grip on a steel railing.

The *Truman* tipped sharply to starboard, like a giant canoe about to capsize. But the *Harry S. Truman* did not go over. With her bow now lined up and facing the oncoming missile, the *Truman* cut through the sea almost with the catlike agility of a small speedboat. This gave the missile a smaller target, from the 1,092 feet of the ship's length to 252 feet, the ship's beam, or width.

"Inbound missile, time to impact sixty seconds, Skipper!"

"Fire interceptors!" Harrison yelled.

"Firing interceptors! Aye, Captain!"

Poof...

Poof...

Two Mk 57 Mod 3 Sea Sparrow missiles shot off the side of the ship and headed east.

"Time to impact forty seconds."

"Fire RAM Launcher!"

"Fire RAM Launcher. Aye, Captain!"

Poof... Poof... Poof... Poof... Poof... Poof... Poof... Poof... Poof... A barrage of short-range blast fragmentation warheads shot off the bow from the portable RIM-116 Rolling Airframe Missile launchers.

"Still closing, Captain. Time to impact thirty seconds!"

"Fire Phalanx!"

"Fire Phalanx! Aye!"

Chit-a-chit-a-chit-a-chit-a-chit-a-chit-a-chit ... The Phalanx sprayed a wall of hundreds of bullets into the air from the electronically controlled "Gatling guns" that looked like the droid R2-D2 from *Star Wars*. If the missiles missed, some of the 20mm armor-piercing tungsten bullets now being fired at the rate of four thousand rounds per minute might connect.

"Time to impact—twenty seconds!"

All eyes on the bridge were glued forward. Every forehead was full of sweat.

"Time to impact—seventeen seconds."

"Come on, baby! Clip that missile," Captain Harrison mumbled.

"Time to impact—fifteen seconds ..."

"Ten seconds ...

"Dear Jesus," Hampton said.

"Nine ...

"Eight ...

"Brace for impact!"

All over the bridge, men grabbed tight onto steel railings. Some closed their eyes.

Boom!

The explosion occurred in the air just in front of the ship, and the fiery wreck of a missile landed on the front of the flight deck and skidded back, running into an F/A-18.

Boom!

The F/A-18 burst into flames. The fireball swooshed around the crew of the RAM missile launcher that had just launched the barrage of shots into the sky. Sailors rushed out of the fireball, their uniforms aflame. Black smoke billowed high from the fighter jet as flames consumed the jet's fuel.

"Fire on the deck! Fire on the deck! Sailors down! All firefighting units! All medical personnel! Report to the flight deck! On the double!"

Kim Yŏng-nam Military Prison Camp

Keith sat at the head of the cot and placed his hand on Robert's forehead.

"How's he doing?" Frank was sitting on the top bunk and looking out into the courtyard.

"Gotta be a hundred and two or a hundred three," Keith said. "Maybe even higher." He reached down and felt for Robert's pulse. "He was doing better, but now his heart's racing."

"Forcing him out in the snow won't help matters," Frank said, his eyes still peeled outside. "I hate those maggots."

"Tell me about it," Keith said. Robert rolled away, his face toward the wall. He was shivering.

"He's got the chills," Keith said. He pulled the blanket up and tucked it around his old friend's shoulders.

Keith looked up and whispered, "Lord, if you are still there, please don't let him die. Not yet anyway."

Robert moaned softly.

"If only we could get this fever to break." He reached down and dipped his right hand into the pan of water and sprinkled a few drops on his friend's head. Then he rubbed the water across Robert's forehead. "He's so hot this water's gonna steam up," he said. "What's going on outside?"

"Not good," Frank said. "Looks like they're getting ready to shoot Pak."

"Dear Lord, no!" Keith said. "Those people are animals."

"She's tied to the tree. The three stooges are lined up with their rifles, the colonel is parading out in front of her, throwing his arms around like a Nazi drill sergeant trying to impress his little woman."

"Aaaahhhh!" Robert rolled over on his back, his face a pasty white, his mouth and eyes locked wide open.

"I've seen that look before." Keith put his hand on the side of Robert's neck. "He's not breathing! His heart's stopped! Dear God, no!"

Keith reached down, cleared Robert's tongue out of the way, pinched his nose, cradled his head back, put his mouth on Robert's mouth, and blew with all his might.

Robert's chest rose, then fell.

"Come on! Breathe, Robert, breathe!" Keith said as he pulled his mouth away from Robert's open mouth.

Frank had scrambled down from the bunk and stood over Keith's shoulder.

"Blow again," Frank said.

Keith inhaled deeply, then repeated the procedure.

Robert's chest rose, then fell again.

And once again ...

Robert's chest rose, then fell, again.

"Come on! Breathe!" Keith shouted, then reached a finger into Robert's mouth and tried again to move his tongue away from the back of his mouth.

USS Harry S. Truman
the Yellow Sea

Move move move!" Fireman Senior Chief Matt Cantor waved an arm, imploring the enlisted members of his hose team to get topside ASAP. The team ran up the steel ladder from the hangar bay, up to the flight deck. The heavy oxygen tanks they carried on their backs added a challenge, and they had to hang on to the ladder railing to avoid falling backward.

Cantor was the second to reach the deck. Flame-heated wind whipped into his face, like the hot *swoosh* gushing from an oven that had been left on broil. The source of the heat was the front section of the carrier's giant flight deck. It was ablaze. Angry flames leaped toward the sky, spewing plumes of black smoke.

Two F/A-18 Super Hornets that had been sitting in the cat position waiting for takeoff burned like dry tinder in a hot desert, the tips of the flames reaching fifty feet into the air. Behind the burning jets, flight crews were pushing two more F/A-18s back away from the flames. A common panic seemed frozen on the faces of men pushing the planes, all aware that a stray flame could set off highly combustible jet fuel. Several men were facedown on the deck opposite the flames.

"Put on your oxygen masks! Grab that hose! Let's go! Move it!" Cantor grabbed the nozzle, and five men picked up the rest of the hose as if they were cradling a giant boa constrictor. "Okay! Hit the water! Let's hose down those planes!"

Cantor donned his mask. And as he did ...

Whoooooooooooshhhh ...

The force of the water rushing through the hose almost knocked Cantor off his feet. "Hang tight, baby!" he yelled at his men as he wrestled the hose under his arms. "Let's go!"

They all moved forward toward the leaping inferno, step by step. Cantor aimed the blast of water at the closest burning plane. Just then ... *Boom!* ... more flames leaped up from the back of the plane! A secondary explosion ...

"Aaaaaaaaaaaaaaaahhhhhhhhhhhhhhh!!"

A sailor, his uniform ablaze, sprinted across the deck. He screamed and waved his arms and ran toward the side of the flight deck.

"Hose down that guy!" Cantor redirected the water toward the burning sailor. The water hit the sailor, pushing him in the back, knocking him off his feet. He pushed himself back up. His uniform still on fire, he turned his burning back to the gushing water. At that moment, a hot crosswind swept back across the deck, knocking the sailor off his feet again and pushing him almost to the edge of the deck.

"Hold off! Hold off!" Cantor yelled, pulling the hose away from the sailor.

Another powerful gust of heat-generated wind swooshed across the deck and the sailor disappeared over the side.

"Man overboard! Man overboard!"

T*weet ... tweet ... tweet ... tweet ... tweet ... tweet ....*
One level below the flight deck, where hot flames still lapped the front of the vessel, six sharp blasts of the alarm whistle bounced off the steel bulkheads of the hangar deck.

"Man overboard! Man overboard! Man overboard! Starboard side!"

Boatswains Mate Chief Walter Drodz, in command of Rescue Team 2, donned a white hard hat and a red life preserver and sprinted around two F/A-18s to the starboard side of the ship, to the bullet-shaped rubber-ringed rescue craft with its outboard engine.

Four other men, all wearing red life preservers and different color hard hats, raced toward the rubber-ringed boat. They were the man-overboard squad. They stepped one by one into the craft that was dangling in the air, hanging by three giant ropes attached to winches just on the underside of the massive flight deck.

"Lower the boat!" Drodz shouted. The winches, working in reverse, lowered the boat down, down, down. *Splash*. "Crank it!" he ordered. A second later, the outboard fired up. "Let's go!"

Detached from the ship, they moved out across rolling swells, out toward where the man had been spotted moments ago in the watchman's binoculars.

Drodz, seated in the front of the boat, could not resist the temptation to look back over his shoulder. Thick smoke and flames were rising from the front of the carrier.

"There he is!" one of the men shouted. That brought Drodz's head back around. The sailor was floating facedown. Only the back of his charred blue shirt was visible. The uniform had been ablaze, but the fire-repellant substances had worked, at least partially.

"Pull over to his left." The boat moved alongside the floating sailor. Just then a large swell rolled under the boat, raising it and moving it away from the floating body. The two came back together as they slid down the back of the swell into the trough.

"Let's get him out of the water!"

Two of the sailors reached over the side, and, as the next mound of water began raising the boat and the body, they snatched the sea-soaked sailor into the boat. He rolled in, face up. His face was bluish and his hair was scorched. The name on his uniform shirt was "Martinez."

"Out of the way!" Drodz scrambled to the center of the boat, put his crossed hands over the sailor's chest, and pushed down hard.

Water gushed from the sailor's mouth. Drodz pushed again. More water. Then he pushed Martinez's head back and clamped his mouth on the sailor's mouth and blew.

The sailor gagged. Drodz rolled him on his side. More water spewed from his mouth.

The boat rode yet another swell to its peak.

"Atta boy, Martinez," Drodz said, thumping the sailor on the back. More coughing. A little more water from the sailor's mouth.

"Martinez. We've got you! You're gonna be okay!"

CHAPTER 11

Kim Yŏng-nam Military Prison Camp

Firing squad! Atten-hut!" The colonel's booming voice echoed across the courtyard as the sound of clicking boots snapped together.

Pak opened her eyes. Squinting through her tears, she saw her three executioners standing about twenty feet in front of her, all in a line standing at attention, their rifles pointing up. The colonel was standing off to one side. He was in full uniform. In his hand was something that looked like a long black club. The colonel's assistant, who had a large black cloth in her hand, was standing to the other side of the guards.

"Staff Sergeant Mang!" the colonel snapped.

"Sir! Yes, sir!" she snapped back.

"Proceed to blindfold the condemned."

"Sir! Yes, sir!" she snapped again and shot the colonel a stiff salute. She then turned, focused her eyes on Pak, and began marching toward her.

"Dear Jesus," Pak whispered and closed her eyes. "The Lord is my shepherd, I shall not want ..."

Pak opened her eyes. Mang was standing right in front of her.

In a whisper that could not be heard by the men standing behind her, Mang said, "It might be in your best interests to continue babbling that propagandistic religious garbage so that you will appear to be insane." Then, in a loud voice she said, "I am going to blindfold you now. Close your eyes, cooperate, and this will be over soon."

126

Come on, Robert! Breathe!" Keith yelled, as he pulled his mouth away, exhaled, then blew back into Robert's mouth, trying desperately to get air into his lungs.

Inhale.

Exhale. Chest rising. Chest dropping.

Inhale.

Exhale.

Chest rising. Chest dropping.

"Keith." Frank tapped him on the shoulder.

Keith heard Frank's voice, as if it was far away. He ignored it. He wasn't going to surrender. Running through his mind were the words: *Marines don't abandon Marines.*

Inhale.

Exhale.

Chest rising. Chest dropping.

"Keith." Another gentle tap on the shoulder.

"Shut up, Frank! I'm not giving up! He's a Marine!"

Inhale.

Exhale.

Chest rising. Chest dropping.

"Keith, I'm sorry. It's over."

Inhale.

Exhale.

Chest rising. Chest dropping.

No pulse.

"Keith, stop. He knew you would've given your life for him. Come on, it's over. He's gone."

"Noooooo!" Keith pushed himself to his feet. "Not Robert! Noooooo!"

He picked up the metal pan with water and slung it at the barred window.

Clang-a-lang-a-lang.

"Nooooooo!"

The metal trash can. Near the door. He rushed at it and kicked it across the concrete floor.

"No! No! Nooooo!"

Another kick of the trash can.

"You've got to get hold of yourself, Keith!"

Firing squad. Ready!" Colonel Song Kwang-sun's commanding voice echoed across the courtyard.

"Firing squad, aim!" In sharp precision, three rifles clacked to the shoulders of the firing squad, their barrels aimed at Pak, roped to the tree.

Clang-a-lang-a-lang.

Colonel Song looked off to his left. "What is that noise?"

"It sounds like it is coming from the barracks, Colonel," his assistant said.

"It sounds like a riot in there."

"But from old men?" Kang said.

"Firing squad, stand down!"

"But, Colonel," Kang said, "we could finish the execution first."

"I said, stand down!"

The men lowered their rifles.

"Chung, go check out the situation in the barracks."

"Yes, Colonel." Chung slung his rifle over his shoulder and jogged over to the barracks. He opened the door and walked in. "What is going on in here?"

Silence.

Moments later, Chung walked back out and yelled, "One of the prisoners has died, Colonel!"

"Which one?" the colonel yelled.

"The one who was sick!" Chung shouted back.

Silence. No one moved. The only sound was the sighing of the wind whipping through the trees as if in mourning for the old man.

Colonel Song sensed the stare of his mistress, and her words came back to him in a rush: "Using someone like her helps to make sure that they do not die on your watch ... die on your watch ... " He couldn't look at her. He just couldn't.

"We are prepared to proceed with the execution, my colonel," Kang said. "We can bury the dead prisoner later. And, if you would like, we can execute the one who was rioting in the barracks. I have a feeling I know which one it was! Sir!"

Colonel Song glanced at Mang Hyo-Sonn.

"The execution shall be postponed for thirty minutes—"

"But, Colonel," Kang said.

"During which time . . . we shall secure the two remaining prisoners . . . to ensure that they do not interrupt the execution."

"But Colonel," Kang persisted. "We can secure the prisoners in five minutes. I will personally secure the prisoners if you would like to keep the remaining members of the firing squad in position."

"Did you not understand my order, Staff Sergeant?" He stared at his very ambitious guard. "We will reconvene in thirty minutes. Do you understand me?"

"Sir! Yes, sir!"

USS Harry S. Truman
the Yellow Sea

Admiral Hampton folded his arms and surveyed the scene of destruction in front of him. Powerful water gushed from high-pressure hoses onto the smoking hulks of the planes. The flames had subsided, but black smoke still plumed high into the sky. Water also poured onto the wreck of what moments ago had been a North Korean missile, destroyed by Phalanx fire just before it would have crashed into the ship.

The entire front section of the carrier had morphed from leaping hot flames to choking black smoke. For now, the fire teams were winning this battle. It would be some time before the flight deck was again operational. And that was a problem.

The *Truman* had survived. But the admiral knew that the ship's defense system had failed. And he needed to find out just what had happened, what went wrong. Damage and injury reports were not all in yet.

He walked over to Captain Charles Harrison, who was issuing orders for the cleanup operations of his ship. "Skipper? Damage reports?"

"Lost two birds, Admiral," the captain said. "RAM crew was wiped out on the flight deck when the missile exploded. Still unclear on how many men we have missing, but the number appears small. One man overboard, but recovered. They're bringing him back onboard now. Medical teams treating the wounded. No final count on fatalities. Once we finish hosing down the flight deck, we'll get these planes bulldozed overboard. We'll be back in the business of fighting a war within thirty minutes."

Hampton checked his watch with a tinge of impatience. "I don't want to push you, Captain, but as soon as you can turn the ship over to the XO for a few minutes, I need to see you and the CAG on the flag bridge. We've gotta get some answers as to what happened and why."

Captain Harrison checked his watch and glanced out at the flight deck. "Actually, Admiral, this might be a good time to turn the ball over to the XO for a few."

"Very well, Captain. Make the transition and put out a call for the CAG and my deputy intel officer to meet us on the flag bridge. We need information for Washington."

"Aye, sir," Captain Harrison said.

He turned to the ship's number-two officer, Commander Rawlinson Petty, who was standing next to him. "XO, take the conn. And would you round up Garcia and Porter for me?"

"Aye, Skipper." Commander Petty said. The executive officer stepped over and took a seat in the captain's chair.

"After you, Admiral." Captain Harrison pushed open the door of the bridge for Admiral Hampton. Captain Tony Farrow, Hampton's chief of staff, followed the admiral.

"Attention on deck!" the two petty officers standing guard outside the bridge barked.

"Carry on," Hampton said.

Admiral Hampton led the two captains down a passageway, then down a short set of stairs, past at least a half dozen young sailors who jumped to stiff attention as the trio passed, before finally arriving at the flag bridge.

Just then a voice boomed over the 1MC. "Captain Garcia, Lieutenant Porter, report to the flag bridge."

"Attention on deck! Admiral's on the flag bridge!" a navy lieutenant announced.

"Carry on," Hampton said.

"CAG on the flag bridge," the OOD said.

Hampton turned and nodded to Captain Mark "Maverick" Garcia, the CAG—the Carrier Air Group Commander.

"Admiral. Skipper," Garcia said.

The flag bridge door opened again. But this time, the officer entering did not rate an announcement. Lieutenant Jim Porter, the junior intelligence officer, said, "Good afternoon, Admiral."

"Well, it looks like we're all here, gentlemen," Hampton said. "Have a seat."

Harrison and Garcia sat on a long sofa anchored to the bulkhead. Farrow sat in a chair beside the long sofa. Hampton sat in another chair on the other side of the sofa. Porter remained standing.

"Gentlemen, I want to know what the heck happened. We've just had an antiship missile crash-land on our flight deck. I have to explain this to Washington."

The senior officers exchanged glances, as if uncertain who should start.

Harrison spoke up. "Admiral, as commanding officer of this ship, the burden for defending the ship is on my shoulders. So with your permission, sir, I'd like to start."

Hampton nodded. "Go ahead, Captain."

"Well, sir, the North Koreans slipped a missile through our missile-defense screen. Two missiles were fired. USS *Lake Erie* engaged the missiles with interceptors and took one out. The other got through."

"SM-3s?" Hampton asked.

"Yes, sir. *Lake Erie* tried taking them out with SM-3s. Word from Captain Bennett, the CO of *Lake Erie*, is that one of the SM-3s failed to detonate."

"Mmm. I've never trusted the reliability of the SM-3s," Hampton said. "Guess this proves it."

"Once *Lake Erie* informed us that the missile slipped through," Harrison said, "we threw everything we had at it. The forward port Phalanx clipped it and blew it up, or it would have been a lot worse."

There was a pause.

"What kind of a missile was it?"

No answer.

"Lieutenant Porter?" Hampton said. "Intel's your department. You got anything on North Korean antiship missiles?"

The junior intel officer twitched and cleared his throat. "Well, sir, Commander McCormick had put together a file on North Korean missiles before he left, and I brought that up in case you asked about it ..." He paused and fiddled with some papers in an accordion file.

"Dang straight I'm asking about it," Hampton snapped. "Come on, son, I don't have all day."

"Sorry, sir," Porter said, as he pulled a memo out of the file. "Here it is." He sounded relieved. "Commander McCormick in his memo indicates that any missiles fired from North Korea are probably either Chinese-made CSSC-3 Seersuckers or KN-01s, which are a North Korean – enhanced version of the Seersucker."

"What's the range on these missiles?" Hampton said.

"Uh ..." — he read the memo — "up to 161 kilometers, or 100 miles, sir."

Hampton shook his head. "Captain Farrow, let's get the chart up. I want to have a look at our current position and the position of our battle group."

"Aye, sir," his chief of staff said, then nodded at the officer of the watch. "Lieutenant? Chart, please."

"Aye, aye, sir."

A second later, the lieutenant wheeled a chart out on an easel.

"Captain Harrison, please brief us on our current position and the position of the ships in the group."

"Aye, aye, sir."

"This chart marks the current position of the surface ships in the strike force. The carrier is represented by the star symbol in the middle. Now as you can see, we have seven ships positioned around the *Truman* to defend the carrier from missile and torpedo attack.

"Our heavy cruisers *Lake Erie* and *Hue City*, the biggest of our missile-defense ships, are represented by the two deltas, out to port and starboard of the carrier. The destroyers and frigates out on the perimeter are represented by lightning bolts.

"The ships, arrayed around the carrier in a circular position, in theory give us equal level of firepower against incoming missiles from any direction.

"Notice our current position. We are operating in the narrowest part of the Yellow Sea. Out to the west, approximately fifty miles, is this finger of land, Cape Chengshan, in China." The captain tapped the chart. "As you can see, the USS *Hue City* is operating between our current position and Cape Chengshan.

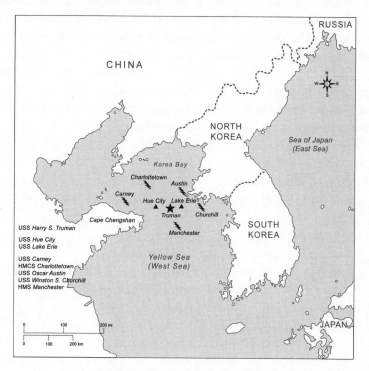

Navy warships, positions in Yellow Sea, Korea Bay

"Out to the east, about seventy miles, is the North Korean province of South Wanghae. We are approximately seventy miles from the westernmost tip of the province, which is here." He tapped the chart again. "USS *Lake Erie* has been buffering us to the east. *Lake Erie*'s job was to take those missiles out. And, as you know, she took out one of them.

"East of *Lake Erie* the USS *Oscar Austin* is moving into place to provide an additional screen against future missile attacks from Korea. *Austin* was south of this position when those missiles were launched and is not quite on station where we're showing her on this chart."

"So we're moving *Austin* into place with *Lake Erie* to provide additional ABM assistance, but she's not actually in place yet?" Hampton asked.

"Yes, sir, Admiral. That is correct. The skipper of *Lake Erie* radioed the skipper of *Oscar Austin* right after that missile got by, requesting emergency assistance, and the skipper of *Oscar Austin* set a course to the northeast to provide the additional missile screen. He also sent a flash message asking approval for the movement."

Captain Farrow, the admiral's chief of staff, said, "We got a top-secret flash message from both captains requesting your approval for repositioning of *Oscar Austin* to flank *Lake Erie*. I hadn't had a chance to present it to you yet because of all the chaos."

"Approve it," Hampton snapped. "Maybe *OA*'s interceptors will work better than *Lake Erie*'s."

"Aye, sir," Farrow said.

"And Tony, try to make me aware of these things before, not after, the fact."

"Aye, sir. My apologies."

"Captain Harrison, continue your briefing."

"Aye, Admiral. As you can see, we have the British destroyer HMS *Manchester* covering us to the south and the Canadian frigate HMCS *Charlottetown* to our northwest running the point.

"And as I mentioned, *Hue City*, our other heavy cruiser, is watching our western flank against anything that might come flying out of China.

"And finally, just out to the west of *Hue City*, we have the guided-missile destroyer USS *Carney*." He tapped the chart with a pointer.

Silence.

Hampton studied the chart. "Captain Garcia." His eyes shifted to the air wing commander.

"Yes, sir."

"What if I ordered our entire western-posted destroyer screens out to the east of the ship?"

The three captains stared at one another. Captain Harrison looked most worried.

"You mean move our escort vessels now guarding our air and sea space between here and China and put them out to the east for added defense against further missile attacks from North Korea?"

Harrison's eyes locked on to Hampton's. Hampton looked back at Garcia.

"Here's what we know," Hampton said. "We just had one North Korean missile out of two fired get in way too close. If that Phalanx gun hadn't taken that missile out at the last second, we'd have had the largest American catastrophe since 9/11. I don't think Captain Harrison here has enough lifeboats for five thousand sailors. And I don't want the largest American disaster since 9/11 on my shoulders."

"But, sir," Captain Harrison interjected, "if we move all our screens to the North Korean side, that means we're exposed if the Chinese launch a missile. Sir, with all due respect, I've read Sun Tsu's *Art of War*. Chapter 6, as I recall, sir, emphasizes hitting the enemy at his point of weakness."

Hampton looked back at the carrier commander. "The Chinese are smarter than the North Koreans. They might attack, but I don't think they will attack hastily. I think the North Koreans are far more likely to fire another missile at us. Maybe even a barrage of missiles.

"Which leads me back to my original question, Captain Garcia." He looked again at the CAG commander. "If I order part or all of the ships on our Chinese flank over to the east to guard the sea lanes on the Korean side, could your planes protect us against missile attack?"

Captain Garcia hesitated. He appeared to be rolling his tongue around the inside of his mouth. "Well, Admiral, we can shoot down any CHICOM plane that would fire a missile at the carrier, and we can take out any land-based missile battery. Raytheon has been experimenting with some fighter-based ABM weapons. But as you know, our planes right now don't have great shoot-down capabilities against other missiles."

The other captains nodded.

"We might deter an attack on the carrier by patroling just outside their airspace, particularly if they think we might be carrying nuclear-tipped missiles," Garcia said. "But shooting down other missiles?" He shook his head. "I'm afraid that's the bailiwick of our surface vessels, sir."

"Umph." Hampton considered the options. "Lieutenant Porter, what's the position of the nearest-known Chinese shore missile batteries?"

Porter fumbled through the files again, his face sporting that scared fish-out-of-water look that Hampton had seen on the faces of junior officers throughout his thirty years in the Navy. "I ... I don't see it here, but I'm pretty sure that Commander McCormick did a memo of the positions of all Chinese missile batteries. If you'd like, sir, I will be happy to run down to the intel office and look for that memo."

Hampton tried suppressing his irritation. "No, Lieutenant. Not now. But get it to me as soon as we break, and make sure that Captain Garcia's staff is briefed on the locations."

"Aye, sir."

"Okay. Here's what we're going to do." Hampton stood, prompting everyone else to stand. "Everybody, sit down," he said as he stepped over to the chart. "I'm leaving *Hue City* out to our west ... just in case. But I'm moving *Carney*, *Charlottetown*, and *Manchester* out to our eastern flank, which gives us six ships with antimissile capabilities if the North Koreans fire again."

The captains seemed relieved at the news that *Hue City* was staying put.

"Captain Farrow."

"Yes, sir."

"Draft operational orders to commanders of all surface ships involved to reposition the aforementioned ships as ordered. Flash. Top secret."

"Aye, Admiral."

CHAPTER 12

The White House
Washington, DC

Mack Williams walked quickly down the middle of the West Colonnade, the long, half-covered open portico that connects the main residential portion of the White House with the West Wing. The open-columned walkway, a picturesque backdrop for events held in the Rose Garden, was a cold walk in late November for the president and his staff.

At three-something in the morning, the temperature flirted with thirty-two degrees. The president, though a native Kansan, did not like freezing weather. Roused from his warm bed by two Secret Service agents, Mack had thrown on a pair of blue jeans, a white shirt, his trademark navy blue blazer, and penny loafers without socks. Now he wished he had taken time to slip on socks. As he hurried along the walkway, feeling like he was walking through a giant refrigerator, he realized he should have at least grabbed an overcoat.

All he knew was that he was needed at an emergency meeting of the National Security Council in the Situation Room. Something on Korea. He wished now he had stayed at Camp David for the remainder of the Thanksgiving weekend. Even emergencies seemed less stressful there.

"What's going on, fellows?" he asked again as the agents escorted him through the cold.

"We don't know, Mr. President," one of the agents said. "About Korea, as I understand it. Mr. Brubaker has all the details."

"Ah, yes. Mr. Brubaker has the details," Mack said. His White House chief of staff, Arnie Brubaker, was so guarded in the flow of information that sometimes even Mack, who had picked Brubacker as his chief of staff, viewed him as a shadow president of sorts.

The trio quick-stepped down the colonnade, the soles of their shoes clicking and echoing on the slate walkway as they hurried toward the light streaming from the entrance to the West Wing. As they approached, the door swung open.

Out walked White House Chief of Staff Arnie Brubaker, wearing a blue pinstripe suit, perfectly pressed white shirt, and red tie.

"It's three in the morning, Arnie," Mack said. "What's up?"

"A missile attack on the *Harry Truman*, sir," Brubaker said when they stepped into the heated entrance of the West Wing.

"What?" Mack said. "A missile attack on the carrier?"

"Yes, sir."

"Did we lose her?"

"No, sir, but the ship suffered some significant damage."

"Who attacked the *Truman*?"

"The North Koreans, sir. A land-based missile slipped through our missile screens. A little over an hour ago. Apparently they were retaliating because two of our Super Hornets splashed two of their MiGs, after a MiG fired on the Hornets."

Brubacker walked alongside the president. The two Secret Service agents followed behind them as they headed for the elevator that would take them down to the basement of the West Wing.

"How bad is it?" Mack asked.

The chief of staff punched the elevator button. "Pretty bad, sir. But we didn't lose the ship. Thank God for that."

The doors closed and the elevator dropped down one level.

"A direct hit?" Mack snapped. "How many men lost?"

The elevator doors opened and the men stepped out into the hallway, right across from the Situation Room.

"The carrier is still afloat, sir," Brubacker said as he pushed open a door of the Situation Room.

"Attention on deck!"

Immediately, six high-ranking members of the armed services rose to their feet. They all held four-star rank. Two were from the Navy, two from the Marines, one from the Army, and one from the Air Force.

Three civilians, all in their fifties—the vice president, the secretary of state, and secretary of defense—also stood. The lone woman in the room, who held the office of national security adviser to the president, also stood.

"Sit down, gentlemen, ma'am," Mack said. He looked at the chairman of the Joint Chiefs of Staff, Navy Admiral Roscoe Jones, who was by law the highest-ranking military officer in the United States armed forces. "Brubaker's details are a little sketchy. What's going on with the *Harry Truman*?"

"Mr. President, the *Harry Truman* took a hit from what we think is a Chinese-made missile fired from North Korea," the Arkansas native said in a bit of a drawn-out Southern accent. "They fired two missiles at us. They apparently fired the missiles because two of our Hornets splashed two of their MiGs after one of the MiGs fired on the Hornets.

"Our cruiser-destroyer screens shot one missile down. The other got through the screen. The *Truman*'s Phalanx system finally intercepted the missile in midair at the very last second. The missile exploded just before it hit the ship, but the burning wreckage of the missile landed on the forward deck of the carrier. This set off a significant fire, destroying two F-18s, that has now been brought under control."

"What are our losses?" the president asked.

"The two F-18s on the cat that went up in smoke. Four confirmed dead."

"Umph." Mack slammed his fist on the table as he stood and leaned forward. "Admiral, I want to know how those missiles got through our defensive interceptors."

Admiral Jones looked over to the other admiral in the room. "Admiral Arthur, would you take that one?"

Mack stared at his chief of naval operations, Admiral Chester A. Arthur VII, who was the great-grandson, several times removed, of the nation's twenty-first president.

"Yes, sir, I'll take that question," Admiral Arthur said. He slipped on a pair of black half-rimmed reading glasses, perching them halfway down his nose. "Sir, USS *Lake Erie* was the lead ship shielding the *Truman* to her east. When the missiles were spotted inbound, *Lake Erie* fired two SM-3 antiballistic missiles.

"Our interceptor missiles launched successfully, sir, and by all accounts tracked the inbound missiles on target. One detonated and took out one of the Seersuckers. Unfortunately, the second SM-3 simply failed to detonate." The admiral paused.

"Simply failed to detonate." Mack parroted the admiral's words.

"Yes, sir, afraid so," Admiral Arthur said. "That's the preliminary indication. Sir, the government bought a lot of SM-3s during the Obama administration because they were cheap. They didn't meet the specs the Navy would have wanted, but the administration rammed them through anyway."

"All right, I know," Mack said. "I know … Obama wasn't much on the military. But what I want to know is why the Phalanx system on board the *Lake Erie* didn't fire as a backup to the SM-3 to take the missile out."

Jones and Arthur looked at each other. Arthur said, "Mr. President, that's a good question. We don't yet know why. We're trying to determine why the Phalanx system on *Lake Erie* wasn't fired."

"Dang straight we need to know why," Mack said. "And when you put that question to the skipper of the *Lake Erie*, his answer better be good or I'll order him removed from command tonight and make whoever the XO is the acting CO. Are we clear on that?"

"Perfectly clear, sir," Jones said.

"Mr. President?" Arthur said.

"Yes, Admiral."

"In defense of the skipper of the *Lake Erie*, sir, the Phalanx is a close-in defensive gun of last resort. It is to be used only if the interceptors have missed and an attacking missile is closing in on the ship. The *Truman* used Phalanx properly and it did work. It's possible the Seersucker never got within range of the *Lake Erie*'s system."

"Let's hope for the skipper's sake that's the case," Mack muttered.

"Yes, sir," Arthur said.

"Now," Mack said, "what are we doing to make sure our carrier isn't threatened again? Because, gentlemen, I will not be the first president in United States history to lose five thousand sailors in one swoop."

Another brief pause. Then Arthur spoke up again. "Sir, the carrier strike group is under the command of Rear Admiral James Hampton. Admiral Hampton himself is an ex-carrier commander and shares everyone's concerns about making sure that no more missiles get anywhere close to the *Truman*. He's already repositioned most of our ships, except for one, out to the east of the *Truman* to provide additional missile screens in the event of another attack."

"Let me get this straight," Mack said. "We've now got all our ships between the carrier and the North Koreans, except one. And that one is supposed to screen against the Chinese on the other side in the event that the Chinese decide to attack?"

"Mr. President," Jones said, "Admiral Hampton is taking a calculated gamble that the Chinese won't attack. He feels that the ships should be positioned in this array to best protect the *Truman* if the North Koreans fire another missile."

Mack stood up from the table and folded his arms. "What ship is flanking the *Truman* on the left?"

"USS *Hue City*," Arthur said. "Ticonderoga-class cruiser."

"Another Ticonderoga-class cruiser," Mack said, "with the same suspect SM-3s, just like the *Lake Erie*?" As an ex-naval officer, the president had a good understanding of what had just happened and the deadly risks of faulty weaponry. "I suppose that's the right decision," he muttered. "But if the Chinese attack our carrier, it's the start of World War III."

"Yes, sir," Arthur said.

Mack looked at the two admirals. "Tell every skipper of every surface ship in this task force to use every means available to defend against any missile attacks, and that means I expect them to employ the Aegis system if an attacking missile comes within range."

"Yes, sir," Jones and Arthur said almost simultaneously.

"Okay, here's what we're going to do," Mack said. "As an ex-naval officer, I take it real personal when someone tries to attack one of our ships. No one attacks a US warship, especially a nuclear-powered aircraft carrier, without paying a heavy price." He paused. "Admiral Jones, what nuclear subs do we have near North Korea at the moment?"

"USS *Virginia* is in the Yellow Sea with the carrier strike group. USS *Boise* is in the Sea of Japan, sir."

"Admiral Jones, contact the skipper of the *Boise* and tell him he's got an assignment. By order of the president, he is to hunt down and sink the nearest North Korean Navy frigate that he can find."

"But, Mr. President," Secretary of State Robert Mauney said, "the

State Department's concern would be that this could lead to unnecessary escalation. I recommend that we first try to open a dialogue to Kim Jong-il to defuse the situation diplomatically."

"Humph. Diplomacy. After they tried to sink an aircraft carrier with five thousand men aboard?" The president looked at the secretary of state. "Dear Leader will understand, in no uncertain terms, that when he tries to toy with the United States Navy, he will pay a heavy price."

Mack then turned to Admiral Jones. "And while you're at it, Admiral Jones, tell the skipper of the *Virginia* that he is to hunt down the nearest North Korean Communist frigate in the Yellow Sea, to follow it like a bloodhound on the trail of a bleeding deer, and if I decide to give the order, he is to send that one to the bottom of the sea too."

"Yes, sir," the chairman of the Joint Chiefs said.

"But, Mr. President," Secretary of State Mauney said, clearly agitated, "if we take out one and possibly two North Korean vessels, not only have we escalated this thing, sir, but I'm sure North Korea will ask for an emergency meeting of the United Nations Security Council. At the very least, the council would introduce a measure to condemn the action. I'm afraid that taking these retaliatory measures without first consulting the UN will make it much more difficult for us to build a consensus of nations against North Korea to condemn their attack."

"That's enough." Mack held up his hand to cut off the arguments of his secretary of state. "I appreciate the State Department and all you do. But you know how I feel about the United Nations. From the beginning, it's functioned as a one-world-order organization whose sole function is to look down its collective nose at the one nation that funds it, the United States. The UN has advocated the transfer of wealth out of the United States, the elimination of international borders, the establishment of a single global currency, international gun control, and the elimination of American jobs. It's become a friendly forum for radical and scientifically absurd ideas like global warming and has advocated cockamamie international tax schemes like cap-and-trade. It has done everything it can to end the sovereignty of the United States."

Mack looked around the table. "Let me tell you this, Mr. Secretary, this president is an American. And I am *first* an American." He was now jabbing his finger in the air. Something about the secretary of state's comments had needled him. "This president is not a globalist and never will be. My allegiance is to the Constitution of the United States of America and not to the Council on Foreign Relations, not to the Trilateral Commission, not to the so-called Bilderburg Group, or any other group of fancy billionaire globalist financiers. They sacrifice this republic and line their pockets with their one-world-order schemes."

He paused. "No, sir. No one-world order. Not on my watch. We are Americans. We have been attacked in international waters. And we shall respond as Americans have responded from the beginning of the republic. We shall defend ourselves, if necessary with overwhelming force. And in the words of President Reagan, our military shall respond with such strength that no potential adversary should ever test its strength."

Mack sat back down in his chair. "Now, I'm going to walk back over to the Lincoln bedroom and get some much-needed shut-eye. Unless there is an attack or some other catastrophe, I don't want anyone to wake me.

"But when I do wake up, Admiral Jones, I expect you to bring me the news that you have put a North Korean warship at the bottom of the sea." Mack stood, prompting the generals and admirals to stand in response. "Are there any questions?"

"No questions, Mr. President," Admiral Jones said.

"Good. We are adjourned."

CHAPTER 13

Approaching Tongy'mak Municipal Airport
South Korea

The jagged mountains off to the right cast shadows across the winding road. Contrasted against that, off to the left, as the road snaked south along the coastline, Gunner found tranquility in catching views of the deep blue waters of the Sea of Japan.

The three men had spoken little on the ride along the superhighway through the mountainous South Korean heartland. From the front passenger side, Gunner looked over into the back of the pickup's crew cab, where Jackrabbit was lying flat-backed, mouth wide open, sawing logs in a consistent droning rhythm. Jackrabbit, in fact, had slept through most of the winding turns along the way and was, by all accounts, oblivious or unconcerned that he would soon begin a mission that could cost him his life.

In the driver's seat, Jung-Hoon, wearing shades against the bright afternoon sun, seemed equally unconcerned, as if another possible brush with danger amounted to nothing more than a Sunday afternoon stroll in Central Park.

The sun would set at 5:16 p.m. If the funds transfer had been completed, they would be airborne by three. As the black pickup got closer to the small South Korean airport, Gunner wondered what changes the dusk would bring. Would the weapons and supplies arrive? Would the plane be ready?

"How much longer, Jung-Hoon?"

"Five kilometers to the turnoff for airport."

Was this mission the right thing? Gunner could not get his mind off what might be happening in the Yellow Sea at the moment. Nor could he stop the tug-of-war going on with his conscience.

Admiral Hampton had not ordered him to check in periodically, and Gunner had left his hotel as the place to contact him. Technically, Gunner had not disobeyed any orders.

At least not yet.

The turn signal clicked for a right turn. The black pickup sped off the main road, and the centrifugal force seemed to get Jackrabbit stirring. Another quick right turn put them on the road leading to the airstrip. Jackrabbit sat up, rubbed his eyes, and looked out just as the black pickup pulled into the gravel parking lot in front of the airport's small terminal.

Two other vehicles were parked there, a silver Hyundai in front of the door to the building and a white flat-nosed panel truck parked a few feet behind it. A man sat inside the panel truck.

"Our contact has arrived." Jung-Hoon nodded toward the panel truck. "Jackrabbit, check with the driver to verify that all weapons and other supplies are present. The commander and I will check with the airport owner about the plane."

"Got it," Jackrabbit said.

The pickup rolled to a crunching stop on the gravel. "Wait here," Jung-Hoon said. He opened the door, letting in a cold gush of wind, and then stepped out and walked over to the panel truck. The driver opened the door, and Jung-Hoon and the driver talked. A moment later, Jung-Hoon turned and motioned for Gunner and Jackrabbit to get out of the truck.

"That's our cue," Jackrabbit said.

"Looks like it," Gunner replied.

Both men opened their doors. Gunner stepped out, put on his jacket, and walked with Jackrabbit toward the panel truck. The long-haired driver had rolled the window down. He wore a black T-shirt despite the cold. A dragon figure tattoo on his bulging bicep made him look, Gunner thought, like a gang member. He was maybe in his midthirties.

"This is Mr. Kim," Jung-Hoon said, nodding to the driver.

"Right," Gunner muttered to Jackrabbit. "And I'm Mr. Smith."

"You better hope he doesn't understand English." Jackrabbit snickered.

"Mr. Kim says everything's here. Jackrabbit will check while we go talk to the airport owner. When we are through, Mr. Kim will help load materials onboard the plane."

"Sounds like a plan," Gunner said.

"Let me see if I can get acquainted with our friend Mr. Kim." Jackrabbit said. He walked over to the panel truck and stuck out his hand to the stranger, then launched into Korean with a Southern accent.

"Come with me," Jung-Hoon said to Gunner. They walked across the gravel to the front door of the small terminal. Jung-Hoon pulled the door open.

To their left, a lean middle-aged Korean man stood behind the counter. On the wall behind him hung color photographs of airplanes in flight, mostly single- and twin-engine. This could have been any private one-horse airport in the United States except for the fact that the writing on the aviation posters was in Korean.

The lobby was empty.

The man shot a nervous-looking grin at them, and as they walked to the front counter, Jung-Hoon and the man commenced rattling in rapid-fire Korean. Gunner wasn't sure who started the conversation.

A moment later, at a pause in the chatter, the man looked at Gunner and nodded.

"This is Mr. Kim," Jung-Hoon said.

"Aah, another Mr. Kim." Gunner grinned. "Why am I not surprised?"

"He says he has received the wire transfer for purchase of plane and he thanks you."

The man smiled and bowed to Gunner.

"Tell him it is my pleasure," Gunner said.

More Korean. More smiling and half bowing. Gunner had a feeling that the guy understands English. The man reached under a counter, pulled out a pad, and began writing.

"He says the plane is fueled and ready for takeoff. I told him to file a flight plan to Hamada, Japan. He is working on the flight plan now."

"How far from here to Hamada?" Gunner asked.

"A little over three hundred miles."

More Korean.

"He is writing my name, your name, and Jackrabbit's name on the flight manifest, just as we discussed."

"Excellent," Gunner said, as the man nodded and smiled but did not look up.

Silence followed. Gunner's eyes wandered around the empty lobby. In the back, behind two rows of empty plastic chairs, stood a Coke machine and a Nab machine, both with selections written in English.

"Flight plan complete," the man said.

"So you understand English?" Gunner said.

"Little bit," the man said. "Come. I show you plane."

"I think that's our cue," Gunner said.

"This way," the man said. He stepped from behind the counter and led the men through the lobby to a glass door at the back of the building. They walked out into the late-afternoon cold onto an asphalt tarmac.

Two planes, one a red-and-white single-engine Cessna, the other a yellow single-engine Bonanza with wings below the cabin windows, sat on the tarmac. The planes were parked about a hundred feet behind the building and to the right of a yellow hangar.

Behind the planes, a long asphalt runway stretched from left to right. "Here is your plane." Mr. Kim pointed to the yellow Beechcraft Bonanza Model G36. "This is my best plane. Congratulations. You will love it. I will miss it."

"Your English is pretty good, Mr. Kim," Gunner said.

"I spent five years as pilot in South Korean Air Force," the man said. "Stationed at Osan. Flew F-15s. Worked with many Americans. I picked up English from that. But I do not get to practice much anymore."

"I see," Gunner said.

"I love this plane more than fighter jet. Not as fast, but easy to fly. I did not want to sell it. But I thank you for your purchase. This will help save my airport. I have money problems."

"Glad to oblige," Gunner said. "You said it's ready to fly?"

"Yes, ready. Full of gas. Extra sealing in case of emergency water landing on your trip to Japan, as you requested."

"Excellent," Gunner said. "Guess we need to check with Jackrabbit."

"I will call him." Jung-Hoon flipped out his cell phone and punched a button. "How does it look? All there?... Excellent.... We'll come get the crates out of the truck."

"No need for that," Mr. Kim said. "He can drive the truck back around here."

"Hang on," Jung-Hoon said. "The airport manager just said that our friend Mr. Kim can drive the truck back here."

"Wait one second," the airport manager said. "I will unlock gate, then he can drive through."

"Excellent," Jung-Hoon said. "The airport manager is walking around to unlock the gate."

"I be right back," the manager said. He walked toward the end of the building.

"So what's his real name?" Gunner asked.

"Perhaps I will tell you when we get in the air," Jung-Hoon said.

"Fair enough."

A few moments later, the panel truck wheeled around the end of the building, with the tattooed Mr. Kim still at the wheel and Jackrabbit in the passenger seat.

The truck rolled to a stop behind the plane's left wing. Jackrabbit and Mr. Kim opened their doors and got out.

"We got three crates, boss," Jackrabbit said. "Everything's here."

The driver opened the twin doors on the side of the panel truck. He stepped into the truck and motioned for Jackrabbit to follow. A moment later they emerged, carrying a plywood crate about the size of a small coffin. "Two more in the truck," Jackrabbit said. "If y'all want to grab one, we'll get this one in the plane."

"Got it," Gunner said.

At that point, the younger Mr. Kim said something in Korean to the older airport-manager Mr. Kim, and the airport-manager Mr. Kim stepped up onto the wing of the aircraft next to the door of the fuselage. It struck Gunner that the two Mr. Kims were in on something. He hoped they did not work for the South Korean government and that they would keep their mouths shut.

Jackrabbit and Kim the younger carried the crate to the aircraft. They passed the wooden crate up to Kim the elder, who pulled the crate into the aircraft. Gunner noticed the *S* painted in red on the side of the crate.

"Let's get another one," Gunner said.

"Okay," Jung-Hoon said, and they stepped into the back of the panel truck and lifted the crate, which had a *W* painted in red on it. The crate was not too heavy, perhaps fifty pounds. They quickly brought it out of the van onto the asphalt tarmac.

Jackrabbit and the two Mr. Kims formed a human assembly line — on the tarmac, on the wing, and in the aircraft. Passing the second crate up through their outstretched arms proved to be an easy task.

"One more," Jackrabbit said.

"I saw it," Gunner said. "We'll get it."

He motioned Jung-Hoon back to the truck. "We gotta hurry," he said.

The third crate, slightly larger than the other two, had the letters *CRRC* painted on it. "I have this end," Gunner said. "Okay. Lift."

The third crate was heavier than the other two, but they quickly got it loaded into the aircraft.

"Y'all ready to take off?" Jackrabbit asked.

"Are you ready, Commander?"

Gunner savored the moment, gazing out over the small airstrip, relishing this, his last possible glimpse of a free nation, knowing that they may not return. At that moment, a car, a blue Hyundai, was speeding down the road, headed toward the airport. Suddenly, blue lights flashed from the car's roof.

"Police!" Kim the elder said. "Probably nothing. But you better take off."

Kim the younger dashed to his panel truck, started it, and squealed off the tarmac.

"Let's go!" Gunner yelled from the plane. He strapped into the back jump seat, just beside the crates. Jung-Hoon jumped into the cockpit and cranked the engine. Jackrabbit climbed in.

The propeller turned about ten times, then stopped.

"Come on, baby," Gunner said. He looked out the window. The police car had disappeared. The panel truck was speeding around the end of the building.

The single-engine prop wheezed and coughed, and the propeller spun twice and stopped.

Silence.

Jung-Hoon cranked the engine again. Finally, pay dirt! The deep, steady roar of the spinning prop whined in the air. Jung-Hoon pushed down on the throttle, and the Bonanza began rolling. The plane started its quick taxi toward the west end of the runway, toward giant snow-capped mountains.

Gunner looked back at the terminal building as they rolled. So far, nothing.

A moment later, the plane reached the west end of the runway. Jung-Hoon did a quick U-turn and nosed the plane back to the east. "Ready for takeoff," he said and pushed down hard on the throttle. The roar of the single engine intensified. The plane shook, then started rolling, picking up speed.

Off to the left, as the plane rushed down the runway, the doors to the brick terminal flew open. Two blue-clad Korean police officers ran out, waving their arms.

"Looks like they've got something on their mind," Jackrabbit said.

"I do not see anything," Jung-Hoon said as the Bonanza raced down the runway, past the officers, and nosed up into the air. A second later, the plane reached two hundred feet and kept climbing to the east.

Gunner looked back at the small terminal, now shrinking to post-age-stamp size. Blue and red lights on the police car swirled in circles.

"Must have something to do with the weapons," Jackrabbit said.

"I've got a bad feeling you're right," Gunner said.

The plane climbed out of the shadows of the mountains and into the late-afternoon sunshine, the bright orange ball of the sun behind them. Soon the deep blue waters of the Sea of Japan spread out in front of them.

They crossed over the shoreline, flying to the east. The plane kept climbing, then began banking to the right, slightly, toward the south-east, headed toward its official destination in Japan.

"Okay, we just flew out of South Korean airspace," Jung-Hoon said.

"How much daylight left?" Gunner asked.

"A little over an hour," Jung-Hoon said. "Barely enough to get to our ditch location."

The plane kept climbing.

"Okay," Jung-Hoon said, "we will be losing power soon. Double-check those boxes to make sure everything is secure. Don't want things sliding around. And get them ready to unload. Once we get down on the water, I cannot take off again."

"Good idea," Jackrabbit said. He moved into the back area with Gunner. "Pass me that crowbar, Commander." He pointed at a crowbar taped to the box marked with the red *S*.

Gunner reached over, pulled the duct tape off, and passed the crowbar to Jackrabbit.

"Box with the *S* is our supply box," Jackrabbit said. "The box with the *W* is our weapons box. Let's start with the supply box." He popped open the top of the crate.

"Bonanza Whiskey-Four-Niner. Gangneung Control."

A voice came over the loudspeaker in English, with a heavy Korean accent. "Set course for zero-niner-niner degrees. Climb to five thousand feet. Maintain until further instruction."

Jung-Hoon clicked on the microphone. "Gangneung Control. Whiskey-Four-Niner. Setting course for zero-niner-niner. Climb to five thousand. Await further instructions. Roger that." Jung-Hoon looked back over his shoulder as the plane turned slightly. "I take it they included the wetsuits?"

Jackrabbit held up a black rubber wetsuit and examined it. "Looks about your size, boss," he said to Gunner

"We'd better get suited up quickly," Jung-Hoon said. "That water is freezing." He looked over his shoulder. "Commander, change places with me and let me get suited up first."

"You want me in the cockpit?" Gunner swallowed hard. "I know nothing about flying."

"Do not worry, Commander. Set on automatic pilot. Not enough room for three in the back."

"Okay." Gunner exhaled. He crouched and slipped himself between the two cockpit seats and nestled his fanny in the right seat, opposite Jung-Hoon, who then slipped into the back.

Gunner watched the plane's altimeter change: 3,500 feet, 3,750 feet, 4,000 feet. The plane remained in a climb, on automatic pilot, with Jung-Hoon in the back and away from the controls. This did not resonate well in the pit of Gunner's stomach. He surveyed the seascape below. A few ships, miles apart, cut through the water in the late-afternoon sunshine, but from four thousand feet above the surface, the water seemed calm. From the back of the plane, short zipping noises cut through the roar of the engine.

Jung-Hoon, now covered in black rubber except for his face, which was partially covered with a black shoe-polish goo, slipped through the space between the two front seats and back into the cockpit. "You had better get your wetsuit on, Commander. We will be in the water soon."

"Got it," Gunner said. He moved to the back of the cabin, where Jackrabbit, also in a black wetsuit, was applying grease to his face.

"Your wetsuit's right there, Commander," Jackrabbit said. "Better hurry."

"Right," Gunner said. He started with the suit inside out, put his feet in first, then peeled up the rubber, making sure it was plenty tight. A few minutes later, he zipped the suit up under his chin.

"Here. Paint your face. It'll help keep your face warm if you go in the water. Plus, it'll make it harder for the enemy to find a target."

"Got it," Gunner said as he started smearing black grease on his face.

Jackrabbit opened the largest crate, the one with the letters *CRRC* painted on it, for Combat Rubber Raiding Craft. Inside was a model FC 470 manufactured by the Zodiac Group for the Navy SEALs and for Marines. "Perfect," he said. "Sure need it on a mission like this one."

"Is the Zodiac ready?" Jung-Hoon asked.

"It's here. Got a CO_2 tank to inflate it. Got the motor. Let's hope that sucker inflates before the plane sinks."

"Weapons?"

Jackrabbit opened the *W* box. "Rifles, pistols, bullets, grenades. Everything the commander bought."

"Supplies?"

Jackrabbit checked the *S* box again. "GPS device. MREs. Clothes. Thermal tent. Wire cutters, et cetera. All here."

The radio sqawked again. "Bonanza Whiskey-Four-Niner. Gangneung Control."

"Gangneung Control. Whiskey-Four-Niner."

"Bonanza Whiskey-Four-Niner. Contact Pohang Control on frequency two-one-eight."

"Gangneung Control. Whiskey-Four-Niner. Contacting Pohang Control on frequency two-one-eight."

"Whiskey-Four-Niner. Have a nice day."

Jung-Hoon switched to frequency 218. "Pohang Control. Bonanza Whiskey-Four-Niner is with you at five thousand feet. Course zero-niner-niner degrees. Destination, Hamada, Japan."

"Bonanza Whiskey-Four-Niner. Pohang Control. Roger that and welcome aboard. Maintain course zero-niner-niner degrees at five thousand."

"Pohang Control. Roger that. Whiskey-Four-Niner maintaining five thousand feet at course zero-niner-niner."

A few moments later, Jung-Hoon asked, "Do you gentlemen like riding roller coasters?"

"Used to ride 'em at King's Dominion near Richmond when I was a kid," Gunner said. "Loved 'em."

"Strap in. I'm getting ready to take us down."

Gunner sat in the jump seat and strapped on his shoulder harness. *Clicks* from latching seat belts reverberated throughout the plane.

"Everyone ready?" Jung-Hoon asked.

"Ready," Jackrabbit said.

"Ready," Gunner said, though his heart pounded like a jackhammer within his wetsuit.

"Okay," Jackrabbit said, "here we go."

"Pohang Control. Bonanza Whiskey-Four-Niner. Still at five thousand and course zero-niner-niner. Be advised we are having electrical and engine trouble. I am concerned that we may lose power."

"Whiskey-Four-Niner. Pohang Control. Copy that. Do you want to set a course back to Pohang?"

"Pohang Control. I think we need to set down. I don't know if we can get close enough in for a glide landing."

"Whiskey-Four-Niner. Pohang Control. Copy that. Right now, you are still closer to Korea than Japan. If you have to make emergency water landing, you are better off closer in to shore."

"Pohang Control. Roger that. Request permission to set course for emergency landing at Pohang."

"Whiskey-Four-Niner. Go to ten thousand if possible. Set course for two-five-three degrees to Pohang."

"Roger that. Whiskey-Four-Niner is climbing to ten thousand, setting course for two-five-three." Jung-Hoon pulled back on the stick. The plane began to climb. He flipped off the radio and flipped off the transponder. "I just turned off our transponder. Let me get us on the right course, and then I'll drop us out of here."

He executed a wide loop to the left. The compass showed the plane changing directions: 099 degrees ... 085 ... 060 ... 040 ... 000 ... 350 ...

"There, that should do it," Jung-Hoon said. "Three-five-zero degrees sets us on a course slightly to the west of due north. Okay, hold it there." The nose of the Bonanza locked straight out at three-five-zero. "I'll call them and we'll make a little dive. This will make it more difficult for them to track us via radar. He flipped the radio back on. "Pohang! Whiskey-Four-Niner! I have total engine failure! Losing power! Losing control of the aircraft! Whiskey-Four-Niner! Mayday! Mayday! Whiskey-Four-Niner declaring emergency!"

"Whiskey-Four-Niner! This is Pohang! Copy that. Declaring emergency. Whiskey-Four—"

Jung-Hoon shut off the radio, silencing the air traffic controller midstream. "Okay, Commander. Let's see if this is as much fun as your roller coaster at King's Dominion."

Jung-Hoon pushed down on the stick. The plane nosed down, at first into a shallow angle, then at a steep angle. Gunner's stomach flew into his throat. The plane shook as it dropped like a rock. Gunner looked over Jung-Hoon's shoulder. A wall of blue-green water rushed up at them ... faster ... faster ...

Gunner clung to a handle bolted inside the cockpit. The altimeter kept dropping: 3,500 ... 3,000 ... 2,500 ... 2,000 ... He had not done much praying in the last couple of days, but at this point, instinct took over. "Jesus, help us!" ... 1,500 ... 1,000 ...

"Hang on!" Jung-Hoon shouted.

The plane dropped like an out-of-control roller coaster. Gunner saw Jung-Hoon pull up on the stick.

"Respond! Respond!" Jung-Hoon said.

... 750 ... 500 ... 250 ...

The rotation of the altimeter slowed, and the Bonanza's nose seemed to come up as the plane's angle flattened out.

... 200 ... 150 ... 100 ...

Gunner looked out. They were still racing at the water, but at a shallower angle now.

... 75 ... 50 ...

The Bonanza leveled off and now flew just over the water, so low they seemed to be skimming the waves.

"Thank God," Jung-Hoon muttered. "I am going to have to bring us down a little lower to make sure we stay below shore radar." He feathered down on the stick just a touch.

... 50 ... 35 ... 25 ...

"Okay, that puts us at twenty-five feet over the water," Jung-Hoon said. "That's a risky altitude at this speed, but that should keep us below their radar."

Pohang Airport Control Tower
South Korea

He declared an emergency and went into a loop to head back here. When he reached three-five-five degrees, he started losing altitude." The air traffic controller kept his eyes on his radar screen as he explained this to his supervisor, who was peering over his shoulder. "At that point he reported power failure and continued dropping. We lost communication with him, and we lost him off the radar screen."

"Pass me your microphone," the supervisor said. "Open emergency frequency to all planes."

"Yes, sir." He passed the microphone back to the supervisor.

"To all planes in the area. This is Pohang Control. Be advised that we have lost contact with a yellow Beechcraft Bonanza en route to Hamada, Japan. Call letters Romeo-Hotel-Xray-Whiskey-Four-Niner. The plane disappeared off our radar two minutes ago. Coordinates thirty-six degrees, thirty-four minutes, eight seconds north latitude, one hundred thirty-one degrees, two minutes, fourteen seconds east longitude. Repeat, all planes in the area, be on the lookout for yellow ..."

British Airways 777
en route from Tokyo, Japan, to Seoul, Korea

Repeat, all planes in the area, be on the lookout for yellow ..."
Captain Martin Fletcher, the RAF veteran in command of the Boeing 777 owned and operated by British Airways, looked up and checked his coordinates. "By golly that looks like about ten miles from here," he said to his copilot, Commander Todd Hemmings.

"Looks about right," Hemmings said. "About ten miles to our south and about ten thousand feet below."

"Be on the lookout. These single-engine puddle jumpers have no business over international waterways, if you ask me," Fletcher said. He looked out and down. Mostly blue water below. A few clouds a thousand feet below, blocking visibility down to the surface.

"You really think a Beechcraft Bonanza is a puddle jumper?" Hemmings asked.

"Any rotary aircraft that tries to jump across international waters with only a single engine in my book becomes a puddle jumper."

Silence.

"Hey, I think I see something down there!" Hemmings said.

"Where?"

"Check this out."

Fletcher jumped from his seat on the left side of the cockpit and rushed over to the right side. He peered out over the shoulder of his copilot.

"Where?"

"Down there." He pointed down, almost right below the aircraft. "Looks like a small yellow single-engine aircraft."

He removed his aviator shades. "I see it." From their altitude, it looked almost like a small plastic toy plane skimming across the water. But definitely, there was something. And then it disappeared behind the clouds.

"What do you make of that?" Hemmings asked.

"Don't know," Fletcher said, "but we'd better report it."

Pohang Airport Control Tower
South Korea

Pohang Control. British Airways Golf-Echo-Bravo Four-Eight-Heavy."

"Bravo Four-Eight-Heavy. Pohang Control. Go ahead."

"Pohang Control. Be advised, we had a visual on an unidentified aircraft, fitting the description of the Bonanza you called in. The aircraft was below us, ten to twelve thousand feet, so it was hard to get a good look. We lost it under the clouds, but it was heading almost due north when we lost visual contact."

The air traffic controller turned and waved at his supervisor. "Hey, boss! We have a call from a British Airways 777. The pilot thinks they saw something. Small yellow plane way below them. They said it was flying almost due north, then disappeared behind low clouds."

The supervisor rushed back over to the controller. "When did they spot it? Before or after we transmitted our emergency call?"

"I am not sure," the controller said.

"What do you mean, you are not sure?" the supervisor said, raising his voice.

"I assumed the spotting must have come after because the call came in right after our emergency notice went out."

"Did you not clarify?" the supervisor screamed.

"No, I assumed," the controller said.

"Look, I know you are new to this job, but you cannot assume! Lives depend on accuracy! Give me that microphone." He snatched the mike from the controller. "What's their call sign?"

"British Airways Golf-Echo-Bravo Four-Eight-Heavy," the controller said. "British Airways Golf-Echo-Bravo Four-Eight-Heavy. Pohang Control!"

"Pohang Control. Bravo Four-Eight-Heavy," the voice came back in a distinctive British accent.

"Following up on your report. Did you spot the unidentified small craft before or after our emergency notice?"

Static.

"Pohang Control. Bravo Four-Eight-Heavy," the British voice said.

"We estimate that we spotted the unidentified craft one minute after you aired the emergency notice. Hope this helps."

"Bravo Four-Eight-Heavy, thank you for clarifying. Let us know if you see anything else."

"Bravo Four-Eight-Heavy. Will do."

The supervisor set the microphone down, his voice tone now having morphed from anger to curiosity, which brought a temporary sense of relief to the controller, who had for the moment worried about losing his job for not asking a simple question.

"It makes no sense," the supervisor said. "Why would they be flying north more than two minutes after declaring an emergency?"

"Perhaps the plane that the 777 spotted was not the Bonanza," the controller said. "After all, the 777 was two miles above the surface of the water. Depending on the aircraft's altitude, and with low cloud cover, a positive visual identification from that altitude would be a challenge."

"Perhaps," the supervisor said. "But yellow is an unusual color for an aircraft. This would make an identification a bit easier. And why would any small aircraft be flying that low so far out? And why heading north?"

"Good questions, boss," the controller said. "If the heavy did spot the Bonanza, it is possible the Bonanza lost ability to steer the plane and could fly in only one direction. He was making a loop back to the west but was headed north when he declared an emergency and we lost him."

The supervisor seemed to think about that for a moment. "That is possible, I suppose." He put his hand on Kim's shoulder. "I am sorry for raising my voice. This is a tense situation."

"I understand, boss."

"We need to message the ROK Navy and all vessels operating in the area to be on the lookout for wreckage."

"Right away, boss."

Beechcraft Bonanza G36
over the Sea of Japan

The Bonanza raced north, just over the surface of the water under a slight cloud cover. Rays of midafternoon sunshine streaked down through the spotty clouds. Patches of orange-blue sky colored the horizon to the west.

Gunner and Jackrabbit had again switched places. Gunner moved to the right cockpit seat and Jackrabbit moved to the back of the plane, where he continued unpacking the supplies and weapons in the three wooden crates, getting them ready for transfer to the Zodiac.

No boats or ships were anywhere in sight, which was a good thing, Gunner thought, relieved that they seemed alone in the world, undetected by enemy eyes.

Not much had been said since the fake power loss, as if each man had reverted to self-reflection.

"What's the game plan, Jung-Hoon?" Gunner asked. "How much longer until we ditch the plane?"

"Our speed is two hundred miles per hour, and we have enough fuel for five hundred miles. We will continue on this course for one hour and hope that we are not spotted by surface craft. This course will keep us between ninety and one hundred twenty miles off South Korea's coastline. Our main risk comes in about twenty minutes, when we will fly twenty miles east of Ulleung-do Island, which is seventy-five miles from the South Korean coastline."

He punched a button and a GPS map appeared on the screen.

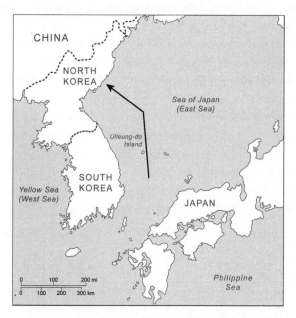

Flight path in Sea of Japan past Ulleung-do Island

"This is our flight path," he said. "Bottom of the arrow is where we started our fake crash. We are flying at twenty-five feet on a course just west of due north, low enough that it is impossible for shore radar to pick us up.

"Right now, we are southeast of the island. In about twenty minutes we will fly past Ulleung-do. The island is jagged with many steep cliffs and craters. It has no airport and no radar. However, there are three ferryboats that run from the small fishing village of Dodong on the island back to the mainland. We will be close enough to the ferry lanes that we could be spotted, but we should pass at least ten miles east of the closest ferry lane.

"If we are able to clear Ulleung-do Island, we fly another forty minutes to the break point, about two hundred miles from where we called in the fake emergency. There we change course to the northwest and fly right toward the North Korean coastline. We arrive at the ditch spot, twenty miles off the North Korean coastline, just before sunset. It will then take about two hours to reach shore."

The plane roared on to the north. "So how much risk do we run of being detected by North Korean radar when we get within twenty miles of the coastline?" Gunner asked.

"Risk would be low if we could stay at twenty-five feet because the curvature of the earth makes it difficult for shore radar to see us. But we can't hit the water at this speed or we will break apart. I will have to bring us up to a thousand feet to get enough altitude to glide back down to the sea. When I bring the plane back up, that will make us visible to radar for a few minutes. Radar operators probably will see us for a few moments, before we drop back down. But even if they call for a search, it will soon be dark. Hard to conduct a search. We'll have to sink the plane, just to be safe."

Gunner wished they could somehow keep the plane ... in case ...

CHAPTER 14

USS **Harry S. Truman**
the Yellow Sea

Admiral Hampton stared through his binoculars out toward the east. Somewhere out there, beyond the scope of his binoculars, the cruisers and destroyers under his command had begun executing his orders to beef up the missile screen between the carrier and North Korea. So far, since that first attack, all had been quiet. No other missile barrages had been fired at the carrier.

The curtain of darkness would soon drape over the ships of the battle group, and Hampton worried about deadly missiles flying out of the night sky. He hoped his ships would make a better account of themselves if or when that happened again.

"Excuse me, Admiral."

Hampton lowered his binoculars and turned around. His chief of staff, Captain Tony Farrow, had returned to the flag bridge.

"Whatcha got, Tony?"

"Sir, we have some information on the whereabouts of Commander McCormick."

"Excellent," Hampton said. "About time we got some good news. You ordered him back to the ship, I take it?"

An anxious look crossed Farrow's face.

"What's the matter?"

"I'm afraid that the news on Commander McCormick is not good, sir."

"Not good? What do you mean? Spit it out."

"Well, sir, Commander McCormick apparently was on a private plane flying from the east coast of South Korea to Japan. The plane issued a distress call, then declared an emergency about halfway out. The South Koreans think the plane went down, sir."

"What the ..." Hampton ran his hand through his hair. "Are you sure about all this?"

"What we know, Admiral, is that a single-engine plane, a Bonanza G36, took off from a small airport in eastern South Korea, a place called Tongy'mak in Kangwon-do Province. The pilot filed a flight plan for Hamada, Japan. That's about a one-hour flight to the southeast across the Sea of Japan, a little over two hundred miles, well within range of the Bonanza.

"Thirty minutes or so after takeoff—and I'm not clear on the time frame here—the pilot declared an emergency. Radar showed the plane losing altitude and then it disappeared from the radar screen."

"Umph." Hampton grunted. "Son of a—" He slammed his fist onto the back of his chair and stared out over the ocean. "Why in the world would McCormick be flying to Japan?" His eyes met Farrow's.

"Well, you did sign the order for him to take leave, Admiral."

"Yes, I did. I was trying to help the guy clear his head." He slammed his hand onto the back of the chair again. "This is unreal. Now I've got to write a letter to his mother informing her of his death. As if she hasn't already lost enough."

Farrow waited for a few moments, then said, "Sir, there are a couple of odd things about all this."

Hampton looked over at his chief of staff. "What do you mean?"

"Well, a British airliner claims to have spotted a small plane fitting the description of the Bonanza headed north just minutes after Commander McCormick's plane declared an emergency."

"North?"

"Yes, sir."

"Don't understand that one. But at least it gives us some hope."

"Yes, sir," Farrow said. "One other thing."

"What's that?"

"A South Korean reserve unit reports that someone stole a cache of weapons earlier today. South Korean police suspect an arms dealer named Kim. Police tracked this Kim guy to the same airport that this plane took off from. It appears that Kim was at the airport when the Bonanza took off."

"So?"

"Well, the police were able to apprehend Kim. They did not find any weapons. The airport is small, sir. Very light traffic. The police suspect the weapons were on that plane when it took off."

Hampton ran his hand back across the top of his head. "What kind of weapons are we talking about?"

"Small cache of light weapons, sir. A few M-16s. Handguns. Grenades. Some navigational equipment. That sort of thing."

"Very odd," Hampton said. He folded his arms and walked over to the window and stared out to the east. "I don't have time for speculation, Captain. Do we have an approximate location of where the plane went down?"

"Yes, sir, we do. The Koreans have the location. It's at thirty-six degrees, thirty-four minutes, eight seconds north latitude and one hundred thirty-one degrees, two minutes, fourteen seconds east longitude."

"Very well. Alert the Pentagon. Request any US ships in the vicinity to conduct search-and-rescue efforts. Let them know that Commander McCormick was on board. I'm sure that the president will have a personal interest in that."

"Aye, aye, Admiral. I'll send a flash message, giving it highest urgency. That will get an immediate response."

Beechcraft Bonanza G36
over the Sea of Japan

We are approaching our position off Ulleung-do Island," Jung-Hoon said. "The island will be about twenty miles over to our left, and the ferry lane is about ten miles to our left. They come from the Korean peninsula and loop out east of the island before going into Dodong. Be on the lookout for any vessels."

"I'll check it out," Gunner said. He unbuckled his harness, got out of the right cockpit seat, and slipped into the back of the plane, where Jackrabbit was loading .223-caliber bullets into magazines.

The jump seat right behind Jung-Hoon was empty, and Gunner took it and peered out the window. The cloud cover had cleared. An orange-pink late-afternoon seascape painted the sea and the sky to the west. The sun was large and low in the sky.

His eyes scanned the horizon. Still nothing but the empty waters of the Sea of Japan.

He pondered the absurdity of it all. What if he did see a ship? So what? Would that change their mission? Of course they could always dump their weapons overboard and make an emergency landing in Japan, and Jackrabbit could tell the Japanese that they'd gotten disoriented or something. That was one of the contingency plans.

Gunner dismissed that thought. At this point, they were in. There was no turning back.

The brave men of the American Revolution had a saying, "Live free or die," that had spurred freedom-loving Americans since the early days of the republic. Most modern-day Americans, addicted to their iPods and smartphones and social networks and unreal reality TV shows, did not understand the saying. Most had never even heard it. Too many modern-day Americans, lorded over by their masters, never complained as long as their fat bellies were full, he thought. Freedom, sadly, no longer mattered. Free was now the goal. Get something for nothing. Get free goodies from the government. Let someone else pay.

But a precious few still remembered and understood the saying that was attributed to the great Revolutionary War hero General John Stark, a great New Hampshireite. General Stark, the hero of the Battle of Bennington, was invited to a reunion, but because of his failing health had to decline. He scribbled a toast on parchment that was carried by horseback courier to the celebration, a toast to which his former men raised their glasses. On the parchment, since yellowed with age, the general wrote the immortal words: "Live free or die: Death is not the worst of evils."

And thus the phrase "Live free or die" became the state motto of New Hampshire and the war cry for freedom-loving Americans who would rather die than be lorded over by a tyrannical government bent on taking away the basic freedoms guaranteed in the Bill of Rights.

"Live free or die." Gunner mumbled the words that were lost in the roar of the plane's single-rotor engine.

If any American soldiers remained in North Korea, he would draw back the curtain on their imprisonment. He would set them free or he would die trying. If the end of his days on earth was imminent, at least his life would have been worthwhile.

He squinted off toward the western horizon. Rubbed his eyes and squinted again. "Jackrabbit, pass me the binoculars."

"Sure, Commander."

Gunner, his squinting gaze fixed on a location to the southwest, held his arm out toward Jackrabbit. When he felt the binoculars in his hand, he brought them up to his eyes. The vessel was cutting through the water, moving from left to right.

"I've got a vessel near the horizon, gentlemen," Gunner announced. "Looks four to five miles out."

"Let me take a look," Jackrabbit said, squeezing himself into the left side of the cabin beside Gunner. Gunner handed him the binoculars.

"Which direction?" Jung-Hoon asked.

"Well, if we're still flying north, looks to be just south of due west from us," Jackrabbit said.

"That's the direction of the ferry routes going into Ulleung-do Island," Jung-Hoon said. "They may not be able to see us from this distance. It depends on how the sun is hitting the plane."

South Korean fishing trawler MinCho
the Sea of Japan

The seventy-five-foot white wooden trawler *MinCho* plowed through choppy seas. Standing on the starboard front deck, Park Chan-Ho checked his watch. The *MinCho* should be approaching its homeport of Dongdo on Ulleung-do Island within the next thirty minutes.

The strong afternoon wind was blowing out of the west, which meant the closer they got to the island, the calmer the water would get as the jagged mountains on the island blocked the west winds.

The day was good. They had been blessed with a large haul of yellowtail tuna and amberjack. Park, the fifty-five-year-old longtime first mate aboard the trawler, was tired, sore, and looking forward to getting back to Dongdo and unloading the haul, some time with his woman, and a good night's sleep. Then back out to sea before dawn the next day.

He stuck a cigarette in his mouth, cupped his hand against the breeze, and flicked the wheel on the lighter.

Aah. Nicotine. He held the smoke in for a moment, then exhaled.

Off toward the eastern horizon, where the dark-blue waters of the sea meshed with the darkening skies in the direction of Japan, he noticed something small and yellow, lit by the orange rays of the afternoon sun, flying low over the water. He squinted and looked again. What was it? An airplane? A helicopter? A low-flying missile? No. He took a drag on the cigarette. A missile would not be yellow. And flying north? Not possible.

He looked hard again and convinced himself that it was a small aircraft. Probably a single-engine plane.

Park stepped into the cabin area, out of the wind, where his friend and longtime sea dog, Captain Cha Du-ri, stood at the wheel of the trawler.

"Captain, there is a small aircraft on the horizon. It's yellow. The same color on the all-vessels notice we heard a while ago. You should have a look."

"Take the wheel," the captain said to the second mate, a twenty-two-year-old recent hire.

"Yes, sir," the second mate said and stepped behind the wheel with a tinge of excitement lighting his face at the notion of taking the wheel.

Park opened the wheelhouse door and stepped out on the wooden deck with the captain.

"Where?" the captain asked.

Park scanned the skies for a moment. "I don't see it now, Captain, but it was out there." He pointed to the east. "Flying from right to left, very low, going north."

"You have an extra cigarette?" Captain Cha asked.

Park handed his boss a cigarette and the lighter. A second later, a cloud of smoke rose from the captain's lips and blew out to sea, following the direction of Park's smoke. "You believe this may be the same plane we received the distress call about?"

"I cannot say, Captain. Probably not. We are way north of those coordinates. But I am sure I saw a small plane and it was yellow."

The captain took a drag on his cigarette. "You are sure it was yellow? Perhaps it looked yellowish in the late-afternoon rays of the setting sun."

The captain had a point. This late in the day, the sun did indeed have a way of distorting colors. "I wish you had seen it. The plane looked like a bright painted yellow. I do not think it was the reflection of the late-afternoon sun."

The captain, who liked cigarettes as much if not more than Park did, seemed more enthralled with his tobacco than discussing a mysterious airplane in the distance that had vanished. Through a smoke cloud, he said, "You feel confident enough in your spotting to recommend that I call it in to the Coast Guard?"

"That is up to you, sir."

"And I did not see what you saw. You did not answer my question. If I call it in, and if the Coast Guard officers then meet us in Dongdo, they will question you about what you saw. That means you will not help me and our young new second mate haul all these fish out of the hold. We'll have to clean up the boat by ourselves too. We'll have to get the trawler ready to go out again in the morning. And since our young apprentice in there has little experience in these matters, you know what that will mean, do you not?"

"Yes, sir," Park said. "That means that you would be left to do the bulk of the work by yourself."

"That is correct, Park." Another drag on the cigarette. "I will call the Coast Guard if you feel certain that you spotted the missing plane, not just any plane. So my question is, do you feel confident enough in your spotting to recommend that I call it in to the Coast Guard?"

Park flipped his ashes over the side of the trawler. A gust of wind blew smoking ambers back along the side and out past the churning waters in the wake of the stern. "Perhaps you are right, Captain. Perhaps I saw the yellow reflection of the sun's rays on the fuselage. It makes no sense that the missing aircraft would have wandered this far north."

"You are a good man," the captain said, patting Park on the back. "Now, go in the wheelhouse and relieve our young friend. I am afraid with him steering we might wind up in Tokyo."

"Yes, Captain."

CHAPTER 15

Beechcraft Bonanza G36
over the Sea of Japan

We are now slightly north of the DMZ," Jung-Hoon said, "and approaching our midcourse correction to the west-northwest. I will climb to one thousand feet and glide the plane down into the water. Once we ditch, we may have five minutes to get the raft inflated, get our equipment, and get out. That's if we are lucky. Jackrabbit, is everything ready to go?"

"Zodiac boat, check," Jackrabbit said. "Weapons, check. MREs, check. Tent, check. Electronics, check. We're ready to take a swim if we need to. It's now or never."

"Okay," Jung-Hoon said. "I'm breaking to the northwest in ... stand by ... three ... two ... one ... setting course for three-zero-zero degrees."

Gunner felt the plane bank in a loop to the left, low over the water. He looked at the GPS map now blinking in the center of the plane's instrument panel.

They had turned in a west-northwesterly direction and were flying straight toward the North Korean shoreline. This marked their final course change. Gunner's heart pounded, for with this turn, there was no turning back.

Down below, swells rolled gently. No whitecaps were in sight.

Gunner turned around and saw Jackrabbit putting gun oil on the barrel of one of the M-16s. He caressed the barrel with his hands as if it were some sort of idol-god. With the droning roar of the plane's engine filling the cabin, Jackrabbit's eyes danced and sparkled as they ran up and down the barrel of the rifle. And that grotesque scar on his face morphed into a wicked smile as he touched the weapon with what seemed like a sense of reverence. He almost looked like a crazed killer in a trance, Gunner thought.

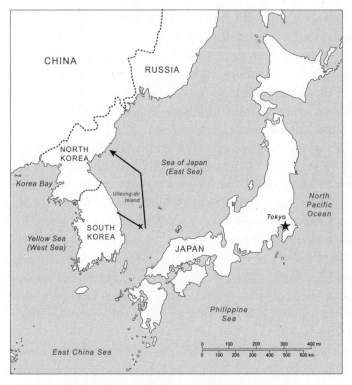

Sea of Japan, full flight path with fake Mayday site,
North and South Korea, Japan

Maybe that's exactly what he was ... a crazed killer in a trance. Of course, how could one serve in the Special Forces without being a crazy, ruthless killer at heart?

Maybe there was a reason he had expatriated from the United States to Korea.

"Hey, Jackrabbit." Gunner broke the trance. Jackrabbit's eyes left the gun, and the scar changed from a wicked smile to a grotesque scar.

"What?"

"Question."

"Fire away."

"Well, don't take this the wrong way, but if I'm getting ready to go into battle with somebody named 'Jackrabbit,' I'd like to know why he's named Jackrabbit."

Jackrabbit snickered, laid the gun down, and leaned forward. "It started when I was eighteen years old, just before I joined the Army. We were huntin' for deer down around Lake Phelps, near my hometown of Creswell, North Carolina. Me and my daddy and a couple of buddies.

"Well, we were in the corner of a peanut field, over by the edge of the woods, when out from the other side there ran up the biggest buck I ever saw. Must've been a fourteen-pointer.

"It was my turn to take a shot, so I cocked that little Winchester 30-30 I'd gotten for my sixteenth birthday, and I bore down on the deer. I knew I had him good. Had his neck right in my gun sights. And just before I squeezed the trigger, something spooked him. That ole buck turned tail and ran right back across that field, zigzagging away from me as fast as he could run.

"Well, I was mad as all get out when I looked down and saw what spooked that buck. Standing right there on his haunches beside where the buck had been, eatin' peanuts, was the biggest jackrabbit I ever saw. At least it looked like a jackrabbit to me. Must've been four foot on its hind legs!

"I was hacked off at that rabbit. So I bore my sights down on him and pulled the trigger. I thought I had him, but he danced over to the left and stood there and laughed at me. So I recocked the Winchester and fired again. Same dang thing. That ole rabbit stood there and danced to the left and danced to the right. I must've shot six or seven times and never could hit him.

"So when we got back to the truck, they started calling me 'Jackrabbit.' Guess it sort of stuck."

He picked up the gun again.

"Dang, Jackrabbit," Gunner said, "I sure hope you can shoot better than that."

Jackrabbit snickered. "Don't worry, Commander. That ole jackrabbit is the only target I ever missed. Haven't missed anything since, and I'm not going to start—"

The roar of the engine swallowed his last words.

"You ever heard that story, Jung-Hoon?" Gunner asked, raising his voice to be heard.

"Yes," the pilot said, smiling, "many times."

Gunner looked out the window. A school of porpoises leaped in the water below them. They were headed toward the west. Toward North Korea.

"One more question, Jackrabbit," Gunner said.

"Let me guess," the voice came from the back of the plane. "You want to know about the scar."

Gunner half laughed. "Well, it's got a history. And if I'm going into combat with a man, I figure I want to know the story behind it."

The porpoises had disappeared, leaving nothing below but deep blue rolling swells.

"Knife fight," Jackrabbit said. "Special Forces recon mission in Indochina. The jungles of Cambodia. A Communist special forces thug dropped out of a tree, right in my face.

"Got me with his knife. I got his heart with mine. I drug his body about fifteen feet off the path. Later, when I came back through there, I checked on him. The buzzards and snakes had taken care of most of the poor sucker. End of story."

Gunner shook his head. "So are you better with a knife or a rifle?"

"Put it this way, Commander. I've killed more men with a knife than you've got toes on your feet, and I've killed more men with a rifle than you've got fingers on your hands."

"Dang," Gunner said.

"Dang is right, Commander."

Gunner let that thought lie as the plane flew on its course toward the North Korean coast. "Thanks, Jackrabbit. I'm glad you're on my team."

"Dang straight I'm on your team. I can't promise you won't get killed. But I can promise you this. They might kill you, but they'll have to kill me first."

What a great idea to have a deranged killer on the side of

righteousness, Gunner thought. He smiled. "Well, Jackrabbit, I'm glad you've got my back."

"Bank on it, Commander. You don't die unless I die first."

Corbin Hall
Suffolk, Virginia

In the midst of the king-sized bed, covered with satin sheets and blankets and with her head resting upon a puffy pink satin pillow, Margaret Pendleton McCormick rolled to her left. Then she rolled to her right. And when that didn't work, she rolled to her left again.

From this position on her left side, her ear buried deep in the pillow, she opened her eyes. The digital alarm clock on the nightstand showed three in the morning.

Why couldn't she sleep?

After twisting and turning a couple more times, Margaret succumbed to the notion that sleeplessness had won the battle. She pushed the covers off, swung her legs over the side of the bed, and slipped her feet into soft slippers. She stood up and grabbed her flannel robe, draped on the recliner beside her bed.

She had come to the conclusion years ago that when she could not sleep, the Good Lord was rousing her to tell her something. She headed for the hallway with an unexplained unease knotted in her stomach.

She went to the kitchen, flipped on the overhead lights, then went to the den and turned on a lamp. Off in the corner of the stately room, the majestic ten-foot fir tree that her son Gorman Jr. had brought in the night before stood waiting to be adorned with the family's traditional Christmas decorations.

She thought about hanging a few ornaments on the tree. Her better judgment stopped her. The Thanksgiving tradition at Corbin Hall was all about the grandchildren, Tyler and Jill. The youngest grandchild always hung the first ornaments on the tree the day after Thanksgiving, and decorating the tree was planned for right after breakfast in just a few hours.

"Leave the tree alone," she said aloud, then plopped into the leather wingback chair and reached for the remote control. She punched the

"On" button. The venerable Tom Miller, longtime CNN anchor, appeared on the screen.

She turned up the volume. "Why's he on air at this time of morning?" she muttered.

"CNN has learned that a North Korean missile has hit the aircraft carrier USS *Harry S. Truman*. The ship is in the Yellow Sea, to the west of the North Korean peninsula."

"Dear Lord," Margaret said. "That's Gunner's ship!"

"The White House is reporting that the National Security Council is meeting at this hour to discuss the situation in Korea and the attack on the *Harry Truman*." The screen switched to file footage of the aircraft carrier. "We're looking at file footage here from three months ago of the USS *Harry S. Truman* sailing out from the port of San Diego. According to the White House, the ship is still afloat but did sustain damage as a result of the attack. There was some loss of life."

The screen switched back to Miller, who was slipping on his trademark wire-rimmed glasses. "Again, the White House is reporting an attack on the nuclear carrier USS *Harry S. Truman* by North Korea."

Margaret could not control her sudden breathlessness and her pounding heart. She muted the television and fell to her knees in front of the wingback chair. "Oh, dear Jesus! I have already lost a father in that place called Korea. Please, please, don't let me lose a son too!"

Beechcraft Bonanza G36
over the Sea of Japan

The sun, now a large orange ball, was sinking below the horizon, spreading an orange carpet across the water as if guiding the plane to its deadly destination.

"We are approaching our ditch point," Jung-Hoon said. "I am going into a steep climb to one thousand feet. We could be detected by radar. I will do a circular glide path down to the water. The seas do not look too rough. Have all flotation devices ready. Jackrabbit, are you ready to deploy the Zodiac?"

"All ready," Jackrabbit said from the back of the cabin.

"You ready, Commander?"

"Do I have a choice?"

"Beginning ascent." Jung-Hoon pulled back on the yoke. The plane nosed up into a steep climb, pushing Gunner back into his seat. He looked at the instruments and saw the numbers on the altimeter beginning to increase.

100 feet ...
200 feet ...
250 feet ...

NKN Frigate Najin
the Sea of Japan

The North Korean Navy frigate *Najin*, on patrol off the North Korean coast, was 328 feet from bow to stern, had a maximum speed of 25 knots, or 28 miles per hour, and carried a crew of 180 black-jacketed sailors and officers of the proud North Korean Navy.

As the sun began setting below the horizon of the darkening waters of the Sea of Japan, all over the ship, from the bridge to the engine room, from the forward to the aft watch, the news spread like fire upon a sea of gasoline. The *Najin*'s comrades serving in the Western Fleet of the North Korean Navy patrolling in the Yellow Sea had delivered the first fatal blow to a powerful United States aircraft carrier!

The excitement from the news had spread throughout the crew, but was soon dampened by frustration. The announcement by the ship's executive officer over the ship's loudspeaker system thirty minutes ago was proof that all the action was taking place on the west side of the peninsula, in the Yellow Sea, not on the east side, where the *Najin* was stationed.

The brave crew of the *Najin* was anxious to get into the fight with the Americans. They wanted to show the Yankees that their superior naval force could teach the Americans the folly of sailing the waters off the Democratic People's Republic, for the Navy of the Democratic People's Republic of Korea was a great tiger ready to roar.

This fervor for war swept into every crevice of the ship. In the *Najin*'s radar control room, Petty Officer First Class Jong Tae-se, distracted by the news, tried to concentrate on the boring sweep of the empty black-and-green radar screen, which continued to show that the *Najin* was alone in this sector of the Sea of Japan.

Sweep ... Sweep ... Sweep ... Round and round and round.

Like a fast-moving, lit-up green electronic second hand sweeping around the black face of a round and numberless watch, the sweeps for ships and planes came up empty.

Sweep ... Sweep ... Sweep ... Still nothing.

If they were in the Yellow Sea at the moment, he thought, the sweeps would be lit up with American warships and planes. Their fire-control radars would be fixed on the enemy. The crew members of the *Najin* would be poised to take their place in history—indeed, in destiny.

The Yellow Sea fleet always seemed to get more money and glory, he thought, than ships like the *Najin* in the Sea of Japan. Did those in Pyongyang not remember the fact that Japan remains a strong ally of the hated US and as such is an enemy and poses a threat to the Democratic People's Republic? Could it be that the Yellow Sea fleet got all the attention because Pyongyang, and thus the Dear Leader himself, is much closer to the Yellow Sea than he is to the Sea of Japan?

But Jong's duty was not to question, but rather to continue watching the ship's radar screen. Sweep ... Sweep ... Round and round and round ...

Beep beep beep beep beep beep beep ...

What was that?

"Lieutenant! Over here! Something just popped up on my screen!"

Beechcraft Bonanza G36
over the Sea of Japan

The altimeter on the instrument panel kept climbing. As his heart pounded like a submachine gun firing on full automatic, Gunner kept his eyes on the plane's altimeter as it climbed to a thousand feet.

"Going down now," Jung-Hoon said. "Get ready to inflate that Zodiac."

"It's ready."

The blanket of tension that descended on the cockpit was as real and as thick as choking smoke. With the last few minutes of sunlight casting an orange reflection on the Bonanza's yellow wings, the altimeter began reversing itself, then dropped fast.

Gunner processed the mental checklist of his duties when they splashed down. Jackrabbit would open the door and deploy the Zodiac. Once deployed and secured by a temporary line inside the plane, Jackrabbit would get in and they would quickly load the gear. That was the plan anyway.

500 feet ...

400 feet ...

300 feet ...

"I'll cut the engine at fifty feet," Jung-Hoon said rapidly. "Can't have the engine running when we hit or the prop might flip us. Hang on."

200 feet ...

100 feet ...

The roaring engine went silent. Air whisked past as the water rushed closer to the wings and the nose started to come up ... then *SPLASH!*

The plane hit nose first with a shocking thud. Dark water rushed over the windshield. Icy seawater streamed in around the doors ...

NKN Frigate Najin
the Sea of Japan

Lieutenant, the blip is gone!" Petty Officer First Class Jong Tae-se shouted at the radar officer.

"What do you mean it's gone?" The radar officer looked over his shoulder.

"I tracked it about ten miles west of our position, and it disappeared as quickly as it appeared."

"That is strange," the radar officer said. "Mark the coordinates. I will notify the captain."

Beechcraft Bonanza G36
the Sea of Japan

The water pouring in around the edges of the aircraft door was icy cold. The cabin, still submerged in the sea, was pitch dark. The nose of the plane, buoyant with the air trapped in the cockpit, started rising, then popped straight up out of the water. Graying light of dusk streamed into the cabin. Outside, the wings were a couple of inches under water, but the plane was still afloat—for now.

"We gotta move," Jackrabbit said. "I'm going to open the door and inflate the boat. Once it's up, Commander, move in the back and start passing me supplies. We've got to move fast. This plane could sink to the bottom any second."

"Got it," Gunner said.

Jackrabbit turned the cabin latch counterclockwise and pushed the door open. Cold air rushed into the plane. Some water sloshed in from the wing.

The waves were long and rolling, and the plane rode them up and down.

Jackrabbit quickly unrolled the black rubber raft out on the partially submerged wing. A long black hose tethered the raft to a CO_2 tank inside the plane. The uninflated rubber floated gently on top of the cold saltwater.

Jackrabbit pivoted back toward the CO_2 tank and turned a valve.

Hisssssssssssssssss . . .

Nothing. No life in the raft. Nothing. Just more seawater sloshing in. The Zodiac remained a flat, uninflated sheet of rubber floating over the wing.

"Come on, dang it!" Jackrabbit uttered an obscenity under his breath. "Something's not right. Let me check the line." He shut off the valve. The hissing stopped. "Hope I've not used up all the CO_2." He started tinkering with the line between the CO_2 tank and the boat.

The plane rose on a long swell. Then it dropped down into the trough of the swell. *Slooooooooooosh.* Water rushed into the cabin, and then, as the plane rode up again on the next swell, the water that had just sloshed in, or most of it, drained back out.

"Late afternoon breeze picking up at sundown," Jung-Hoon said in a voice so calm he could have been ordering a Big Mac in the drive-through at McDonald's. Gunner shook his head. The total lack of fear displayed by both men was amazing. It was as if they were both unfazed by the fact that they were on a sinking aircraft on a faraway sea thousands of miles from home, and if that CO_2 tank didn't work soon, they would never see home again.

"You boys might want to get life jackets on," Jackrabbit said as he twiddled with the line.

Another large swell lifted the plane up toward the darkening sky, followed by another dip down into the trough of the swell, followed by another *slooooooooooshhhh.*

More water in . . . more water draining back out.

But each time, more water stayed in the plane. By now, about a half inch covered the floor of the cabin. To make matters worse, the nose of the plane had sunk several inches lower into the sea.

"We are starting to sink," Jung-Hoon said, again in a voice of calm.

"Hang on, boys," Jackrabbit said. "I'm working on it." He kept fiddling, twisting something attached to the long black hose.

The plane started rising again on the next swell. *Slooooooooooooshhhh.* Another sheet of cold water sloshed in.

"There's a bad connection where the hose from the tank is screwed into the extension hose. Hang on." Slumped over, Jackrabbit moved across the watery floor of the plane and put his hands on the valve of the CO_2 tank. "Let's hope this works or we're gonna have a long swim."

Let's hope . . . and pray, Gunner thought.

More water sloshed into the cabin. Jackrabbit twisted the valve again.

Hisssssssssssssssssssssssssssss . . .

The graying skies and twinkling starlight cast a grayish but still visible hue on the lifeless rubber form floating on the water. Daylight had surrendered to nightfall. But the fading vestiges of dim light revealed that the boat remained a useless, lifeless sheet of rubber floating about an inch now above the sinking wing.

"Come on . . . dangit . . . come on . . ."

Now for the first time, Gunner sensed uncertainty in Jackrabbit's voice.

CHAPTER 16

Corbin Hall
Suffolk, Virginia

The silence of the morning calm tormented her. How could she sleep after hearing this ominous news?

Loneliness overwhelmed her. Who could she talk to? All of Tidewater was asleep at this hour, and when they awoke, many would head to Lynhaven and Greenbrier Mall and Military Circle and the other malls for those day-after-Thanksgiving sales that marked the beginning of the commercial rush toward the Christmas season. The thought of hundreds of thousands of shoppers traipsing the malls in a shopping frenzy while her youngest was in harm's way made her sick to her stomach and intensified her utter isolation.

She thought about calling Gorman, but what good would that do? Why ruin his sleep? And maybe Gunner wasn't near that missile. In fact, CNN did report that the ship was still afloat, but with *some* loss of life. And *some* loss of life implied there were lots of survivors.

Did it not?

That meant that statistically, Gunner was probably all right.

Did it not?

But if Gunner was okay—as he surely must be—then why this uncontrollable twisting in her stomach?

Margaret Pendleton McCormick could do only one thing. With the undecorated fir tree standing like a silent sentry across the room, she got down on her knees on the Persian rug in front the coffee table, and

179

she cried from the depths of her heart. Then she wiped her tears and looked up.

"Heavenly Father ... since you took my earthly father away from me all those years ago, I've had no one to lean on other than you." She looked down. More teardrops splattered on the mahogany coffee table. She wiped it with her hand. "You say to be anxious for nothing, but in everything, by prayer and supplication, and with thanksgiving to bring all our requests to you.

"Well, heavenly Father, I am calling on you right here and now. And on this lonely morning after Thanksgiving, protect my boy, Father, and bring him home safely. Please. For you know that your servant is too old and too feeble to lose another family member in the service to his country.

"Please do not make me sacrifice yet another loved one on the altar of freedom!

"In the name of Christ Jesus, the one who is and who was and who is to come, I pray. Amen."

Beechcraft Bonanza G36
the Sea of Japan

Come on!" Jackrabbit blurted out. He kept twisting the cord and had turned the CO_2 off and on several times. Nothing but hissing and a flat sheet of rubber still floating on the sea under a dark sky.

From the cockpit, Jung-Hoon pointed a flashlight at the tubing to give Jackrabbit light to work. More water flooded the cabin. The plane had sunk another inch.

"Let's try this baby one more time." Jackrabbit reached over and turned on the valve again.

Hisssssssssssssssssssssssssssssssssssssssssssssssssss.

Jackrabbit looked out onto the wing. Nothing. He blurted out another obscenity. "If y'all are praying gentlemen, and I've not always been much of a praying man, I suggest you start now. I've done about everything I know how to do. We're about out of time, and we're about to go down."

Another wave raised the sinking plane up. Another trough brought more water sloshing in.

Hissssssssssssssssssssssssssssssssssssssssssss.

"Hand me the flashlight, Jung-Hoon."

"Sure thing, Commander."

Gunner aimed the beam of the flashlight inside the plane. Would this be his last vision of life? There were three life preservers in the back. "Let's get these life jackets on," Gunner said. "Maybe we'll get picked up by the North Korean Navy. It looks like our mission here is over."

"Commander," Jackrabbit said, "I'd rather borrow one slug from an M-16. That water out there's too cold to survive very long, and even if the North Korean Navy is out there, I'm not lettin' em take me alive."

Gunner looked over at the pilot. "Jung-Hoon? You want a life jacket?"

"No life jacket," Jung-Hoon said. "I agree with Jackrabbit. Give me a rifle."

Slosh . . .

A larger wave, the largest yet, raised the plane almost on its side. Gunner dropped the flashlight on the floor. When he picked it up, he pointed it out toward the wing.

The rubber . . . it was moving!

"Jackrabbit! Check the raft!"

"Yeeeeee hiiiiiiiiiiiiiiiiiii!" Jackrabbit screamed. "We struck pay dirt!"

Gunner pointed the flashlight back outside. Sure enough, a rubber tube was inflating like a balloon coming to life and starting to turn the flat rubber into a genuine Navy SEAL Zodiac boat.

"Unbelievable!" Gunner shouted.

"All right!" Jackrabbit yelled with renewed enthusiasm. "That sucker's finally blowin' up! I'm going out, finish it up, then pull the boat off the wing and get in. Start passing stuff to me. We gotta get everything in that boat before this puppy sinks."

"I'm with you, my man!"

Gunner heard a splash as Jackrabbit dropped out of the plane's door and into the Sea of Japan. Jackrabbit pulled the Zodiac off the wing and guided it to a position just behind the cockpit.

The boat was fully inflated now, and Jackrabbit pulled himself up and rolled over the side. "Dang, this water's cold!" Jackrabbit said with the excitement of a kid who'd gotten a ten-dollar bill from the tooth fairy. "Why don't one of y'all get over here in the boat with me. No point in having both of you drown if the plane goes down."

"You go, Commander," Jung-Hoon said.

"No," Gunner said, "you go. The two of you have a better chance of finding those prisoners. Besides, you might have to steal a plane and fly out, and I don't know how to fly a plane." *Slooooshhh.* More water in the plane. "Come on, man, get a move on or we're both going down. Now!"

"As you wish, Commander," Jung-Hoon said. He crawled past Gunner and slipped out the door of the plane.

Splash.

A moment later, Jackrabbit reached his hand over the side of the boat and pulled Jung-Hoon aboard. "All right, Commander. You ready?"

"Ready," Gunner said.

"First, unscrew that CO_2 line. There's no point getting pulled down with the plane. I'll have Jung-Hoon here hang on the propeller to keep us from drifting off."

"Check," Gunner said. He leaned over, turned off the valve, and unscrewed the line tethering the boat to the plane. "Done."

"Start with that outboard motor and gas tank ... it's in the bottom of the crate that the boat was in."

Gunner looked into the crate. "Got it." He picked up the small outboard and headed to the door of the plane.

"Don't drop that thing in the water, Commander. It won't float."

"I'm not dropping it. He passed the motor out of the plane toward the boat. Got it?"

"Got it," Jackrabbit said. "There's a fuel tank in there too. We need that."

Gunner got the fuel tank out, which was full of gasoline, and lugged it over to the open door and passed it out of the plane.

"I got it," Jackrabbit said. "Okay, now let's start loading weapons."

NKN Frigate Najin
the Sea of Japan

The captain of the North Korean Navy's frigate *Najin* stood on the bridge of his ship, scanning the western horizon with his binoculars. The whole notion of looking in the general direction of the strange disappearing blip he believed was somewhat pointless. Sunset was more than five minutes ago, at 1715 hours, and the waxing crescent moon did not yet provide much light. Nevertheless, he was the captain, and it was his warship. He could do what he wanted, whether what he was doing was pointless or not. Actually, it was Dear Leader's warship, he reminded himself.

He lowered his binoculars and checked his wristwatch, then looked back out to sea with renewed resolve. Since Dear Leader had entrusted him with this type of awesome power and responsibility, he was determined to not let Dear Leader down.

Yet, the mysterious blip on the radar screen that had been visible for such a short time confounded the captain. And the executive officer. And the other officers on the ship. The radar operator on duty in the radar room was the only one who saw the blip and actually tracked it for a couple minutes. He had since checked his equipment and determined that the blip was not the product of equipment malfunction.

The executive officer joined the captain on the bridge. "Anything else?" the captain said.

"Nothing else from the radar room, Captain," the executive officer said. "It has gone quiet out there again."

The captain brought his binoculars to his eyes again.

"Bridge. Radio room."

"Radio. Bridge. Go ahead," the captain said.

"Sir, we received a flash message in from T'oejo-dong." This news grabbed the captain's interest. For T'oejo-dong was the naval headquarters for North Korea's East Sea Fleet, the ships responsible for security in the Sea of Japan.

"Bring it up immediately," the captain ordered.

"Right away, Captain."

"Interesting," the captain said as he laid his binoculars down on the chart table and lit a cigarette. "I wonder what that could be about."

"Perhaps they are ordering us to reinforce the Yellow Sea fleet against the Americans."

"You and I both know that is just a dream. Pyongyang never transfers any ships from the East Sea Fleet."

"Yes, I know, Captain. Of course everyone always thought that our next great naval encounter with the Americans would come here in the East Sea since we are the ones who guard the Motherland from the US stooge allies in Japan."

"Yes, of course," the captain said, sucking in a satisfying drag of nicotine. "Such is our luck."

A petty officer from the radar room joined them on the bridge and flashed a proud salute to the captain. "You wanted this, sir." He handed the captain an envelope.

"Thank you, petty officer. Return to your station."

"Yes, sir."

The captain ripped open the envelope and laid the message on the chart table next to the helm.

FLASH MESSAGE

FROM: HEADQUARTERS EAST SEA FLEET—T'OEJO-DONG
TO: NKN FRIGATE NAJIN
DATE: 25 NOVEMBER
TIME: 1717 HOURS
SUBJ: RADAR BLIP SPOTTING EAST SEA
        SE SECTION OF TANCH'ON-HUNGNAM SECTOR

1. Be advised multiple shore-based radars have spotted aerial blip between 1700–1705 hours, location East Sea, southeast quadrant of Tanch'on-Hungnam Sector.
2. Blip last spotted at coordinates 40 degrees, 08 minutes north latitude, 129 degrees, 40 minutes east longitude.
3. In view of the current situation in the Yellow Sea, this occurrence is of highest concern.
4. You are instructed to proceed immediately to that location to investigate.
5. You are instructed to take all measures necessary, including use

of force, to protect and defend the interests of the Democratic People's Republic of Korea.

6. Intercept, sink, or capture any vessels or aircraft that refuse to provide identification or that proceed toward coastal waters of the Democratic People's Republic of Korea.

7. Report findings to Headquarters, East Sea Fleet, NLT 2300 Hours, 25 November.

It is so ordered,
Rhee In-gu
Commanding Admiral
East Sea Fleet

"Looks like we are in business, XO." The captain handed the orders to his second in command. "Helmsman. Plot a course to 40 degrees, 8 minutes north latitude, 129 degrees, 40 minutes east longitude. Advise of distance and course setting."

"Yes, Captain," the helmsman said, then started punching the coordinates into the ship's GPS guidance computer. "Stand by, Captain." A few seconds passed. A revolving circle rotated on the computer screen. And then the coordinates appeared.

"Coordinates plotted, Captain," the helmsman said. "That position is ten miles to our east."

"Very well," the Captain said. He hit the intercom button, opening a channel to the radio room.

"Radio. Bridge."

"Radio. Go ahead, Captain."

"Send flash message to East Sea Fleet Headquarters, T'oejo-dong. Acknowledge receipt of your orders and proceeding to coordinates stat."

"Aye, Captain."

"Helmsman. Plot course zero-nine-zero degrees. All ahead full."

"Aye, sir. Plotting course zero-nine-zero degrees. Engines all ahead full. Aye, Captain."

The *Najin* began her turn in the water, her bow cutting a course toward the east. The captain picked up the microphone and clicked the button activating the ship's loudspeaker system. "Now hear this! This is the captain speaking! Our shipboard radar and land-based radar have detected a mysterious blip that appeared and disappeared on our screen just a few minutes ago, ten miles to the east of our current position. Fleet headquarters in T'oejo-dong has determined that we are the nearest vessel and has ordered us to steam to that position to investigate. All lookouts, pay close attention to anything suspicious on the sea or in the air. I know it is dark, and I want all lookouts sweeping the seas with searchlights. Our orders are to report back to T'oejo-dong no later than 2300 hours. This is the captain speaking."

Beechcraft Bonanza G36
the Sea of Japan

Cold water now stood three inches deep on the floor of the cabin, and the Bonanza's nose section sunk deeper into the sea with each rise and plunge of the aircraft.

"Commander! Hurry! Get the heck out of there!" Jackrabbit yelled.

"Almost done," Gunner said. "A few more MREs and we've got everything."

Gunner sloshed to the back to grab the MREs. Each packet contained a ready-to-eat 1,200-calorie meal, albeit not tasty, wrapped in airtight and watertight packages. Mr. Kim, if that was his name, had purchased sixty-three such packets, enough for a seven-day supply of three meals a day for the three of them without having to forage or steal anything to eat from the North Koreans.

The waves were getting much larger. "The wind's whipping up, Commander!" Jackrabbit yelled. "Leave the rest!"

Jackrabbit's right, Gunner thought. Better get out of here. "I'm coming!"

As Gunner reached for the doorway, a wave raised the plane up much higher than any of the previous waves. The monster wave felt like the surge of a tsunami. At the crest, the plane suddenly dipped, then tipped, sliding down the back of the wave like a roller-coaster car starting a long drop. Gunner lost his balance and tumbled into the tail section of the cabin.

Seawater gushed through the open door with a fury. The plane's tail section sank quickly, tipping the nose up, dumping the seawater in the nose compartment down into the cabin.

Gunner had pulled himself up, but then fell back down and slid again into the back of the flooded cabin. He fought to keep his head up for air. The cold water pouring in through the door was like a strong undertow keeping him from fighting his way out.

"Help!" he screamed. "Help me! Help!"

CHAPTER 17

USS Boise
depth 100 feet in the Sea of Japan

S kipper, target is starting to move. She's setting a new course. Looks like course zero-nine-zero degrees. She's moving out pretty fast, sir. Looks like all ahead full."

From the center of the sub's control room, Commander Graham Hardison, the experienced captain of the Los Angeles–class nuclear-powered submarine USS *Boise*, calmly finished his swig of steaming black coffee and set it on the plotting table behind the periscope. *Boise* had been patrolling the waters off the east coast of North Korea for a week now, monitoring the naval activities of the Democratic People's Republic. At depths varying from one hundred to three hundred feet, she was invisible to the world. Only those in the United States Navy with a need to know knew her location.

"Very well, Lieutenant." Hardison acknowledged the sonar officer, then turned to the sailor sitting in the chair in the far-left corner of the control room. "Helmsman, let's get in her wake and follow her. We'll see where she goes. As loud as that old bucket is, she'll never know we're down here. Set course zero-nine-zero degrees. All ahead full."

"Aye, aye, Captain. Setting course zero-nine-zero degrees." The sub started a turn in the water. "All ahead full. Getting on his fanny right now, sir."

"Very well," Hardison said. "Steady as she goes."

Beechcraft Bonanza G36
the Sea of Japan

Only a small portion of the Bonanza's cockpit and the propeller were still above the surface. The plane was almost vertical in the water. Gunner clung to the pilot's seat, trying to keep his face and nose up in the rapidly shrinking air pocket. He pressed his head against the windshield and sucked in the precious oxygen from the six or seven inches of space that was not yet flooded.

The torrent of water gushing into the plane had been like a powerful fire hose blocking him from even trying to get out the door for fear he'd lose his grip and be tumbled backward again. He clung to the seat, his heart pounding so hard he could feel the rapid beat. He was cold all over. He began shivering despite the thermal wetsuit. He wasn't sure if fear, shock, the cold water, or the realization that he was about to die had caused the shivering.

Gunner knew he had one chance. In a few seconds, as the last air pocket filled with water, the water would stop rushing in through the door. The pressure of the fire hose that had pushed him back would be gone. His life or death hinged on his ability to swim back through the cabin to the open door and pull himself out before the plane sank to the bottom, taking him with it.

With the air pocket gone, if he could not get out within thirty seconds, he calculated, his life would be over.

Jung-Hoon! Hit it with that flashlight!" Jackrabbit said.

The Korean complied, flashing the high-beam utility light in the direction of where the plane had been only moments before.

With no time to mount the outboard and get it running, they had drifted twenty, perhaps thirty feet from the sinking plane. Only part of the yellow nose section remained visible in the swells.

"I've lost him! I don't see him anywhere!" Jackrabbit said. "I'm going in after him."

"No!" Jung-Hoon protested. "The plane is going down. If you jump in, there's a good chance both of you will drown."

"I gotta go," Jackrabbit said. "He's risking his life for a good cause. He's a good man. Americans either live together or we die together."

Jackrabbit stood up and dove headfirst into the frigid waters of the Sea of Japan.

G unner pressed his nose tight against the glass windshield, gasping to inhale the last of the oxygen from the tiny pocket of air.

A light flashed through the windshield and into the water that filled the cockpit. The bright beam set his mind into a panic. A searchlight? A flashlight! Help was on the way! Instinctively, he beat his fist against the inside of the windshield, and then ...

Cold water swirled around his ears and forehead. He sucked the last ounce of air into his lungs. Water now covered his face and nose.

Like a submarine diving, the plane slid under the surface and disappeared from view.

Gunner closed his eyes. It was time ...

J ung-Hoon tried standing in the Zodiac so he could see better, but lost his balance and slipped to his knees. He flashed his high beam in the direction that he had last seen the plane. Nothing. "Jackrabbit!" He had lost sight of Jackrabbit. He could not hear or see any splash of kicking in the water.

"The plane is gone! Get back to the boat!"

He swept the flashlight back and forth. Nothing but rolling swells. "Jackrabbit! Get back to the boat!"

I nside the plane, total darkness had snuffed the slight semblance of light that had still existed before the wreck had gone under. Gunner felt around for something to grab. Cold, dark panic gripped his body. He found the passenger's seat beside the captain's chair. The door leading out of the plane he knew was behind that seat. But he had to be fast.

The pressure was mounting like a crushing vice on his skull as the plane continued its way to the bottom. It seemed as if the plane was twirling as it sank deeper through black water. Floating between the two cockpit seats, Gunner pulled himself toward the doorway. He blew out a bit of air and reached into the dark watery abyss. Something wooden.

One of the wooden crates floating inside the plane was in the way.

Panic gripped him. He pushed the crate aside and swam toward the door. If he could just get out through it.

His hands walked along the inside of the fuselage.

Where was the door? Where was the opening?

Then he felt it.

The latch.

The door had closed shut!

The Zodiac had drifted fifty to sixty feet from where the plane had sunk, and from this point, even the high-beam flashlight was useless.

Jung-Hoon realized that if the boat kept drifting away, Jackrabbit too would be lost at sea, and there would be no chance of finding Gunner.

He lifted the outboard and carefully positioned it on the mounting board on the back of the rubber inflatable. He pushed down hard on the vice clamps to secure the outboard. He screwed the rubber hose from the gas tank into the side of the engine. He squeezed several times on the pressure bulb on the gas tank hose and pulled out the choke. Then he pulled hard on the rope to start the outboard.

Nothing.

He pulled again.

RRRRRRRRRRRRRRRRRRRRRRRRRRRRRRRRRR ...

The outboard ignited! He pushed the choke in. Jung-Hoon exhaled in relief, then sat down and put his hand on the throttle and twisted. The boat moved forward, and he steered in the direction that he had last seen Jackrabbit swimming.

The latch ... Gunner tried twisting one way, then the other. Somehow he could not get a good grip on the latch. It seemed slippery in the cold water.

He blew out a little more air and tried again.

He released more air.

Suddenly he felt dizzy. Very dizzy.

His chest reflexes commanded him to inhale.

Why not? He had done all he could do.

He twisted the latch once more.

The door popped open!

He pushed his head against the door, holding tight on each side of the door to give himself more leverage, and it gave way. He kicked with his legs and pulled hard with his arms. Suddenly, he floated free of the plane.

He was out of the plane, but which way was up?

He blew out the last bit of air in his lungs and kicked with what little strength was left in his legs. With his arms, he pulled against the water, hoping that the direction he was trying to swim was up.

Jung-Hoon headed to where he thought he had last seen the nose section of the plane bobbing in the water. The blanketing darkness and the large swells made it hard to judge where the plane had been. At this slow speed, barely a sputter, and with the swells as they were, he could not have moved more than a hundred feet from where he started.

This seemed like the right spot where the Bonanza had sunk. He turned the throttle down to idle and slid the gearshift lever to neutral.

He remembered that they had put one pair of night-vision binoculars on their checklist. He aimed the flashlight on the gear in the boat. There. Beside the ammo case. Crouching low, he moved halfway up the boat and grabbed the binoculars.

The night-vision binoculars made the huge swells look menacing. The seascape glowed a ghastly green through the scopes.

No sign of either American. He looked all around in a full circle. Still nothing.

He cut the engine to save gas.

Swooooooooooooosh ... Swooooooooooooooosh ...

He held his breath trying to listen, but heard only the sound of the wind and the roar of the sea.

"Help!"

A voice!

"Over here!"

"Where are you?" The howling wind made it impossible to track the direction.

"Here!"

Jung-Hoon swept the flashlight beam to the left and to the right. Nothing but waves.

"Jung-Hoon." He swept the light around to the other side of the boat. "Here!"

There! About fifty yards away! Hands splashing the surface of the water!

"Hang on! I'm coming!" He turned and pulled the starter rope. The outboard ignited. With one hand on the tiller-throttle and the other pointing the light in the direction of the flailing hands, he steered toward the swimmer.

The Zodiac crested and troughed straight across a couple of large waves. It then peaked up on a third wave that seemed as big as Mount Hallasan. When he came down on the back side of the wave, a black-painted face gasping for air was right in front of the boat.

Jung-Hoon quickly steered to the right to avoid ramming the face with the bow. He cut the engine back to idle, shifted to neutral, and reached down over the left side of the boat.

"I got him right here." It was Jackrabbit. "I'm all right. See if you can pull him back in."

Jackrabbit was treading water with one arm and holding the commander face up with the other. The commander's neck was secured in the crook of Jackrabbit's elbow.

Jung-Hoon reached over the side of the boat and grabbed the commander's limp arm. "I have him!"

"Keep his head up," Jackrabbit said. "Hang on and I'll help you get him in."

Jackrabbit disappeared below the water. A second later, Jung-Hoon felt a pull on the boat from the back. He looked over his shoulder. Jackrabbit was hoisting himself into the boat on the other side.

"Okay, let's pull," Jackrabbit said, "but try not to flip this thing. On my count. One ... two ... three!"

The two men tried to pull Gunner up on the tube on the left side of the boat, but the Zodiac nearly flipped from all the weight, and four or five MRE packages fell overboard.

Jackrabbit held Gunner against the side of the boat and said, "Jung-Hoon, go sit on the other side to balance this thing out. I'll pull him up."

"Okay," Jung-Hoon said and crawled over to the right side.

Just then, the boat got caught broadside to a large swell. Down in the trough they went. Then they were lifted up and up as the swell moved under them. Sliding down the back side of the swell, Jackrabbit hoisted Commander McCormick into the boat.

"Okay, give me some light."

Jung-Hoon grabbed the flashlight as Jackrabbit dragged the commander to the middle of the boat.

"He's not breathing," Jackrabbit said. He turned Gunner over, face down, and pushed down in the middle of his back.

A gush of water came out of the commander's mouth.

Jackrabbit pushed down again.

Nothing.

Jackrabbit quickly turned the commander over on his back. He pushed the commander's head back and with a finger quickly swiped his mouth out to clear his airway. Then he started mouth-to-mouth resuscitation. The commander's chest rose and dropped. Jackrabbit repeated it. Again it rose and dropped. Then Jackrabbit crossed his palms and pushed down three times hard at the center of the commander's chest. Then he blew air into his lungs again. Once again, the lifeless chest rose and dropped.

"Come on, man! Breathe!" Jackrabbit screamed into the dark.

NKN Frigate **Najin**
the Sea of Japan

Word spread quickly all over the ship about the strange disappearing blip spotted ten miles to their east. And now the *Najin*'s new mission was of vital national importance!

The blip could have been anything. A ship. A missile. Some sort of aircraft. Whatever it was, the crew was certain that it was hostile to the Democratic People's Republic and to Dear Leader.

From his position at the bow of this ship, on the forward lookout post, Petty Officer Cheong Tae-hee saw himself as the eyes and ears not only of the ship but also of the DPRK and of Dear Leader. The watch he was now standing, in the very front of this warship, could be pivotal in the burgeoning war with the Americans and to the future of the republic.

He flipped on the powerful searchlight and swept the beam across the waters in front of the *Najin*. He swept to the left, then to the right. Nothing.

But they were out there.

Somewhere.

He knew it in the deepest recesses of his soul. The Americans were out there. They would not only attack from the west but they would attack from the east too. They possessed the resources to attack from both directions, and when they did, the Navy of Dear Leader would be more than capable of defending the country.

He always took pride in his performance as the ship's forward watch. But tonight he took a special pride in his duties. For tonight, he was certain, he would rendezvous with history!

Kim Yŏng-nam Military Prison Camp

A sliver of light slid in through the crack under the door of the windowless isolation cell. Outside, the guards' clicking boots beat a rhythmic pattern on the floor.

Pak was curled up on the concrete floor in the far-left corner of the cell. Her arms were wrapped around her shivering body. Ironically, the death of the old prisoner she had tried to save had delayed her own death. The colonel, ignoring Kang's protests about delaying Pak's execution, had stayed her sentence—for now—to deal with the disposal of the dead body. But then the colonel, as if to show his own cruel streak to Kang, had shoved a lit cigarette against her neck just before the guards cut the ropes tying her to the tree. The burn was to teach her a lesson for stealing property of the state, he had said.

Pak gingerly touched her neck. The burn had turned into a large blister. She could barely move her head because doing so exacerbated the pain. With each heartbeat, a hot, throbbing pain pulsed in her neck.

Why had they spared her? But the more she wondered the more convinced she became that the Lord himself had spared her, at least for a few hours, perhaps less. But for what? She could only wait through the pain. The cold. The hot. The shivering.

Into the dark, against the echoing clicks of the jackboots outside, she whispered, "Lord, why me? Why am I here? Why did you spare me, if only for a little while? Do you still have a purpose for my life?"

The door opened. She squinted against the bright light glaring from the hallway and could see only a dark silhouette.

"Get up, traitor!"

She recognized the voice as that of the enthusiastic new guard, Kang, the one who had promised to kill her when he cut her down from the tree. Perhaps he had come to fulfill his promise.

"We are taking you to another location." This time a woman's voice. It sounded like the colonel's assistant, but Pak couldn't be sure. The woman's voice did not display the same level of hatred that the man's voice revealed.

Pak had learned that when officials of the government speak, it is best to comply and offer no resistance. She stood up and walked to the doorway. Kang and the colonel's assistant were standing there.

"Hands out," Kang ordered.

She obeyed, and steel handcuffs were clamped tightly around her wrists.

"What I told you earlier still stands," he said in a low voice.

She did not respond. If he wanted to shoot her here, what difference did it make?

"Let's go."

Kang and the woman each took her by an arm, turned her to the right, and led her down the long hallway of the camp's main building. They walked past the colonel's office on the right, the office where all this had started, where she had stolen the penicillin to help the old prisoner who was so sick. And the old man had died anyway. Was it worth it?

She reminded herself of the verse in Deuteronomy that she sometimes read in her small apartment when she was alone.

"Do what is right," it said.

And trying to help the old man in his misery, even though he died, had been the right thing to do. Even if she had to pay the price with a permanent scar on her neck ... or with her life.

They reached the exit at the end of the long hall. Kang released his grip on her upper arm and pushed open the door to the outside. Darkness had fallen over the snow-mounded camp. The blast of freezing wind that whipped against her blister accentuated the painful throbbing.

Kang walked down the three steps to the circular gravel driveway in front of the building and opened the back door of the jeep parked a few feet away. The motor was running and the headlights were on.

"Get in," Kang ordered.

Pak complied, stumbling clumsily into the backseat. The colonel's assistant got in the back with her. Then Kang slammed the door, walked around the back of the vehicle, and got into the driver's seat. The jeep rolled forward. A moment later, they drove through the front gate and past the two armed guards, who closed the gate after they left the camp.

Kang turned the jeep left onto the single-lane asphalt road in front of the camp, and they sped off into the night.

Pak leaned her head back and closed her eyes.

"The Lord is my shepherd ... I shall not want ... "

Zodiac boat
the Sea of Japan

Cough ... *cough ... cough ... cough ... cough ...*
Lying flat on his back, Gunner opened his eyes to a bright glare and heard a familiar voice.

"You all right, Commander?"

Cough … cough … "Jackrabbit?" … *Cough …*

"Take it easy, sir," the voice said. "This is what happens when you take too long of a dip in too cold of a pond this time of year. Happened to me one time when I went duck huntin' in January down at Lake Mattamuskeet in eastern North Carolina. I made the mistake of standin' up in the canoe with my .20-gauge, and the next thing ya know …"

Cough … Gunner was half coughing and half laughing at Jackrabbit's story. The ole warrior knew exactly what to say and when to say it.

"Whoever pulled me out of the drink, thank you."

"Jung-Hoon did it, Commander," Jackrabbit said. "You can thank him."

"He is a liar, Commander," Jung-Hoon said. "He jumped in the water like an idiot after I warned him that you both would drown."

A laugh. Another cough. "Get that flashlight out of my face. You're blinding me."

"Yes, sorry."

The light disappeared. After a while, after his eyes adjusted, Gunner looked up and saw a host of stars shining brilliantly across the late November sky. He remembered as a boy how his mother would come into his room at bedtime and throw open the curtains, and they would gaze at the stars in the southeastern Virginia skies. "The heavens declare the glory of the Lord," she would say.

"Oh, no. We got more problems," Jackrabbit said.

"What now?" Gunner said.

"Look out there."

Gunner pushed himself up into a sitting position and saw what Jackrabbit was pointing toward on the horizon. A beam of light out in the distance was sweeping back and forth, back and forth.

"Looks like somebody's lookin' for somebody," Jackrabbit said, "and my guess is that whoever they are, they aren't the good guys."

"North Korean Navy," Jung-Hoon said. "They probably spotted us on radar when we climbed to one thousand before our descent."

"Now what?" Gunner asked.

"One thing's for sure," Jackrabbit said, "we sure aren't gonna shine Jung-Hoon's flashlight in that direction."

"Maybe we should crank the engine and get out of here," Gunner said.

"Where we gonna go?" Jackrabbit asked. "GPS says that's the direction that we've got to go." He pointed at the light. "We go back that way"—he pointed in the opposite direction—"and we're headed to Japan. If we go any direction other than toward the light, we run out of gas, and we got no place to go. So what do we do?"

"We sit and wait, hope they don't come this way," Jung-Hoon said.

They waited, watching the light sweep back and forth in the distance.

Gunner said, "I hate to tell you, but that light's getting bigger and brighter. They're coming this way."

Swooosh ... swoosh ...

The wind had picked up. The swells had turned into waves that were carrying the boat up and down. The wind whistled and wheezed. Gunner looked over and saw Jackrabbit peering through binoculars at the sweeping searchlight.

"I'm afraid you're right, Commander," Jackrabbit said. "That's a ship headed in this direction."

"So are we going to sit here and let them find us?" Gunner asked.

"You're the Navy guy, Commander," Jackrabbit said. "Me and Jung-Hoon here, we're ole retired Army hacks. But we don't have enough gas to go in any direction but one, and we can't paddle very far. Look. It's a big ocean, and this boat is black, and we're all painted up in black. Even with that searchlight, it's almost like looking for a needle in a haystack. I say we got no choice but to wait it out till they leave."

A faint roar came into earshot, just over the sound of the wind and waves. A mechanical roar.

"I hear their engines," Gunner said.

"I hear it too," Jackrabbit said.

Jung-Hoon said, "I hate to ... what is the phrase you Americans like to use? Bust your babble?"

"You mean burst your bubble," Gunner said.

"Yes. I hate to burst your bubble, but I think there is a better chance than Jackrabbit thinks that they will find us."

The sound of the ship's engines grew louder. The sweeping light kept getting brighter.

"Why do you say that, Jung-Hoon?"

"Because I assume they spotted us on their radar systems just before we ditched the plane. They got a GPS fix on our last airborne position. That could not be far from here. Perhaps a half mile. A mile at the most. That would put them on a course for this sector. Straight for the coordinates last picked up on their radar. This being the case, we may not be so much of—what did you say—a needle in haystack?"

"Great," Gunner said. "One of you thinks they'll find us, the other thinks they won't." The wind died down a bit, making the noise of the coming ship more profound. "So what do you think, Jung-Hoon? Should we crank the engine and get the heck out of here?"

"No," the Korean said. "I agree with Jackrabbit on that. Not enough gas. However, I think we should get guns ready."

"M-16s? Against a ship?" Gunner raised an eyebrow.

"If they decide to take us alive," Jung-Hoon said, "they would send a boarding craft from the ship, full of armed sailors or North Korean Marines."

"That's assuming they're North Korean Navy, and it's also assuming they decide to capture us rather than blow us out of the water," Gunner said.

"Yes," Jung-Hoon said. "Assuming all that. I will let no Communist pig capture me alive. I will fight them to the death. And I will take out several Communist pigs before they kill me. Therefore, my advice is to get guns ready."

The roar of the approaching ship's engines now rivaled the volume of the wind and the waves.

"Jackrabbit?" Gunner looked at the American, who was still peering at the approaching ship through his binoculars. "What do you think about that?"

"Well ..." Jackrabbit paused. "I don't know if they'll find us or not. But I agree with Jung-Hoon on one thing." He spit in the ocean. "Let's get the guns ready."

"Probably a good idea to get the night-vision goggles out too," Jung-Hoon added.

"They're in the backpacks in the back of the boat," Jackrabbit said. "I'll get the guns ready."

CHAPTER 18

NKN Frigate **Najin**
the Sea of Japan

Petty Officer Cheong Tae-hee stood at the ship's bow, watching the sea with his binoculars. Just to his right, his assistant, Junior Petty Officer Kim Won-tu, manned the high-power spotlight. Nothing, other than rolling seas, had yet come into their view.

"This is the captain speaking!" The voice boomed in Korean all over the *Najin's* intercom system. "We are now approaching the GPS coordinates where the radar blip was last spotted. Be alert. We will remain at this location as we search. Assume that whatever we spotted represents interests hostile to the Democratic People's Republic and to Dear Leader. Forward watch station. Arm machine guns. Be prepared to fire upon my order."

The captain's voice sent chills down Cheong's spine. "Be prepared to fire." He lowered his binoculars and rushed to the forward machine gun station.

The mounted weapon for close-range attacks on smaller vessels was the Soviet-manufactured NSV machine gun. Named for its Soviet designer, the late Nikitna Sokolova-Volkova, the machine gun sported a five-foot-long barrel, fired 800 rounds of 12.7mm cartridges in belts containing fifty rounds each, and had the flexibility to be mounted anywhere on the ship. In this case, the Navy of the Democratic People's Republic had mounted the NSV at the bow of its flagship frigate.

Cheong had taken target practice on the gun last week, and with the captain and the first officer watching over his shoulder, he busted plastic floating targets out of the water at a range of at least two hundred and fifty yards. Even the captain had mentioned his proficiency with the gun and had bragged that Cheong was the best machine gunner in the Navy. Carefully, Cheong threaded the first fifty-round belt into the gun.

If anyone was out there and if he was ordered to fire, the single fifty-round belt should be more than enough to get the job done. There. The belt was threaded. Ready to fire when ordered.

"Petty Officer Cheong! I see something!" Junior Petty Officer Kim Won-tu yelled as he pointed frantically.

"What?" Cheong sprinted back across the fifteen-foot deck space between the machine gun and the forward searchlight.

"A boat! A small boat! It has men in it! They appear to be armed!"

Zodiac boat

They've spotted us." Jackrabbit held his hand up to block the blinding searchlight from his eyes. "Jung-Hoon, I know we don't have much gas to burn, but my guess is that they'll send a boarding party out to grab us. When I tell you to crank that motor, do it and get us the heck out from under that light. Got it?"

"Got it."

NKN *Frigate* Najin

Petty Officer Cheong Tae-hee held the binoculars to his eyes and watched the small black boat about two hundred yards off the ship's port bow. Three men, dressed in black, wearing black scuba gear and holding guns, were crouched low in the boat.

Navy SEALs. There was no other explanation, he decided. The United States must have dropped them out in parachutes from a stealth bomber, which would account for the fact that no aircraft had been detected inbound. And then, when they parachuted down, the parachutes were picked up on radar. Yes, this would explain it.

Cheong could not contain himself! He picked up the forward-deck telephone with a direct connection to the bridge. His hand shook with excitement as he punched the button alerting the bridge.

"Bridge! Forward lookout."

"This is the bridge. Go ahead, Petty Officer."

"Sir! We have discovered a small craft in the water. Approximately two hundred yards off the port bow. The craft is manned with three individuals in scuba gear. Believed to be armed US Navy SEALs, sir!"

"Very well, Petty Officer. Keep them in your sights and await further instructions."

"Yes, Captain," Cheong said.

"We see the boat from here. Good work, Petty Officer. We are sending a boarding team to bring them in. Keep the spotlight on them and cover the boarding party until the SEALs are taken into custody. Do you understand your instructions?"

"Understood, sir!"

"Now hear this! This is the captain speaking! All members of the marine boarding party, report to debarkation station. Repeat, all members of the marine boarding party, report to debarkation station.

"Forward watch has spotted an unidentified small craft approximately two hundred yards off our port bow. The craft is manned and believed to be armed and hostile to the Democratic People's Republic. The craft could be manned by US Navy SEALs.

"Battle stations! Battle stations!"

Zodiac boat

Ding-ding-ding-ding-ding-ding-ding-ding-ding. The shrill sound of alarm bells from the ship clanged. With the searchlight blinding their eyes, they heard authoritarian voices from the ship's loudspeaker bellowing across the water.

"What are they saying?" Gunner asked.

"I heard the captain say that they are going to battle stations," Jung-Hoon said. "They think that we are Navy SEALs."

"Navy SEALs. Sheesh," Jackrabbit said mockingly. "Paranoid Communists will believe anything."

"I've got a feeling we could use some Navy SEALs right now," Gunner said.

"You got retired US Army Special Forces protecting you, Commander," Jackrabbit said. "You're in good hands! You don't need Navy SEALs!"

Gunner shook his head. "Jackrabbit, you're crazy."

"I decided a long time ago," Jackrabbit said, still holding his hands up to block the glare from the spotlight, "that crazy is the only way to live, and crazy is the only way to die."

"Attention. You on the boat! Attention! We see you, and we know who you are . . ." The ship's loudspeaker thundered out over the water.

"I think it's about time to crank that motor, Jung-Hoon," Jackrabbit said.

"Got it," Jung-Hoon said.

Vrooooooooooooooommmmmmmmmmmmm. The outboard ignited like a dried-out Christmas tree lit up by a blow torch.

The ship's loudspeaker boomed across the water again. "You have violated the territorial waters of the Democratic People's Republic. You are now in the custody of the Navy of the Democratic People's Republic."

"Like heck we are," Jackrabbit muttered.

The announcement switched back and forth from Korean to English. "In a few moments you will be boarded by Marines of the Democratic People's Republic. You shall surrender, and you shall transfer to our boat for transportation back to the ship. If you do not cooperate, you will be shot."

A moment later, the sound of another outboard ripped across the water. Out of the shadows of the blinding light, the smaller craft came into view, cutting its way across the water from the ship.

The small craft had six men aboard, all armed with rifles. It pulled to within one hundred feet of the Zodiac and slowed. "You will now raise your hands in the air."

"Got your rifle ready, Commander?" At this point, Jackrabbit, who sat in the center of the Zodiac boat, had taken *de facto* control of the mission. Gunner, crouched in the front of the boat, was fine with Jackrabbit assuming command.

"Got it right here, Jackrabbit."

"Can you boys from Virginia shoot some turkey?"

"Between the eyes at a hundred yards," Gunner said.

USS Boise
depth 100 feet in the Sea of Japan

Skipper, the target has stopped. Plus this flash message just came in from CINCPAC. I think you'll find it interesting."

"Very well. All stop!"

"All stop. Aye, sir."

"Hand me that message."

Commander Hardison, a blond and blue-eyed officer who had almost an Aryan look about him, unfolded the message.

"XO. Mister COB," Hardison said to the sub's executive officer and the senior enlisted sailor, known as the chief of the boat, "why don't the two of you join me for the reading of this fine message."

Hardison unfolded the orders and spread the paper on the table.

FROM: NATIONAL COMMAND AUTHORITY
TO: USS BOISE
      VIA CINCPAC FLEET
      SEVENTH FLEET
SUBJ: ATTACK ORDERS

1. In light of the recent missile attack by North Korean forces on the USS *Harry S. Truman*, you are ordered to attack and sink the North Korean frigate NKN *Najin*.
2. It is important that North Korea be sent the message in no uncertain terms that attacks upon United States naval forces will not be tolerated and shall not go unpunished.
3. You are to carry out these orders immediately.
4. By direction of the president.

                Respectfully,
                Roscoe S. Jones, ADM, USN
                Chairman, Joint Chiefs of Staff

"Man," Hardison said, "I've never gotten an order directly from the National Command Authority before."

"That means this order is straight from the president, sir," the XO said.

"That's exactly what it means, XO," Hardison said. "Very well. Helmsman, all ahead one-third. Swing us out to a ninety-degree angle for a broadside torpedo launch. Set us five hundred yards from target."

"Aye, sir. All ahead one-third, swinging for broadside launch at five hundred yards."

"Fire control, serve me up two Mark 48 torps. One in tube one, the other in tube three."

"Aye, Skipper," the fire control officer said. "Arming tubes one and three."

"XO, sound general quarters."

"Aye, Skipper. Sounding general quarters." The XO picked up the ship's microphone system. "General quarters! General quarters! This is not a drill." Bells clanged all over the sub. "General quarters! General quarters!"

Hardison smiled. "Looks like the president wants a little post-Thanksgiving turkey shoot."

Zodiac boat

The black, piercing eyes of the enemy sparkled through the lens of Gunner's binoculars. There were six of them—North Korean Marines with rifles in dark blue and black uniforms. They sat in a whipping wind in three rows of two in the white North Korean navy launch, which was now inside the perimeter of the beam of the bright spotlight surrounding the Zodiac. The Korean boat chugged toward the Zodiac boat, closing to less than twenty-five feet. Their rifles were pointed at the three men in the Zodiac. One of the sailors in the launch started barking instructions in broken English through a bullhorn.

Gunner and Jackrabbit were on their knees in the front and center of the fifteen-foot Zodiac. Jung-Hoon crouched on his knees in the back, his hands on the throttle of the running outboard. "Prepare to be boarded! Put your hands in the air!" the voice cracked over the bullhorn.

"I think they want us to put our hands up," Gunner said.

"Not ... quite ... yet," Jackrabbit said.

Whatever game of Russian roulette Jackrabbit was playing, it was getting too hot for Gunner.

"We will drift in closer and throw you a line." The voice from the bullhorn. "You. In the front of the boat. You will catch the line, and we will pull your boat in close to ours. If you do not cooperate, you will be shot."

"I think he's talking to me," Gunner said. "Sounds like a friendly guy."

"Okay, listen up," Jackrabbit said. "When I say *now*, Commander, drop to the bottom of the boat. I'll do the same. Hopefully, between that and these swells, it won't be a turkey shoot for 'em."

"You! In the boat! Put your hands up and prepare to receive the line!"

"Let's get our hands up to play along. Jung-Hoon, don't get your hands too far away from that motor."

"Got it."

Gunner raised both of his hands in the air. He looked around and saw that Jackrabbit had done the same. Except that Jackrabbit was also flashing a cheesy grin right at the North Koreans. "Jung-Hoon," Jackrabbit said, "when I give the word, crank the throttle as hard as you can and stay down. Commander, as soon as I say 'Fire,' come up shootin'. We'll be moving and we've got these swells to contend with, so the shots won't be easy, but be accurate. We need to take these guys out."

The North Korean launch inched closer and started turning in the water. "We are about to throw you a line. Prepare to receive line."

"Hey, Jackrabbit, if we shake these guys in this boat, what about that ship over there?"

"One problem at a time, Commander."

"Got it."

The North Korean launch was now cutting through the swells, chugging toward the Zodiac. A sailor stood in the bow with a looped line, preparing to throw it. The sailor with the bullhorn stood beside him, aiming the bullhorn directly at Gunner.

"Get ready, boys," Jackrabbit said.

"We will now throw you the line!"

"Now!" Jackrabbit shouted just as the North Korean Marine slung the line toward Gunner.

The outboard revved and the Zodiac jumped. Gunner fell back onto the floor of the boat. He felt the boat turn and lunge forward. He heard an immediate torrent of angry Korean words blaring over the bullhorn.

Pow-pow-pow-pow-pow-pow-pow. Rifle fire cracked the night air. Whizzing bullets flew inches over the top of the boat, just as the glare of the bright spotlight turned into darkness.

Gunner felt the boat turning in the water and then slowing almost to a drift.

"All right, let's let 'em have it, boys!" Jackrabbit yelled.

Gunner got up from the floor of the boat. The Zodiac was drifting just outside the glare of the spotlight. Jackrabbit was already up, his M-16 on his shoulder and aimed at the North Korean launch, which was still illuminated by the searchlight from the ship.

Bang bang bang bang bang bang! Jackrabbit's rifle unleashed six quick shots.

"Aaaaahhhh!" Screams from the Korean launch filled the air. Two North Korean sailors fell overboard, both clutching their throats. Two others, whose heads had just exploded, slumped lifeless in the boat. The two others, the one who had been snapping with the bullhorn and the one who had thrown the rope, scrambled in the boat like a couple of panicked chickens.

"Holy smokes, Jackrabbit!"

"Commander, fire about ten rounds in the engine. I'll take the other two out."

Bang! Bang!

Before Gunner could even bring his rifle to his shoulder, the heads of the bullhorn guy and the line thrower exploded like watermelons smashing against concrete. One body fell into the ocean, the other fell into the boat.

"Hold your fire, Commander," Jackrabbit said. "No point in wasting valuable ammunition on an engine when there's nobody in the boat to drive it. I got a feeling we're gonna need those bullets later."

"I guess you're right," Gunner said. He sat back down in the front of the boat and put his M-16 on the floor beside him.

"Jung-Hoon, cut a course due west at full power. Let's get as far away from that spotlight as possible. They might find us out here again, but no point in making it any easier on them than we have to."

"Got it."

The engine revved again, and the boat shot across rolling waves, headed in a direction that would take it across the pathway of the ship's bow, from the left to the right, on a course straight for the North Korean coastline.

NKN *Frigate* Najin

Get the spotlight off our boat, you stupid idiot!" Petty Officer Cheong Tae-hee screamed at the junior petty officer, Kim Won-tu, who had stood there with the spotlight on the North Korean launch while bullets whizzed in from the dark. "You have made them blind sitting ducks for the Navy SEALs!"

Cheong rushed over and pushed the junior petty officer out of the way. He retook control of the spotlight and started sweeping out over the black rolling waves. "Which way did they go, Petty Officer?"

"I think that way." He pointed off to the left of the bow.

"You *think* that way?" He swung the light off the lifeless North Korean boat, concentrating on the black waters off the port bow.

Nothing.

"Why did you not follow the SEALs with the light when they got away? Why did you keep the light on our sailors and Marines?" he yelled as he moved the searchlight to the right and swept the waters right in front of the ship.

"I ... I do not know. I did not know what to do. I ... I froze."

"You froze!" Cheong screamed. "You froze! And now they could be anywhere out there!" Still nothing. "I am the one who will get blamed by the captain for this! If the Navy does not court-martial you, I will personally shoot you."

He swung the light farther to the right. Then ... there! Scooting across swells and now out to the right side of the ship's path, the Zodiac sped away from the ship.

"Petty Officer, you hold this light on that boat while I get the machine gun. If you lose that boat again, I will shoot you on the spot. Do you understand?"

"Yes, sir."

Zodiac boat

The searchlight lit them up again, causing Jackrabbit to unleash a string of expletives.

"Commander, get down! I'm gonna see if I can take out that spotlight!"

Gunner went head down again, behind the inflated tube of the small rubber craft. He looked back and saw Jackrabbit crawling with his rifle to the back of the boat. Jung-Hoon moved over to the back left, hand still on the throttle of the outboard. Jackrabbit slipped into the back right and started firing multiple volleys back toward the ship.

USS Boise
depth 100 feet in the Sea of Japan

Skipper, we're now broadside to the target. Range to target, five hundred yards. Awaiting your orders."

"Very well," Commander Hardison said. "Fire torp one!"

"Fire torp one! Aye, sir."

Swish. The sensation of a huge air puff rocked the sub as the first Mark 48 torpedo shot from the bow of the submarine.

"Fire torp three!"

"Fire torp three! Aye, sir."

Swish ... Another air puff sensation. The second torpedo raced away through the water toward the target.

Hardison said, "Range to target."

"Sir, torp one range to target is three hundred fifty yards and closing. Torp two range is four hundred fifty yards and closing."

"Any indication that we've been detected?" Hardison asked.

"Sir, there's a Russian Yankee class out of Vladivostok in the general area, but nothing to indicate that either the North Korean frigate or the Russian sub has detected us," the XO said.

"Good," Hardison said. "Let's sit back and enjoy the fireworks."

NKN Frigate Najin

Because the Zodiac had moved from the forward left of the ship, at about ten o'clock, to the forward right of the ship, now at about two o'clock, Cheong moved the machine gun onto the right forward bow. His assistant had kept the spotlight on the Zodiac.

Ping ... ping ...

What was that?

"Aahhhhhhhhhhh? I'm hit! I'm hit! Oh, my arm!"

Cheong glanced over at the junior petty officer, Kim Won-tu. Kim was grasping his bleeding forearm.

Ping ... ping ...

The Navy SEALs had opened fire! Cheong pulled back on the firing mechanism and aimed the powerful machine gun out toward the SEALs' boat. He pulled the trigger. The jackhammer sound of the mighty NSV echoed at the front of the ship.

Chit-a-chit-a—chit-a—chit-a—chit-a—chit-a—chit-a—chit.

Zodiac boat

S*plash-slash-splash—slash-splash—slash-splash—slash-splash.* "They're banging us with machine gun fire!" Jackrabbit said, as water sprayed all around the boat.

"Take this, sucker." Jackrabbit, ignoring the machine gun fire, aimed his rifle back at the ship and pulled the trigger in quick succession.

Bam-bam-bam-bam-bam.

The fireball erupted from the forward section of the ship just as Jackrabbit fired his fourth shot. A loud booming noise rumbled across the water.

The second fireball amidships was more blinding than the first. Then a second later another *BOOM!*

The rain of deadly bullets that had peppered the sea around the Zodiac stopped. Screams from the ship could be heard against the roaring sound of crackling flames leaping into the night air.

"Slow down, Jung-Hoon. I want to see this."

The Zodiac slowed to a crawl, riding the waves as its occupants witnessed the shocking, fiery display. The ship, a sudden and magnificent flaming hulk, cast a bright reflection on the rolling swells. Gunner looked through his binoculars. Multiple fireballs exploded along the deck. Against the image of the exploding fireballs, they saw silhouettes of men diving into the cold water of the Sea of Japan.

"Am I seeing what I think I'm seeing?" Gunner asked. "I think it's breaking in half."

"Sure is, Commander," Jackrabbit said. "Right down the middle."

The two sections of the ship, both now burning silhouettes in the water, had separated. The front two-thirds, which contained the ship's superstructure and command center, was drifting away from the aft section.

The aft section started rising up into the night sky, the propellers pointing up to the crescent moon like one end of a giant see-saw.

As the aft section continued rising, the forward section, floating perhaps a hundred yards off to the right, started doing the same thing, The bow rose from the water as the other end sank. Haunting metallic groaning sounds, the eerie sounds of a ship dying, filled the air.

"That baby's going down fast," Jackrabbit said. And no sooner had he said it, than the aft section slid under the surface.

The front section, now almost vertical in the water, seemed to be pointing up at the North Star. A moment later, as if someone had opened the trapdoor to the graveyard of the sea, the front section slipped under the water and disappeared.

Fire on the water, from oil and fuel, flickered for a while and then burned out.

The three men stared at the empty sea where, moments before, an enemy warship had been firing at them. Even the sailors who had jumped overboard seemed to have vanished. All that was left was the Korean launch, bobbing aimlessly in the swells.

Peace, almost a supernatural peace, enveloped the Zodiac and its occupants.

"I wonder what hit it," Gunner said.

"It sure wasn't my M-16," Jackrabbit said. "Although I'd love to take credit for it."

Jung-Hoon said, "I would guess either a floating mine or possibly a missile fired by a plane over the horizon out to the east of here. Or a submarine."

"Whatever it was, I thank the Good Lord," Gunner said. "That ship was a whole lot bigger than this little boat and had a whole lot more firepower." He exhaled as if he had been holding his breath. "I sure didn't want to become the first American naval officer captured by those Communists since the *Pueblo*."

"You a praying man, Commander?" Jackrabbit asked.

"Not like I should be, Jackrabbit, but I sure have been praying like crazy today."

"Seems like God's in a listening mood," Jackrabbit said. "But right now, we got work to do. The portable GPS device is in that pack over there, Commander. Can you get it for me?"

"You got it."

"Jung-Hoon, give us some light over here."

The powerful flashlight lit up the interior of the Zodiac again. Jackrabbit turned on the GPS and pulled out a nautical chart.

"Okay, we must assume the ship got off a distress message before she went down. This area will be crawling with search planes and other ships looking for survivors. We need to get the heck outa here.

"Look at this nautical chart. Here is our last position when we ditched." Jackrabbit looked at the GPS. "According to the GPS, we should be right here." He pointed to a position on the chart. "That means our nearest landfall is twenty-five miles northwest ... right about here"—he fingered a section of shoreline on the chart—"between the towns of Sinch'ang and Iwŏn. I know I've kind of taken control out here, but once we hit land, Jung-Hoon, you speak their language and you look like 'em. So you're in charge."

The distant roar of a propeller aircraft droned in the skies from the west.

"Search parties are headed this way," Jackrabbit said. "We better get this boat moving. The GPS is ready. I set a course for the northwest, three-one-five. Gunner, you sit up front. I'll sit in the middle. We'll make better time if we even out the weight. Less drag. I'll watch our track on the GPS, Jung-Hoon, to make sure we stay on course."

"I'm ready," Jung-Hoon said, his hand on the throttle of the idling outboard. Jackrabbit held up the GPS and pointed out the direction. Jung-Hoon throttled up the engine just enough to get the boat turned toward the northwest.

"Ready, Commander?"

"Ready."

"Let 'er rip, Jung-Hoon."

Jung-Hoon revved the engine, and the boat picked up speed as it cut across the rolling black water, bouncing and splashing across the swells.

Spurts of cold water sprayed Gunner as the boat moved out, running from the area of the sunken ship.

Gunner checked his watch. In two hours, they would be approaching the North Korean coastline, with a whole host of dangers and challenges that he probably had not even contemplated. He looked back at the two men who had so willingly taken on this rescue mission. And he thanked God.

Soon, with the hum of the engine and the splash of the waves and the sliver crescent of the moon offering a peaceful respite, Gunner closed his eyes, thought of his grandfather, and prayed for protection.

CHAPTER 19

Hongwŏn State Psychiatric Hospital
Hongwŏn, North Korea

Hongwŏn, a town on the east coast of North Korea, sat forty miles as the crow flies from the prison. As they drove there, Staff Sergeant Kang seemed bent on driving as fast as the jeep would go, slinging them around steep curves in the road and then pressing down hard on the accelerator again to pick up more speed, always checking the rearview to see how his passengers were reacting to the ride. Pak sensed that his anger was not only directed at her. She decided that his anger was also focused against Staff Sergeant Mang, who sat beside Pak in the back all the while glaring back at Kang via the rearview mirror.

As they approached the outskirts of Hongwŏn, Kang hit the brakes, slowed the jeep, and turned off the winding, two-lane concrete road onto a long gravel drive with thick woods on both sides.

Kang's words reverberated in her mind—*I am going to kill you.*

Did his turn down this long winding gravel road mark the beginning of the end? The jeep rounded a curve and came to a large opening in the trees.

In the distance was a large single-story stone building. Lights shone in some of the windows, but most were dark. Parked outside were four cars and three vans. The sign over the main entrance proclaimed in large red letters on a white background "Hongwŏn State Psychiatric Hospital." Next to the sign hung a side-view photographic profile of Dear Leader, Kim Jong-il.

Kang slowed as he turned onto the circular driveway, passing by the cars parked on it. He stopped in front of the building.

A solitary guard, dressed in an Army uniform, stood watch at the entrance. Pak decided the guard did not look like Dear Leader's finest.

"Wait here," the colonel's assistant said. She stepped out of the jeep, slammed the door behind her, and strutted past the guard, who did not even acknowledge her. She opened the door of the hospital and marched straight in.

Silence.

Pak could see Kang's eyes in the rearview mirror, leering at her with hatred, ablaze with fury. But still, no words came from him.

Slowly, carefully, he pulled his pistol out and held it up in the air.

Chi-chink.

He chambered a bullet into firing position. Then he turned around and glared at her. He pointed his pistol at her head. "You think you can get away with embarrassing me like this?"

She did not respond. Instead, the words she had memorized came back to her: *A soft answer turneth away wrath.*

"Do you think I am going to let you live, you everlastingly worthless female sheep?" He stuck the barrel against her forehead and pressed hard. "You think you can fool anyone with all that religious garbage about Christianity, do you?" He shoved the barrel so hard against the middle of her forehead that it knocked her back in the seat.

"Do you not know what Marx said? 'Religion is the opiate of the people.' Christianity is for losers! Of all religions, this Christianity of yours is the most despicable! It is more despicable than Islam! More despicable than Buddhism! Than Shintoism! You believe your claims that someone would rise from the dead? Why do you not just deny such despicable lies, and perhaps I shall let you live, you traitorous hog!"

The Lord is in his holy temple. Let all the earth keep silent . . .

"Your Christianity garbage. You do not fool me. It's all a calculated ruse. All you Christians use God talk as a diversionary tactic to manipulate others to get your way! I *hate* you! I hate you all! Now deny your God!" He was screaming in a shrill voice she had not heard before. "Deny him or I will shoot you on the spot! Right now! I said deny!" He again rammed the gun barrel against her skull.

Her head throbbed. Tears welled up in her eyes. In a soft voice she said, "I am sorry, but I cannot and I will not deny him."

Whack!

The butt of his pistol smacked against her lips and teeth. Blood gushed from her mouth and ran down on her clothes.

Just then the front door opened. "Kang, what are you doing?" the colonel's assistant snapped.

"This woman, while you were gone," Kang said, "began a slanderous tirade against Dear Leader himself. She became recalcitrant, calling the Dear Leader a homosexual. I told her to shut up. I reminded her that insults against Dear Leader would not be tolerated. But instead of obeying me, she became more defiant. And she went on, not only to repeat the slanderous charge against Dear Leader, but said that he had received and given sexually transmitted diseases to both men and women alike!"

A pause.

"Yes, Kang," the colonel's assistant said, "I am sure that this wretched refuse of a beaten-up woman said all of these things about Dear Leader in the three or four minutes that I was gone." She closed the door and walked around the back of the jeep. She opened the rear passenger door. "Get out, Pak."

Pak swung her feet down onto the rocky driveway and stood up.

Mang closed the back door and opened the driver's door. She leaned down to look directly at Kang. "You stay here. I will deal with you later."

"You? Deal with me?" Kang screamed. "Will you deal with me by sleeping your way into greater influence with the colonel? I will remind you that I am the one who—"

The colonel's assistant slammed the door, cutting off Kang's tirade and morphing his voice into a garbled mumble inside the jeep.

"Come with me," she said to Pak.

They walked past the old guard and in the front door of the hospital.

The entryway was empty. It sounded hollow. No one manned the nurse's station up front. In fact, the whole front part of the hospital seemed abandoned. Still, Pak sensed someone's eyes upon her.

"This way," the assistant said. They walked down a long abandoned-looking hallway, past two older life-sized photos of Dear Leader that adorned the walls, one on each side.

Some of the hall lights were burned out. All of the doors they passed were closed. About halfway down the main hallway, another hallway went off to the right. "This way," the assistant said, and they made a quick right. Over the second door on the right hung a sign that said EXAMINATION ROOM.

Sergeant Mang delivered three sharp knocks on the door. From within the room, a female voice said, "Enter."

Mang opened the door and walked past an empty examination table with white sheets and restraining straps dangling down to the floor. To the right, seated at a Spartan-looking desk and wearing a long white nurse's uniform, a nurse was bent over a clipboard writing something with a pen.

The nurse turned and looked up with piercing eyes behind plastic, black-rimmed glasses. "This is the patient, I presume?"

"This is the patient," the colonel's assistant snapped.

"Well, well." The nurse stood and turned toward Pak. "Looks like we've had a little burn on the neck." She adjusted her glasses and came in for a closer look. "Hmm, that blister is nearly the size of a Ping Pong ball. This is one of the biggest I've seen in a while." The nurse picked up her clipboard and wrote a note on it. "And what about these cuts on the mouth? They look fresh. They're still bleeding." She took some paper towels and dabbed the right side of Pak's mouth, where most of the blood had collected. "I hate wasting the state's valuable resources on such a thing as this wretch's blood." The nurse held the paper towel up against Pak's lip for a few seconds. "Our records will need to reflect what happened here also, Sergeant. Regulations, you know."

"Yes, of course," the colonel's assistant said. "This was the result of disciplinary measures taken by the driver a few moments ago when I first came in to announce our arrival. I was not in the jeep at the moment, but the official report that he seeks to file indicates that she made certain derogatory comments about Dear Leader."

The nurse shifted her eyes back and forth between Pak and Staff Sergeant Mang. "Derogatory comments about Dear Leader?" She took the blood-soaked paper towel away and tossed it into a white trash can. "If she insulted Dear Leader, she is fortunate to still have her teeth."

The nurse dabbed another paper towel against Pak's mouth. This one did not seem to absorb as much blood. "That should stop the bleed-ing." The nurse removed the second paper towel and tossed it in the trash can with the first. She picked up her clipboard and started writ-ing again. "My compliments to the disciplinary practices at Kim Yŏng-nam." She scribbled a few more notes. "I take it that the blister also is a result of a well-deserved disciplinary matter?"

"Yes," the colonel's assistant said. "She is an employee at the prison. However, she was disciplined because she was caught stealing."

"Caught stealing?" The nurse looked up from her pad. "Stealing what?"

"Medicine."

"Medicine?"

"Yes. She stole medicine and attempted to administer it to one of the prisoners."

The nurse slammed her clipboard down on her desk. "Does she not realize that medicine is an expensive and rare commodity?"

"I do believe after our little disciplinary session, she now realizes this."

"Do not fear, Sergeant Mang," the nurse said, "by the time we have finished our readjustment procedures here at the hospital, I do not believe you will have any other problems from this patient."

"Excellent, nurse. I will report this to the colonel," Mang said. "Would you like for me to remove her handcuffs now?"

"Hmm . . ." The nurse looked at Pak. "Let us get her on the examination table and put the restraining straps on her. Once we do that, then you can remove the handcuffs."

"Certainly. Lie down, Pak."

Pak positioned herself on the table, face up.

The nurse tightened the straps, first across her feet, then across her shoulders.

"All right, Sergeant, I don't think she is going anywhere. You can take the cuffs off."

The nurse grabbed Pak's arms and held them. When she did, the sergeant reached over, inserted a key into each handcuff, and the tight cuffs, which had been cutting into her wrists, fell off.

"Be still and I will tie one more strap," the nurse said.

Pak didn't move, and the nurse tightened a third strap around her waist area. The restraining straps now held her down at her shoulders, her waist, and her feet. The straps weren't too tight, and she was able to breathe.

"There," the nurse said. "I do not think she is going anywhere.

Now we can begin our testing." She walked back over to the desk and picked up her clipboard and began scribbling again. "Sergeant, I understand there is an issue as to whether she is competent to understand the charges against her, and whether she is competent to face a firing squad?"

"Yes," the colonel's assistant said. "That is one of the issues that Colonel Song is instructing us to look into."

"Very well, Sergeant," the nurse said. "Please tell the good colonel that we will make competency determinations on her ability to face a firing squad, and that he will have his determination soon."

Pak's heart beat with a renewed fervor. *Whatever your will, Lord.*

The nurse wrote some more. "Sergeant, you are welcome to stay if you care to observe our testing. But this could take a while."

"That won't be necessary. There is business to attend to back at the camp," she said and checked her watch to see if there still was time for her meeting with the colonel. "I will leave the patient in your hands."

"As you wish, Sergeant." The nurse stood and extended a stiff arm to the sergeant, who took her hand and shook it and then walked out the door. The door closed behind her with a click.

Lord, not my will but thy will be done. For thine is the kingdom and the power and the glory forever.

Pak opened her eyes. The nurse was standing next to her. The black plastic glasses were gone. So was the black angry look in her eyes.

"So what was your *real* crime, my sister?" The woman's voice and tone had softened. "You tried to give some medicine to one of the poor old Americans?"

Even a fool is deemed wise when he is silent.

"Oh, you do not think anyone knows about the old Americans up there? Do you not know it is the worst-kept secret in this region?"

She is trying to trick me. If I acknowledge that Americans are there, she will report that I revealed a state secret, and they will behead me.

"For what it is worth, I think you did the right thing trying to help the old man. It is a shame that they will all be gone soon, and no one will ever know that they have been there all these years. Let me take a closer look at that blister."

The nurse bent down and looked carefully at the blister on Pak's neck.

"Dear Leader brags about capturing the *Pueblo* and how we supposedly beat the Americans in the Great War sixty-some years ago. But then he hides this dirty little state secret. Of course we in the hospital know because they have brought them up here for treatment for years. They swear us to secrecy and make it a capital offense if anyone talks. So only hush-hush rumors percolate. They have shot a few people who talked too much about the old Americans and even shot some people who innocently heard too much information.

"Of course, if you ask me, it is typical Pyongyang hypocrisy. It is as if they are afraid that the Americans would nuke us if they knew. Brag about the *Pueblo*. But keep this under the covers. It sounds like the great Dear Leader is not as brave as he would have his subjects believe. Hmm . . ." She eyed Pak's neck. "A second-degree burn. A cigarette?"

Surely this was all part of the psychological testing, Pak thought. How could a woman go from so harsh to so soft in such a short period of time?

"Don't want to talk? Okay. Hold still while I apply some antiseptic on that blister. I won't touch it, just drip a little of this on it."

She held a bottle over Pak's neck. Three drops fell on the blister. The soothing was instantaneous. "I am sorry, but that is all the antiseptic we have at the moment. They do not give us much. Medicine is scarce. But do not worry. I will send the doctor into town to the pharmacy for more tomorrow. He is a good man. He is one of us."

One of us? What does she mean? Pak wondered.

"I will loosen these straps in a moment." She turned and walked back across the room. "As soon as our friend has had time to get back on the road. I must put on a show to convince her and her superiors that I will treat you in the same brutal fashion that they treat you. But do not worry. It is all a show." The nurse reached up into a cabinet. "We have a small amount of ointment called aloe vera. Smuggled in by Christian missionaries from Seoul. A local pharmacist gets it for us. He is a good man. He is one of us."

She removed the tube from the cabinet and walked back over to Pak. "I will apply a small amount around the base of the blister. But I warn you, it can be cold at first."

Pak watched the woman squirt green ointment onto her finger. "I'll try not to touch the blister. So be still."

At first, the ointment felt cold, and Pak cringed when it touched her skin. But then the woman rubbed the ointment onto her neck in slow, circular motions, carefully avoiding the blister. "That feels good," she said, forgetting her self-imposed vow of silence. "Thank you."

"You are welcome. Let me do this a bit longer. Then I will loosen these straps." She continued to rub gently around the blister.

"There," she said. "No more aloe. We shall pray that the doctor gets more from the pharmacist tomorrow."

The nurse removed the restraints from Pak's feet. Next she removed the waist strap, and finally she took off the collarbone strap.

"I am sorry we had to do that. I tried not to make the straps too tight. I hope you could breathe okay."

"Yes, I could," Pak said.

The nurse examined her mouth. "What really happened here? Did the dog hit you with a pistol?"

"How did you know?"

"And let me also guess. You never said a word about the great Dear Leader, but the dog made that up as a story to give to the lady sergeant."

Pak was not sure what to think. "How do you know these things?"

"What is your name, my dear?"

"Pak. I am Pak."

"Well, Pak, I know how they operate. If they want to strike you, they make up a reason. If they want to cut you, they invent an accusation against you. If they want to torture you or shoot you, then they make up stories that you have slandered Dear Leader. That way, they have a range of options, all the way up to murdering you, if that is what they wish to do. Now then, is there anything you want to ask me?"

Pak hesitated. "What did you mean a moment ago when you described both the doctor who works here and the pharmacist as 'one of us'?"

The nurse flashed a beatific smile and then rubbed Pak's hair. "What do you think I meant?"

"Perhaps ... perhaps you are suggesting that we share a ... a common philosophy?" Pak asked.

"Communism is a philosophy," the nurse said. "Would you like a glass of water?"

"Yes, please. Thank you."

The nurse walked over to a sink and ran water from the faucet into a glass. "Let me help you sit up. There. Lean forward and I will put pillows behind your back."

Pak leaned forward, and the nurse fluffed three pillows and slid them under her back. The pillows felt so soothing. She sipped the water.

"No," the nurse said, "a philosophy is something shared by the likes of the animals who burned your neck and tried breaking your teeth by hitting you with a pistol. Philosophies come from man. What we share is not a common philosophy, but rather a common relationship with one who is living, who makes us sisters."

Their eyes met. Pak said, "A relationship with one who was and who is and who is to come."

The nurse smiled. "A relationship with the one who lived, and died, and rose again, and lives forevermore." She reached over and opened her arms. They hugged and tears flooded Pak's eyes. The nurse squeezed her tight in her arms. "It is all right, Pak. We will protect you. The doctor will declare that you are insane and unable to stand trial. Whatever it takes, we will do."

CHAPTER 20

Zodiac boat
nearing North Korean coastline

In an earlier life, before he left the private sector to return to the Navy, Lieutenant Commander Gunner McCormick worked as a commodities analyst in the mammoth building of the New York Mercantile Exchange located in the heart of Manhattan's financial district, on the bank of the Hudson River. He worked nights and monitored the prices of overseas commodities coming from foreign markets. The job paid him considerably more than his Navy job—not that he needed the money. But the hours were bad. He worked the midnight shift, from just before twelve to eight and sometimes nine in the morning. After work he would go home to his posh Manhattan flat, sleep most of the day, get up in the afternoon, have breakfast, and then do it all over again.

The night shifts were lonely, and oftentimes, between the reports streaming in from overseas markets, Gunner would grab a cup of black coffee, wander over to the large windows overlooking the Hudson River and, from his tenth-floor office, gaze out in the black of night at the river, at the occasional boat passing by, and at all the lights shining on the Jersey shore across the way.

The few lights he was now seeing on the other side of the narrowing band of black water that separated the Zodiac from the world's most oppressive Communist regime provided a stark visual contrast. He thought back to the myriad of blinking lights and colors reflecting on the water of the Hudson, a symbol of a powerful economic life, a bustling capitalistic democracy. As they moved closer to shore, Gunner could see only two or three solitary lights on land. There was no loom of city lights anywhere onshore. There was no reflection of lights on the black water. There was only darkness, a darkness that was the end result of a government taking, and taking, and taking some more. In the end, lifelessness.

Finally, Gunner could see a dim outline of the land that somehow, some way, had taken his grandfather. Somewhere beyond the dark and desolate shoreline and the mountains rising behind it, in this land of mystery and evil, were the answers to his questions.

Their gasoline was almost gone. They had two options: they could remain at sea and die or go ashore and fight to survive. And maybe solve the mystery of the missing Americans that had gone on for so many years.

"Let's hold up for a minute and get organized," Jackrabbit said. "GPS says we're one mile from the shoreline."

Jung-Hoon let up on the throttle. The boat eased along at idle speed.

"Okay," Jackrabbit said, "let's review the first phase of our landing plan. We hit the beach right straight ahead of us, about ten miles northeast of the town of Sinch'ang. There's a road snaking along the coastline." He stopped and took hold of his left upper arm, took a deep breath, and continued with, "We're sixty miles from the Hamhung area. So we've got sixty miles to cover to see if the camps really are there.

"When we hit the beach, we need to keep moving as far as we can and as fast as we can while it's still dark. I figure if we don't have to stop for anything, we can move about five miles in an hour and a half. Doing the math, that's about ten miles in three hours … if we're on foot.

"Right now, it's twenty-thirty-hundred hours local time. We hit the beach in thirty minutes, assuming we don't run into any Koreans who distract us with target practice. We change clothes, deflate the raft, and bury it in the sand along with the motor. Then we move inland and head southwest along the road. We need to take advantage of the night and move as far as we can toward Hongwŏn.

"By oh-four-hundred, we move up into the mountains, establish base camp, and stand alternating watches while the others get shut-eye. Jung-Hoon will go into town to collect intel. When he gets back, he hits the rack.

"Remember. The night is our friend. We move quickly, rapidly, silently." He paused for a moment and again pulled his left upper arm against his body.

The wind had died down some, and the boat floated in toward shore, the outboard at idle speed. They could hear the soft rhythmic murmur of the waves breaking against the shoreline.

"Questions?" Jackrabbit said.

"I've got one," Gunner said.

"Fire away, Commander."

"What's wrong with your arm?"

"Nothing's wrong with my arm," Jackrabbit snapped.

"Nothing wrong with your arm? Then why do you keep holding it? Sure looks like something's wrong."

"Like I said," Jackrabbit snapped again, "nothing's wrong with it. We've gotta get moving. No time to mess with anybody's arm."

Gunner quickly ran his finger down Jackrabbit's upper arm and felt a tear in the wetsuit. "You've been hit."

"Nothing to it," Jackrabbit insisted. "Not the first time I've had a little ole bullet graze me. I've been splashing it with some cold saltwater. Keeps the bleeding down. It's nothing."

It struck Gunner that with all the hasty planning to get the mission started, one thing had been left out. Antibiotics. In fact, they had no first-aid supplies. Nothing.

"Jung-Hoon, when we get to a town, a store, take some money and find some first-aid stuff, especially some antibiotics to get on that wound."

"That isn't necessary." Jackrabbit snorted. "That's a waste of valuable time and resources. You aren't a real man unless you've taken at least one bullet in your lifetime. Flesh wound. It'll be all right."

"You heard me, Jung-Hoon."

"Got it, boss. In fact, one of the underground contacts that Reverend Lee gave us is a pharmacist."

"Great," Gunner said, "let's get this boat moving again."

Jung-Hoon revved the outboard and steered the Zodiac back toward the northwest. The roar of the outboard blended harmonically with the *swish, swish, swish* as the Zodiac cut a path across the swells.

Gunner forced his mind to rest. The next fifteen minutes might be his last chance to relax before he either escaped North Korea or died there. He stared straight ahead. There. The dark mass of land, outlined dimly against the sky, seemed to rise higher as they came in closer to shore. Above the dark expanse of land, an army of stars spread out. The sharp black division between the darkness rising from the sea and the field of stars clearly showed the tops of the great mountains that dominate the country. He remembered the words of an American colonel serving in the Korean War who, in describing the Korean landscape, said, "Behind every mountain, there was another mountain."

Jung-Hoon shut off the outboard.

"Okay, we're about two hundred yards from shore," Jackrabbit said. "Jung-Hoon and I paddle in the rest of the way. No noise. When I give you the cue, Commander, you get out of the boat and pull us in. No more talking until we hit the beach. If anybody's out there, well … put it this way … they don't need to know we're here. We've wasted enough valuable ammunition already this evening."

"Got it," Gunner said. "Mum 'til we hit the beach."

Jung-Hoon and Jackrabbit each grabbed one of the two small paddles.

This was their last push in to shore. The sound of the breakers crashing on the beach was now much louder. This was the same sound that Gunner had heard over and over, thousands of times, during summer vacations at Nags Head and Cape Hatteras.

The moment had arrived.

Gunner turned around and saw Jackrabbit give a thumbs-up. He waited for the next breaker to shove the boat a bit farther along. Then, in the respite between waves, with the Zodiac still moving toward shore, he put his right leg over the side of the boat and waited for the next wave to shove them in closer to shore.

Even the thermal suit could not totally block the cold of the frigid water. A second later, his foot touched bottom, and he remembered Neil Armstrong making that "one small step for man." On the moon, there was no evil. But the land on which he would soon stand was a land full of evil, from the DMZ to the Chinese border, from the East Sea to the West Sea. "Deliver us from evil," Gunner whispered as he slid out of the Zodiac, landing with both feet on the bottom.

He stood on the sand of North Korea, waist deep in water. He held his thumb up to the two men in the boat. Jackrabbit slipped over the left side of the boat. With Gunner stabilizing the boat on one side and Jackrabbit on the other, another thumbs-up signal brought Jung-Hoon out of the boat at the back. He had already tilted up the outboard to keep it from dragging on the bottom.

The three men each grabbed a handle on the boat and pulled it along through the surf and up onto the beach.

Jackrabbit leaned over and whispered to Gunner, "Get your NVDs, your night visions, Commander. Screw the silencer on your M-16. Stay here and guard the boat. Jung-Hoon and I will check out the beach. Make sure the coast is clear."

Gunner nodded.

"Let's get moving."

Gunner pulled out his night-vision goggles and strapped them on his head. The dark world was suddenly lit in a ghastly green. A ledge of rocks, perhaps ten feet high, rose just beyond the wide expanse of beach. And beyond that, mountains. The beach looked empty. Jung-Hoon and Jackrabbit were jogging in opposite directions to survey the situation.

Gunner reached for his M-16, popped in a thirty-round magazine, and screwed the silencer on the end of the barrel. He mounted the night-vision scope on his rifle and twisted the thumb screw to lock it in place.

Gunner fixed his eyes on the natural rocky ledge. Until now, Jackrabbit had done all the killing on this mission. But if someone crossed that ledge, with both Jackrabbit and Jung-Hoon out of range, the responsibility for killing would fall on his shoulders.

In the solitude of the moment, with the swishing of the waves peacefully lapping the dark beach behind him, he felt, for the first time, a tinge of loneliness. He had resolved that he might have to take a life, maybe more than one, during the course of this mission. But what if a teenager traversed the rocks? Or a young couple looking for a place to make out? Or an old man trying to make it down to the surf to do a little night fishing? What if he had to take an innocent life to protect the secrecy of the mission?

More waves washed up on the beach, now in increasing frequency with the rising tide, each time reaching closer to the boat. Gunner had read about the rapid tide changes in the Yellow Sea, which made MacArthur's heroic landing at Inchon that much more risky. He was less sure about tide fluctuations in the Sea of Japan. He wished now that he had put more time into advance planning. They had forgotten about antibiotics. First-aid supplies. Now he was dealing with the uncertainty on the timing and level of the tide.

The water seemed to be rising at an alarming rate, running up closer with each cycle. Or was it his imagination? . . . No, not his imagination.

Gunner decided to pull the boat up farther before the tide took it back out to sea. Crouching low, he dragged it across the sand to the base of the rock barrier. The scraping sound of rubber against sand blended with the crashing waves of the surf. He dragged the stern of the Zodiac around so the boat was now resting against the rocks, as snug against the rock wall as he could get it.

Thump.

What was that?

The noise came from above his head, from on the rock ledge. His heart pounded.

He pressed his body against the base of the rock wall and froze. The only sound was from the wind and the surf.

Two beams of light flashed on above his head and pointed out to sea. Headlights.

Gunner pressed harder against the jagged rocks and looked up. The light beams disappeared. Then, voices!

Chi-chink.

He worked the action on the M-16, sliding a bullet into the firing chamber. He tried to suppress the sound of his breathing.

The voices grew louder. Whoever they were, they were coming closer. He heard two voices. Male. Possibly more. Definitely two.

Gunner craned his head back and looked up, back across his left shoulder in the direction of the voices.

A second or two later, two silhouettes appeared at the edge of the ledge. He could clearly see them from his position. They wore the rounded caps with short bills of military uniforms.

He slid off the NVDs, letting them dangle by a strap, and brought the rifle to his shoulder. Through the night scope, he trained the crosshairs on the chest of the one on the left. His right finger caressed the trigger.

Back as a hunter in his native Virginia, even on the grounds and in the woods at Corbin Hall, he'd shot plenty of ducks and deer. But never had he come close to training his sights on a man, even as a SEAL in Afghanistan.

Through the infrared crosshairs, he could watch the two guards or police or whatever they were as they chatted in what seemed excited tones and pointed out to sea. Then one, the one on the right, looked down, right toward him!

Gunner centered the crosshairs between the man's eyes and held his aim. Had he been spotted? The man kept looking down in his direction and speaking in an excited voice.

Do I take them both out? he wondered. I might not be as good as Jackrabbit, but I'm good enough to pick off these two.

The other man looked down in Gunner's direction. Could they see him? He was all in black, even his face. Was he blending in against the dark rocks? Was the Zodiac in far enough?

If they could see him, he had to take them out. He slowed his breathing. Then he froze.

The two men turned and walked away.

He heard the sound of a cranking vehicle.

Headlights again.

The sound of tires against gravel.

"North Korean National Guard." Gunner looked to his right. Jung-Hoon was a few feet away. "I do not think they saw us, but we cannot know with certainty," he whispered.

Then Jackrabbit joined them, jogging in from the opposite direction. "You did the right thing not to shoot 'em, Commander," he whispered. "Last thing we need is to start a massive manhunt this early in the game."

"You saw?"

"The whole thing."

"You think they saw anything?"

"I don't think so," Jackrabbit said. "Probably wouldn't have left if they did. Good thing you hauled the Zodiac up. But we need to assume they did. If they saw us and thought we were a commando unit, they may have gone back for reinforcements rather than try to take us on by themselves."

"So what do we do?" Gunner asked.

"We need to get out of here now," Jackrabbit said. "No time to bury the boat and motor. Let's change clothes, deflate the boat, and hide the boat and motor behind these rocks. Jung-Hoon, stand watch while the commander and I change."

"Got it," Jung-Hoon said.

Gunner stripped off the wetsuit. The cold air felt like he was standing in a freezer with a wind tunnel. Goose bumps popped out all over his body. He reached down into one of the seabags for thermal underwear and pulled it on. The warmth was immediate. He then slipped into black jeans, a black T-shirt, a black pullover, and a heavily insulated black jacket. He put on thermal socks, gloves, a black knitted skull cap, and black combat boots.

He looked over and saw that Jackrabbit had beaten him again and was already dressed and letting air out of the Zodiac.

"Pull some of those rocks back, Commander," Jackrabbit said.

The rocks were about the size of cement blocks, not too heavy to move by hand. Gunner chucked roughly twenty of them out of the way. Then he and Jackrabbit dragged the deflated Zodiac, along with the outboard, and shoved it up against the base of the rocks, rolling the deflated boat into a narrow ridge of black, the outboard sticking out behind it.

"Let's cover 'em up," Jackrabbit said and started piling the rocks back against the ledge, covering the evidence.

Soon there was no sign that anyone had been on the beach.

Jung-Hoon washed the black grease from his face, since he would have to talk with North Korean civilians, but Jackrabbit and Gunner kept their faces black.

"I'll go up first to see if anybody's up there," Jackrabbit said. "Wait for my signal."

The rock wall in one area rose off the sand at an angle a little steeper than forty-five degrees. It did not appear to be an impossible climb, but was not an easy one either.

Gunner watched as Jackrabbit put his foot on the first rock, then the second, and then the third. With a few more steps, Jackrabbit reached the top of the ledge. He looked to the left and then to the right. He looked down and waved a come-on signal with his arm.

Gunner stepped on the first rock, then the second, the third, and finally reached up and clasped Jackrabbit's hand. With a yanking heave from Jackrabbit, he sprang to the top of the ledge. Jackrabbit reached down to assist Jung-Hoon.

Gunner stood there, taking in his first full view of North Korea. They were on a rocky plateau area, rising about ten feet above the beach, that stretched north and south along the coast for as far as he could see with his NVDs. About a hundred yards or so in from the edge of the plateau, a two-lane road snaked along the coastline.

The three stood as if explorers of old reaching the New World, but with a few major differences. They were a three-man, self-financed commando squad dressed in state-of-the-art black thermal gear in a hostile, foreign land, each with an M-16 with night scope and silencer slung over his shoulder, and with a large backpack containing supplies needed for the mission. Each man also packed a .45-caliber pistol with ten rounds of deadly Winchester "silvertip" bullets.

Jung-Hoon had a coded list of local contacts opposed to the regime in Pyongyang. Many on the list were Christians worshiping in underground churches whose names and contact information had been supplied by Pastor Lee. Other names on the list Jung-Hoon had accumulated from his own sources. Every person on the list would be tortured and/or executed if Dear Leader or any of the government officials in Pyongyang learned of their opposition to the regime.

Jackrabbit pulled his arm tight against his body, but kept turned away from the others to keep them from seeing his pain. "We'll cross the road and move south, following it as long as we can. If we can get past the next town without being seen, it'll clip twelve to fifteen miles off the distance to where we'll set up camp, get some shut-eye when daylight gets here."

"Let's do it," Gunner said.

"If a vehicle approaches," Jackrabbit said, "hit the deck. Let's roll."

Jackrabbit jogged across the narrow road and moved through the ditch and up the other side into a field of dead grass. Gunner and Jung-Hoon were right behind him, matching almost step for step.

"Head to the treeline," Jackrabbit said.

A couple minutes later, they approached a line of fir trees, which marked the beginning of the steep rise of rock and earth along the coast, leading to the rugged mountainous heart of the country to their west. The treeline stood closer than Gunner first thought, perhaps only ten yards from the road.

"This treeline runs along the road. Let's move as fast and as far as we can. We'll keep pushing until an hour before light, then look for a place to pitch camp. Tomorrow, Jung-Hoon here can spend some of your cash, Commander, and buy us a vehicle to get around in. That should help." He held on to his arm again and almost seemed to grimace. "Okay, let's go."

The trio headed south into the dark and cold Korean night.

CHAPTER 21

Headquarters
East Sea Fleet
Navy of the Democratic People's Republic
T'oejo-dong, North Korea

What do you mean the *Najin* has been sunk?" Admiral Rhee In-gu screamed at his aide, Senior Captain Choo Shin-so, as if Captain Choo had done something wrong. Rhee was commander of the North Korean Navy's East Sea Fleet, one of two four-star admirals in the Navy of the Democratic People's Republic.

"The *Najin* is the flagship of the entire fleet! Do you not understand that the *Najin* is Dear Leader's pride and joy? He has said as much many times!" Admiral Rhee threw his arms in the air. "Do *you* want to be the one to tell the general admiral? Do *you* want to be the one to break the news to Dear Leader? That his flagship is gone? That you and all your subordinates failed to carry out all defensive measures to protect her?"

The admiral turned and walked away from his ornate desk. He walked over to the back wall of his office and stood before two life-size oil paintings, each lit by a spotlight. One painting showed Dear Leader, resplendent in his green medal-adorned Army uniform. All senior officers in the North Korean military were commanded to display this portrait. The other, of an elderly officer in his service dress-blue Navy uniform, portrayed the legendary General Admiral Kim Il-chol, the five-star commander of all naval forces of the Democratic People's Republic, who was retired at the age of eighty.

From the canvases on the wall, their eyes bore into him. Dear Leader had entrusted to him command of the entire East Sea Fleet and, with it, the flagship *Najin*. He was one of only two four-star admirals who served in the Navy. His East Sea Fleet was bigger than the Yellow Sea Fleet. Rumors flowed that he, Fleet Admiral Rhee In-gu, stood next in line to pin a fifth star to his collar and become the next general admiral of the Navy.

But now, this? How could it be? All gone ... his ambitions of becoming general admiral had just sunk with the *Najin*. His East Sea Fleet had lost the nation's most prestigious flagship.

And now his rival, West Fleet Admiral Cha, would surely be anointed with the fifth star.

Rhee knew the price of failure. He would be lucky if Dear Leader let him keep any of his stars. He would be lucky if Dear Leader did not order him shot by a firing squad.

He turned back and glared at Captain Choo, who was still standing at attention. "I wish for you to explain two things to me, Captain." He slammed his fist on the desk, which startled the captain. Rhee believed the captain needed startling. His senior officers had become soft. "One, how did this happen? And two, how many survivors do we have?"

"Fleet Admiral, sir." The captain adjusted his blue tie, as if that adjustment would somehow make what he was about to say more acceptable. "From the information we have been able to gather, by all accounts, it appears that a special commando unit of US Navy SEALs is responsible for the sinking of the *Najin*."

"US Navy SEALs?" The fleet admiral slammed his desk again. "I know that American propaganda boasts that the SEALs are the world's most elite commando unit. But sink a great warship? In North Korean territorial waters?" He swiped his hand through his hair. "Explain! Explain *that* to me, Captain!"

"Sir, we believe the Americans dropped the SEALs in by parachute from a stealth bomber. We believe this because of a brief blip on the radar screen that disappeared in the vicinity of the ship. We did not detect the airplane on our radar because it was stealth. But we spotted on the radar screen the parachute deployment.

"Our theory is that the SEALs swam under the ship and attached magnetic explosives to the hull and then detonated the explosives remotely."

"Magnetic explosives?" Admiral Rhee shook his head. "That is the stupidest explanation I ever heard! Did you ever consider the possibility that the South Koreans or the Americans launched a submarine attack?"

"We did consider all that, Admiral. But one of the survivors, the ship's forward lookout, reported seeing a SEAL team in the water near the ship. In fact, the ship went to general quarters before she blew and had opened fire on the SEAL team with a bow-mounted NSV machine gun. The captain of the *Najin* tried to take the SEALs captive and sent a launch with Marines to capture them. But the SEALs got into a gunfight with the Marines and shot them all before the ship opened fire with the machine gun. These SEALs, they are excellent sharpshooters." The senior captain spoke with a tinge of admiration in his voice for the SEALs.

Admiral Rhee glared at the captain, not appreciating his praise of the SEALs' marksmanship.

The senior captain adjusted his tie again. "The other survivor, the ship's radar operator, corroborated seeing the blip on the screen. Shore radar operators had spotted this same blip."

"Wait ... did you say the *other* survivor?"

The captain hesitated. His contorted facial expression suggested something ominous. "The *Najin* went down rapidly, sir. And I regret to inform you, my fleet admiral"—he hesitated, stammered, and looked down at the floor—"there were only two survivors."

"What?"

Admiral Rhee walked behind his desk and reached up into a cabinet for a greenish bottle half full of Chamisul soju. He poured a healthy dose into a glass and gulped a huge swallow of the potent liquor. He would have downed the whole glass, but he had to remain sober. This was a crisis, and he was in charge. Tomorrow was tomorrow.

He looked back at the captain. "We have rescue boats in the area continuing the search for possible survivors?"

"Yes, sir, Admiral. We have three Komar-class missile boats crisscrossing the area now, sir, with two more on the way."

"What have they found so far?" the admiral demanded.

"The debris you typically find floating after a sinking. Plastic bottles. Items of clothing." The senior captain paused. "But perhaps the most interesting thing they found, my admiral, is this."

The captain reached into his attaché case, pulled out a brown plastic container, and slid it across the admiral's desk. "This was found in the water less than one kilometer from where the *Najin* went down, sir. Three of these were floating on the surface."

Admiral Rhee picked up the container and examined it. Like most senior military officers in the DPRK, Rhee could understand enough English to comprehend what he was reading.

Three large letters, "MRE," were printed across the top of the sealed bag.

Just under the letters was a sketch of two men sitting with propped-up guns. And to the right of the sketch were the words "Menu #19 Beef Roast with Vegetables." Below that, the words "US Government Property" were followed by "Ameriqual Packaging, Evansville, IN."

Rhee slammed the MRE down on his desk. "So it *was* the Americans!"

"Yes, Admiral," Captain Choo said. "Because we found three of these packages, it had to be the Americans. There is no other explanation as to why these were found floating in the water. And this finding, sir, corroborates the theory that SEAL-team commandos blew up the ship. It weakens the submarine-torpedo theory. Submarines have regular food on board. They do not use MREs. They would not eject sealed MREs into the water."

"Yes, I am beginning to give some credibility to that theory," the admiral said. He turned and walked back over to the portraits. He crossed his arms across his chest and tipped his head to one side as he looked up at the portrait of Dear Leader. He tapped his chin with his fist. "Assuming that we are right and this crime is the work of Navy SEALs, then we must ask this question: Is this a one-time hit against our ship? Perhaps in retaliation for our attack on their carrier? This I would guess to be the case."

He did an about-face, pivoting back to face Captain Choo.

"If it is a one-time hit, then we have to assume that the SEALs headed out to sea, presumably to rendezvous with a Los Angeles–class submarine." He picked up the glass of soju and took another swig. "But if not ... what if they are not finished? That is a question we must examine. Would you not agree, Captain?"

"Yes, that is a good question, Admiral." The captain nodded, as if in relieved agreement that the admiral was seeking his advice rather than preparing to order punishment.

"What if," Rhee continued, "they were on a reconnaissance mission to infiltrate our beaches, but the *Najin* got in their way?"

"A good question, Admiral." Captain Choo nodded again.

"Or what if ... what if their mission was twofold? First, to sink the *Najin*, to make it appear that a sub had done it, and then to infiltrate our coastline?"

"An even better question, Admiral," the captain said, becoming more enthusiastic as he realized the admiral was no longer focused on him. "We must consider this possibility, sir."

"They had hoped to secretly attach explosives to the hull of the *Najin* and not be seen, thus making us think a torpedo did it. But"—Rhee held up his index finger—"but things did not go as they planned. They were spotted by the crew of the *Najin*. A firefight broke out, and during the firefight, they dropped evidence in the water, which we have recovered, and now we know they were there."

"Yes, and may I add one other observation, Admiral?" the captain said.

Rhee finished off the soju and poured another glass. "Yes, go ahead, Captain. What is it?"

"It would seem to me, sir, that a SEAL team going in for a quick hit-and-run mission would not bring a supply of food. As I said, sir, we discovered three of these floating on the surface, and we assume they have more in their boat. To me, sir, this says they are on a longer mission."

Rhee took another sip. He was beginning to feel the warming effect of the soju. The captain was beginning to make sense. "This means, Captain, that somewhere along a ... say fifty-mile stretch of coastline, is an American Navy SEAL team, a team of professional killers with the expertise to sink a mighty warship and the marksmanship skills that pose a threat to anyone in the DPRK, including Dear Leader. They are either preparing to hit our beaches or already have hit the beach."

"Yes, I think that is a reasonable assumption, Admiral." The captain nodded.

"We must be ready," Admiral Rhee said. "Post Marine units on the coast at one-mile intervals along a stretch of beach starting at"—he walked over to the wall beside the inside door to his office—"Tanch'on, north of the attack on our ship, and southwest along the coast all the way to Hongwŏn. That is a stretch of about sixty miles. If the SEALs attempt to come ashore, we will give them a royal dose of hospitality, courtesy of the Democratic People's Republic of Korea."

"Yes, my admiral. And if I may add, sir, this is an example of brilliant leadership under fire, sir. This is another example of why Dear Leader appointed you over your rival admirals to command the East Sea Fleet. Your superior leadership, sir, will soon lead to your ascension to command over the entire Navy!"

"Perhaps," Rhee said, knowing the captain's comments were mostly about protecting his own future. The captain hoped to become the senior aide to the general admiral of the Navy and to become a fleet commander himself. "But you're wasting time, Captain. Get those Marines posted. Now."

"Yes, Admiral. Right away, sir!"

"Also, get as many boats into the area as possible. Continue search activities in the East Sea throughout the night. There may be other survivors. Resume search by air first thing in the morning."

"Yes, sir."

"Also notify Army Command. I don't need General Sokcho up in a wad and complaining to Dear Leader that the Navy is overstepping the Army's boundaries by posting Marine guards along the coast without consulting him. In fact, tell him that we would request and welcome the assistance of some of his National Guard units, despite their incompetence, along the coast at points north of Tanch'on and south of Hongwŏn. That will make them feel like they are part of the operation and give them something to do but will keep his bumbling tin-horn soldiers out of the way of our Marines, guarding sections of the beach that this SEAL team is not likely to land on."

"Understood, sir."

"That will be all, Captain."

"Aye, sir."

The aide turned and left Rhee's office.

Rhee looked at the red telephone on his desk—the secure telephone to Pyongyang. He grabbed the bottle of soju, sat down in the swivel chair behind his desk, and commenced a bottoms-up maneuver. He would need every drop of soju to calm his nerves for what he was about to do.

To break the news to Dear Leader that the Navy's pride-and-joy flagship had been sunk by American Navy commandos? Or even to tell the general admiral? To admit that he had failed?

His last act had been to give orders. And indeed, he knew these were good orders that would be carried out. These were the correct orders under these circumstances of colossal failure.

But hope? Where was hope? His destiny, always, had been to become general admiral of the Navy.

And now? With the flagship of the East Sea Fleet sunk on his watch? With 180 sailors and officers drowned in an instant?

Often he had wondered why Communism had officially banned Christianity all those years ago. Was Marx right? Was Christianity really the opiate of the people? At least those fanatical Christians had something to hope for, even if their hope was in a man who had been crucified so long ago ... a man they claimed rose from the dead. How could that be?

He finished the soju.

Was it so wrong to give someone a bit of hope? No. Not wrong. Especially if that hope could somehow deaden the pain.

Soju deadened pain. But not enough. Soju was temporary. It could not alter reality.

The admiral opened the center drawer of his desk. His pistol was loaded and ready to end his pain. If only ...

He thought again of what the Christians said. Would Christianity have given him hope? Could it now give him hope? Were the Communists liars? Would he ever know the truth?

He closed the drawer and sat there, his head down. He leaned forward, staring down at his desktop.

No hope.

His career was finished.

Indeed, *he* was finished.

No reason to live.

He opened the center drawer and pulled out his pistol.

He cocked it, put the barrel in his mouth, and pulled the trigger.

East coast of North Korea
along the road between Iwŏn and Sinch'ang

The snow had started falling a little while ago and was getting progressively heavier as the three-man invasion force moved parallel to the road, along the edge of the treeline. They had been on the move for the better part of an hour. According to their GPS handheld, they had covered five miles and were less than five miles from the town of Sinch'ang, their first destination point. They were headed toward Hamhung, which was in the general area where the prison camps were rumored to be located.

The distance between the edge of the treeline and the side of the winding, two-lane coastal road had narrowed. The men were moving through snow accumulation on the side of a ravine next to the treeline, perhaps twenty feet from the road's edge.

The temperature hovered just below freezing. The wind had died down, which helped them stay surprisingly warm in their thermal winter gear.

Based on what he had seen so far, Gunner had come to one of two conclusions. One, either they had landed in a desolate and isolated section of the North Korean coastline, or two, North Koreans do not drive much at night. Since the close call with the two North Korean National Guardsmen back on the beach, not a single vehicle had passed them.

He then came to another conclusion — nature called, and it called with a vengeance.

"Hey, Jackrabbit," Gunner said, still walking in line between Jackrabbit and Jung-Hoon.

"What, Commander?"

"I need to make a head call, man."

"A head call?" That announcement brought the moving line to a halt. "You Navy guys. Hmmph." Jackrabbit stopped and turned around. "Only the Navy and the Marine Corps would call a latrine a head. Okay, make it quick."

"Got it," Gunner said. He stepped into the woods and then ...

Headlights!

Twin light beams shot out from around a corner.

"Hit the deck!" Jackrabbit said.

Gunner dove facedown in the snow.

Vroooooooooooooooom ... They heard the roar of a truck and the crunching and whining of gear shifts as the vehicle shifted down to keep moving on a steep section of road. The truck was coming right at them from the direction of Sinch'ang, the town they were headed toward.

Just inside the treeline, Gunner kept his head down. He wanted to grab his M-16. It had fallen in the snow a couple of feet away. But he resisted the temptation to avoid any movement that might be spotted from the truck.

As the truck rounded a bend in the road, its headlights flashed all around and over the men, hidden behind tree trunks and old snow drifts.

The roar of the truck engine and the crunching rumble of tires on pavement grew louder and louder. There was more than one truck. A troop transport! Only twenty feet away!

"North Korean military," Jung-Hoon said. "Stay down!"

A small convoy of four vehicles crept up the coast, toward the northeast. Just as the convoy had passed Gunner's position, brake lights flashed in the night. The last truck rolled to a stop in the road.

"Shhhhhhhhhhhh!"

Doors slammed. The sound of voices. Gunner brought his NVDs to his eyes. Three soldiers with rifles slung over their shoulders were standing outside one of the the covered troop transport trucks. One was waving his hands and pointing, as if he was giving directions. The other two fired up cigarettes, the orange glow of burning tobacco casting a dim light on their faces as they sucked in.

"I heard something about a checkpoint on the ocean," Jung-Hoon whispered.

"Maybe they're looking for something in the water," Gunner whispered back.

"Or for somebody," Jackrabbit said. "Gotta keep moving. Stay low. Stay inside this treeline until we round the next bend. Let's move."

Corbin Hall
Suffolk, Virginia

The morning sun blazed in a clear blue Virginia sky. Wearing comfortable old blue jeans and the red sweater Gunner gave her last

Christmas Eve, Margaret McCormick walked out onto her front porch, highly sweetened coffee in hand, and gazed across the large lawn of brown grass, beyond the long drive that led to the brick-pillared gates on Pendleton Road.

She hoped that the warm sunshine on a cool morning would calm her raging nerves. Her hands shook as she gripped her steaming cup of coffee.

Her stomach, churning like a tornado, had whirled all night. At six, she had called Gorman. He already had heard. As a good son would, he had tried reassuring her. "Don't panic, Mother. Gunner's probably fine. He doesn't work on the flight deck of the carrier and would have no reason to be down there where the missile hit."

Still, nothing had calmed her—not Gorman's reassurances, not the morning sunshine, not even the cozy feel of the sweater that Gunner had given her last Christmas.

She turned around and walked back inside the grand entrance of Corbin Hall.

The cinnamon smell of warm apple cider, a Friday-after-Thanksgiving tradition for the grandchildren, permeated the downstairs and seeped up the curved staircase of the house.

Margaret walked into the kitchen and poured herself half a cup of cider. The warm cider soothed her throat, and the sweet apple flavor gave her the sensation of an energy burst.

The doorbell rang.

She checked her watch. For the first time in hours, she felt a smile creep across her face. What a tonic for a bad day. Her grandchildren could make her smile no matter what.

She walked back out of the kitchen, cider in hand, and opened the front door.

"Granny!"

"Grandma!"

From both sides, they wrapped their arms tightly around her waist. "Okay, okay," she said. "Grandma has to breathe."

"Let's decorate the tree!" Jill said.

"No! I want apple cider and cookies!" Tyler tugged on her dress.

"Okay! Cider's in the kitchen," Margaret said. "I've got a batch of chocolate-chip cookies too. Go help yourselves. Grandma needs to talk to Mama and Daddy."

"Yippee!" Tyler said. They released her and galloped like a thundering herd of ponies straight to the kitchen.

"Bri, I thought you would have hit the mall by now," Margaret said. She managed a smile at her daughter-in-law, who reciprocated, while swiping a loose strand of long blonde hair from across her green eyes.

"The mall isn't going anywhere," Bri said. "They're open all day, and I don't want to get trampled under that idiotic stampede that's been waiting out there since midnight. Besides, I wanted to come check on my favorite mother-in-law."

"You're sweet." Margaret set the mug of cider on the small marble table in the foyer and moved into Bri's warm embrace.

"Mother, Bri's heading to the mall, but I'm staying with you and the kids," Gorman said.

"Don't be silly, Gorman. Go with Bri. She'll need all the help she can get carrying those bags around."

"She'll be fine," Gorman argued. "Besides, I haven't decorated a Christmas tree in years. Bri and the kids have all the fun in that department. I figured it'd be a good way to get into the Christmas spirit."

Looking over Gorman's shoulder, out on Pendleton Road, Margaret saw a small white car slow down, then turn and drive through the main gate and head down the long driveway.

"Looks like we've got company," Margaret said.

"Who could that be at this hour?" Gorman said.

The car turned onto the circular driveway in front the house. As it turned, they all saw its silver-and-black front tag with the words "US Government."

"Uh-oh," Gorman said. "You paid your taxes, Mother?"

The car rolled to a stop and the right passenger door opened. A tall Navy officer, dressed in his dress-blue uniform, stepped out. He had two gold stripes on his coat with a star sewn above the stripes, which Margaret recognized as being the rank of a lieutenant. A gold cord hung from his right shoulder.

Then the driver's door opened. An enlisted Navy man emerged, wearing a dark blue "cracker jack" uniform and a white "Dixie-cup" style cap.

A second later, the other passenger door opened. Another officer got out. He sported the four gold stripes of a Navy captain. A gold cross was sewn on his sleeve right above the four stripes. The cross, which normally brought peace to her soul, sent Margaret's heart racing. "Dear God, no ... no ..." she said, as the captain affixed his white-black-and-gold officer's cover on his head.

"What is it?" Bri asked.

"He's a chaplain." Margaret buried her face in her hands. "Please, Jesus. Not my son too. Please." She felt Gorman's arm wrap around her. Tears flooded her eyes.

"Mrs. McCormick?" The captain removed his cap.

"I'm Margaret McCormick." She wiped the tears from her eyes, but more kept coming.

"Mrs. McCormick." The captain's voice was soft and kind. "I'm Chaplain Roberson from the Norfolk Naval Station." The chaplain offered her a white handkerchief from his pocket.

"Thank you, Captain. I never expected this visit."

"This is Lieutenant Duckworth. He's here on behalf of Admiral Rusotto, who's the commander of the Norfolk Naval Base."

"Lieutenant," she said, acknowledging the junior officer, then turned her eyes back to the captain. "It's Gunner, isn't it, Captain?" Her body started to shake. "I'm so sorry, Captain." Another rainstorm of tears. "But I lost my father in Korea ... and I never thought ..."

"Captain," Gorman said, "I'm Gorman McCormick. I'm Gunner's brother. We heard about the missile attack on the *Harry Truman*. Mother has been unable to sleep knowing that's Gunner's ship. I take it you're here because of that."

"Mr. McCormick, I'm afraid that I do not have good news about your brother."

"I was afraid of that," Gorman said.

"But I'm not here because of the attack on the *Harry Truman*."

Margaret looked up at the chaplain. "What do you mean?"

"Mrs. McCormick, I'm afraid that your son appears to be lost at sea."

"Lost at sea? What?"

"Ma'am, Lieutenant Commander McCormick was not on board the *Harry Truman* at the time of the attack. He'd taken a thirty-day leave the day before and had flown off the ship to Osan. He then took a private plane to Japan. The plane went down in the Sea of Japan sometime yesterday afternoon. We've conducted an extensive search of the area and found nothing. It doesn't look good. I'm sorry."

Margaret stared out across the yard, across the brown grass to the log fence. A flock of geese, flying south for the winter, flew in a perfect V-formation overhead. She let her eyes linger for a moment on the sky.

Then she looked at the chaplain. "Captain, may I ask something of you?"

"Yes, ma'am," he said. "Ask anything you'd like."

She inhaled and exhaled slowly and wiped her eyes with the handkerchief. "If they find his body, would you come back and let me know?"

"Yes, ma'am, I'll do that."

"And one other thing."

"Anything, ma'am."

"I want a military service for him with full honors, with a Navy honor guard. I want a Navy chaplain officiating. Would you consider officiating at the service?"

The chaplain reached out and took both of Margaret's hands in his. "Mrs. McCormick, I'll give you my card with my personal cell number. When you're ready to hold a service, ma'am, it would be my honor to officiate and to assure you that your son will receive the full military honors that he deserves. Lieutenant Roberson here will lodge your request with the admiral's staff."

The lieutenant nodded.

She smiled through streaming tears. "You're a good man, Captain."

"You and your family are in my prayers, Mrs. McCormick." He handed her one of his cards, put his cap on, tipped the bill, and, with a nod to her, said, "Ma'am."

Then he turned and the three men got back in the car. The white car circled back to the long driveway and headed for the gate and Pendleton Road.

Margaret watched it until it disappeared around a bend in the road.

CHAPTER 22

East coast of North Korea
along the road between Iwŏn and Sinch'ang

Freeze!" Jackrabbit whispered.

From inside the treeline paralleling the road, Gunner froze in his steps. Up ahead, across the road to the left and overlooking the beach, he saw the source of Jackrabbit's concern. Three North Korean Marines huddled around a jeep, whooping it up in loud and animated conversation. They all were smoking cigarettes. One would periodically gaze out to sea with a pair of binoculars.

This marked the second such unit they had discovered. Clearly, the North Koreans were establishing watch positions along the coastline to monitor the sea.

Jackrabbit motioned his hand to the right, and the trio moved deeper into the woods, farther away from the loud-mouthed Marines. They kept moving parallel to the road, quietly moving from tree to tree, stopping for a few seconds behind each trunk, hiding in the dark shadows.

When they had gone a hundred yards or a little more beyond the North Korean observation post, the GPS showed they were just over a mile northeast of the outskirts of Sinch'ang.

As they rounded the next bend in the road, Jackrabbit held up his hand. Bright lights shone about a quarter of a mile ahead.

Another checkpoint?

Gunner brought his binoculars to his eyes.

A petrol station.

The parking lot was empty. The cigarette-smoking clerk was walking toward the lone gas pump. He threw down his cigarette, stamped it on the ground, and started fiddling with the pump.

"Pssst." Gunner motioned for Jung-Hoon and Jackrabbit to huddle around him. "I think it's open. I think it would be a good idea for Jung-Hoon to go check things out."

"Bad idea, Commander," Jackrabbit said. "I say we stay in the trees and walk behind the store and keep moving. No point in risking discovery tonight. Not with these Communist Marines hanging around."

Gunner eyed his compatriots for a moment. "Jung-Hoon, go into the store and see if you can find anything for Jackrabbit's gunshot wound. Alcohol. Antiseptic. Bandages. Anything. I'm worried about infection setting in."

"Oh, come on, Commander, that isn't necessary." He reverted to his whining, country-boy, redneck tone. "I told you I splashed a little saltwater on it earlier. It'll be fine."

"Sorry, Jackrabbit. I'm paying for this trip, and I'm just protecting an asset. I've seen the way you shoot, and I need to make sure you keep both arms. I don't want to have to become the number-one sharpshooter around here. Besides, Jung-Hoon might be able to gather some valuable intel."

"But—"

"No buts." This time Gunner held up his hand in a that's-enough gesture. "I'm sure Jung-Hoon can take care of himself for a few minutes while we hang in the woods and pop popcorn or something."

Jackrabbit shook his head. "Jung-Hoon, are you okay with that?"

"That's an excellent idea. I will be back shortly, if you can make Jackrabbit behave himself while I am gone."

"Need me to take that?" Gunner asked, pointing at Jung-Hoon's rifle.

"Good idea." Jung-Hoon handed him the M-16 as Jackrabbit kept shaking his head in protest.

"Got your .45 locked and loaded?"

"In the back of my belt."

Jung-Hoon pulled a bottled water from his pack, poured some in his hands, and slapped his face to wash off the final residue of black grease he had not gotten earlier. Then he squatted down and scooped up some snow and rubbed that against his cheeks.

"You're going to get frostbite," Gunner said.

"Here's a rag," Jackrabbit said. "I don't like this whole idea, but at least finish getting that grease off your face."

Jung-Hoon took the towel from Jackrabbit without comment and wiped it hard across his face like a wash rag. Then he handed it back to Jackrabbit.

Gunner patted Jung-Hoon on the back. "See you in a few minutes."

Jung-Hoon stepped out from behind a fir tree and headed for the gas station, walking along the bank of the ditch that ran next to the road.

Corbin Hall
Suffolk, Virginia

Gorman sat in the large wingback chair at the back of the house and sipped a brandy in stunned disbelief. Just yesterday, they had celebrated a joyous Thanksgiving together. Of course his mother had gotten a bit sentimental at first about her father—the grandfather he never knew—but after that, aside from Gunner's absence, it had been one of the more enjoyable Thanksgivings in several years.

And now this.

For Gorman, reality had not yet melted away the stunned disbelief at the fate of his younger brother. Gorman had always been more stable, the serious family man determined to come home after Virginia Tech to run the family business and take care of his mother. Gunner was five years younger. They never attended high school or college together. While Gorman returned to his peanut-farming roots, Gunner was bent on sowing his wild oats. In the Navy, then in New York. And back to the Navy.

The brothers were never at odds with each other, as brothers from well-to-do families sometimes can be. But then again, their relationship was never close.

Gunner was closer to his niece and nephew, Jill and Tyler, than he was to his own brother. In fact, although Gorman was back here running the farm and Gunner was off playing Navy, Gunner was the mama's boy. Go figure. Gorman didn't think he was jealous. He sipped more brandy and stared out through the large window overlooking the pool and beyond that to the acres of peanut fields, now dormant.

Sipping on the warm brandy, trying to control his thoughts, he suddenly felt a wave of regret. Perhaps, under the surface, he always justified their less-than-cozy relationship as being Gunner's fault. Gunner was the one who left Virginia. If Gunner had wanted a relationship or if he had been interested in farming at Corbin Hall, he would have come home and done his part rather than play sailor.

As he sat there, looking out, Gorman's regret turned to guilt. The preacher last week at First Baptist Church had quoted David and said that "life is like a vapor. Here today. Gone tomorrow."

Did the preacher have a premonition?

His cell phone rang.

"Scott and Stringfellow" popped up on the screen.

The day after Thanksgiving? Why would his broker be calling today? Aren't the markets closed? Odd. Let it go to voice mail, he thought.

No, Todd Stacks was a longtime friend. It might be important. He answered the phone. "Todd? ... Not too well ... Hang on a second, will you?" He stepped out through the glass French doors, out onto the back deck around the pool. "Sorry, Todd, I didn't want the kids to hear this yet." He told him the news they'd received that morning, then listened as Todd gave the reason for his call. "What? Say that again.... How much? ... When? ... Yesterday? ... Yes, I'll let you know if we hear anything else.... Right away. Thanks, Todd. Thanks for calling."

He stuck the phone in his pocket and walked back into the house, past the sunroom where the kids were decorating the tree, and then up the grand staircase.

He knocked twice on his mother's bedroom door. "Mother?"

"Come in." Her voice was weak, tired sounding.

Margaret sat in the chair beside her bed, her Bible in her lap, still holding the chaplain's handkerchief as if it were a security blanket. She looked up at him through glazed, reddened eyes.

"I got a call from Todd Stacks, Mother."

"From Todd? Today?" A curious look crossed her face. "I thought the markets were closed today."

"They are." He sat at the end of the king-sized bed. "Todd called because his computer alerted him about a large transfer from Gunner's trust account yesterday."

"Yesterday?" She cocked her head to one side. "How much?"

"Six hundred thousand dollars."

"What? That's almost his entire cash reserve!"

"That's right, and it looks like he drained another two hundred thousand in cash before he deployed."

"Why would Gunner withdraw that much without telling anyone?"

"I have no idea about the withdrawal, but Todd checked the wire transfers, and a large sum was wired to a private airport owner in South Korea. Todd made a few follow-up calls and found out that money went to buy an airplane."

"An airplane?"

"In Korea."

"Korea?" Her face contorted. "Why would Gunner want an airplane? I never heard him say anything about wanting to fly."

"I have no idea. Gunner's always been more of a daredevil. He always came up with these harebrained ideas. Maybe he wanted to take flying lessons. Maybe he took thirty days off and decided to buy an airplane. And the plane goes down. I mean, what other explanation is there? The timing fits."

Margaret wiped her eyes. "That makes no sense. I mean ..." She buried her face in her hands and started weeping again.

East coast of North Korea
along the road between Iwŏn and Sinch'ang

The falling snow was much thicker now. Visibility was down to about a hundred yards, or the length of a football field. Jung-Hoon was almost to the parking lot of the petrol station.

He stopped at the edge of the parking lot to check the area. He saw one clerk inside, a young man who looked to be in his twenties. The clerk stood behind the counter, smoking a cigarette.

How strange, he thought, that the place remained open so late at night in such a remote area in a nation that does not embrace capitalism. Where there are no cars out this late.

Jung-Hoon walked across the snow-covered parking lot and pulled open the front door of the store.

"Ahn-yahng haseo," he said, the Korean greeting for "Hello."

"Ahn-yahng haseo," the clerk replied with an expression of surprise.

"Are you open?"

"Do I know you?" the clerk asked. "You do not look familiar."

"I am a loyal follower of Dear Leader," Jung-Hoon said. "What else do you need to know?"

The clerk squinted his eyes and sucked on his cigarette. His black eyes danced nervously from the area outside the station, to the door, and to this unknown standing before him. "We are not normally open this late. In fact, I had closed and gone home for the night. But the local provincial leader called and ordered me to reopen in case military vehicles needed petrol. They are doing some kind of military exercise along the coast tonight." Another drag on the cigarette. "So here I am. What are you looking for tonight? Soju? Beer? Can't sell you petrol. Not tonight. That is for military vehicles only."

"Actually, comrade, I am a political officer from Pyongyang, assigned to help oversee political control of the military operations for the night. One of our young privates stupidly cut his hand on a piece of metal. So I ventured out in the dark and in the snow to find some alcohol and perhaps a bandage. I would rather be out in the cold and snow than listen to the stupid private whine and squeal like a stuck pig. Do you know what I mean?"

"Ha! Ha! Ha! Yes."

Good. A laugh.

"I wish I could help you, comrade, but I am afraid that we have nothing here. No medical supplies. No bandages. No medicine. Mostly liquor, cigarettes, and petrol. The only place nearby with such supplies is Hongwŏn. Too far to walk. But, if you would like, I can sell you a bottle of soju. That has enough alcohol in it to help 'til you can find medical alcohol."

"Hmm." Jung-Hoon mulled over the suggestion. "How much?"

"Fifty thousand won."

"That's expensive, isn't it?" Fifty thousand won was equal to roughly twenty US dollars.

The clerk grinned. "Hey, it's late. Not supposed to even be open."

Twin beams of bright lights shown in through the window as Jung-Hoon heard the sound of heavy wheels against ice and gravel. Outside, a North Korean military jeep was pulling up to the single petrol pump.

"Here is fifty thousand won." Jung-Hoon slipped the North Korean currency across the counter, keeping his eyes on the jeep through the glass.

"I will get your bottle." The clerk walked into a back room.

As one of the soldiers pumped petrol into the jeep, two others stood outside talking, gesturing with their hands. One checked his watch, then started walking toward the store. His comrade turned and followed him.

Jung-Hoon stepped back from the counter, back away from the front door of the store. He felt for the gun stashed under the belt in the back of his pants.

He could take them all out. The three soldiers. The clerk. The jeep would come in handy.

The door was flung open. "Hey, comrade, we're getting petrol and we need six bottles of soju," the first soldier yelled out.

"Right away, Sergeant," the clerk said nervously. He sheepishly proceeded to take multiple bottles off the shelf and cradle them in his arms.

As the clerk made his way around the end of the shelf with the bottles, the sergeant spotted Jung-Hoon.

"Hey, Comrade," he said to the clerk, keeping his eyes on Jung-Hoon, "you have a new employee in here tonight?"

"No employee," the clerk said. "He's with the officers' group." He stood the bottles up on the counter, one through six. The bottle for Jung-Hoon stood alone.

"Hey, Comrade," the North Korean sergeant said, clearly speaking to Jung-Hoon. "Where are you from?"

"From Hongwŏn," Jung-Hoon replied.

"Interesting." The soldier picked up one of the bottles from the counter, unscrewed it, and took a sip. "What are you doing all the way out here so late at night?"

"I am here to purchase soju, just like you, Comrade Soldier," Jung-Hoon said.

"Special rate for Korean Army tonight!" the clerk said, sounding as if he was trying to defuse trouble before it started.

"Interesting, Comrade. I am from Hongwŏn." He stared at Jung-Hoon. "I have never seen you there."

The front door again swung open. The third soldier, the driver, walked in. "Don't you have soju yet? We must get moving."

Jung-Hoon's fingers itched to reach for the gun hidden under his jacket. Control. He needed to hide his hatred of the swaggering soldiers. It would be so easy to pull his gun and squeeze the trigger — easy as shooting baby ducks in a pond.

He halfway hoped that the bantam rooster would dare to push the issue, to give him an excuse to blow his brains out. He snapped back at the solider. "In my line of work, Sergeant, there would be no reason for you to ever see me."

"Is that a fact, old man?" the interrogator continued, swigging his soju. "Well, since there would be no reason for me to have seen you before, it would seem to me that now would be the perfect time for us to get acquainted." He sported a cheesy grin, then his face went stern. "Show me your papers!"

"What did you say to me?"

"I said, Show me your papers."

"You do realize that you are speaking to an officer of the National Security Agency who reports directly to Kim Jong-un, the son of Dear Leader himself?"

The sergeant's face took on a pale look of stunned bewilderment. "If you are with the National Security Agency, then why would you be here?" The voice had lost its prosecutorial edge.

Too bad.

Jung-Hoon thought about his brother. Then he remembered why he had agreed to come on this trip — to kill North Koreans for killing his brother.

"Why I am here is none of your business, Sergeant. But know this. Both Kim Jong-un and Dear Leader himself have an interest in knowing how Dear Leader's military performs on domestic missions in guarding the coast. Tonight I, and others like me, am the eyes and ears of Dear Leader to watch and report back on the performance of soldiers like you. Now" — he paused — "do you have any other questions?"

The soldiers exchanged confused glances. Then the original inter-rogator seemed to regain his bearings.

"I still need to see identification papers."

"You want to see papers, do you?" *Now!* He whipped the .45 out from his belt. "My papers, soldier, are pointed between your eyes! Would you like a closer look? Perhaps at the ink on my papers? I will give you a hint! The ink on my papers is made of lead!" He stepped forward, closer to the swine.

"I am Inspector Jung-Hoon of the National Security Agency. No member of the National Security Agency must produce papers to any-one in the Democratic People's Republic, Comrade Soldier, and, no offense, but especially not to an enlisted member of the armed forces. Now what is your name, soldier?"

No response.

"I am speaking to you, Comrade Soldier!" he screamed and walked closer, pistol straight out, gripped in both hands. "Your name ... and place your military identification on the counter! Now!"

The big he-man soldier raised both hands in the air. His hands and arms were shaking. His mouth hung open and a glaze of shock had set into his eyes. The he-man had morphed from a cocky swashbuckling piece of Communist trash to a scared snow dog. His two young Army colleagues did not look much better.

"Do you have a problem hearing, Comrade Soldier?" Jung-Hoon screamed at the top of his lungs. "I am going to count to five. And if your military identification card is not on that counter by then, I will blow your head off! One ... two ..."

"Wait ... wait, Comrade." The bantam cowered. "I will do as you say."

"Then do it!"

The dog-wimp removed his military badge and, like a compliant sheep, laid it on the counter.

"Clerk! Read this man's name."

"Kim. Sergeant Kim. Kim Wong-sai."

"Well now, Sergeant Kim Wong-sai, what are you doing out here in the dead of night? Away from your duty station? Do you think Dear Leader will be happy to learn that you are out getting drunk on soju rather than attending to your military responsibilities?"

The sergeant stared back, speechless.

"Again I ask. What are your duties? I demand an answer!"

"My mission is to form a lookout for three US Navy SEALs believed to be coming ashore from the sea!"

"At last! Now do you believe that you can leave here and focus on your mission and cease harassing citizens and dignitaries whose concern is not part of your mission?"

"Yes, Comrade Inspector!"

"Very well," Jung-Hoon said. "The only reason I did not blow your head off is because of the grave importance of your mission to the national security. But hear this! My eyes are on you the rest of the night, Comrade Sergeant Kim! I will be invisible. I am your worst nightmare. Now if you think you can behave yourself and get to your duty station, I might even let this incident pass without mentioning your bumbling incompetence to your superiors. But one slipup, Comrade, and I will be delivering your brains to your mother for breakfast in the morning. Am I clear on this?"

"Yes, very clear, Comrade Inspector. Thank you, Comrade Inspector."

"Good. Now get out before I change my mind!"

The three hurried out the door, jumped into their jeep, and rolled out of the parking lot, their taillights soon swallowed by the thickening snowfall.

The clerk stood there, wide-eyed. "I just now remember that we do have one bottle of alcohol left, Inspector."

"Excellent!" Jung-Hoon stuck the pistol back inside his belt. "I am pleased to see that your memory has suddenly improved."

The clerk hurried to a back room and returned with the bottle of alcohol.

Just then, another set of headlights flashed into the building from the parking lot. Jung-Hoon reached back for the .45, but as the headlights dimmed, he saw an elderly white-headed man, wrinkles clearly visible from inside the store, get out of the van. The old man closed the door of the van behind him, then limped slowly through the snow toward the store.

"You know him?" Jung-Hoon asked, removing his hand from the pistol.

"He is Eun Ji-won," the clerk said. "A local plumber. Regular customer. Comes for petrol and soju."

The door opened. "Comrade. Comrade." The older man waved and spoke in a friendly tone. He reminded Jung-Hoon of an uncle who had long since passed away. "You are working late tonight, Comrade Clerk."

"A special occasion tonight, Eun Ji-won," the clerk said.

"Perhaps you could sell an old man some soju so he can get to sleep and petrol so he can get up early in the morning and go fix broken toilets in a Hongwŏn apartment building." The old man's voice whined from age and cracked a couple of times.

"I have soju, Eun Ji-won," the clerk said, "but I can only provide petrol to military vehicles until further notice."

"Until further notice?" The man looked perplexed. "What does that mean? I have job in Hongwŏn. I need the money."

"Sorry, old friend," the clerk said. "Perhaps in the morning. Perhaps not. You come back then and I will let you know."

"Old man," Jung-Hoon said, "there is good news for you tonight."

The old man turned and looked at Jung-Hoon.

"I am Inspector Jung-Hoon of the National Security Agency in Pyongyang. I am instructing the clerk that your request for petrol is approved as a special-needs exception to tonight's military-only rule." He looked at the clerk. "Do not worry, Comrade Clerk. I have verbal authority directly from Kim Jong-un personally to override the policy by special exception on a case-by-case basis, and I believe this to be such a case. This man's work is of high importance. Unsanitary conditions in an apartment complex due to malfunctioning toilets are a danger to public health. Do not worry. I will pay you cash immediately from a special government fund." Jung-Hoon whipped out enough won to pay for two tanks of petrol and put it on the counter. "You are authorized to keep the excess for your personal use, to spend as you see fit. However, you are not authorized to tell anyone about this, or the consequences will be grave."

The clerk's eyes widened as he counted the won. "Yes. Thank you, Comrade Inspector."

"Very well," Jung-Hoon said. "I will help our friend here pump his petrol. I will check in on you soon. Remember, you are not to speak to anyone concerning anything that you have seen and heard this night."

"Yes, Inspector!"

Jung-Hoon opened the front door and held it for the old man, who stepped back out into the falling snow. "Does the heater work in your van?"

"Yes, a little."

"Good, then go start the engine and sit in the van and turn the heater on. Get warm. I will pump your petrol."

"Thank you, Inspector."

Jung-Hoon walked the old man back to the van and began pumping his petrol. After the petrol topped off, Jung-Hoon put the nozzle back onto the pump.

He walked around to the driver's side of the van. The old man had rolled his window halfway down. "You are kind, Inspector."

"How much will you make tomorrow, Eun Ji-won?"

When the old man told him, Jung-Hoon asked, "How would you like it if tonight you were paid a whole year's wages and I were to purchase your van for twice what it is worth?"

The old man raised an eyebrow. His wrinkles became more pronounced. "I am afraid I do not understand, Inspector."

"As you heard, there is a military operation going on tonight in the area. Dear Leader is in need of every vehicle available tonight. I can pay you cash now. An entire year's wages and twice the value of your van. Are you interested in serving Dear Leader? Are you willing to accept this token of cash gratitude from Pyongyang?"

The old man's eyes lit up and sparkled like stars on a clear night. "I am happy to serve Dear Leader in any way I can, Comrade Inspector."

"Very well. I will report your cooperation to Dear Leader. But there is one caveat."

"A caveat? What is that?"

"I will pay you now, but I need your van immediately for the state's business. Are you able to make it home?"

"Ha, ha! For that kind of money, I would walk in the dark and snow to Pyongyang! Besides, my house is only two kilometers from here."

"Good." Jung-Hoon pulled out a wad of cash, flipped through it, and handed it to the old man. A wide smile crossed his wrinkled face, revealing a toothless gumline.

"That enough?" Jung-Hoon asked.

"Yes, this will be perfect." The old plumber looked from the money in his hand to Jung-Hoon and smiled.

"Then I ask you to step out of the van now."

"Of course, Inspector." He got out. The limp in his step had almost become a spring. "Thank you again, Inspector," he said, still counting the wad of cash as he headed away from the station, as if he wanted to take the money and run before Jung-Hoon changed his mind.

Jung-Hoon smiled. He got into the driver's seat, closed the door, and put the van in first gear.

East coast of North Korea
along the road between Iwŏn and Sinch'ang

The snowfall had turned into a near blizzard, filling the night air with huge snowflakes. And while the thick snowfall would temporarily help hide their position from the North Korean military, it also obstructed their view of the petrol store.

"I don't like this," Jackrabbit snarled. "Not being able to see. He's been gone twenty minutes."

"I'll bet you'll like it less if that arm of yours develops gangrene," Gunner said.

"Gangrene in this weather? It could wait till tomorrow," Jackrabbit argued. "Besides, Jung-Hoon said he had a pharmacist contact in Hongwŏn. The last thing we need is to get stuck in this God-forsaken place without a translator."

"I thought you spoke Korean, Jackrabbit."

"Yeah, I do, but my Korean sticks out like the color of my skin up here. Enough of a sore thumb to get us both shot."

"Maybe we should go look for him."

Bright headlights flashed through the snowfall from the direction of the store. "Back up, Commander. Got a vehicle coming this way. Get your gun."

"Roger that."

The vehicle moved slowly toward them, its windshield wipers flapping and squeaking, its motor whining. Just before it reached their position, it pulled over and stopped on their side of the road.

His heart pounding, Gunner aimed the M-16 at the van and adjusted his eyes through the night scope. He worked the action—*cha-chink*—

bringing a .223-caliber bullet into firing position. A couple of trees over to his right, Jackrabbit aimed his rifle at the same target.

With the motor still running, the headlights went dark. A second passed. The headlights flashed on again. Gunner held his rifle on the driver's door. A few more seconds passed and the signal was repeated. Lights off. Lights on. Lights off.

A creaking noise cut through the night. The driver's door opened. Gunner tightened his finger on the trigger, waiting.

A figure emerged, hands straight up in the air. "Do not shoot! It is Jung-Hoon."

Gunner brought his night scope on the man's face, then smiled and lowered his rifle.

"I'll be," Jackrabbit said.

"We have a ride!" the Korean shouted through the snow. "Get in the van! Fast, before another Army jeep drives by."

"I don't know how he pulled it off, but let's take him up on it, Commander."

"Right," Gunner said. He picked up his backpack and, with his rifle slung over his shoulder, emerged from the treeline and crossed the shallow ditch to the van on the side of the road.

"Stick the supplies in back, Commander. I bought this ... excuse me ... you bought this from a North Korean plumber. We have all types of tools in the back that might be helpful. Shovels, wire cutters."

"No windows in the back. I like it," Gunner said. He opened the back door of the van and started slinging supplies inside. "Good work, Jung-Hoon."

"One more pack," Jackrabbit said. "I'll get it."

Gunner got into the back of the van. A moment later, Jackrabbit returned with the rest of the supplies, tossed them in the back, and slammed the door. Jung-Hoon got into the driver's seat and Jackrabbit sat in the passenger seat.

"Okay," Jung-Hoon said. "We must get turned around. Hongwin is back that way."

"Let's go!" Gunner said.

Jung-Hoon flipped on the headlights. The snowfall was now so thick that the high beams created a near-blinding reflection. Jung-Hoon dimmed the high beams, then began executing a three-point turn in the road. A moment later, they drove slowly back in the direction of the store.

"How far to Hongwŏn?" Gunner asked.

"Thirty miles," Jung-Hoon replied. "In this weather, that could take a while. At least the road is relatively flat."

"The road may be flat, but the road is not straight," Jackrabbit said. "And the Sea of Japan is over that ledge to our left. I don't want to go back in the water tonight."

"Do not worry," Jung-Hoon said. "No more swimming tonight." They passed the store on their right and continued along the winding, snowy coastal road, their headlights piercing the dark.

"This would be a great time to alternate getting some shut-eye," Jackrabbit said. "We'll go in shifts. Commander, you go first. I'll wake you in two hours. When we get closer to Hongwŏn, we'll pull over on some back road and let Jung-Hoon catch a couple."

"Sounds great," Gunner said. He leaned his head back, closed his eyes, and listened to the roar of the engine and the sound of a wiper against the snow.

Ten minutes later, they approached another parked military jeep on the left. Two soldiers were looking out to sea with binoculars. As the van approached, one soldier turned.

"Guns ready, gentlemen," Jackrabbit said. "If they stop us, we're gonna have to take 'em out."

Gunner held his breath, clutched his gun, and prayed.

CHAPTER 23

East coast of North Korea
on the road to Hongwŏn

The van rolled past the jeep. The soldier who had turned and seen them coming just watched as they drove by. He made no attempt to stop the van. He didn't even alert the other soldier.

Two minutes later, they rounded another curve and were beyond the military observation post, once again alone on the winding, snowy road overlooking the sea.

"That was a break," Gunner said. He leaned his head back again. He needed sleep. They all needed sleep. Two hours. He could sleep for two hours. He closed his eyes.

Hey, Commander. Wake up, sleepin' beauty." Jackrabbit's voice interrupted the rhythmic back-forth, back-forth tranquility of the lone working wiper against the windshield.

Gunner looked out and saw a light snowfall and a dark two-lane road in front of them. "What happened to the snow?"

"Still getting a little bit," Jackrabbit said. "But it's died down."

"What time is it?"

"Three twenty."

"Three twenty? I thought we were taking two-hour shifts."

"We were," Jackrabbit said, "but then we came through the first little town, and then the second little town, and I decided that if anyone needed to take a shot for any reason, it'd be better if I were awake and you were asleep."

"Oh." Gunner rubbed his eyes. "You trying to say I'm not good with a gun? Hey, I'm an ex-NRA junior shooting champ. How do you think I got my nickname? I nailed every bull's-eye they put out in front of me on the range. After that, the name 'Gunner' stuck."

"Impressive, Commander. I've got a feeling that before this trip's over, we'll find out just how good a shooter you are."

"Bring it on. Where are we?"

"A few miles from Hongwŏn," Jung-Hoon said.

"We're going to pull off on the next road," Jackrabbit said, "and wait until dawn. Your turn to carry the watch, Commander. Up to it?"

"Since you let me sleep all night, I should be."

"Up there." Jackrabbit pointed to a side road. "That looks isolated."

"Let's check it." Jung-Hoon turned the van onto the narrow gravel road and drove about a hundred yards.

"Nobody up here, no tracks," Jackrabbit said. "Looks like we're in the back forty."

Jung-Hoon executed a three-point turn very carefully, for the road had a layer of fresh snow on it and deep ditches. He then pulled onto the side of the road. The van was facing east, toward the Sea of Japan, headed in the direction of the main road they had just been on.

"Looks good to me," Jackrabbit said. "We've got a long day ahead. You ready to take the watch, Commander?"

Gunner picked up his rifle and moved to the front of the van. "You boys get some shut-eye back there. You're in good hands."

Kim Yŏng-nam Prison Camp

The body of his dearest friend was wrapped in a blanket just a few feet from where Keith was digging his grave. He'd been told to dig in a spot where a grave had already been started but not used. He needed to dig deeper. He slammed the shovel down again and got the tip to cut in. He stepped on the shovel with his foot, and it dug in more. He picked up a small clod of earth and slung it out of the hole. He kept working, promising his friend that he'd have a proper grave.

The thick clouds that had brought the snow had departed. The sky was a rich blue.

Perhaps it was never true, Keith thought as he worked. That saying that was pounded into his head all those years ago during that sweltering sand-gnat-infested summer in the salt marshes around Parris Island, South Carolina. He was but a teenager back then. A young boot camp recruit. Boys on the verge of manhood are prone to believe anything they are told. The words came back to him, as if playing on some unstoppable mental tape.

Once a Marine always a Marine.

Marines don't let themselves get captured—especially not Marine Corps officers.

Marines don't cry.

If all that was really true, he thought, as he slammed the shovel into the ground again, if Marines don't cry, then why were tears dripping from his eyes, falling in the grave?

Either the saying was a lie—and he had been fooled in boot camp—or he was never a true Marine to begin with.

Keith slammed the shovel in the ground again and threw the chunk of earth he broke loose out of the hole. His knees ached and his arms burned as he worked. Again and again he slammed the shovel down, breaking through small clods of ground, picking them up, heaving them out of the grave, sometimes with his bare hands. A knifing pain shot through his back as he chucked more dirt out of the grave.

But no matter how much pain he suffered, no matter how much burning, no matter how many tears dropped to the ground, Keith knew he would not give up. Robert was his friend, his best friend, and Robert would be laid to rest among their comrades here on this mountain with all the honor and dignity that a United States Marine deserved.

Hongwŏn
North Korea

Gunner looked through the windshield of the moving van and got his first view of the downtown area of a North Korean city. If not for the snow piled along the sidewalks and the snow-covered mountains to the west, Hongwŏn could have passed for a ghost town in the West. The streets were nearly empty. Only a few small cars were moving. Empty parking places abounded in front of empty and abandoned buildings. Most of the storefronts were boarded up, barred up, empty.

The town's main drag, Kim-Il-sung Boulevard, had only a few people milling about. A couple were ambling in and out of the business establishments. Gunner watched one man walk down the street aimlessly, as if he had nowhere to go. Several came out of a building and headed toward the van. The faces were expressionless, like stone. The number of civilians seemed matched by an equal number of green-jacketed Army personnel and a matching number of blue-jacketed police officers walking along the street.

"If GPS is correct, the pharmacy should be on the right," Jung-Hoon said. "I will pull over here." He parked the van on the right side of the street and turned off the key. "Here, take the keys, Jackrabbit. If something goes wrong, drive to the spot where we spent the night. I will find you. I will be back in a few minutes."

"Good luck, Jung-Hoon," Gunner said.

Jung-Hoon got out of the van, slammed the door, and headed down the sidewalk.

Jung-Hoon looked up, trying to find the sign for the pharmacy that he thought should be about three doors down. He almost collided with two policemen who stepped from a storefront just a few feet ahead of him, but he moved out of their way just in time. Each wore a black service belt with a pistol holster on one side and a riot stick on the other. They were deep in conversation, talking and gesturing with their hands, when suddenly they saw him and stopped talking.

"*Ahn yang haseo*, officers," Jung-Hoon said, dipping his head slightly.

"*Ahn yang haseo*, citizen," one officer replied.

Jung-Hoon walked on, eyes straight ahead, and held his breath as he waited for some order to stop. To turn around. But none came. The two kept right on walking and talking. They were headed toward the van.

Jung-Hoon took four more steps, then glanced back over his shoulder. The police had not yet reached the van. He wondered if the old van's presence, parked alone on the side of the street with no other vehicles nearby, would snag their attention. Not that either of them stood an ice cube's chance in hell of winning a shootout with Jackrabbit, but a bloody shootout here and now would be a serious complication.

Jung-Hoon slowed his pace, took a few more steps, then quickly glanced over his shoulder again. The officers had passed the van and were walking briskly on down the sidewalk.

When he turned back, he saw the small sign, maybe three feet in length, hung over the next stone storefront: EAST SEA PHARMACY — A DPRK CLINIC.

Jung-Hoon pulled open the door. The front area was empty. No customers, no clerk. He walked to the back of the store, where a man and a woman, both middle-aged, both dressed in white pharmacy coats, stood behind a counter. They were looking down and shuffling paperwork.

The man looked up.

Jung-Hoon said, "Pardon me, Comrade Pharmacist, but I need topical antibiotic for a cut to prevent infection."

"I am sorry. Pharmacy opens at nine," the man said. "Come back then. First we must complete government paperwork. I shall check for antibiotics. Supplies are low from the government these days."

The man looked down and resumed his paperwork. The woman never looked up. Jung-Hoon was not surprised. Korean women, especially North Korean women living under the totalitarian regime of Dear Leader, were often reluctant to make eye contact with men.

Jung-Hoon let a few seconds pass, then spoke again. "Peace be with you."

These words brought the eyes of both pharmacists up from the paperwork. "And also with you," the man said.

"Fear not," Jung-Hoon said, "for I am with thee."

The woman responded with, "Thy rod and thy staff they comfort me."

Then Jung-Hoon said, "In my father's house, there are many mansions."

"You are from Pastor Lee!" The woman's face beamed from ear to ear.

"Yes," Jung-Hoon said. "I am from Pastor Lee."

"Wait, please," the man said. "I must lock the front door." The man rushed to the front of the store, twisted the dead bolt in place, then turned and, with a smile on his face bigger than the woman's smile, rushed back. "Welcome, my brother." The pharmacist threw his arms wide open and held Jung-Hoon in a bear hug. "We are Mr. and Mrs. Jeong. Any friend of Pastor Lee is a friend of ours." They each gave a half bow.

"*Ahn yang haseo*, Mister and Mrs. Jeong, of whom I have heard many good things from Pastor Lee. I am Jung-Hoon." He returned a half bow to each of them.

Their faces changed from smiles to looks of astonishment. They exchanged glances, then Mr. Jeong said, "Was it your brother . . ."

"Yes," Jung-Hoon said, "they murdered my brother. He was on a mission trip through Pastor Lee."

"We are sorry," Mr. Jeong said. "We met your brother once. He was a wonderful Christian man."

"My brother was a better Christian than me," Jung-Hoon said. "Although I am a friend of Pastor Lee, I do not go to church like my brother did. I want to kill Communists too much to be a good Christian."

"We know your reputation, Jung-Hoon. Many in the North know of you. You are a great freedom fighter for Korea. We stand with you."

"Thank you," Jung-Hoon said. "Pastor Lee said you might be able to help."

"Anything."

"First, it is true, I do need topical antibiotic."

"What sort of injury?"

"Gunshot."

"I see. We are low on inventory. Government supplies always low. I think we have one tube. Would you please check, my dear?"

"Of course." Mrs. Jeong nodded and walked down an aisle about halfway. She reached up on a high shelf. "We have one." She gave the yellow tube to Jung-Hoon.

"*Kamsamnida.*" He thanked her in Korean.

"*Chu-man-ay-oh,*" she responded and nodded.

"Second, Pastor Lee said I should ask you about escape routes out of North Korea."

"Do you know the military already thinks there are Navy SEALs in the area?"

"Yes, thank you for the warning."

"Hmm. You want to escape by land, sea, or air?"

"By air if we can find a private plane."

"Hmm." The pharmacist looked down at the counter, then back up at Jung-Hoon. "Not many private aircraft in North Korea. Most planes are controlled by Dear Leader and the government. But if you can make it across the border, across the Amnok River—you know it as the Yalu—we have missionary friends with access to a seaplane in Dandong, China."

"Really?" Jung-Hoon raised an eyebrow. "What kind of seaplane?"

"Not big. Small with pontoons. Carries five, maybe six people. They keep it in the Yalu River on the Chinese side, several miles downstream from Dandong."

"Interesting," Jung Hoon said. "And we could use this plane?"

"The plane is officially a charter tourist plane run by Christians. All Christian missionaries in China and North Korea must operate some sort of front business. But I know the owner. It is part of a network of Christians who help people escape from the North. He has helped North Koreans escape, and if I ask him, I think he will let you use the plane. But you have to pay for fuel."

Jung-Hoon smiled. "We may end up paying for more than fuel if we make it that far."

"I do not understand," the pharmacist said.

"Perhaps we could buy the plane? For a very good price, of course. You could ask them?"

The pharmacist thought about what Jung-Hoon had said, then he nodded. "I will ask them. I can see how that might be necessary."

"Good. You have a map? It would help for me to see the route on a map."

"Yes, of course." The pharmacist reached in a drawer, pulled out a map, and spread it out on the counter in front of them.

"Here you can see Hongwŏn. It is marked with the star right here on the east coast," the pharmacist said. "To the west, straight across the Korean peninsula, almost due west of us and across the Yalu River, is Dandong, China. It is marked with the other star. If you can cross the border, we have Christian contacts in China to help you get to Dandong."

North Korea, two white stars, Hongwŏn and Dandong, China

"Excellent," Jung-Hoon said. "Please contact your friends in China. Ask them to be on standby to help us get to Dandong if we get across the border. And to please have the plane ready."

"Yes, of course, Jung-Hoon." The man bowed. "How else may I be of service to you, my friend?"

"You have cigarette?"

"My wife and I, we do not smoke. But we sell Chinese cigarettes. Here. You like one for free?"

"Not for free." Jung-Hoon slipped enough North Korean won across the table to more than compensate for the pack and the antibiotic. Then he picked up the cigarettes, took one out, lit it, and took a drag. Then, lowering his voice, he said, "I have heard these hush-hush rumors of elderly Americans still being held from the Korean War. These rumors, in my opinion, come from credible sources." Another drag. "What do you think, my friend?"

Mr. Jeong slid him an ashtray. "Rumors are true. Only one camp, and only a few Americans are left. We hear one died yesterday."

"Oh? What caused him to die?"

"We do not know."

"Hmm," Jung-Hoon mused. "And where is this camp located?"

"About forty miles away. Near the small town of Youngwang, on Sŏngch'ŏn River. North of Hamhung. I have never seen it. You should speak with Dr. Kaesong at Hongwŏn State Psychiatric Hospital. He is the director of the hospital. It is more like a small state-funded clinic. Not many employees and few patients anymore. Unless the state needs to teach someone a lesson. Dr. Kaesong is a Christian, he is one of us, and has Christians on staff. He came here earlier this morning. He has a woman patient who works at the prison camp. The commanding officer of the prison camp burned the woman on the neck with cigarettes because she took medicine to try and help one of the old American prisoners who was sick."

"Some lesson." He flicked ashes into the ashtray.

"Yes, they do that."

"And you say this woman is still a patient at the hospital?"

"Yes. The doctor says she will be there several days."

"And do you think it would be possible for me to speak with this Dr. Kaesong and his patient?"

The couple looked at each other and exchanged nods. "Yes. I will take you to the hospital now if you like. My wife will stay here and run pharmacy. Let me call the doctor and tell him we are coming."

"Excellent," Jung-Hoon said. He stuffed the antibiotic, the cigarettes, and the matches in a front pocket. "And I have some American friends I want you to meet."

Kim Yŏng-nam Prison Camp

Two guards, the two older ones, lowered Robert's body into the grave. Then they reached down and pulled the blanket over Robert's head.

Kang, the whipmaster, stood at the head of the grave, lording over the whole procedure like a god, a look of hatred on his face.

The two guards stood up. They reached over and took the shovels that Keith and Frank had used to dig the grave, effectively relieving the old men of any further grave-digging duties.

The two guards silently began shoveling chunks of earth on top of the blanket-covered body. The way they worked seemed like a small act of human kindness in a prison camp so focused on brutality.

As soon as dirt completely covered the body of his friend, Keith could no longer hold back the tears, Marine or no Marine. He still had Frank, but Robert was his brother. Their bond had been forged forever the day Robert saved his life. And the bond had held through all they had endured as prisoners through all the many years.

Now Robert was gone. The image of his friend disappearing forever under the soil of the earth ripped apart Keith's soul.

What now did he have to live for? Where was hope? Where was joy?

"Let me die fast, Lord. If you are still there, take me home," he whispered.

Approaching Hongwŏn State Psychiatric Hospital Hongwŏn
North Korea

The gravel road snaked through a forest of evergreens. Snow covered the ground. They saw no tire tracks.

Jung-Hoon was behind the wheel, and their new pharmacist friend, Mr. Jeong, sat in the passenger seat, speaking Korean and pointing out front as if giving directions.

According to Jung-Hoon, who translated the words of Mr. Jeong as he drove, they would soon arrive at the hospital. Mr. Jeong described it as a poorly funded and largely forgotten state-run psychiatric clinic. The doctor in charge of the place, a Christian nurse who is his ally, and the patient from the prison camp would be waiting for them. All would verify the existence of the camp still holding the elderly Americans, Mr. Jeong assured them.

This confirmation, that there actually were Americans nearby, had sent Gunner's heart racing. The information seemed too good to be true, obtained too easily, too soon. In fact, since their firefight with the North Korean sailors in the boarding craft, their travel down the coast to this point had been relatively unobstructed, without any serious opposition that Jung-Hoon couldn't handle. Was it really this easy to move around North Korea? And now, to have the information they were looking for suddenly fall into their laps! Gunner felt an uneasiness. Was their luck about to run out? Were they headed into a trap?

They rounded the last bend in the road and entered a large clearing in the woods, a quarter of the size of one of the family peanut fields back at Corbin Hall. At the far end of the clearing was a one-story building with a couple of cars parked in front. The building looked like a large medical clinic or a small hospital. The few windows boarded over made it look dilapidated.

The circular driveway at the front appeared to continue all the way around to the back of the building. At the front door stood a single North Korean guard with a pistol. Mr. Jeong said something to Jung-Hoon.

"What'd he say?" Gunner asked.

"He says get in the far back of the van, out of sight. He will tell the guard that we are going to deliver pharmacy supplies to the director at the back of the building."

Gunner and Jackrabbit moved to the far back corner of the van with their M-16s. Mr. Jeong opened the door and got out. A few seconds later, he returned, speaking rapid Korean to Jung-Hoon.

"He says the guard cleared us to go around back. The doctor will be waiting for us there. No one is in the back of the building except the doctor, nurse, and patient."

"Excellent," Gunner said.

Jung-Hoon drove around to the back of the hospital and parked. Gunner and Jackrabbit heard more Korean spoken. Then Jung-Hoon said, "He says wait here a minute."

They heard a tap on the driver's-side window. Gunner pointed his rifle toward the back doors of the van as Jung-Hoon rolled the window down. A voice in broken but understandable English said, "Colonel Jung-Hoon. I am Doctor Kaesong. This is an honor. You and your friends, follow me."

"Peace be with you," Jung-Hoon said.

"And also with you," the doctor responded.

"Fear not," Jung-Hoon said, "for I am with thee."

The doctor responded with, "Thy rod and thy staff they comfort me."

"You do that well even in English, Doctor," Jung-Hoon said.

Gunner and Jackrabbit looked at each other. Jung-Hoon opened the door and stepped out.

No shots yet.

Gunner looked at Jackrabbit. "I'll go. You cover. You know what to do if this is a setup."

"Got your back, Commander."

Gunner laid down his rifle—too intimidating if these people really were allies—but he tucked his pistol in the back of his belt. He opened the back door of the van—light poured in—and he stepped out.

A smiling middle-aged Korean man wearing a white medical jacket and an old stethoscope stood beside Jung-Hoon.

Jackrabbit, apparently satisfied there was no immediate danger, got out of the van without his rifle.

"Please follow me," the doctor said.

Jackrabbit gave Gunner a quick and subtle it's-okay nod, and they fell in line behind Jung-Hoon and the pharmacist.

The doctor opened the door of the building, and they hurried down a long hallway that stretched all the way to the front of the building, where the guard was posted outside. They walked down the hall about fifteen feet. The doctor opened a door on the left and said, "Please, come in."

Gunner was last to enter the large room, which resembled an operating room, complete with an operating table in the middle of the floor. Two women, both midthirtyish, stood up when they entered. One wore a long white nurse's uniform, something that looked vintage 1950s. The other had on a long black dress down to her ankles. On the side of her neck was a gauze patch.

"This is my nurse." The doctor nodded at the woman in white. "If it is okay, I will not give her name. Security reasons."

"That is fine," Gunner said.

"And this is Pak. She is the one I told you about who works at the camp." Pak closed her eyes and bowed toward Gunner. "She was the one they burned with cigarettes because she gave medicine to the elderly American who died. She is lucky to be alive. They lined her up to be shot, tied her to a tree, but changed their minds and decided to burn her neck and commit her here instead."

She looked up at Gunner. Her black eyes had a soft, haunting beauty about them.

"So it is true," Gunner said, "Americans are still alive here."

Pak looked at the doctor, then at the nurse, then at Jung-Hoon. She appeared to be terrified.

The nurse put her hand on her shoulder and whispered something in her ear.

"She is afraid to talk about the camp," Jung-Hoon said. "Dear Leader makes it a capital offense for anyone to mention it. She thinks we may be North Korean agents seeking to trap her so we have an excuse to cut off her head."

The nurse kept talking to Pak.

"The nurse is telling her that no one here will report her to Dear Leader or to anyone at the prison. She says we all are against Dear Leader and are against Communists."

Pak kept nodding as the nurse spoke to her.

Finally, when the nurse's explanations seemed over, Jung-Hoon said, "Pak, let me show you something." He took off his jacket and rolled up his sleeve. He pointed at the tattoo of the man shoveling dirt on the North Korean flag.

Pak looked at it and smiled. Then she burst into laughter.

"Jackrabbit, show her yours," Jung-Hoon said.

"Sure, anything it takes." Jackrabbit rolled up his sleeve, revealing the same tattoo.

More laughter and head nodding. Even Gunner could not contain his laughter.

Pak smiled and put up both hands, as if to say she needed no more convincing. "For the two old men who are left, I will tell what I know. If you are agents ... I will have done what is right."

Gunner came back to his last question. "So it is true? There are Americans still in the camp?"

"Yes," she said. "It is true."

"How many?"

"Only two left now. There were three. One died yesterday. The one I tried to help."

"You know his name?"

"His name was Robert. That is all I know."

Dear God, no! Gunner thought, then he asked, "Do you know his last name? Where he was from?"

"No. Don't know last name. He from USA."

"No, I mean where? Where in USA?"

"Don't know. Sorry. One time he mention ... Vur ..."

Gunner's heart jack-hammered. "Was it Virginia? Maybe Vermont?"

"Not sure. Don't know those places."

He took out the photograph of his grandfather in uniform. "This was my grandfather. He disappeared in Korea. Did he look anything like this?"

Pak studied the photograph. "This young man. These old men. No recognize. Sorry." She handed the photograph back.

"Okay, okay," Jackrabbit said. "It may or may not have been your grandfather, Commander. We've known all along that was a long shot. But the point is, this lady says some old Americans are in a camp somewhere nearby. I say if that's the case, then let's go get 'em. Get 'em out of there."

"Amen," Gunner said.

"Mind if I ask you a few questions, ma'am?" Jackrabbit said.

Pak nodded.

"What's the name of this camp and how far away is it?"

"Camp is Kim Yŏng-nam Military Prison Camp. I think from here, it is forty miles. I am not good with distances. Takes about one hour."

"She is right," the doctor said. "About forty miles is right."

"Which direction?"

"It is on Sŏngch'ŏn River near small town of Youngwang," she said.

"That is west of here," Dr. Kaesong said.

"How many guards are there?" Jackrabbit asked. "What kind of guns do they have? What does the camp have to keep people out? Walls? Fences?"

"Not many guards. Two at front gate all the time. They stay outside with guns and guard front gate. Fence all around has much barbed wire at top. Inside, there are three guards. One very mean new guard named Kang. He takes bullwhip to prisoners and spits in their faces. The other day, he hit one of the prisoners across his foot with bullwhip. The colonel is commander of the camp. He has an assistant, a sergeant, who is ... how you say ... his mistress.

"Three kitchen workers come and prepare meals. Arrive about eight and leave at seven. Not many people working at camp. Once many more people working there. More guards, more workers. More prisoners. But so many prisoners die. Now only two."

Gunner, Jackrabbit, and Jung-Hoon looked at one another. "Pak, can you draw us a map of the inside of the prison camp grounds?" Jackrabbit asked.

"Yes, I can draw map."

The doctor passed her a sheet of paper, and she began to sketch. Finally she was satisfied. "Here," she said, handing over the drawing.

Gunner and Jung-Hoon hovered over Jackrabbit's shoulders. "Hmm," Jackrabbit said. "Looks like a simple layout. Main administration building. Guard residence. Prisoners' residences. Mess hall. Nothing too complicated." He looked at Pak. "Only one entrance into the camp?"

"Yes. At the front guard station. Here." She pointed.

Jackrabbit eyed Jung-Hoon. "Sounds doable to me."

"Agreed," Jung-Hoon said.

"When it gets dark, we move in," Jackrabbit said. "Pop off the guards at the front and try the heavy wire cutters at the gate. If that doesn't work, we rig a little C4 and *poof*. We're in. Jung-Hoon, you find the colonel and take him out. The commander and I take out the other three guards. We grab the prisoners and get the heck out of Dodge."

"Dodge?" Jung-Hoon said, a puzzled look on his face.

"Forget it," Jackrabbit said. "Doctor, we've got lots of supplies, but we're short on medical stuff. Could we buy a couple of light stretchers and bandages? That sort of thing?"

"Of course. Anything you need."

Jackrabbit looked at Pak. "Ma'am, we sure could use your help if you would be willing to come with us. You could help us locate the prisoners. But this could be very dangerous. We'll understand if you don't want to come."

Pak looked over at the nurse as if seeking her approval.

Gunner spoke up. "Pak, if we can rescue these men, we are going to take them out of the country. We'll take you with us too, if you want to come. You can request asylum in South Korea or America. My family can help you."

Pak again glanced at the nurse. The nurse nodded.

"Yes, I will come."

"Thank you," Gunner said. He turned to the doctor. "Once we get these guys out of the camp, what's the best way out of here?"

The pharmacist reached in his pocket and took out a folded paper. "I have a map of the escape route."

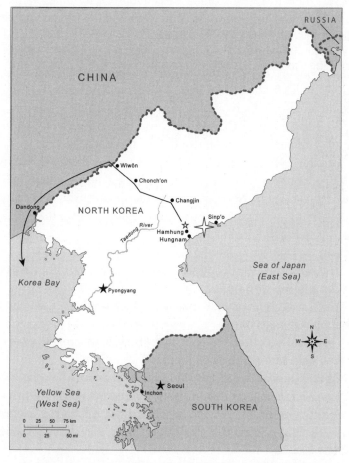

Route from prison (small white star) to China and into Korea Bay

"That is fabulous," Gunner said.

Mr. Jeong spread out the map on a table. "This is the route we use to get people into China from this area.

"We are here, near the four-point star, between Sinp'o and Hungnam. Prison camp is here, north of Hamhung. I have small white star there. Near town of Youngwang. A single-lane road goes north out of Youngwang about thirty miles. All roads in this area are narrow. Not much traffic and no big cities.

"When you get to the town of Changjin, you turn left on road across mountains to Chonch'on. From there you take road to Wiwŏn, where you cross Yalu River into China. It is about eighty miles across the mountains from Changjin to the Yalu River and the Chinese border. It could take you three, maybe four hours.

"When you get across the river, the missionaries will pick you up. You are about one hundred miles from Dandong, China. The seaplane is about ten miles farther. From there to Inchon, South Korea, is about a three-hundred-mile flight over Korea Bay and the Yellow Sea."

"So if all goes well," Gunner said, "we could cross into China sometime after midnight and be aboard that plane by sunrise."

"Possibly," Mr. Jeong said. "The good news—there are not many cars or police or Army on this route. But the bad news—the Yalu River is heavily guarded by North Korean border guards who shoot anyone they see trying to cross. And if the Chinese capture you, they turn you back over to North Korean authorities."

"Can the Chinese be bought?" Gunner asked.

"Yes, some can," Mr. Jeong said. "Not all. Depends. If they are hard-core Communist, then no."

"You'll need to save your money for that seaplane, Commander," Jackrabbit reminded him.

"One other question," Gunner said. "How do we cross the river?"

"You walk across," Mr. Jeong said.

"Walk?" Gunner said. "Only one man ever walked on water."

"Hah!" Mr. Jeong said. "Actually, two. Jesus and Peter. But this river is shallow and is frozen over from late November till March. So you will walk across. But be careful. Very slippery. And if they see you, there will be deadly gunfire."

"I appreciate the warning," Gunner said.

"I will pray that the One who first walked on water will be with you."

"Thank you, Mr. Jeong."

Jackrabbit looked at his watch. "I say we strike one hour after sundown. That gives us plenty of time to take care of business, get the men out of there, and get to China before the North Koreans wake up and realize what hit 'em."

"Agreed," Gunner said. "We strike one hour after sundown. Tonight is the night."

CHAPTER 24

Kim Yŏng-nam Military Prison Camp

Night had fallen over North Korea, and looming snow clouds had once again moved in from the Sea of Japan. This snow, however, differed from any that Gunner had ever seen. The large snowflakes floated down from clouds that flashed with lightning bolts, and after the flashes of lightning came booms of thunder.

Thundersnow.

Flash ... Boom.

He had heard of it. It was reported to have occurred in Manhattan in the Boxing Day blizzard of 2010. But Gunner had never before witnessed this rare phenomenon. Perhaps the snow, combined with the flashing and the booming thunderclaps, would serve as a well-timed distraction for what they were about to do.

The prison camp was now less than a mile away. This was his plan, his brainchild. All that had tortured and twisted within him was racing toward a dramatic life-or-death climax. With this realization, a surprising case of nerves caught him off guard.

He was an intelligence officer. He was not a Special Forces commando. But the plan called for him to perform like a commando. He and Jackrabbit were to advance on foot and eliminate the two front-gate guards while Jung-Hoon remained behind with the van.

Once the guards were eliminated, Jung-Hoon would move up with the van to better position it for the getaway. That was the plan.

"This is as close as we can get without being seen," Pak said.

Jung-Hoon pulled the van over to the side of the road.

"Sounds good," Jackrabbit said with an air of supreme confidence. "Let's do it. Commander, quick checklist." He sounded like a pilot preparing for takeoff. "Rifle?"

"Check."

"Silencer and night scope?"

"Check."

"NVDs?"

"Check."

"Pistol?"

"Check."

"Ammo for pistol and rifle?"

"Check."

"Then let's rock 'n' roll."

"Rock 'n' roll."

Jackrabbit opened the back van door and stepped out onto the road. Gunner followed him. They quietly closed the door.

"Stay low and silent," Jackrabbit said, crouching and moving in a double-time jog just in front of Gunner. They quietly moved forward about a hundred yards and, at a bend in the road, Jackrabbit stopped and held up his hand. He turned and gave Gunner the *shusssh*, with index finger over lips. Gunner didn't move as Jackrabbit advanced, crouched down to get a better look at whatever was ahead. He gave Gunner the come-on motion with his hand.

Gunner moved out and, a few seconds later, crouched beside Jackrabbit.

Before them was the prison camp. The high fence with its tangle of barbed wire at the top ran about twenty-five feet to their left, then snaked off into the woods out of view. The two guards at the front gate were about a hundred yards away, the alternating red glow of the cigarettes they were puffing on clearly marking their positions. Each flash of lightning was like a spotlight on the area.

"Okay, Commander, let's get a bead on 'em. You take the one on the right. I'll take the one on the left. Get his head in your crosshairs, and when I give the go-ahead, drop him."

"Got it." Gunner noted that because of the angle, the guard on the right was the easier target.

"Can you make that shot, Commander?"

"In my sleep."

"Get ready."

Gunner braced himself on one knee and brought the M-16 with night scope to his shoulder. He brought the crosshairs right onto the middle of the Korean's nose and watched the guard enjoy the last cigarette he would ever smoke.

"On my mark ... Ready ... Aim ... Fire!"

Gunner squeezed the trigger. The gun jumped, but silencers muted the sound. Both guards dropped to the ground in a heap.

"Keep your gun ready in case one of 'em is still alive. Let's go!"

Jackrabbit took off in a sprint, rifle forward, a soldier charging the enemy camp. Gunner sprinted behind him, following him to the front gate.

Just outside the gate were the two guards, transformed into lifeless heaps. Their mouths and eyes were frozen open. Seeing what the bullets had done going through their heads nearly made Gunner sick on the spot. He took a few quick breaths and looked away.

"Good shootin', Commander." Jackrabbit slapped Gunner on the back. He clicked the walkie-talkie. "Phase one complete. Move in."

Jung-Hoon's voice came back, "Roger that. Moving now."

More lightning lit up the snow-covered landscape. More thunder boomed and shook the earth.

Jackrabbit examined the locking mechanism on the front gate. "See if you can find a key on one of those guys, Commander."

Gunner reached down and felt for a key, a ring of keys, anything—first on one body, then on the other. "Nothing here."

Jung-Hoon pulled up in the van with headlights off. Jackrabbit jogged over to Jung-Hoon in the van. "No keys. Wire cutters will take too long. Grab the C4. Let's blow this baby."

He turned to Gunner. "Commander, we're going to use C4. Stay back and cover us. If anybody shows, you know what to do."

"Got it," Gunner said.

Jackrabbit grabbed the malleable C4 and meshed it into the gate lock as Jung-Hoon strung detonator wire from the gate back to the van, about fifty feet away. They worked with amazing efficiency, not wasting a second.

"Okay, stand back," Jackrabbit said. "Cover your ears!"

The explosion sounded like a double-barrel .12-gauge shotgun going off.

The gates blew wide open, as if the waters of the Red Sea had been parted in the midst of an ice storm.

"Jung-Hoon, you and Pak head to the colonel's quarters," Jackrabbit said. "The commander and I will get the guards' quarters, over to the right of the main building. After we've wasted those guys, you two meet us in front of the guards' quarters and we'll go find the prisoners.

"One other thing. Let's pull the silencers off. I want to intimidate the living heck out of these goons. I want 'em to know what hit 'em. Got it?"

"Got it."

"Let's go!"

Guards' quarters

Did you hear that?" First Sergeant Chung Nam-gyu, lying on the right bottom bunk of the four-bunk concrete guards' residence, dropped his copy of the *Pyongyang Times* on the floor and pushed up on the rack. "Was that an explosion?"

"I didn't hear anything," First Sergeant Cho Doo-soon said. He was reading the sports section of the newspaper.

Chung listened again. The wind was whistling around the building. Cold air seeped in through the cracks. The chimney on the stove in the middle of the concrete floor rattled as the wind shook its top.

"You two are stupid idiots." Staff Sergeant Kang Ho-soon had become a big-mouthed know-it-all who didn't hesitate to say whatever he wanted to say. "One thinks he heard an explosion. The other heard nothing. You idiots do not know the difference between thunder and an explosion. It amazes me how you two ever got cleared to serve in a secret and prestigious post like this one."

Chung stared at the loudmouth. "Kang, if you do not shut up, I'll report you for insubordination."

"Hah." Kang snorted. "Do it fast, First Sergeant. In a matter of weeks, I will outrank both of you. You are idiots!"

Chung said nothing. He watched Kang for a while, then lay back down and picked up the *Pyongyang Times*.

Another booming sound outside.

That, definitely, was thunder.

Office of Colonel Song Kwang-sun

They crept forward carefully, opened the door of the main administration building, and headed down the hall.

"This is the door," Pak whispered. "Lights are on. He is probably still in there. There are two offices. The first is his assistant's office. That is where his girlfriend works. Colonel's office is in the back."

Jung-Hoon held up his .45-caliber pistol in his right hand and turned the doorknob with his left. The door cracked open. The desk out front was empty.

A jumble of giggling, groaning, and moaning came from the back office. It sounded like two voices—one male, the other female. With his pistol leading the way, Jung-Hoon tiptoed past the desk and headed toward the door to the back office, which was slightly ajar.

More moaning. More giggling.

Jung-Hoon put his hand on the door and pushed it open. Two bottles of liquor sat on the big desk. Behind it, a woman in a slinky red dress sat on a man's lap. They were kissing passionately, oblivious to anything other than themselves.

Then the man saw Jung-Hoon.

"Who are you? What are you doing in my office?" the man demanded, pushing the woman to get off his lap. The woman flipped her head around, flopping her long dark hair across her shoulders, and stared at Jung-Hoon with a look of shock. Her mouth was smeared with bright red lipstick.

"You! In the red dress! Get down on the floor. Out here beside the desk! On your hands and knees!" Jung-Hoon ordered.

The woman scrambled off the colonel's lap and went down on all fours, like a dog, next to the desk. She looked up at Jung-Hoon.

"Keep your head down!" he snapped.

"How dare you!" the colonel said. "Do you know who I am? I am

Colonel Song Kwang-sun of the Army of the Democratic People's Republic of Korea! I have the highest access to authorities in Pyong-yang, even to Dear Leader himself! I demand that you put down that gun. Do it now! Or you will not live."

Jung-Hoon did not blink. "Aah. You invoke the name of the almighty Dear Leader, do you? Kim Jong-il! Son of Kim Il-sung! The self-proclaimed king of the North and the Son of the Morning Calm!" He looked around. A photograph of a much younger Song Kwang-sun taking the hand of and bowing to Dear Leader hung on the wall next to the desk. "That you and your king, Colonel?"

"Dear Leader is no king. He is the *king* of kings!"

"I know some people who would disagree with that." Keeping his gun on the colonel, he walked over to the photograph, took it off the wall, and mockingly pretended to admire it. "Dear Leader ever rise from the dead?"

"He is the immortal Dear Leader!"

"Oh, he is, is he?" Jung-Hoon spat on the picture and slammed it down. Glass shattered all over the floor.

"How dare you desecrate the image of Dear Leader!"

"Colonel, I do not believe Dear Leader would be too pleased with you at the moment."

"What … what do you mean?"

"Being the great servant of Dear Leader that you are, it has come to my attention that you are not much of a gentleman with the fairer sex."

"Leave her alone!" The colonel looked down at his red-dressed paramour. "She is *my* woman."

"Oh, I was not referring to her." He snapped his fingers twice, crisply.

Pak entered from the outer office, a bandage covering the cigarette burn on her neck. The colonel's eyes widened.

"You know this woman, Colonel Song Kwang-sun? Hmm?"

"Traitor!" Song snapped at Pak.

"I understand you like to scorch a lady's neck with the burning end of a cigarette. *Tsk. Tsk.* Surely such rumors cannot be true, Colonel. Surely not. A gentleman of such high esteem as yourself!"

"The internal security procedures of the Democratic People's Republic are none of your concern!" Song snapped.

"Democratic? How is it democratic? Why do governments and political parties that would take everything from the people call themselves democratic?" Jung-Hoon laid the gun down on the desk and extracted a cigarette from the pack he'd gotten from Mrs. Jeong at the pharmacy. He lit it, took a drag, and exhaled. A cloud of smoke hung in the air.

"Tell me, dear Colonel, have you ever had *your* neck burned with a cigarette?" He leaned forward, moving the burning cigarette in his fingers closer to the colonel.

Song reached into his front drawer and grabbed a pistol.

Jung-Hoon snatched the .45 from the desk and fired just as Song took aim.

"*Aaaaaahhhh.*" Blood flew from Song's right hand. The pistol dropped on the desk.

"It would not be a good idea to reach for your gun again, Colonel," Jung-Hoon said.

Guards' quarters

T*hat* was not thunder," First-Sergeant Chung said.

Kang looked up. The idiot was right this time. He jumped off the top bunk. "That was gunfire. Something's going on. Grab your rifles." He picked up his AK-47 and worked the action. "Hurry!"

Following Kang's lead, the other guards picked up their guns and snapped on ammunition magazines. Kang barked instructions. "We'll check the guard station at the gate to make sure that's secure. Then we'll check the administration building, then the prisoners. If there is nothing, we'll sweep the perimeter. Any questions?"

"No, sir," Chung said.

Excellent. Chung had just referred to him as "sir," a sign that natural leadership had nothing to do with technical rank. "Follow me."

Kang opened the door. Thick snow blew in on the howling wind. The grounds were dark except for single pole lights at each building. "Let's go," he said. "Stay in formation. Behind me!" Moving in a triangle, with Kang at the point, they headed for the front gate.

Out of the dark a loud voice shouted, "*Sic semper tyrannus! USA!*" Then gunfire.

"Aaahhhhhhhhh!" Kang dropped his AK-47 and grabbed his hand.

Behind him, Cho and Chung were sprawled facedown, blood gushing from their heads and spreading in pools in the white snow.

Lightning briefly lit the camp's grounds. Kang saw no one, just a blank and blinding snowscape. Then he heard the thunder.

He looked for his gun. He had to get his gun. There. Three feet away in the snow. He quickly bent down to pick it up.

Blam! The bullet tore into the snow and sprayed ice into his face.

"Do not touch that gun!" Again, a voice from nowhere.

Kang stood and looked around. Where were they? Behind trees? Where? "Where are you?" he yelled out into the howling wind.

"We are in the wind. We're in the trees. We're in the snow! We are everywhere. You cannot see!"

For the first time, Kang felt fear. He pivoted around, looking ... looking. Perhaps he should run, but which way? What was he to do? He must keep them talking.

"Who are you?"

"I am the Ghost of Christmas Future! And your future is not so bright right now!"

"What do you want?"

"We want to know something. Is it true that you are one who lashes old men with a bullwhip and slaps them and spits in their faces?"

Now! He dove into the snow for his gun.

A single shot echoed in the night.

The bullet cracked the back of his head. He stood, dazed, then the world went into a fast swirl. His face hit the snow. And then ... blackness.

Prisoners' barracks

What do you see out there, Frank?"

Keith sat on the side of the bunk that Robert had slept in before he died. Frank was on the opposite top bunk, trying to peer through the barred window.

"Can't see anything except snow when the lightning flashes," Frank said. "Too dark. Can't see a thing."

"That sounds like gunfire," Keith said. "And it's too cold to go quail hunting."

"I agree," Frank said. "What do you think they're shooting at?"

"I'm worried that they might have decided to finish off Pak."

"With all those shots?"

"You know Kang," Keith said. "He's the crazy type to kill somebody and still keep shooting."

"Nothing we can do," Frank said. "Go back to sleep. Hope they don't come this way."

"I don't care if they do come," Keith said. "If they want to shoot me, let 'em."

"Don't give up, old friend. I know you and Robert were close. It's just the two of us now. We've got to stick together. There is always hope."

"Hope lived once upon a time," Keith said. "Hope died with Robert."

Office of Colonel Song Kwang-sun

Do you hear that, Colonel?" Jung-Hoon puffed on the cigarette, holding it with his left hand, and kept the pistol aimed at Song's head with his right. "Hear that gunfire? Know what that is? Let me give you a hint. That gunfire is not from Russian-made AK-47s. It is from American-made M-16s. And at this very moment, your secret empire of oppression is crumbling in the falling snow."

"You will never get away with this," Song snarled.

"No?" Jung-Hoon said. "Maybe. Maybe not. But you will not be alive to find out. Now then, I believe I asked you a question. Has to do with whether you have ever had your neck scorched by a burning cigarette."

Song defiantly turned his head away, still refusing to answer.

"Pak, while the good colonel decides if he would like to feel the burning end of a cigarette on his neck, tie up our pretty little red-dressed flower. Tie her legs and feet to the legs of the colonel's big fat desk. I have only a limited supply of ammunition to waste tonight."

"Yes, Jung-Hoon."

That brought a raised eyebrow from Colonel Song. "Who *are* you?"

"I am Colonel Jung-Hoon, Army of the Republic of Korea."

"Jung-Hoon." A bewildered look of recognition came across Colonel Song's face. "I have heard of you. I thought you were retired."

Jung-Hoon drew a final drag from the cigarette, then smashed it out on Song's desk. "Colonel, I shall never retire from my hatred of socialism, or communism, or tyrants who seek to control others, taxing them to death and stealing their property. Nor shall I retire from my life's conviction to see my nation, my Korea, reunified and rid forever of the swine Communist dictator in Pyongyang. But you, my friend, you are about to retire. Permanently! Look on the bright side. I am not going to torture you with a cigarette like you did to this nice lady." He looked at Pak. "You have her tied down?"

"Yes, very tight."

"Good. Go into the outer office and wait."

"Yes, Jung-Hoon."

He waited until she left and had closed the door. "I hope your service to the dictator was worth it."

"What do you mean?" Song demanded.

Jung-Hoon pointed the .45 at Song's head. "Your gun is on your desk, Colonel Song. You have two choices, it would seem. You can either get down on your knees before me, and I will have Pak come back in here and gag you and tie you down beside your mistress, or, if you want to be a real hero, you can always try to reach for that gun of yours."

Song glared at him, his black eyes ablaze with anger.

"If I were you, Colonel Song, I'm not so sure I would take my chances with the gun. That blood dripping from your hand is proof that South Korean special forces are vastly superior marksmen than North Korean swine. Seems your poor marksmanship could be a hazard to your health. The much safer alternative would be for you to get on your knees and take the rope. That way you could live to explain to Dear Leader how you lost control of your camp while your attention was distracted by this woman."

"How dare you try and humiliate me!"

"Humiliate you?" Jung-Hoon said. "I am in fact giving you a chance to save your life. Unless, of course, you think you are a quick enough draw to grab that gun off your desk and shoot me before I shoot you."

Jung-Hoon smiled. He felt a brief moment of smug satisfaction as Song glared at him. Time froze. This was a stare-down for the ages, between North and South, between oppression and freedom. It was between mortal enemies—warrior colonels—one trained to kill in defense of freedom, the other trained to kill to further the evils of totalitarianism.

"My dear Colonel Song," Jung-Hoon said, "they do teach you to use your brains here in the Democratic People's Republic, do they not? To think? I would suggest you use your brain and get down on your knees so that I do not have to blow your brains out."

Song did not blink. In a quick, jerking movement, his bleeding hand reached across the desk for his gun.

Blam!

The colonel was thrown back, away from the desk, landing sprawled on the floor against the wall. His assistant whimpered on the floor, certain she would be next.

Jung-Hoon checked both, then walked into the outer office. "He will never harm you again, Pak. Let's go find the commander and Jackrabbit and get the old men out of here."

Prisoners' barracks

Frank, someone's at the door." Keith pushed himself up from his bunk, his eyes on the locked door, which could only be unlocked from the outside.

"You're right," Frank said. "Somebody is jiggling the lock on the door."

"Oh, I don't like the sound of this."

A booming explosion rocked the building. The door flew open. Snow swirled in on a blast of cold air.

Then a figure appeared in the doorway. A woman. She walked into the barracks and turned on the lights.

"Pak!" Keith exclaimed. "Are you all right?"

"I am fine, and now so are you," Pak said. "There is someone here who wants to speak to you."

"To us?"

She nodded.

The two men who walked into the barracks were all in black. Their faces were covered with black grease. Over their shoulders, they each carried a black assault rifle. They were stiff in their bearing, a formal military bearing.

Keith and Frank just stared up at them, their mouths open.

The one on the left stood a bit straighter, with shoulders back, eyes forward, and said, in a voice of confidence, "Gentlemen, we are Americans. We've come to take you home."

CHAPTER 25

On the road between Youngwang and Changjin

The clock showed ten at night. They had been driving along the dark, winding road about an hour. They had seen only two cars. Both were going in the opposite direction. There was no sign of police or the military. There was not much at all along the road. Just ahead lay the town of Changjin, where they would cut northwest across the mountainous heart of the country on the road that would lead them to the Yalu River and the Chinese border.

The phenomenal thunder-and-lightning snowstorm flashed in the sky behind them. Snowfall had lessened, and the road was passable. The two men they had plucked from the camp sat on the floor of the van, opposite Gunner, their legs covered by a blanket. Pak sat between them. She had one arm around each of their shoulders. She had been sobbing when they left the camp. Gunner wasn't sure why and wasn't about to ask.

"Here is our turn," Jung-Hoon said. "About eighty miles to go."

The van swung to the left, onto a different road. "Be ready for curves and mountains ahead," Jung-Hoon said.

Pak and the two old men seemed like an odd, out-of-place family. Their faces were barely visible in the dark interior of the van, their expressions difficult to make out. Pak had been crying off and on, but said nothing. All Gunner knew about the men was their names—Keith and Frank. All three, the old men and Pak, seemed to be in a trance or perhaps were too overcome with emotion to talk.

Gunner had pictured this moment another way. He thought they

292

would be jubilant, talkative, utterly elated to be free. But then, when he thought of what it must have been like to be in brutal captivity for sixty years and then to be suddenly popped out of the cage in which you had been confined—he realized that he knew nothing about what they must be feeling. And, on top of that, sensing the danger that still faced them. No wonder they were speechless.

Against his natural instinct as an intelligence officer to ask question after question, Gunner decided to postpone any questions. His focus had to remain on getting them all out of North Korea, getting them all home safely. And he knew the danger they still faced.

There was one question that Gunner did not yet want to know the answer to. He could not ask about Robert. The pain, the disappointment, were too great.

Pak had warned Gunner, back at the psychiatric hospital, that Keith was very close to Robert, like a brother, and that he would be very upset because of Robert's death. This news gave Gunner a sick-to-the-stomach feeling. His grandfather's name was "Robert." What if his grandfather had died only hours before they arrived? He couldn't dwell on that possibility. Not now. Their mission—his mission—needed every man to remain sharp, alert. The safety of all depended on it.

He had stood at Robert's grave in that frozen and forsaken prison camp. Not knowing. Robert was, after all, a common name. He imagined his grandfather in heaven, looking down and smiling, as his grandson sped north in a plumber's van with the last two prisoners from a forgotten war fought some sixty years ago. That thought brought a smile to Gunner's face.

The intel officer in him allowed him to ask one question: "Are you gentlemen hungry? We've got a bunch of MREs that we haven't opened."

No answer. Finally, Keith said, "No. No, thank you. Not hungry."

"Okay," Gunner said. "Could be a long night. Might be a good idea to try and get some sleep."

Road that runs along the Yalu River

At two in the morning, Jung-Hoon woke up the others. "According to GPS, only two more miles to debarkation point," he said, his eyes searching for Gunner in the rearview mirror. "We should start getting our friends ready."

"Get our rifles ready too," Jackrabbit said. "Got that, Commander? M-16 and night scope. This area is crawling with border guards."

"Rifle and pistol both good to go, Jackrabbit," Gunner said.

The lights from the instrument panel on the dashboard of the van cast a dim glow into the back. Both Keith and Frank appeared to be snoozing, their heads resting on Pak's shoulders. Pak, with her head cocked back and her mouth open and aimed at the van's ceiling, was asleep between them. "Pak. Keith. Frank." Gunner reached over and shook Keith's knee.

"Aaahhh." Keith opened his eyes.

"Sorry. Didn't mean to hurt you. Time to get up. You too, Frank. We're getting ready to cross the river into China. We're going to walk across." He felt the van slow down, then swing right.

"This is the road along the river," Jung-Hoon said. "The Yalu or Amnok River Road. Our destination is one mile northeast of here."

Gunner said, "The river is frozen and will be slippery. So watch your step. We're all going to walk across. Jung-Hoon, could you hit the country map on the GPS so I can show where we are?"

"Sure." Jung-Hoon punched the Back button a couple of times and the national map came up.

"Could you pass it back for a second?"

Jung-Hoon handed the GPS back to Gunner.

"This is called a GPS. Think of it as an ultrasophisticated radar and map. It can show us where we are at any place on the earth at any time."

In the glow from the GPS screen, he could see their faces light up with interest.

"Right now, we're almost at the tip of this arrow, just outside the town of Wiwŏn. We just turned on the road that snakes alongside the river.

"We're going to drive down here a little ways, and then we'll ditch the van and cross the river. When we get to the other side, there are Christian missionaries who will meet us. They have a seaplane waiting for us. They'll drive southwest on the Chinese side of the river all the way down to Dandong to the plane. We'll take off for Inchon at sunrise.

Closeup of escape route, road along river,
prison to Wiwŏn to Dandong, Korea Bay

"From there we'll take you to Osan Air Base, south of Seoul. We're going to get you home." Gunner gave the GPS back to Jung-Hoon.

"There are border guards in this area, so remain silent. We need to be careful."

"Okay," the old men said in unison.

"Here are jackets for you. It's even colder here than it was back at the prison."

A few minutes later, the GPS stated, "Destination is one mile on your right."

"We are looking for a large stone on the right side of the road as the landmark," Jung-Hoon said.

They rolled on for another two minutes.

Jackrabbit pointed over to the side of the road. "There's our rock."

"Okay, I'll pull over to the right," Jung-Hoon said. "I'll park the van in front of the rock to block visibility from the rear at least. Then we unload and go."

"Need to move fast," Jackrabbit said. "China, here we come."

DPRK patrol jeep
Amnok River Road

He had ten kills notched on his gunbelt. Ten times traitors had fallen from a bullet shot from his rifle. Five times he had been decorated in Pyongyang for his heroism in stopping escapes.

Four of his career kills had been at the Tumen River, on the country's northeastern border with China and Russia. Six of his kills had been at this very river, the Amnok.

Now word had leaked of the sinking of the North Korean Navy's frigate *Najin*. US Navy SEALs were said to be behind it. America was retaliating, it seemed, for the Navy's heroic attack on the carrier *Harry S. Truman*.

The Border Patrol had been placed on high alert. First Sergeant Yoo Young-chul had been at his barracks, asleep, when he had been ordered to border patrol duty along Amnok River Road. And *he*, the master sharpshooter in all the Army, was the only member of his patrol to be assigned a night-vision scope.

His driver, Staff Sergeant Oh Se-hoon, who had never before been in combat, was eager to learn at the feet of the master. They drove to the southwest, toward the town of Wiwŏn. To their right, paralleling the road, was the river, about a quarter mile from their position. It flowed southwest to the city of Sinŭiju and from there into Korea Bay and the Yellow Sea.

Most illegal crossings, however, were not in the more populated areas around Sinŭiju, but rather in this region, a desolate area, where there were few people.

Sergeant Yoo, despite being the Army's most decorated border guard, never got complacent or rested on his magnificent laurels. A fire for killing still burned within him. Though he had killed ten, he thirsted to kill more, to kill a thousand. With every head that he shot with his rifle, the killing grew more exhilarating.

Like a deer hunter closing in on his prey, his instinct told him every time that he was about to kill. He knew it, somehow, by the pounding of his heart and the salivation of his mouth. Before the kill, his breathing always quickened. Indeed his instincts made him a great killer. For marksmanship was only half of the equation. The rest was instinct. Yoo became one with the kill.

"Stay alert, Staff Sergeant Oh!" He caressed his Soviet-made Dragunov 7.62x54mm sniper rifle. "Tonight we are going to kill someone."

He looked out of the slow-moving jeep toward the river and the Chinese border. "I feel it. And I am never wrong."

Border-crossing point
Amnok River Road

Gunner stepped out onto the snow-covered and frozen vegetation beside the road. He turned back to the van and held his hand out for Keith. On the other side, Jung-Hoon steadied Frank by the arm.

The old men moved slowly and cautiously, occasionally wincing when they took a step. But they kept moving and seemed remarkably fit for a couple of guys who had been cooped up in a Communist prison camp for sixty years. Whoever they were, whatever town they were from, they were true survivors.

"Let's get across the road," Jackrabbit said, his gun slung over his shoulder. "The river's about a hundred yards in that direction. I'll cover the rear if there's any trouble."

"This way," Jung-Hoon said as he stepped onto the snow-covered road. Gunner steadied Keith's back as they followed Jung-Hoon. Pak walked beside Frank. They took slow, steady steps, and in a few seconds, they had crossed the road without slipping.

Gunner glanced back and saw Jackrabbit standing guard in the middle of the road, rifle in hand, ready to shoot anyone who tried to interfere with their escape.

A minute later, Jackrabbit fell in line behind them as they shuffled across a flat field, a snowy no-man's land between the road and the river.

When they reached the river's edge, they stood staring at the magnificent sheet of white snow and ice stretching out before them. And beyond, on the other side, were trees.

China!

How ironic that the sight of the world's most populated Communist dictatorship, the People's Republic of China, only a hundred yards away across a sheet of ice, could evoke such a sense of relief.

China, the lesser of two evils, represented a better chance for escape to freedom than the monstrous land now to their backs. Despite its evils, China had become a land with a vibrant underground network of Christians that offered hope to those trying to escape the dark world of North Korea.

"Careful where you step," Jung-Hoon said, still leading the way, and now stepping onto the ice on the river. "Not too bad," he said. He turned and waited for the others.

Gunner stepped onto the frozen river and turned back to help Keith. The thick layer of new-fallen snow gave his feet more traction than he expected. It was slippery, but not treacherous like an ice rink. He took a few more steps. Behind him, the entire group was stepping out onto the river.

He focused his eyes on the trees on the other side.

They moved, inch by inch, step by step, knowing that beyond that treeline in China they would be greeted by friends of Pastor Lee.

And from there—freedom!

DPRK patrol jeep
Amnok River Road

What is that up ahead?" the driver asked.

First Sergeant Yoo rubbed his eyes for a better look. The jeep's headlights illuminated a white vehicle parked off the opposite side of the road.

"Looks like a work van. Pull over," Yoo ordered.

The jeep stopped and First Sergeant Yoo turned on his flashlight and stepped out. "Cover me," he said to his driver.

"Yes, sir." Oh got out of the driver's side and aimed his weapon at the parked van.

Yoo approached the driver's side. He shone the powerful flashlight through the window.

Nothing.

He walked around the back and opened the back doors.

Wire. Plastic explosives. Plastic military food packets.

His eyes widened. This *was* the work of Navy SEALs!

Amnok/Yalu River
midway across the Chinese – North Korean border

We've got a problem," Jackrabbit said. He watched as the vehicle with the lights on stopped in front of the abandoned van and two figures emerged.

"Better pick up the pace," Gunner said, stepping out a little more quickly.

"Aah!"

"Oh!"

Gunner turned around. Keith, Frank, and Pak had all slipped and fallen, and all three were lying facedown in the snow. "Okay, don't panic," Jackrabbit said. "Help them get up, guys."

Gunner reached down for Pak's hand, while Jackrabbit and Jung-Hoon each helped Keith and Frank get back to their feet. "Okay, listen," Jackrabbit said. "We may not be able to walk much faster, but we've got to spread out as far as possible. If there's a sniper over there, we can't be bunched together. Otherwise it's like shooting ducks in a pond."

"Good point," Gunner said. "Everybody spread out in a wide line. We've only got a few more yards to go. Keep moving for those trees over there. Spread out! Spread out! Move! Move!"

DPRK patrol jeep
Amnok River Road

First Sergeant Yoo rushed back to the jeep, his heart pounding with excitement. "Pass me my rifle!"

"Yes, sir!" Oh handed it to him.

Yoo looked down. *Tracks in the snow!* Yoo slung the rifle over his shoulder and headed across the road.

"Where are you going?" Oh called.

"To the river," Yoo said. "Cover me from here." How had he missed them earlier? The tracks showed about six men had headed from the van toward the river. A perfect number for an elite SEAL commando team!

His adrenaline was in high gear as he followed the tracks. He had to think. If he followed them all the way down to the river, they could cross into China before he could get off a shot. He needed to fire now!

He stopped, took his rifle off his shoulder, pointed it in the direction of the tracks, and looked through his night scope.

There!

He counted ... one, two, three, four, five ... six in all, strung out like ducks in a shooting gallery! They were traipsing across the river toward the Chinese side.

He brought his scope over to the far left, lining his crosshairs on the back of the head of the Navy SEAL at the left end of the line.

He squeezed the trigger.

The crack of rifle fire reverberated off the frozen riverbed. The SEAL on the left of the line dropped facedown into a limp, lifeless form. He had drawn blood! Kill number eleven!

His body rushed with excitement as the others dived to the ice, going facedown onto the frozen river, trying to make themselves harder targets. Now they crawled like a bunch of squealing pigs across the ice. This should make easy target practice!

Corbin Hall
Suffolk, Virginia

What now, Lord?"

Margaret sat alone in her bedroom. It was early afternoon at Corbin Hall. She was alone. The grandkids had gone home with Gorman and Bri. Margaret had insisted. Told Gorman she would be fine. She just needed some time.

Now, the same feeling that had wrenched at her stomach the day Gunner's plane went down washed over her body again. Could it be Gorman? Would she lose him too?

"Lord, I don't know what I'm supposed to be praying for right now, but please help whoever needs your help. If it's Gorman or whoever. Help them. But please don't take any more from me."

Amnok/Yalu River
North Korean side

First Sergeant Yoo knew that night scopes were rare in the North Korean military. They were issued on a priority basis only to the most elite snipers in the Army. At the moment, he was grateful for the perk that his marksmanship had earned him. Through the greenish glow of his night scope, he watched as the almighty team of US Navy SEALs crawled on their bellies like a pack of petrified swine. He smiled. This was going to be the most glorious moment of his illustrious career.

He brought the crosshairs onto the next pig Navy SEAL crawling across the ice ...

Bang! Bang! Bang!

Snow and ice sprayed his face and eyes. The SEALs were firing back! He should have known! The SEALs had a reputation as deadly marksmen.

He rolled left and fired in the general direction of the SEALs again, but did not have time to aim with the crosshairs.

More shots flew from the river.

Yoo again rolled hard to his left, trying to avoid the bullets whizzing above his head.

He needed to take cover, to reload. He had to stay low, keep moving. To make himself as small a target as possible, he kept rolling over the icy snowbank toward the jeep.

Two shots rang out. Snow sprayed in his face to his left and to his right. Yoo unleashed a string of expletives.

"Staff Sergeant Oh!" he yelled.

"Yes, sir!"

"I need some cover! Drive the jeep down here. Stay low! Keep the driver's side away from the river!"

"Yes, sir!"

S tay down! Keep moving," Jackrabbit said. "Kiss the ice if you have to, but keep your heads down. When you get to the shore, get behind a tree and stay there! I'll keep 'em pinned down for the time being."

Jackrabbit sprawled belly first on the river, his head and his rifle facing North Korea. Over to his right, at two o'clock, the old man's body lay still on the ice, a sniper's bullet having struck the back of his head.

Jackrabbit brought his scope to his eye and searched the other side of the river.

Lights!

The jeep started moving. Blinding high beams shone down toward the river. They were driving down toward the riverbank!

Jackrabbit pulled the trigger twice in rapid succession. Two sharp rifle cracks echoed through the air. The lights on the jeep exploded, then went dark.

The jeep turned. Jackrabbit pumped two more shots into its tires, then fired a third shot through the side window for good measure. The sound of shattering glass carried all the way across the river.

T he SEAL sniper is good, First Sergeant Yoo concluded. The shots into the tires and the window from across the river—into a moving target in the dark—this was impressive marksmanship.

Yoo also concluded that the SEAL had not yet spotted his position, otherwise he would already be dead.

What a thrill this was … to duel an American Navy SEAL sharp-shooting ace in a contest to the death across the Amnok River! This victory could define him forever as an immortal Legend of the North. He just had to survive long enough to shoot back, and that meant taking cover.

Quick.

Staying low, he got up, sprinted through the snow, slipped, then dove behind the jeep.

Crouching down beside the driver's door, he called out for his driver. "Staff Sergeant Oh!" Again. "Staff Sergeant!"

No response.

Yoo reached up and put his hand on the door latch. "Staff Sergeant!" Again no response. He opened the door.

The body dropped from behind the steering wheel, head first, like a marionette whose arm strings had been snipped but whose feet remained tied from above.

A lifeless, upside-down Staff Sergeant Oh dangled from the jeep, arms and fingers reaching into the snow, wide-open eyes and mouth hanging head down between the running board and the ground. Blood seeped from the fresh bullet hole smack through the middle of his forehead.

The American was even better than he thought. And he had thrown down the gauntlet.

Fair enough. May the best man win! He would peep around the back side of the jeep and wait for a better look.

J ackrabbit scrambled up onto the bank and took cover behind one of the large fir trees.

Safety at last!

If that North Korean idiot tried crossing that river—*Hasta la vista,* baby!

He looked over and saw his four fellow escapees all huddled behind big trees, Gunner and Jung-Hoon with their rifles aimed across the river. Pak had buried her face in her hands and was curled up behind a tree.

"Okay," Jackrabbit said. "Let's get it together! These woods are supposed to clear about one hundred yards to the northwest. Hopefully our ride will be waiting for us. We'll see how good Pastor Lee really is. Let's move through this wood cover. Jung-Hoon, you lead. I'll bring up the rear."

"I'm not leaving him!" Keith cried out.

Gunner looked around, shocked, frankly, at Keith's outburst. He looked at Jung-Hoon, who took cover behind a nearby fir tree.

"He's dead," Jung-Hoon said. "We can do nothing for him."

"Marines do not leave Marines!" Keith protested. "Dead or alive! I'm going to get him!"

"No!" Gunner said. "You stay, Keith. I'll get him."

"Commander, that's suicide," Jackrabbit said. "That sniper's still out there, and he's dead accurate."

"Jung-Hoon," Gunner said, "grab Keith. Make sure he stays put. Jackrabbit, you cover me."

"Don't do it, Commander!"

"Cover me, Jackrabbit!"

Shaking his head in disgust, Jackrabbit brought his rifle up against the tree and aimed again across the river, his night scope on the lifeless jeep with shot-out tires.

No sign of anyone.

The sniper was probably behind the jeep, waiting for someone to make a dumb move, like Gunner was about to do. Then he'd pop out for a shot before popping back under cover again.

In his peripheral vision, Jackrabbit saw Gunner crouching low and crawling back toward the river. He shifted his crosshairs back and forth between the front and back of the Jeep. If he got lucky enough to have his crosshairs in the right place when the sniper popped out, Gunner might have a chance. If not, in a matter of minutes, there would be two dead Americans sprawled on the Yalu River.

He brought his night vision scope onto the back of the jeep.

Nothing.

Slowly, carefully, First Sergeant Yoo peered with his rifle around the front of the jeep. He adjusted his eyes through the night scope. One of the SEALs was crawling out to the dead SEAL. Excellent! Yoo held his fire. He retreated behind the jeep. He could get a better angle on his shot from the back bumper.

Jackrabbit swept his scope from the back to the front of the jeep. Nothing. He knew Gunner was crawling down on the river now, but could not take his eye off the scope.

He held his scope on the front for a few seconds, just in front of the hood of the jeep.

"Pop into my crosshairs, sucker. I dare ya."

Even wearing thermal gloves, Gunner's hands throbbed with aching pain from the ice on the river. He breathed heavily and, frankly, found himself surprised that a shot had not yet been fired. He had slithered to within a couple feet of Frank's body. He looked up, reached forward, and grabbed hold of Frank's left foot.

Yoo crouched down behind the back of the jeep. His opponent was over there, somewhere. Waiting with his rifle. Watching. He sensed it. He knew it. The SEAL sniper, hidden behind one of those trees on the Chinese side, was covering for the SEAL with the death wish crawling out on the ice.

Yoo decided to pop out quickly, get a fix on the crawling SEAL, fire, and pop back behind the jeep before the SEAL sniper could react. Energy and adrenaline surged through his body. Life-or-death danger—he was born for this!

He edged to the back of the jeep and peered around the bumper. He brought his rifle to his shoulder and looked through the scope, searching for the SEAL he was about to slaughter.

Nothing at the front of the jeep, Jackrabbit decided. He swept the scope back toward the rear of the jeep again.

Yoo pointed the rifle at the body of the dead SEAL. There! Right behind the body! The target SEAL was reaching for the dead SEAL's leg. Yoo moved the crosshairs up to center on the SEAL's head, his finger on the trigger. Steady . . . steady . . .

There! In the crosshairs at the rear bumper!
The gunman! A rifle!
Jackrabbit pulled the trigger. A shot cracked the freezing night air.
The shot echoed several times off the frozen river. Or was there more than one shot? Had the Korean gotten off a shot? He was not sure.
He readjusted the night scope, for after firing, he had lost his bearings on the target. He found the jeep and moved the crosshairs back to the rear bumper.
There!
The enemy sniper was sprawled in the snow next to the back bumper. Jackrabbit kept the night scope on him for a few seconds to determine if he was dead.
No point in taking any chances, he decided. He pulled the trigger again. The body jumped, as if jolted by a powerful electric shock. The visual result of that shot was rather gruesome, even by Jackrabbit's standards. If he wasn't dead before, he was now.
"Commander, you okay?" Jackrabbit called out.
No response.
"Commander?"
Still nothing.
Then . . . "I'm fine." Gunner's voice from the river.
"Thank God," Jackrabbit said. "Jung-Hoon, the coast is clear. How about helping the commander with the body. I'll cover you."
"Got it."

Jung-Hoon and Gunner dragged Frank's body up to the treeline. They all stood around Frank, a semicircle in the lightly falling snow. Keith and Pak fell to their knees. Pak put her arms around Keith and the two wept there, on their knees, over their friend.

Jackrabbit, Gunner, and Jung-Hoon formed a quiet, protective circle around them and gave them time.

After a few minutes, Gunner said, "Keith, Pak. We have to go. There are some people through those woods that are supposed to be waiting for us. Don't worry. We'll take Frank with us and make sure that he gets a proper burial back home in the United States."

Keith and Pak stood, still arm in arm.

"If you guys help me get him up, I'll carry him over my shoulders," Jackrabbit said.

"No," Gunner said, "even though we aren't in North Korea anymore, this team is better off if you have quick access to your rifle. Hang on to my rifle. I'm sure it has more bullets in the magazine than yours. I'll carry Frank. If he gets too heavy, maybe Jung-Hoon can help me out."

They exchanged glances. "Fair enough, Commander."

Jackrabbit and Jung-Hoon loaded Frank across Gunner's right shoulder, then they all headed northwest through the Chinese forest. Jung-Hoon led the way. Gunner with Frank on his shoulder was next. Pak and Keith followed him.

Jackrabbit was the rear guard.

Yalu River Valley
People's Republic of China
near the village of Liangshu

They trudged solemnly, at a snail's pace, through the remote Chinese woods. Frank wasn't a heavy man, but still, his body weight was wearing down Gunner's shoulder, making each step harder.

"There's the opening," Jung-Hoon said finally. They stepped out into the opening of a valley-like field. The snow had stopped. Brilliant stars shone in the crisp black canopy above.

"I need to put him down for a minute," Gunner said.

"Hang on, Commander." Jackrabbit lifted the body off Gunner and laid it face up on the snowy ground.

"Look!" Pak said.

Gunner looked up. Two silhouettes approached from across the field. Gunner did not have his rifle, but reached for his pistol. Jackrabbit and Jung-Hoon readied their M-16s.

"Commander McCormick," a male voice in Chinese-accented English called out.

Gunner looked over at Jackrabbit, who gave him one simple nod of the head.

"I am McCormick!" Gunner called back.

A second passed. "We are from underground Baptist Church in Liangshu. God bless you!"

Jung-Hoon called out, "Peace be with you!"

"And also with you!" came the reply.

"He is risen!" Jung-Hoon said.

"He is risen indeed."

"We heard gunshots," the voice said. "Is everything okay?"

"One dead," Jackrabbit said. "We're over here." He gave them a quick shot with a flashlight, then turned the flashlight off again.

"We see you." A few seconds later, the two Chinese Christians had joined the small group near the treeline. "I am Brother Qian." He half bowed. "And this is Brother Wang Yong." They both half bowed. "May God bless you all," Qian said.

"God bless both of you too," Gunner said.

Brother Qian knelt down near Frank's body. "Looks like fresh wound. I am sorry."

"He got hit by a sniper as we crossed the river," Jackrabbit said.

"We will help you take him to our van," Qian said. "We have a blanket that we can wrap him in. Let me call our driver. He will bring the van up." Qian made a quick call on his cell phone, spoke in Mandarin, then put the cell phone away. "The road is about two hundred meters in that direction. The van will be here in five minutes. We should start moving toward the road."

"I have a question," Jung-Hoon said. "I am the pilot. Could you tell me what kind of plane we will be flying?"

"It is a Cessna 172 floatplane, moored on a dock on the river several miles southwest of Dandong. An American missionary group donated it for delivering smuggled Bibles all over east Asia and southeast Asia."

"Cessna 172." Jung-Hoon said. "That will be a tight squeeze for six. No chance of taking the pilot to bring it back."

A van rolled up and stopped. "This is our van," Brother Qian said. "We will take your friend for you."

"Thank you." Gunner nodded.

The Chinese lifted Frank's body, Qian locking his arms under Frank's armpits and carefully stepping backward, and the other man taking the old man's feet. The sight of them trudging across the snow in an act of loving service, holding the body of an elderly American they had never met, brought tears to Gunner's eyes.

CHAPTER 26

Road along the Yalu River
fifteen miles southwest of Dandong, China

The drive along the Yalu River during the night had been uneventful. The sun was now rising off to the east, its bright rays a near-blinding brief glare each time the winding road took them east before it again turned to the southwest.

Not much had been said except for the occasional banter from the Chinese Christians. If Keith and Pak had been in shell shock after the attack on the prison camp, the death of their friend seemed to have sent them into a deeper hole of darkness.

Gunner bought the plane, paying the missionaries with both Korean won and US dollars. They would leave the plane in Inchon. It would be returned to Pastor Lee's network to be ready to help others. Gunner was satisfied that he had done everything he could.

The van slowed.

"Here is our turn," Qian said. "This road takes us to the river."

A couple of minutes along a winding road through the woods brought them to an opening. Before them now was a wide expanse of river flowing to the sea. Gunner looked across, to the nation that had taken his grandfather from him, and he felt an overwhelming sadness.

In front of them, a wooden pier stuck out into the river. Tied to the pier was a blue single-engine floatplane. A Caucasian man, fiftyish-looking, walked down the pier toward them.

"Fortunately," Brother Qian said, "the river does not freeze over here for a couple more months. That is Martin Luther. He sometimes flies the plane."

"Martin Luther?" Gunner asked.

"That is not his real name. He is an American missionary pilot, but his sponsoring organization requires him to use another name for security purposes. Officially, Chinese government is hostile to evangelical Christians."

"I see," Gunner said.

The van, with the driver's window partially down, rolled to the edge of the pier. Martin Luther walked up to the driver's window and leaned his head into the van. "She's gassed up and good to go," he said, speaking English in a Southern accent. "Who's flying?"

"Me," Jung-Hoon said.

"I understand you're flying dead-reckoning to Inchon. I've plotted the course and it's waiting for you in the cockpit."

"Thank you," Jung-Hoon said.

"We'll help you load her up."

They got out of the van and exchanged hugs with the Chinese Christians. Then they proceeded to board. Jackrabbit shoved the rifles and a backpack with the rest of the C4 and other gear into the back, ready to be dumped in the sea, then sat up front with Jung-Hoon. Pak sat on Gunner's lap behind the pilot. He wrapped his arms around her waist because the seat belt would not click across them both. Frank's body, wrapped in a blanket, was laid on the floor between the seats. Keith strapped into the seat behind Jackrabbit.

Martin Luther untied the plane, and he and the Chinese pushed it out into the river.

Jung-Hoon hit the starter and the engine started immediately. Its powerful roar shot an unexplained surge of confidence through Gunner. They were going home.

Jung-Hoon pushed down on the throttle and the Cessna moved on the water, gathering speed, then nudged into the air, rising for a few seconds to about ten feet over the water, and then banked upward, climbing higher above the river. They took off to the south, the brilliant sun shining in from their left. A few minutes later, they were flying over Korea Bay, and from there, to the Yellow Sea, and from there, God willing—to freedom.

US Navy F/A-18
over the Yellow Sea

Lieutenant Commander Corey "Werewolf" Jacobs, USN, had been confined to the ship for a brief JAGMAN investigation, which found that he and his wingman, Lieutenant Bill Morrison, had operated properly within the rules of engagement when they shot down the two North Korean MiGs.

Jacobs was glad to be back at the controls of his F/A-18 and in the air again on this glorious sunny morning. His assignment was to patrol the sector north and west of the *Harry S. Truman*. The CAG had put more pressure on the fighter squadrons to guard that sector after Admiral Hampton moved the frigates to the east of the *Truman* to guard against any more missile attacks from North Korea. Still, despite the added pressure, getting back in the air felt like a refreshing swim in the waters of freedom—the exhilarating feeling that only a fighter pilot could understand.

Beep-beep-beep-beep . . .

Jacobs checked the sweeping radar screen. The radar showed an unidentified aircraft approaching from the direction of the Chinese–North Korean sector, altitude 1,000 feet, speed 100 knots.

Its course would take it directly over the *Harry S. Truman*.

"Truman Control. Viper Leader. I've got an unidentified bogie entering the sector. Course one-eight-zero. Range thirty-five miles. Entering our airspace and headed our way."

"Viper Leader. Truman. Proceed to investigate and report. You have your orders. If bogie continues on present course, take it out."

"Truman. Viper Leader. Roger that."

Jacobs pushed on the throttle and hit the afterburners. The jet shot through the air like a rocket. "Estimated time of intercept, one minute."

The Super Hornet descended . . . 1,500 . . . 1,200 . . . 1,000 feet. Jacobs made a large sweeping motion and came up behind the much-slower-moving aircraft.

There. One o'clock.

Visual contact.

Jacobs reduced airspeed to match the bogie's speed, closing to about two hundred yards behind the plane.

"Truman Control. Viper Leader. I've got a visual on the bogie. We've got a single-engine Cessna seaplane. Looks like a 150 or 172. Chinese markings on the tail. I've got it in my gun sights and can take it out if necessary."

"Viper Leader. Truman. Attempt to contact Cessna to determine intentions. Instruct to divert. If no response by radio, send IFF. If no response to IFF and no change of course, assume the ID is foe, not a friendly, and take it out."

"Truman Control. Viper Leader. Roger that." Jacobs switched to a universal frequency. "US Navy warplane to Cessna. You are approaching airspace controlled by the United States Navy. Please identify yourself and identify your intentions."

A pause ...

Then a squawk over the radio, and then ...

"Cessna to US Navy warplane. I am Colonel Jung-Hoon Sohn of the Army of the Republic of Korea ..."

USS Harry S. Truman
the Yellow Sea

Captain Charles Harrison sat in his captain's chair in the center of the bridge of the *Harry S. Truman*, drinking his second mug of black coffee of the morning when his communications officer rushed onto the bridge.

"Skipper, you won't believe this," the officer said.

"Try me," Harrison said, then took another swig.

"The aircraft that Lieutenant Commander Jacobs is tracking is asking for permission to land in the water."

"Land in the water?"

"Yes, sir. It's a small Cessna floatplane. They're also requesting helicopter rescue assistance. Pilot claims to be a Colonel Jung-Hoon Sohn of the ROK Army. They claim to have an American POW from the Korean War on board. They also claim to have ... get this ... Lieutenant Commander Gunner McCormick on board."

"Say what?" Harrison said. "That's crazy. McCormick went down in the Sea of Japan."

"Understand, sir. But Commander Jacobs is right out there on top of him, and he thinks it's credible. In fact, he says the plane is already making the approach for a landing."

"XO, scramble two choppers out to the intercept position for this Cessna. Let's see what we've got."

"Aye, sir."

"And Lieutenant?" He addressed the communications officer.

"Yes, sir."

"Tell Commander Jacobs to order that plane down. And if it gets within a twenty-five-mile zone of this ship, tell him to splash it. The last thing we need is to get fooled by a Communist kamikaze plane masquerading as a social project."

"Aye, Captain."

Chinese Cessna 172 floatplane
the northern Yellow Sea

Jung-Hoon flew low over the water, watching the powerful Navy F/A-18 Super Hornet one hundred yards off his left wing. The radio squawked again.

"Cessna 172. This is US Navy warplane. You are ordered to commence water landing immediately. Rescue helicopters are en route."

"Yes!" Gunner pumped his fist in the air. Even Pak smiled.

"If you proceed much farther on course, you will be shot down."

"US Navy warplane. Cessna 172. I'm putting her down now." Jung-Hoon pulled up on the stick, raising the plane's nose, and cut back on the throttle. "Hang on, ten seconds to splashdown."

The Cessna dropped gradually. Gunner wrapped his arms tight around Pak's waist. A second later, a swishing noise, and the sound and feel much like water skis being pulled behind a powerboat. Jung-Hoon cut the engine. They were floating silently somewhere on the Yellow Sea.

Jackrabbit worked his way back to the weapons and the remaining gear. In case of a second water landing, he had put together a plan B. They could not take the chance that the plane would remain afloat and become treasure for the North Koreans. He lashed everything together, checked the timer on the explosives, and grabbed the remote.

After everyone was off and safe, he would send the plane to the bottom of the sea.

US Navy SH-60B Seahawk
the northern Yellow Sea

Over there!" The chopper's copilot, Navy Lieutenant (JG) Bill Jonson, pointed off to the left.

"I see it," said veteran Seahawk pilot Navy Lieutenant Bill Cameron. The blue seaplane was riding the shallow swells about three hundred yards off their port side.

"Okay, let's drop a couple of swimmers in the water out to the right of the plane. Tell the chief to get ready to lower the life basket."

"Got it, Skipper."

Chinese Cessna 172 floatplane
the northern Yellow Sea

The familiar roar of US Navy helicopters filled the air. Gunner leaned over and saw the gray SH-60B Seahawk with the word *NAVY* painted in black along the tail fuselage and the name USS *Harry S. Truman* in black letters just behind the pilot.

The chopper descended about a hundred yards out to the right of the plane. It hovered at ten feet. The cargo bay opened. Two SAR swimmers in black thermal gear leaped, feet first, into the water. The chopper ascended again as the swimmers surfaced and headed toward the plane with powerful freestyle strokes.

The chopper climbed back to about one hundred feet and feathered over to one side of the plane.

"Attention, Cessna aircraft." A voice boomed from the Seahawk's loudspeaker system. "This is the US Navy. We are lowering a rescue basket from the chopper. Two swimmers are en route to your plane. Stay put. Follow their directions. This is the US Navy."

The swimmers arrived within a minute or so and climbed up on the pontoons. They reached up and guided the metal basket down and opened the door of the aircraft.

They strapped Frank's body in first, and the basket swung out over the water, hanging from the steel cable. Gunner and Keith watched as the basket ascended up into the chopper. A couple of minutes later, the basket was lowered again. "Keith, you're next," Gunner said.

Keith protested. "Marines don't go before ladies," he said, seeming to come back to life.

But Pak refused. "Once you are aboard that helicopter," she said, "you will be almost home in your country again. You have waited many years for this."

Gunner and the others sided with Pak, so Keith went next. He was followed by Pak, then Jung-Hoon, and then Jackrabbit. Gunner insisted on going last.

With everyone finally settled in the helicopter, Jackrabbit quietly told the pilot and copilot that he needed to take care of some unfinished business. He explained how he had rigged the Cessna with explosives to send it to the bottom and keep it out of the hands of the North Koreans.

With the helicopter still within range and angled to look back at the floatplane, Jackrabbit pushed the remote. "Good to go," he told the pilot.

They headed for the *Truman*, and Jackrabbit watched the Cessna as it got smaller and smaller. Then ... *POOF!* A column of black smoke billowed out and hung there like a death shroud, then was lifted up and away by the wind. Jackrabbit smiled. The plane was gone. He saw only the sea.

Fifteen minutes later, the Seahawk flew in over the fantail of the USS *Harry S. Truman*. The chopper hovered over the flight deck and slowly feathered down and landed.

Deck crews rushed to the helicopter and opened the cargo door. Two Navy corpsmen were the first aboard the helicopter. They removed Frank's body, first covering it with a white sheet and loading it on a stretcher.

Commander Lawrence Berman, the ship's senior medical officer, climbed aboard next and walked over to Keith. "Sir, I'm Dr. Berman. I'm the ship's doctor. Would you come with me, please?" Pak, Jackrabbit, and Jung-Hoon then stepped out onto the windy deck. Gunner was last.

Three senior officers formed an arms-folded semicircle outside the chopper. They included the *Truman's* commanding officer, Captain

Charles Harrison; her executive officer, Commander Rawlinson Petty; and Captain Anthony Farrow, Admiral Hampton's chief of staff.

"Good morning, sir," Gunner said to the senior of the three, Captain Harrison.

"Welcome back aboard, Commander," Harrison said.

"Commander," Captain Farrow said, "you just have time to go get cleaned up, get in your uniform, and report to the admiral at ten-thirty hours."

"Yes, sir."

USS Harry S. Truman
the Yellow Sea

Lieutenant Commander McCormick." The admiral dragged out every syllable as if he were about to start the dreaded Chinese waterboard torture. "Where have you been?" Hampton sat back in his chair and played with his pencil as he looked at Gunner.

"Sir, you told me to take leave." Gunner stood at attention in his Navy service dress-blue uniform, staring straight ahead and not daring to make eye contact.

"Yes, I suppose I did, didn't I?"

Gunner did not respond.

"Of course I don't recall ordering you also to transform yourself into a one-man Rambo squad."

"No, sir."

"Or even a three-man Rambo squad."

Gunner hesitated. "No, sir, you did not."

Hampton stood, crossed his arms, and walked over to the side of his office. He didn't look at Gunner. "We've interviewed Colonel Jung-Hoon and Lieutenant Colonel Davenport." The admiral shook his head. "We know what happened."

"Understand, sir."

"Boy, when you decide to associate yourself with retired Special Forces guys, you don't mess around, do you?"

Gunner didn't know what to say. "Unfortunately, sir, there weren't many retired Navy SEALs that I could find in South Korea."

"You sure fooled the North Koreans."

Again, Gunner did not respond.

"Interesting, isn't it? You take leave, as I ordered. You purchase a yellow aircraft. You decide to take that plane, according to the flight plan, to Japan with your two newfound friends, who happen to be the meanest, baddest, fighting machines in all of South Korea not dubbed with the title Navy SEAL. Your pilot calls in a distress signal. Two hours or so after that, the flagship North Korean frigate, the *Najin*, blows up and sinks ... although I can't give you credit for that one." The admiral paused and shook his head. "Less than forty-eight hours later, you show up in another private single-engine plane, flown out of China, this one with pontoons, and right before my fighter pilot shoots it down, your pilot lands it in the Yellow Sea. My choppers pull you and your two buddies out, along with a Korean woman, the body of an old man, plus another old man. Both US Marines who have been in prison in North Korea for sixty years. You entered a Communist dictatorship, without authority, when military tensions are high with the United States. And you proceed to attack and obliterate a Communist military prison and kill who-knows-how-many North Korean soldiers."

Gunner stood there. "I don't know what to say, sir."

"You know I could court-martial you for this, don't you?"

"Sir," Gunner said, "I am prepared to resign my commission and plead guilty to whatever charges JAG wants to throw at me."

Another awkward period of silence.

"Yes, well, I appreciate the offer. That would save me a lot of trouble." The admiral sat back down in his chair and twirled his yellow number 2 pencil between his fingers. "But before you do that, I at least want to tell you what we've found out about the two gentlemen you brought back."

"Yes, sir."

"We did dental impressions of them both and matched them against records held at the National Military Personnel Records Center in St. Louis." He picked up a sheet of paper. "The deceased is HN3 Frank Dinardo, of Oak Park, Illinois. Eighty-four years old. He was a Navy hospital corpsman detached to the First Marine Division. He volunteered for service with the First Marine Division in Korea."

Hampton laid down that paper and picked up another. "The other

is a Second Lieutenant Robert Keith Pendleton, age eighty-three, actually now *Colonel* Robert Keith Pendleton, because he was promoted *in
absentia* as an MIA—of Suffolk, Virginia."

Hampton looked up from the paper. "That name ring a bell?"

Gunner looked down. Had he heard that right? His heart fired into
afterburner mode.

"Yes, I thought that might break that stiff stance of yours." The
admiral's stern face showed a tinge of a smile, but not for long. "Colonel
Pendleton is suffering from shell shock, from fatigue, from dehydra-
tion, from arthritis, from an infected foot as a result of a slice from
a whip, and from malnourishment. They've got an IV in him and are
pumping in antibiotics. Other than that, Dr. Berman says he'll be fine."

Hampton laid the paper down. "Your grandfather, Commander, is
one tough Marine."

Gunner felt tears welling in his eyes.

"At ease, Commander. Relax for a second."

"Thank you, sir." He wiped his eyes. "I thought my grandfather had
died a few days ago. They said they had buried a Marine named Robert."

"Yes, we interviewed Colonel Pendleton about that. That Robert was
Second Lieutenant Robert Harold Ward of North Carolina, your grandfather's best friend. Your grandfather, years ago, started going by his
middle name of Keith to avoid confusion and out of deference to Lieutenant Ward, who saved his life under fire at Chosin Reservoir."

"So that explains the name."

"Yes, that explains your grandfather's name," Hampton said. "It
does not explain my quandary with you, Commander." He eyed Gunner
with a piercing stare. "So the question now is, what do I do about you?
Put another way, has the end justified the means in this case? A means
in which, I might point out, you have violated a whole host of standing
orders and regulations."

Gunner wasn't sure if that was a rhetorical question or one that
required a response. "As I said, sir, I offer my resignation now and plead
guilty to whatever JAG throws at me."

"You know," Admiral Hampton said, seeming to ignore Gunner,
"this ship is named for a guy who had a sign on his desk that said,
'The Buck Stops Here.' I've always admired that about Truman. Fearless
decision maker."

"Yes, sir, he was."

"And out here, at sea"—he crossed his arms and nodded his head—"with the ships of this strike group, the buck stops with me."

"Yes, sir, it does."

"Good. I'm glad you understand that. So here's my official report to Washington that will follow you for the rest of your life." He put on reading glasses and looked down and picked up a sheet of paper and began reading.

Lieutenant Commander CP (Gunner) McCormick, while on leave to the Republic of Korea, chartered a private aircraft with two friends for a Thanksgiving weekend furlough to Japan. While in flight, said aircraft developed engine, electrical, and navigational problems, and with the pilot losing total navigational control of the aircraft, it flew hundreds of miles off course and crash-landed in the Sea of Japan near the North Korean coastline. Miraculously, McCormick and his friends survived and were washed ashore behind enemy lines. Attempting to survive in enemy territory at a time of heightened tensions, with the US and North Korean naval forces exchanging fire, Commander McCormick and his colleagues evaded the enemy and, while attempting to escape, came across South Korean and American sympathizers living in the North. Rebel elements within the North Korean Army opposed to Kim Jong-il informed McCormick of the existence of a secret POW camp reported to house a small number of Americans from the Korean War. This knowledge disturbed Commander McCormick, and he persuaded rebel forces to help him organize an underground commando raid, which resulted in the rescue of two US Marines who had been imprisoned more than sixty years, unbeknownst to the United States government. One of the Marines, unfortunately, was killed during the escape into China. The second, Colonel Robert Keith Pendleton, survived and was safely transported back to USS *Harry S. Truman*, en route to being reunited with his family in the United States.

Therefore, for extreme gallantry and risk of life in actual combat with an armed enemy force and going beyond the call of duty, Lieutenant Commander Christianson Pendleton McCormick is hereby nominated by this command for receipt of the Navy Cross. Also nominated are Lieutenant Colonel John Michael Davenport, US Army (retired), and Colonel Jung-Hoon Sohn of the Army of the Republic of Korea (retired).

"Sir ..."

"Your request to resign is denied. Now get out of my office, you bonehead! You've got some catching up to do!"

CHAPTER 27

US Navy C-40A Clipper
over Havelock, North Carolina

five days later

The big US Navy jet banked to the right, and from the far-right seat next to the window on the first row, Keith looked out and saw the forest of green Carolina pines and the sparkling rivers below. The panorama of green and blue provided his first close-up view of the continental United States in more than sixty years. Though he had kissed the ground at Hickam Field in Hawaii and enjoyed his three days of recuperation at Pearl Harbor Naval Hospital, his heart leaped for joy at the sight of the East Coast. For the trees and rivers of coastal North Carolina were but a few short miles from Camp Lejeune, where he had reported for duty with the Marines as a young butter-bar second lieutenant. Not only that, but when they landed, he would be only 150 miles from home in Suffolk, Virginia.

"Colonel. Commander." The Navy lieutenant copilot, who had stepped out of the cockpit, interrupted his thoughts. "The pilot says we're on final approach for landing at Cherry Point. If you would please strap in, we'll be on the ground in about five minutes."

"Thanks, Lieutenant," Keith said. The click of his seat belt sent his mind racing again.

Only two weeks ago, he had been slashed by the bullwhip of a savage North Korean guard, convinced he would die a forgotten man, never again to see home this side of heaven.

Now, here he was in a modern Navy jet, decked out in the uniform of a full-bird colonel in the United States Marine Corps, sitting beside a naval officer grandson he had never met before, who had not taken his hand off his arm for virtually the whole flight from Hawaii.

In the rows behind them, the commandant of the Marine Corps had flown out from Washington to join them on the flight back from Hawaii, along with the secretary of the Navy, along with CINCPAC, the four-star admiral in command of all the US Pacific forces. In the seat across the aisle, an attractive lady, a public-affairs officer, a Lieutenant Colonel Meg Owens, had tagged along for two days to make sure Keith did and said everything right.

Surely this was all a dream.

The jet descended rapidly now, and Keith's ears registered the descent. He gazed out his window at the tops of the loblolly pines blurring by outside the window, and then the concrete runway came rushing toward them.

A slight bump signaled the plane had touched down, then a rushing windy sound as the jet braked on the runway.

As the plane taxied around, the Cherry Point control tower came into view, and under it, on the tarmac, Keith saw a sea of men and women in Marine Corps green and navy blue behind an army of cameramen and reporters. Several reporters stood with their backs to the plane, talking into their microphones, obviously hoping to film the arriving jet as a visual backdrop to their reports.

The plane came to a stop.

"Welcome home, Granddaddy." Gunner smiled and patted him on the hand.

"Almost home, son," Keith said. "Not quite yet."

Outside, two Marine staff sergeants rolled a portable stairway up to the jet's cabin door. The copilot stepped out of the cockpit and opened the door. A rush of chilly air blew into the cabin.

The public-affairs officer looked over at Keith. "Okay, sir, just to remind you of the itinerary, the honor guard will remove Petty Officer Dinardo's casket from the rear of the aircraft. We will watch those ceremonies on closed-circuit television from here in our seats. After that, you will descend the ladder along with Lieutenant Commander McCormick. The president will be waiting for you at the bottom of the stairway. He will have a few prepared remarks. After that, your daughter will greet you. We have a Marine Corps helicopter waiting to take you, your daughter, and Commander McCormick directly to Corbin Hall."

Keith smiled at the mention of Corbin Hall.

"Any questions, sir?"

"No, I think that has it. Thank you."

Television screens over the seats flashed on, showing the tail section of the aircraft. A coffin draped with the flag of the United States of America slowly descended on a lift from the rear of the plane. Standing at attention waiting for it were six enlisted Marines who made up the pallbearer honor guard and a United States Navy chaplain. They wore dress-blue uniforms with white belts and white gloves. Swords dangled from their belts.

The Marines stepped forward and lifted the casket. Then, moving in perfect unison, they took one step backward away from the lift. The Marine Corps band began a slow, mournful rendition of the "Navy Hymn." The Marines moved slowly, step by step, carrying the flag-draped coffin to a black hearse parked on the tarmac. The Marine band stopped playing, and the US Navy Chorus, standing in blue crackerjack uniforms beside the hearse, began to sing *a cappella* the words of the hymn as the Marines loaded the coffin into the hearse.

Eternal Father, strong to save,
Whose arm hath bound the restless wave,
Who bidd'st the mighty ocean deep,
Its own appointed limits keep.

Oh hear us as we cry to Thee,
For those in peril on the sea!

"Color guard. Pree-zent ... arms!"

"Fire!"... *BOOM!*

"Fire!"... *BOOM!*

"Fire!"... *BOOM!*

Three volleys of rifle shots cracked the Carolina blue sky. Then a reverent silence blanketed the tarmac.

Keith watched as the hearse moved forward and drove out of view. They were home. Frank was gone.

A moment passed.

"Colonel. Commander McCormick," the public-affairs officer said. "It's time."

Keith and Gunner stood and walked to the entrance of the aircraft as the Marine Band trumpet section broke into "Ruffles and Flourishes." Then the red-jacketed band began playing a piece of music that Keith had feared he would never hear again.

From the Halls of Montezuma
To the shores of Tripoli;

They stepped out into the sunshine at the top of the portable stairway to thunderous sustained applause.

We will fight our country's battles
In the air, on land and sea;

They walked down the stairway, waving to a sea of a thousand camera flashes.

First to fight for right and freedom
And to keep our honor clean;

At the bottom, they walked together out on the tarmac. The applause continued.

We are proud to claim the title
Of United States Marine.

The applause kept on and on. Keith realized that the PAO officer and the commandant of the Marine Corps and several other dignitaries were now standing close behind him.

"This way, Colonel," the public-affairs officer said. They walked toward the podium set up on the field. And there, to one side of the podium with a blue covering and a round emblem with the phrase "Seal of the President of the United States," stood a smiling salt-and-pepper-haired man in a navy blue suit and red tie. He was applauding. A limousine with the presidential seal on the back passenger door was parked nearby.

When the applause finally subsided, the man stepped behind the microphones and said, "Colonel Pendleton. I'm Mack Williams. I'm your new commander in chief. Welcome home!"

Keith shot the president a sharp salute. "Nice to meet you, Mr. President."

That reignited thunderous applause, this time peppered with cheers and whistling and the sound of Marines grunting "Ooooo-rah."

"My first order," the president said, then waited as more whistles and applause threatened to drown out his words. When the applause subsided again, he said, "My first order is for you to come stand behind the podium with me."

Keith complied, and the president greeted him with a big bear hug.

More applause.

"Colonel, I know you are anxious to get home, and we have a Marine chopper waiting to take you to a place called Corbin Hall." Cheers ... whistles. "But first, there is something you should know. While you were in flight from Hawaii, the Senate, at my recommendation, approved your promotion to brigadier general. You will retire from the Marine Corps at that rank and, though I haven't checked lately, I suspect that might improve your retirement pay a tad."

More cheering.

"Thank you, Mr. President."

"I'll ask Lieutenant Commander McCormick, your grandson, to help me here, and we're going to remove those birds from your collar and replace them with stars."

"With pleasure, Mr. President," Gunner said.

Keith stood at attention while Gunner removed the eagle off his left collar, and the president removed the eagle from his right collar. Then they each pinned a single silver star onto each collar, officially making him a brigadier general in the United States Marine Corps.

"Congratulations, General Pendleton," the president said. More applause. "And now ... and now ... there is someone who is very anxious to see you." He turned around and said, "Captain."

A trim Marine officer, standing by the black limousine, opened the back door. An attractive woman who looked to be in her sixties got out, took the arm of the Marine officer, and walked toward the podium. With her free hand, she wiped tears from her eyes.

He had last seen her when she was a baby. But still, somehow, he knew. Daddy never forgets his little girl.

She walked up to him and fell into his arms.

"My little Margaret," he said, holding her tight.

"I always knew you were alive," she said. "I never stopped praying."

They hugged, oblivious of the sustained cheering around them.

"Let's go home," he said.

"Yes, let's." She stepped back, smiling, tears flooding her eyes.

The president said, "General, I know you've got a chopper to catch and a lot of catching up to do. But before you do, is there anything you'd like to say?"

"Yes, sir, Mr. President, there is." Keith stepped to the microphone. The crowd went stone silent. All eyes were focused on him.

"Thank you for being here. You have made this one grand welcome home. I am grateful. And I was grateful for my country when I was captured sixty years ago as a young man. I am no less grateful for my country today as an old man. I am grateful to my grandson Lieutenant Commander Gunner McCormick and to all who risked their lives to save me. And I am most grateful that my final days on this earth will be spent at home, with my family, in the glorious sunset of freedom.

"May God bless America."

EPILOGUE

Corbin Hall
Suffolk, Virginia

Brigadier General Robert Keith Pendleton, United States Marine Corps, retired, sat at the head of the table and absorbed the sights of Christmas. His daughter, Margaret, wearing her red Christmas sweater, sat to his right, beaming like the happiest woman in the world. His grandson Gunner, the real hero of the hour, sat at his left. Right beside Gunner, in a radiant new red dress, the product of her first visit to an American shopping mall, Pak looked stunning and happy with her new adopted American family.

Grandson Gorman sat at the other end of the table, surrounded by his wife, Bri, and their two children, Jill and Tyler.

Keith looked down and eyed the turkey, dressing, mashed potatoes, gravy, and squash casserole on his plate. It was a white plate that had the Marine Corps globe-and-anchor emblem on it. Margaret had insisted that he use this plate, although he was the only one with such a plate.

Whatever Margaret wanted. He wasn't going to argue.

Off to the side, the Christmas tree glowed with a myriad of colored lights, some shining constantly and some blinking. And on top, an angel looked down with outstretched arms.

He wondered if this could all be a dream and he would soon wake up back in the perpetual nightmare of his real life.

The doorbell rang.

This was no dream. This was real.

The doorbell rang again.

Although the turkey was freshly carved and on the table, Keith was grateful for the interruption. He got up with the family and walked to the front door.

Since his return home, Christmas carolers had descended on Corbin Hall like an invading army of goodwill. They were bused in from churches around Tidewater. One church youth group even trekked in from Rocky Mount, North Carolina.

They would park along the road, offload from their buses, and walk down the long driveway singing all the carols that he had not heard for so long—"Silent Night," "Joy to the World," "O Come, O Come, Emanuel," "We Wish You a Merry Christmas"—then they would walk back singing, board their buses, and go back to spend the rest of Christmas with their families.

Standing out front in a light falling snow was another group of carolers. The last time he had seen snow, it was like frozen ice falling into the cold pit of hell that was Korea. But tonight, as he stretched out his hand and looked up, Keith smiled. The falling snow was like manna from heaven.

A smiling young woman, perhaps seventeen years old, stood in front of the other smiling teenagers.

"General Pendleton?"

"Yes, ma'am?"

"We're the youth group from First Baptist in Elizabeth City, North Carolina."

"Thank you all for coming tonight."

"May we ask a question?"

"Certainly you may."

"May we sing you something a little unusual for Christmas?" The girl's blue eyes twinkled with excitement.

"My dear, you can sing anything you would like."

She smiled and turned around. She held up her hands in a director's pose and said, "Slow and meaningful," then hummed a single note for pitch.

Then came the most beautiful blend of melody and harmony his ears had ever heard.

Oh beautiful
For spacious skies
For amber waves of grain,
For purple mountain majesties
Above the fruited plain,
America, America, God shed his grace on thee!
And crown thy good with brotherhood,
From sea to shining sea!

Keith stood there, his right arm around Margaret, and wiped his eyes.

Maybe he really wasn't a Marine.

Marines don't cry.

"Merry Christmas, General Pendleton!"

Black Sea Affair

Don Brown

It's a mission that could bring the world to the brink of nuclear war.

Now time is running out.

It starts with a high-stakes theft: weapons-grade plutonium is stolen from Russia. The Russian army is about to attack Chechnya to get it back, but U.S. intelligence discovers that the stolen shipment is actually on a rogue Russian freighter in the Black Sea manned by terrorists.

It turns into a global nightmare: a secret mission gone awry. An American submarine commander is arrested and hauled before a military tribunal in Moscow, starting a game of brinksmanship so dangerous that war might be its only possible conclusion.

A submarine mishap escalates in international crisis. With the world watching, JAG Officer Zack Brewer is called to Moscow to defend submarine skipper Pete Miranda and his entire crew. It is a heart-stopping race against the clock. With Russian missiles activated and programmed for American cities, Brewer stalls for time as the U.S. Navy frantically searches the high seas for a floating hydrogen bomb that could threaten New York Harbor.

Available in stores and online!

Defiance

Don Brown

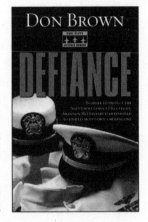

From a murder in Paris to a courtroom in California to a terrorist camp in the Gobi Desert, Don Brown's follow-up to *Treason* and *Hostage* plunges into a suspense-filled journey of danger, duty, and hope.

The commander's bodyguard is Shannon McGilverry, a crack NCIS agent assigned to protect Navy JAG Officer Zack Brewer. Zack is being hunted by terrorists, stalked by a psychopath, and is working his way through a perilous, politically-charged trial. When another Navy JAG officer is murdered, it's clear that Zack is in harm's way.

As his bodyguard, Shannon must do more than protect Zack. She also must set aside her growing feelings for the brilliant attorney and investigate rumors that the love of his life, Diane Colcernian, may still be alive. Zack finds himself in need of his faith more than ever as Navy SEALs launch a daring rescue attempt that has the potential to trigger World War III.

Available in stores and online!

The Navy Justice Series

Hostage

Don Brown

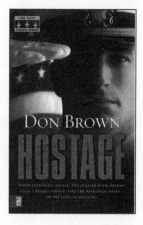

JAG Officer Zack Brewer's prosecution of three terrorists posing as Navy chaplains was called the "court martial of the century" by the press. Now, with the limelight behind him, all Zack wants to do is forget. But the radical Islamic organization behind the chaplains has a long memory—and a thirst for revenge.

Now the Navy has a need for Zack that eclipses all else. When an unthinkable act of aggression brings Israel and its Arab neighbors to the brink of war, Zack and co-counsel Diane Colcernian are called to the case of a lifetime. As leading nations focus their gaze upon these two, other eyes are watching as well.

Zack and Diane are in harm's way.

A kidnapping, an ultimatum…and suddenly, Zack faces an impossible choice. If he loses this case, the world could explode into war. If he wins, his partner—the woman he loves—will die.

And Zack himself may not survive to make the decision.

Available in stores and online!

ZONDERVAN®
.com

The Malacca Conspiracy

Don Brown,
Author of the Navy Justice Series

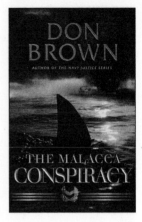

Set in Singapore, Indonesia, Malaysia, and the United States, *The Malacca Conspiracy* is a bone-chilling tale of terrorism on the high seas, political assassination, and nuclear brinkmanship. And for Zack and Diane—your favorite JAG characters from Don Brown's popular Navy Justice Series—a story of hope for a long-standing romance that is now or never.

When a dastardly plot is hatched in the Malaysian seaport of Malacca to attack civilian oil tankers at sea, to drive up the price of crude oil futures, to assassinate the Indonesian president, and use fat windfall profits to finance a nuclear attack against American cities, Navy JAG officers Zack Brewer and Diane Colcernian reunite in a sizzling race against the clock to foil the conspiracy before disaster strikes.

But as President Mack Williams sends ships of the U.S. Seventh Fleet towards the Malacca Straights to reassert control over the sea lanes, will Zack and Diane survive this dangerous and final high-stakes drama of life and death?

You won't be able to put this thriller down until you find out.

Available in stores and online!

Treason

Don Brown

The stakes are high . . . and the entire world is waiting for the verdict.

The Navy has uncovered a group of radical Islamic clerics who have infiltrated the Navy Chaplain Corps, inciting sailors and marines to acts of terrorism. And Lieutenant Zack Brewer has been chosen to prosecute them for treason and murder.

Only three years out of law school, Zack has already made a name for himself, winning the coveted Navy Commendation Medal. Just coming off a high-profile win, this case will challenge the very core of Zack's skills and his Christian beliefs—beliefs that could cost him the case and his career.

With Diane Colcernian, his staunchest rival, as assistant prosecutor, Zack takes on internationally acclaimed criminal defense lawyer Wells Levinson. And when Zack and Diane finally agree to put aside their animosity, it causes more problems than they realize.

Available in stores and online!

Share Your Thoughts

With the Author: Your comments will be forwarded to the author when you send them to *zauthor@zondervan.com*.

With Zondervan: Submit your review of this book by writing to *zreview@zondervan.com*.

Free Online Resources at
www.zondervan.com

Zondervan AuthorTracker: Be notified whenever your favorite authors publish new books, go on tour, or post an update about what's happening in their lives at www.zondervan.com/authortracker.

Daily Bible Verses and Devotions: Enrich your life with daily Bible verses or devotions that help you start every morning focused on God. Visit www.zondervan.com/newsletters.

Free Email Publications: Sign up for newsletters on Christian living, academic resources, church ministry, fiction, children's resources, and more. Visit www.zondervan.com/newsletters.

Zondervan Bible Search: Find and compare Bible passages in a variety of translations at www.zondervanbiblesearch.com.

Other Benefits: Register to receive online benefits like coupons and special offers, or to participate in research.

ZONDERVAN®

ZONDERVAN.com/
AUTHORTRACKER
follow your favorite authors